Dragon Wish

by

Judith Leger

Dragon Wish

Cover Art by *Jennifer Greeff*

The Wild Rose Press, Inc.
PO Box 708
Adams Basin, NY 14410-0708
Visit us at www.thewildrosepress.com

Publishing History
First Edition, 2023
Trade Paperback ISBN 978-1-5092-5287-9
Digital ISBN 978-1-5092-5288-6

Previously Published Wild Child Publishing
Published in the United States of America

Dedication

Terri, Jerri, and Leslie

Chapter One

Afraid to blink in case the dragon's image appeared behind her lids, Seren glanced around her spotless, steam filled bathroom. Eyes burning from fatigue, she repeated the plea in her mind. *Show me what you want or leave me alone.* Whatever was causing the dragon to appear needed to know she'd had enough. She'd force an end to the vision.

Low classical music emanated from the radio. She'd plugged it into the nearest socket so it sat on the smooth angled slope of the tub's lip. The soft, lulling notes did little to ease her restless thoughts.

She wanted to relax after using her psychic abilities to help the police solve a string of murders. In the past, the resulting closure for the families helped her to go forward with her life too. However, this time, a week before catching the killer, the first vision struck, leaving her emotionally drained and physically exhausted. The images of the dragon dug deep into the darkened sections of her mind. They stirred old memories of fear and pain she longed to forget.

Terror made her shiver as wispy strands of horrors from her past drifted through her mind. She couldn't focus on anything solid as crimson flooded her memories. Seren fought against the rise of utter helplessness. In an effort to escape, she squeezed her eyes shut. The vision appeared, seeking to destroy her sense of normalcy.

A single dragon, cold and menacing, rested atop a pinnacle. In profile, under the heavy brow crowned by six curving horns, one blue eye with its slit pupil watched her. Wings hung straight at its sides. They concealed most of the creature's body. Pearly white scales glistened in a darkness that swirled with charcoal and silver clouds. With the first touch of its gaze on her, a tremendous weight settled over her body. On the outer edges of her awareness, the force of an unseen entity threatened to drain the life from her.

She snapped her eyes open. The mental pictures evaporated, but left her trembling. She studied the clear water gushing in glimmering streams from the faucet. What was she missing? The message lay hidden, beyond her comprehension. She rested her head against the back of the tub.

Sirens echoed outside her apartment, announcing another emergency on the streets of New Orleans. Eyes burning from lack of sleep, she hoped the police didn't call her to work for them again. She needed rest, but the vision's hold on her tightened with each new day.

With a soft sigh she sank lower in the tub, knees bent. Damp air chilled the bare skin on her knees. Ripples in the water moved out from her as the liquid covered her shoulders and the heated wetness licked against her clenched jaw. The tub's rim hid the rest of the room from her. A strong scent of herbal shampoo mingled with the mist rising from the water.

Seren tried to connect something from her past to the present—anything to trigger this sort of reaction. She'd married and became a mother at eighteen. Ten years later, she was single. Her husband and daughter, the child she'd loved so much, gone forever. Over the last two years she'd tried to be happy, or at least content to exist alone.

In a flash, ten years of her life had disappeared along with everything she'd loved.

She drew in a deep soothing breath and released it by slow degrees. She'd decided two years ago that she would live the rest of her life without a man or children. No emotional ties connecting her with anyone. The thought of love along with loss sent bone-deep chills through her soul. The very idea frightened her so much that she'd buried herself in work. She hadn't wanted to spread the word about her psychic ability but word had gotten out, and during the last few years, her slight psychic ability had increased to the point where she was called upon many times to aid local law enforcers with some of their most daunting cases. She'd been happy helping others find resolution for their own losses since she'd never found any for her own.

She frowned, concentrating on the last case. Nothing concerning the murders should have triggered this kind of reaction. No, the image of the dragon was real, yet not. She grunted. *Dragons*, they were nothing but myths created by the over-active imaginations of ancient people. They didn't exist—except man-made ones.

The thought ended, and the vision erupted in her mind with a screeching cry.

Darkness surrounded her. The wind buffeted her with a constant stream of cold. She stood on a high peak across from where the dragon waited. Like before, its eye was focused on her. Moonlit-rimmed clouds drifted overhead. The sting of salt in the air burned her nostrils. Her breath caught in her throat. She tried to scream a question at the beast, but no words came.

In an instant, the bathroom materialized. She jerked, struggling to maintain control. Water splashed against the side of the tub, sloshing over the rim to pour down the side and pool on the floor. She gripped the sloped edges, taking deep cleansing breaths to control her pounding pulse. Was this what the vision meant? Had it been warning her of what to expect in her future—cold emptiness?

Once calm, she raised her foot, and with her toes, pulled the knob down to shut off the hot water. Determined to finish her bath in peace, she shoved her troubling thoughts aside. A slow drip slipped from the faucet, plopping below, sending ripples in the water to circle outward. Seren braced her feet against the tub. With a slight push, she forced her body forward. She reached toward the Sweet-Pea scented soap sitting next to the radio. Hand trembling, she sent one last heartfelt plea for release from the vision. When she picked up the soap, she brushed against the side of the radio.

The radio slipped toward the water.

****

Avaris, 1111
Age of the Great and Mighty White Dragon

The Crakkintaw Inn boasted the best drink, but lacked the niceties richer places in the port city of Gilliesport offered. Numbed by the overindulgence of the potent house drink, Captain Paladin Fulcan weaved down the dim paneled hallway of the second floor. Musty clouds of dust rose with each step from his booted feet. The wicks in the wall lanterns needed a trim. The blue flames gave off barely enough light to see by, and the smoke rising from them added to the stale odor in the building. He grunted. The place needed a thorough cleaning. He had not chosen this place for its finer aspects, but for the solitude along with the liquor.

He'd passed on an earlier opportunity to attend a dinner gathering at a friend's home. The idea of a night spent eating a delicious, savory meal and visiting with several high-ranking men alongside their splendidly robed families seemed appropriate, but the thought of mouthing platitudes while whispers swept across the room turned his stomach. Sympathetic, the guests would have offered comfort, yet at the same time, averted their eyes, none of them bold enough to meet Paladin's steady stare. Everyone would have been uncomfortable with him there. So instead, he had come here to drink and mourn alone.

Through the grimy multi-pane window at the end of the hall, stars glinted in the night sky. Paladin narrowed his eyes, concentrating on the glittering beacons as he approached his room. He needed to get to the second door from the end— almost there.

A shooting star blazed across the sky beyond the window. At the sight, he stumbled. It was beautiful, so fleeting. Much like life.

He made a wish, violating the one cardinal rule for all dragonseeds of Avaris. The dragons would know and their decision to grant him a child would, most likely, lead to dire consequences.

What had he done?

Regret flared in his heart. He clenched his teeth to fight the pain.

Fool.

His wife was gone, lost to him along with his unborn child. His wish for a son was impossible now. He had no intention of ever marrying again. To do so meant he must trust another female, which was unlikely to happen.

He stopped and rubbed the heels of his palms over his eyes in an effort to erase the horror of finding her along with their babe. The burning hatred the memory provoked threatened to overwhelm him. He lowered his hands and staggered forward, wanting to reach his room where the comfort of his bed waited. Once stopped in front of the door, he fumbled with the key.

A brilliant light burst against the window where he'd viewed the shooting star. He stiffened, surprise rendering him motionless. The other end of the hall disappeared in a blinding whiteness. Within it, a solid white door formed.

Caught off guard by the strange sight, he stepped away from his room, a chill moved down his back. Out of habit, his right hand grasped the cool, solid handle of his long sword. What magic worked in this inn? Paladin tried to recall if there were any wizard apprentices in the building, but there were none that he knew of.

He took one step closer and lifted his free hand to touch the door inside the bright glow. He snorted then half smiled. Excellent sorcery. The power radiating from the light amazed him. None but the six great dragons acting in conjunction possessed such strength.

At this thought, horror over his regretted wish widened his eyes. Was this the dragon's answer to his plea? He should turn and go to his room but curiosity drove him forward. Without any further consideration, he twisted the golden knob then gave the door a shove. The door swung wide, banging into the wall on the other side.

A room appeared before him with its smooth floors,

walls, and even the ceiling painted white. Amazed at the difference between this room and the dank, dim hallway, Paladin stepped over the threshold.

Across the room, a woman, her short dark hair slicked against her scalp from the abundance of steam in the air, leaned forward in a vessel filled with water. Her hand stretched toward the opposite end, but her gaze was caught by a strange box emitting a tune. The silver box slipped toward the water.

Fire flared in his veins. His dragonblood roared to life. It warned him of danger with the box. In one long leap, he clasped its sides a moment before it touched the water. With a swift jerk, he flung the contraption behind him.

****

The radio crashed against the wall, pieces flew out, scattering the floor with debris. Seren, at first unable to tear her eyes from the broken pieces, glanced toward the stranger.

He was bent over next to the tub, his body twisted at the waist with his back hunched. A long-fitted coat flared around his middle and fell to his knees. From her side, she saw underneath the coat, gold hued skin of a solid chest peeked through the gap in his white shirt which opened from the neck to mid chest. Lower, a wide black leather belt wrapped around his slender waist, holding up dark pants which clung to his long legs; the hems of his pants were tucked into knee-high black boots.

Golden hair fell in strands angled toward his face and shoulders. His light blue eyes were narrowed in his lean face. Just past him, a brilliant light from the doorway added brightness to the gold strands.

She glanced at the water. Then, unable to stop, her

stare moved toward the shattered radio. What the hell had just happened? Was she imagining this or was it part of another vision? Her body felt numb, but her mind raced through the events of the last few seconds. Yes, it had to be another vision, just another weight to add to her already miserable day. She reached out and poked the arm closest to her. He faced her, straightening and staring down at her with a cool, almost curious look in his eyes.

He was real. Oh, God! How had he gotten into her apartment? The shock of having a strange man in her bathroom added to the fact she came close to death sent adrenalin rushing through her body. Only one other time had she experienced such a feeling, and that was when Mandy had died. Without thought of her nakedness, she grabbed the tub to stand, determined to escape. A phone—she had to call the police.

He gripped her hand. She wasn't sure if he meant to capture her or help her stand. A sense of security came over her, but she wasn't going to take the chance his intentions were good.

"Let me go," she demanded, pulling from his hold. He held tighter. She gave one fierce tug. He released her. Free, she splashed back, landing with a dull thump against the far corner of the tub. She watched in slow motion as water flew out and a drop landed at the corner of his eye. Pain lanced up her left side, ending in her shoulder.

Their gazes clashed; his pupils dilated. The water droplet slowly drifted down his check like a tear. A second later, he wrapped his arms around her and lifted. He set her on her feet and made sure she was steady. Water cascaded in streams off her body and his soaked sleeves to pool on the floor. The drop on his cheek fell free.

He touched her lips and muttered words she couldn't understand. She had no idea what he was doing. Whatever it was, he'd better stop and get the hell out of her bathroom. In one sweep, he shrugged his coat off and wrapped it around her. Heat raced up her neck to end in her cheeks as she realized her nakedness was covered. How had she forgotten she was nude? He hadn't thrown her down or hurt her. Maybe he didn't plan on hurting her.

"What do you want?" Seren tried to shove him and his coat away, but she slipped on the wet floor. Her body tilted forward, she started to fall, but his body stopped her from hitting the ground. Instead, she landed hard against the width of his solid chest.

Stunned, she panted, gathering the strength to fight this strange man. He picked her up. His voice, so deep and melodious, lilted around her. "There'll be no death in this place tonight. If you desire to place yourself in danger once more, kindly wait until I have departed."

She wanted to scream, hit him, anything that would force this man…this intruder to leave, but her strength ebbed. Her muscles refused to obey the fight or flight message her brain sent. She lay in his arms staring horrified at him, trying hard to ignore the increasing feeling of security that wove around her. She searched his face and whispered, "Leave me alone."

He turned toward the open door, glancing at her. "One day, but not this one."

In that second, his clear, intense look landed on her. The bathroom disappeared. *Cold wind whipped over her face. Closer now, still silent and foreboding, the dragon stared at her.* In the next instant, the image vanished. She gasped in surprise and found she was once more captured by this man's cool blue eyes.

The vision came upon her so fast then disappeared just as quickly. She studied his lean face, the smooth jaw, sculptured lips, straight nose, and strong forehead. Arched golden brows matched his light hair. His looks reminded her of drawings she had seen of glorious archangels. He appeared like a saint, untouchable and pure, yet the dragon's image nudged her to whisper while fear of his answer tightened her muscles. "Are you the dragon?"

He stopped at the open door, a frown marring his smooth brow. His attention stayed focused ahead of them. A strong citrus odor floated in the air separating them. She inhaled the intoxicating scent.

"Depends on which dragon."

"A white one with blue eyes."

He glanced at her, one brow cocked before he looked away. For a second, a flicker of surprise and recognition appeared in his eyes.

"Perhaps."

Unsettled by his answer, she tried to understand his reaction to the question. He moved toward the door. The moment he walked out of her bathroom, the blazing light just outside the doorway dissipated. Darkness crept in on them. She looked around, blinking to give her vision time to adjust.

Stale air assaulted her. She wrinkled her nose. Memories of her grandmother's house flittered through her mind. Old, dusty furniture, tainted with a moldy scent, filled each room in the elderly woman's home. Here, though, dim, bluish light from lamps situated in tarnished brackets lined the scarred, paneled walls. The air pressed in on her, pulling her body toward the floor. With the heaviness around her, she had to concentrate to shift closer against his broad chest.

Shadows danced along the hallway. Cool air touched her bare legs. Curiosity warred with panic inside her mind.

"Please, tell me where we are?" she whispered. Glad her voice didn't reveal her fear, Seren continued to search for some reminder of her pristine condominium. "What do you want with me?"

"Just to help. You are safe. I intend to keep you close until I have departed on the rising," he murmured, stopping at a closed door.

Her mind awoke with his words. "No, you won't. You'll take me home."

Before he had a chance to respond, slurred phrases mingled with unsteady steps stomping up a staircase that seemed to be coming from the far end of the corridor. Seren glanced over her shoulder, and tightened her hold around his neck.

"To return you to your home, I fear, is impossible at present. If you desire, I can leave you here, but I will take my coat with me."

Seren's heart dropped. He didn't actually intend to leave her here, did he? Where was this place exactly? Her stomach roiled, nausea threatened to make this a more memorable night. She hadn't believed the day could get any worse, but it had decidedly gotten much more than worse. Horrified, she met his piercing stare and opened her mouth to speak only to find no words would come out.

One golden brow lifted in question. "Interesting

situation. What do you suppose those men will assume when they reach the top of the stairs and discover a naked woman?"

She balled her fists. How dare he do this to her? She wouldn't be humiliated like this. The heat of fury started to rise within her, overriding the shock and setting her in motion. "All right. I'll go with you," she ground out between clenched teeth.

He had taken her choice away from her. She fumed, nostrils flaring, inhaling to fill her lungs. She regretted the deep intake of his scent. It filled her mind with his intoxicating aroma and made her press her fingers into the solid muscles of his shoulders.

With a nod, he tightened his grip on her with one arm. He managed to unlock, twist the handle, and push the door open. Once inside the room, he kicked it shut behind them.

"Where are we? What are you going to do to me?" She searched his face, seeking some answer.

He blinked. His eyes remained closed longer than she thought necessary. Moments continued to slip by. Why wouldn't he answer her? The wet streak on his cheek caught her attention. She reached over and wiped it off. He moved his head back away from her fingers and spoke. Her body jerked in reaction, her nerves stretched taut by everything that had happened to her. His words, though, had nothing to do with her questions. "You are here with me because I saw a shooting star, and fool that I am, made a wish."

"Wishes on stars don't come true."

Curtains at the window were pulled wide, admitting more light than the small blue-flamed candles situated around the room. The soft moonlight emphasized the shadows on his face, giving him a menacing look. She swallowed against the lump of fear tightening her throat.

His low laugh rumbled in his chest as he moved to a small bed against the far wall. "Perhaps for those who do not believe."

He leaned over and slid his arms from under her. She sank into the soft mattress. The coat's edges separated. Her hands braced behind her, she stared at him. He towered above her, his features half-shaded.

She held her breath for a few seconds.

He tilted his head. His gaze roamed over her face, glided down her throat to linger on her breasts, her waist, and stopped lower, at the junction of her legs.

Frightened of him, she should have curled away, but right now, she cared little that the coat had fallen off, and she sat with her arms behind her, her legs bent at the knees, spreading her body for his view. A sharp slice of desire cut into her, hardening her nipples and swelling her nether lips. Shame followed, chasing away the sudden rise of passion. She jerked the edges of the coat over herself. Her body heated in embarrassment.

He turned his back to her, took several deep breaths before moving with slow steps to the windows. "Go to sleep. The night is yet young, but I am tired. Crawl under the covers. I'll not have you sickened because you are wet and might catch a chill."

Each step echoed in the quiet room. For the first time, Seren saw the true length of his hair. The light strands streamed down his back and were tied just below his shoulders with a black band. Thick and straight, the pointed tips ended at his hips.

Cold numbness swept over her mind and body, mingling with the heaviness in the air. She struggled to scoot up in the bed to tug the covers back. Breathless, she slid under them. Once settled, she noticed the coat where she'd left it, crumpled and spread on the edge of the bed. She reached out and touched the satiny material, wondering if she could read something about him through the cloth. Seren rubbed the softness between her fingers. Nothing came to her. She recalled his comment concerning a wish. Had he wished for her? No, not her in particular, but any woman? But she'd brought him bad luck by being the answer for his wish. She stifled an insane need to giggle. He came out the loser on his wish. She was useless to a man.

The smooth fabric calmed her tremulous thoughts some. She stared at the cloth. Why did she notice such a mundane thing like the soft material? Instead, she should figure out a way to escape. A means to return home.

Anger pulled at her. She considered slipping the coat on and making a run for the door. She glanced at where he stood before the window, staring into the night sky. He'd stop her, even just to retrieve his coat.

Her anger melted into consternation. She didn't even know where she was. He'd never answered her. She considered asking him again, but something inside her warned that he wouldn't respond. She jerked the coat up and tossed it over the end of the bed. Refusing to lie down, she sat, keeping her focus on him.

Silently, Seren waited for him to move. Her mind raced with a menagerie of scenes from earlier. She tried to find an explanation for what had happened tonight but failed. She narrowed her gaze at his profile. He'd saved her life. If the radio had hit the water in the tub, she'd be dead. She released a shaky breath. Minutes slipped by. The weeks of sleeplessness crashed over her, making her sag, no longer able to fight the exhaustion.

****

Paladin studied her, hoping the shadows concealed his features so she wouldn't notice his stare. He had never expected to find a woman on the other side of the doorway.

Over a thousand years ago, the connection between Avaris and all other worlds he'd learned about during the history lessons of his youth had been destroyed. Time had brought about the realization that the worlds beyond were found to be unsuitable for magic and deadly to dragons—that was incomprehensible. But all this knowledge had not prepared him for her. A chill touched his back. He stiffened under the frigid tingles moving up his spine. From the moment her haunted glance met his, he had experienced a flood of desire. Something he hadn't expected or yearned for since his dead wife's betrayal.

He glanced out at the dark sky with the multitude of twinkling stars while his mind whipped through all that had occurred on this night. Had the dragons reacted to his wish? The magical blood in his veins would have responded to his desire. The great clan leaders, each a mighty and terrible creature, would have felt his need. He gritted his teeth but kept his body relaxed. Why his wish and none other? There had been others, wizards along with their apprentices, who had tried to invoke the dragons to open the portal, but their efforts had always failed. Yet his had not only opened a doorway but brought him this woman.

His gaze strayed back to her. She held no answer to his wish. His body reacted to her, but he still maintained control over his baser needs. The dragons must have a purpose for her presence on Avaris. His desire for a son had nothing to do with their manipulations. Or did it?

Her question came to him. *Are you the dragon?* Coming from a different world, how had she known of his relationship to the dragons? In particular, a white one.

Time would reveal why this had happened. He would keep her close until he departed in the morning. Afterward, he intended to put her from his mind. Let the dragons find her since they had brought her here.

Mind still dulled by the liquor he'd consumed earlier and no longer able think clearly, he gave up trying to figure out the meaning for what had occurred for the moment.

****

The click of his heels forced Seren's drooping lids open. He moved to a chair on the side of a small round table in the center of the room. There, he started to undress.

She narrowed her eyes, trying to see clearer in the room's dimness. He slid the long and short swords free before unclasping his belt. He laid them on the table. Next came his shirt. He draped it over the back of the chair. Seren's breath caught in her throat. The outrage from moments ago vanished with the slow slide of material over bare skin. As the moonbeams highlighted his back, revealing valleys and peaks of muscle, she was enthralled by the beauty of his body. Dark smudges marked his left arm from wrist to shoulder. Puzzled, she just managed to make out a design on the mark—a raised tattoo with frills and sharp angles. He sat and pulled off one boot then the other before he stood to remove his pants.

Seren, more awake now, stared at the man before

her. At twenty-eight and living in New Orleans, she had seen a lot, but she'd never viewed such a fine specimen of the male body. Flawless, his long legs rose to meet his tapered waist which accented the width of his shoulders and joined to his muscled chest. And his...

Heat crept into her cheeks. As hard as it was, she forced herself to look away. She enjoyed the view, but she would not be caught staring at him!

He extinguished the candles. On silent feet, he returned to the bed. Keeping her face averted, she whispered. "How can you be so perfect?"

His low answer reached her. "I am not perfect. Now sleep."

"You're not sleeping here."

He grunted at her comment and sat on the side of the mattress a moment before he snuffed out the lamp on the table next to the bed. He lay with his back to her. The mattress shifted. After she sat there for a couple of minutes, the reality that he did intend to sleep next to her struck. She glanced toward the foot of the bed, trying to decide what to do. Emotionally tired, her body sluggish, she sighed. She had nowhere to go. Several quiet seconds passed. She scooted down and curled into a ball.

Turbulent thoughts about the events of the night, what happened, and how she'd ended up in bed with him rifled through her mind. Had the radio fallen into the water? Had she died? She'd seen the light mentioned by people after near death experiences, but she didn't feel dead. Maybe she was insane. Had the vision gripping her mind these last few weeks forced her to slip away from the real world and to this place?

Too upset to voice her thoughts, she clasped a hand over her mouth, cutting off a cry of denial. Tremors racked her body. She was so cold, empty. Alone.

At her muffled sound, he released a low sigh. The bed sank under his weight as he turned. He wrapped his arms around her, pulling her against his chest. She stiffened. "Easy, my sweet. I mean you no harm," he murmured against her hair. Soon, his warmth seeped into her frozen flesh. She relaxed, the tension oozing out.

After a soft sigh, she swiped her tongue over her lips to wet the dryness there. Unable to stop, she scrubbed her cheek against his muscled chest and drifted off to sleep, his wonderful smell surrounding her.

Chapter Two

Seren dreamed of a glorious angel.

She inhaled the sandalwood scent which had a slight citrus flare that had followed her into sleep. Her angel held her clasped against him. She pressed her lips against the pulsing vein in his neck. From the back of his throat, a needy groan rumbled.

He lowered his head, grasped her jaw and kissed her. She opened her mouth wider to allow his entrance, wanting him to stop her terrorizing visions of the dragon. Only he had the power to erase the nightmare she'd lived in over the last few weeks. She wanted to feel alive, no longer heavy with worry. She didn't want to be alone any more. She needed someone to love, to desire her without conditions.

Her hands smoothed down his chest to his abdomen. Slick skin over hard muscles tensed beneath her palms. He rolled over, his hands under her hips, lifting them. One heartbeat later, he thrust deep inside her, sliding with ease into her slick entrance.

A moan escaped her. Yes, she needed this, no one but he would do. Her angel. Freeing her lips, she begged, "Please, please."

"Always," he groaned, capturing her mouth with his once more.

Seren slid her fingertips over the sleek muscles of his back to the curve of his buttocks. She grasped them, pulling him harder, faster into her. She wanted him to…

White streaks flared behind her eyelids. Her entire body jerked with her climax, followed by warm lassitude, numbing her limbs. He stiffened and emptied himself into her womb. She cried out, unable to hold the sound in. Gasping, she kissed his shoulder, his neck, her tongue tasting the saltiness she found there. He lifted her chin, claiming her lips again. "Sweet," she whispered. He shifted off her and pulled her close to him. Wrapping a leg over his hip, she dozed.

Twice more before sunrise, she dreamed of her angel. Each time, he brought her pleasure the likes of which she'd never before experienced. No foreplay, no sex toys, all she needed was his kiss, his heavenly touch, and the hard length of him buried inside her. Each climax burned her like a Roman candle exploding on the fourth of July.

He remained silent during their lovemaking. She liked that. She'd tried to discuss the dragon with friends and associates, but their responses failed to solve the puzzle of the vision. Helpful advice and assumed suggestions hadn't worked to eliminate the problem. The vision continued. So she'd had enough of talk.

Right now, she wanted someone to give her peace, and for a short time, allow her to rest. He succeeded.

****

Warmth and the orange glow of light beat against her closed eyelids. He shifted away. She groaned. Her body felt weighed down, yet nothing but the covers were on top of her. She cracked open her eyes. Across the room, past where he sat on the edge of the mattress, angled sunbeams came through the windows. The golden light struck him in a framed picture, branding it into her memory for life. For a moment, broad shoulders slumped as his chin rested against his chest. He inhaled deep, and then pushed up off the bed.

Her breath caught in her throat. She hadn't imagined it. He was beautiful. Every muscled curve, each firm line rippled with perfection.

Her thoughts whirled with memories of last night. She'd dreamed of him. She straightened to a more comfortable position. Soreness pulled between her legs. Her gaze, widened. Shocked, she stared at the back of his head.

Oh, God, what had she done? She'd let him make love to her during the night. She tried to remember if he'd worn any protection.

She bit her bottom lip. Her palm covered the base of her belly. She might, even now, carry his child. She released a shaky breath, hoping that never happened.

Memories of long sweltering summer days playing in the park, laughing while wet, tiny arms embraced her after a warm bath, the first day of school, and then…Seren squeezed her eyes shut in an attempt to stop the images of her daughter's death and the days—no, years which followed.

She attempted to quell the familiar resentment of her psychic ability as it was now compared to before she lost Mandy, but failed. The anger never left her. She should have known and somehow saved her daughter from the drunk driver. Because of this, she'd decided never to have any more children, a fact her ex-husband, Lance, hadn't been able to understand.

Lance had assumed she'd change her mind, but this was a decision she'd stood by. Seren refused to chance losing another child. He'd filed for divorce two years later.

Sunlight streamed through the windows and cast a glow, surrounding the stranger's body. Golden hair rippled over his shoulders. The beauty of his hair captured her attention. The strands shifted to one side, revealing muscled buttocks. Seren's turbulent thoughts ended with a rush of intense desire flooding her body. She gritted her teeth, confused at her reaction and tried hard to fight her own passion.

Every movement was slow, almost lazy, yet she sensed a layer of steel beneath the quiet veneer. She stared at him, unable to tear her focus away while he poured water from a pitcher into a bowl.

Droplets, sparkling in the light, flung wide while he washed. Her gaze wandered over his lean legs, up his sculptured back, and across broad shoulders. She stopped at the strange mark on his left arm. A raised tattoo in the shape of a white dragon spiraled from his wrist to end just above his left breast.

Her breath caught in her throat. Sore muscles in her back stiffened. He was the dragon. The mark was proof. She met his stare in the small mirror on the upright chest where the wash bowl sat. She froze, heart thudding against her chest at being caught studying him.

He lifted the pitcher.

"The water is from yesterday, but it is still clean if you choose to freshen up," he told her, lowering his eyelids, hiding the blue. "I am going below to break my fast. I will let the Innkeeper know you are here and to bring some clothing. Once you dress, you are welcome to join me."

"Where is this place?" She sat up, pulling the covers to her neck. "What is the meaning of the dragon?"

"Gilliesport."

She frowned in confusion. The unfamiliar name hung in the air between them. She swallowed before asking, "Where is that?"

The left side of his mouth curved up. "Where are you from?"

She hesitated. He'd been in her home last night, yet he acted like he didn't know where she lived. She narrowed her eyes, trying to see into his mind without any results. Did he think she was stupid? His expression never changed. "New Orleans."

A vee formed between his brows. He appeared to not understand what she meant. He was silent as he dragged on his pants.

"Louisiana," she added, frustrated with his lack of response. What game was he playing?

Tugging on his boots, he stopped and glanced at her. "I have never heard of loueezzeeaannah."

"It's in the U.S. You have to know the United States." She looked at him and rolled her eyes. "Of America." With no recognition evident in his eyes, her heart thumped harder, its beats increasing, pounding an erratic rhythm in her chest. Her blood surged through her veins, and her head throbbed. She spoke low, the words edged with anger. "North America. It's on Earth."

He nodded with a slight smile on his lips. "Ah, Earth. Now, I have heard that before. Sister planet to Avaris." Dressed in his shirt and pants, he fastened the wide black belt at his lean middle. After he slipped his coat on, he slid the two scabbards through the belt, one on each side of his waist.

Seren stared at the weapons. He'd worn them last night. Now, she wondered why. The black handles reflected the sun's light, and each was tipped with a clear, round, gold encased stone. Once he finished, his gaze met hers. "There is a man in Dene. He claims he, too, is from Earth. Perhaps, you should speak with him."

"You're nuts, aren't you? There's no way I could have traveled from one planet to another. Tell me the truth, where am I?" The news of someone else who knew the places she mentioned had little if any impact on her. The sudden rise of her fear threatened to turn into panic. "How can we talk to each other if we come from separate planets?"

"You are, indeed, on Avaris. Both Earth and Avaris are connected to one another by the dragons' magic. The portal can only be opened at the gathering of the great ones, or perhaps, by combining the powers of several talented wizards." He stopped and shrugged before his stare met hers. "We have magic so powerful we are able to understand what anyone says at any time. It is a common spell placed on all babes at the time of their births. The one I placed on you when I found you enables me to understand you and to speak in your language. You now also have the ability to speak and understand my language."

Unable to fully believe him, she stared wide-eyed at him.

The door rattled under a heavy fist. A rasping voice sounded from the other side. "Ready to depart in an hour, Cap'an."

She twitched and tightened her hold on the blanket.

He glanced from the door to her. Their eyes locked. His voice remained soft, gentle, and calming. "Only the cosmos knows how the two planets became connected. No one that I know of has ever questioned it."

Her voice trembled with unshed tears, frustration, and the hot embers of her anger. "Well, I do. I want to go home. I want to know what the dragon means. What do you intend to do with me? Last night, we—oh, God, I just want to go home."

With a slow gait, he walked to the door. He lifted one hand and grasped the knob. Without looking at her, he said, "I cannot send you home."

"Why not?" Frightened, overwhelmed with what had happened to her, Seren gripped the covers, her knuckles white. Tears scalded the lids of her eyes, shame and despair built in her mind.

"The only way I know of is to have the great dragon clan leaders open a portal."

"Then tell them to do it."

He shook his head, a sad smile forming on his lips. "One does not go to the dragons to demand something. It is by their will that peace is possible on Avaris, therefore, we are obligated to them."

"They have to send me home. I don't want to be here!"

"I suppose I shouldn't have brought you through the portal. It seemed right to do so."

"For who? You?" Furious and more than a little frightened for the future, she lashed out at him. "We had sex last night. There might be complications I don't want."

His response followed on the heels of her statement. "I agree. Even now, I travel to return my *beloved* wife to her family. She bled to death trying to rid her body of my child. If I had a choice between a willing and an unwilling mother to a babe of mine, I would much prefer to do without either."

25

Horrified, Seren's eyes widened. She started to speak, but he opened the door and left, shutting it with gentle care behind him.

His words still echoing in her ears, Seren huddled under the blankets. The shock of what had happened to him surprised her enough to forget her own troubles for a moment. Guilt at her callous manner toward him came over her. She shook her head then clenched her fists, fighting the need to call out to him, begging him to return. He didn't appear the type to accept an apology. She bit her lips, sucking them between her teeth.

Who was this man? Where was Avaris? What kind of world was it where dragons ruled? For a second, she stilled. The warmth of the sun fell across her face and upper body. She hadn't even asked his name.

She shifted on the over-soft mattress. Muscles, unfamiliar with the type of exertion she had asked of them last night, pulled and tightened. No, she was alive. Vivid memories from the last few hours spread fiery heat up her chest to fill her face. Sex. No other word described what had occurred between them the night before. Hot, lurid sex with a complete stranger.

She tried to pull in a deep breath, but her lungs refused to expand far. With just the physical act, he had accomplished what her husband hadn't been able to achieve even after hours of foreplay. She had climaxed every time. Once, she'd reached her peak twice, her body tightening around the entire length of him stronger than the first instance. He'd reached his also.

After a shuddering breath, she waited for the appearance of the vision. Nothing happened. The terrifying image seemed to be gone. She still felt the remnants of the pressing weight the vision put on her, but the bone-deep fear remained absent.

Scratching came from the door. She glanced at the wooden barrier. Her voice cracked when she spoke, "Who's there?"

"Be Alice, mum. The cap'an sent me 'ere to give ye these clothes."

Seren's gaze bounced from one spot to another around the room. What now? Should she let this woman in? The news of the clothes tempted her. Knowing she had to get out of bed sometime, she tightened her hold on the covers and called, "Come in."

The door opened, revealing a full-bosomed woman. She swept in, her long black curls bobbed about her head, swirling over her shoulders. Her wide brown eyes scanned the room. When she spied Seren, she stopped and grinned, showing off a mouth full of white teeth.

A narrow scarf held the mass of hair away from round, rosy cheeks and a broad forehead. The yellow peasant shirt with a low scooped neck and a brown, ruffled, long skirt clung to the generous curves of her body. The sandals she wore revealed bright red painted toenails.

"So, you're the one keeping the cap'an up most of the night. I sleep right above 'ere. I could 'ear that bed a movin' all night. W'at a man, the cap'an is." A dreamy expression covered the woman's face as she sashayed across the room, a bundle clutched in one hand. She plopped on the bed at Seren's feet. Her skirts floated up then settled over well-rounded legs.

This woman had heard them. Seren's face flamed hotter. She pressed her hands over her cheeks. *Oh, please let me live through this.*

Observant eyes flickered over Seren, a mischievous

glint in them. "I brung ye some clothes, though from the looks of ye, they won't fit. Dinna know the cap'an liked 'em so young."

Seren reached out, clasping the offered bundle. Untying the dull brown sleeves crisscrossed over the folded cloth, she lifted a blouse. Much too large, the oval neckline would fall low on her chest, revealing more than she wanted. The woman may be outspoken, but she was a good judge of size.

Letting her hands drop to her lap, the shirt wadded on the bedcovers, Seren lifted her gaze to the woman. "Do you have some men's clothes, maybe boy's pants and shirt?" "Well, I might be able to find ye somethin'. Cap'an says he brun' ye 'ere. Couldn't 'elp wonderin' w'at 'appened to yer clothes." Eyes bright with curiosity, the woman leaned closer, anticipation heavy in her husky voice. "Tell me, w'at's it like, bein' with him?"

Amazed that this woman, a complete stranger, dared to question her concerning something so personal, Seren swallowed and leaned back, putting distance between them. Did this woman believe she had such loose morals? The answer showed in the bright look angled at her. Embarrassed by what had occurred last night, Seren shook her head. "I don't think the captain would appreciate me talking about him."

The woman straightened, her mouth twisted into a pout before she huffed out a sigh. "So ye know 'im well, do ye? Of course, ye right. The cap'an 's a secretive man. A real gent, 'e is. But when 'e's around us common folk, 'e don't put no airs on. Right favorite 'e is to us. So be careful 'ow ye treat 'im." In a flurry of flying skirts, the woman jumped up and hurried to the door. "I'll be back in a blink. Wash up, mum, ye still got the cap'an's smell on ye. Lovely as it is, I think ye'll feel much better cleaned up a bit."

With this last comment, the woman flounced out, hips swaying, banging the door closed behind her.

Seren fiddled with the coarse cloth of the blouse, trying to keep the tears of embarrassment at bay. How many others had heard them last night? She searched for the strength to rise, clean up and go below to meet him. Strangers would look at her. Would they know what they'd done? She stopped moving and frowned. Why should she even care?

If what he said was true, a new world existed outside these walls. She didn't have to follow the same rules she always had. There were new ones on this planet. She'd learn to survive and be strong until she returned home.

Memories of Earth flittered in her mind. Her little girl was buried in New Orleans. Tears filled her eyes, threatening to fall. Seren squeezed her eyes shut, allowing the tears to roll down her cheeks. Somehow she had to find a way back home.

Without fully comprehending what she did, her hands cupped her lower belly. She frowned, hoping she hadn't conceived, yet she felt like a new life grew inside her. She shook her head. That was all impossible. She hadn't known she was pregnant with Mandy until she had missed her first period. But right now she sensed the joining of his sperm with her egg.

She shoved the covers aside and slid her legs over the side of the bed. Once on her feet, she tugged a sheet from the bed. She wrapped it around her with the top edges tucked under her arms, leaving her neck and shoulders bare.

Feeling dirty, she washed in the clean water he'd left

for her. Using a fresh cloth, she poured a few drops from the pitcher to wipe her teeth and tongue. Re-wrapping the sheet around her body, she gazed around the room. A heavy table, the one she had noticed the night before, stood in the center. Three carved wooden chairs, two pushed in while the one he'd used still stood sideways to the others, were situated around the scratched round surface. Dust gathered in the corners of the room. The bureau's counter and the table carried a layer of dust. She wrinkled her nose, but continued her scrutiny of her surroundings. Her survey stopped on a satchel sitting on a faded cushion of the window seat.

The dark brown leather was worn with several crease lines. She glanced at the door. He'd never know if she peeked inside. Her curiosity propelled her forward until she reached the bag.

Hands trembling, she unclasped the belted hooks and raised the flap. A metallic blue shirt, exactly like the one he put on this morning, lay wadded on top. She smiled. He wasn't perfect then. She had expected neatness, instead she'd found disorder. Pulling the shirt free, she brought it to her face and inhaled. His scent filled her mind.

Unexpected desire flared. She wanted him again. She longed to feel him joined with her, moving until she reached the blinding pleasure she had experienced the night before.

She swallowed, lowering the shirt and eased down onto the thin cushion of the window seat. With the side of her head resting against the pane, she looked outside.

The sky and ocean met on the horizon, the varying blues merging into one hazy color. The Inn had been built on a high bluff overlooking a bustling city. To the right, the cliffs dropped off. She tried to see the beach, but it lay hidden out of sight. Cut from white stone, wide water channels sliced through the streets rowed with two-story, some three level houses along with businesses. The narrow canals emptied over the edge of the cliffs. It seemed strange that the people here had built above the water's edge. She tried to find a logical explanation, even searching her memory for a resemblance of any place on Earth.

A noise below brought her stare down and she saw her rescuer-kidnapper, the captain, walk from a doorway somewhere beneath her window. She followed him with her steady look until he stopped in the middle of the busy yard.

People dressed in out of period clothing hustled back and forth. Some shouted instructions or welcomes while others worked at loading and unloading barrels, baskets, and an assortment of boxes from wooden wagons harnessed to huge, long-haired beasts that reminded her of oxen. Their clothing brought to mind those worn during the eighteenth century.

The wind gusted, lifting the sides of the captain's frock coat. The shorter strands of his light gold hair fluttered over his shoulders.

Her breath caught in her throat. He appeared so tall, so easy to look at. Her body throbbed, igniting with need. Wetness gathered between her legs. She craved his touch— now. She squeezed her eyes shut, battling the embarrassment in her mind and the passion growing throughout her body. How could she feel like this? What kind of person was she? One she no longer knew, or did she? Had a darker part of her soul been born last night?

She opened her eyes, hoping to stop her thoughts,

and found that he had turned and now stood staring at her. Their gazes met. She refused to yield. Temptation reared its head. She wanted to crook a finger at him, telling him to come to her.

Just as she was ready to give in to her desire, a broadchested man jogged from the doorway below her to the captain's side and said something. The captain half-smiled at her then followed the other man inside. Relieved she hadn't given in to her baser sensibilities, she stuffed his shirt back into the satchel without looking at anything else. With a flip of her wrist, she closed the bag. Disappointment soon followed, mingling with her relief.

Her thoughts wandered to how the inhabitants in this new world would treat her once they learned she came from another planet? She would have to work to fit in until she returned home, but she didn't know what this meant to these people. Most of all, while she tried to acclimate herself to this place, she would make sure she never had another child. Which meant the intimate moments with him were at an end.

She had learned a hard lesson with Mandy. One she swore she'd never forget.

Alice swung the door wide, and flounced across the room. "'ere ye go, mum."

Seren jumped, her hands clutching the sheet tighter around her. Heat rose to her cheeks at being caught near the captain's belongings.

"Ooo, goodness, ye are a tiny bit of t'ing. I'd say ye'd barely reach the cap'an's shoulder, ye would, iffin ye stood side by side. Well, come on, let's see 'ow ye look in t'eses." The woman held out a pair of pants similar to narrow-legged capris in one hand. A white billowy shirt was draped over her other hand.

"Thank you," Seren said, accepting the woman's offering. She pulled the shirt over her head and tugged it down. The seam across the shoulders fit, but the length came to the top of her thighs. A little too short for her tastes, but she had no other choice.

Under the cover of the sheet, she slipped her feet into the pants. Using one hand, she slid them up. They were a little snug, but she could deal with that, she decided, buttoning the double-sided front flaps. She raised the hem of the shirt to study how she looked. Yes, they'd do.

"Do ye want a bindin' for yer chest? I don't t'ink ye need one. Don't 'ave much up t'ere to bind."

Seren glared at the woman. Maybe she was small busted, but the captain hadn't minded last night. "No, I don't need any binding."

Alice handed her a pair of thick wool socks along with a black cap. "Well, now, 'ere's ye a 'at. The cap'an's down below waitin' for ya. 'E's ordered ye a right 'effy morning repast, 'e 'as. Now, come along. Don't wanna keep 'im waitin'."

"Wait, I don't have any shoes. I can't go down in socks." Seren dug in her heels. Fear interlaced with uncertainty rushed through her. She wasn't ready to see him. Not again. Not so soon.

"Come on wit' ye. We'll stop in my room. It's just above us. I t'ink t'ere might be a pair of clogs t'ere. It's all I gots." The woman grabbed her wrist and pulled her toward the door.

Realizing how useless it was to argue, Seren allowed Alice to guide her down the paneled hall. At the landing, the serving woman veered to the right, thumping up a short flight of stairs. "Come on, up 'ere with ye."

The slight detour took just a few minutes. Seren reveled in the small delay. At the top of the stairs leading below, she inhaled a deep breath, hoping to calm her nerves. Once steady, she proceeded down the stairs. The time to face the captain had arrived.

Chapter Three

"So ye're still determined to return her body to her family?" Calis Mer asked.

Paladin glanced at the barrel-chested man sitting across from him. Short dark hair stuck out from his head, and keen gray eyes studied the contents inside his mug. A large, beefy hand curved around the gray tankard. Eyes, similar in color to the mug, rose to meet his look.

"It is my duty as her husband. My last duty," Paladin replied. He sliced a thin sliver of beef steak and ate. His first mate would never understand. Paladin took his marriagebond duty seriously. His honor required it of him even though the woman he'd married had broken those same vows time and again. Calis understood the skies from all the voyages they went a journeying on. The man comprehended life and death, but honoring a woman who was also a wife seemed impossible for him to comprehend.

Calis grunted before he took a long pull from his tankard, straining the foam through his front teeth. The man had little manners, but Paladin hadn't hired him for his social refinements.

His first mate arched a bushy black brow at him, his tone teasing. "Heard ye had a bit of fluff during the night. Where'd ye find her? I don't recall any new faces in the place last evening."

Paladin half smiled. He refused to meet the other

man's look. His ship was set to sail in less than an hour. If time had permitted, he would have brought the strange woman the clothes instead of asking the serving wench to do it. He should have known she would have rattled her tongue to others. "She isn't anyone you know," he commented. He cut another slice. He took his time chewing it. The food carried no taste to him. The texture was dry, even tough.

Last night still haunted him.

He had inquired of the innkeeper to see if anyone complained of any strange happenings in the night, but the man had shaken his head. Satisfied none of the locals suspected what had occurred, he had proceeded to order his morning meal along with the bill for the room.

He chewed another bite, hiding the disgust floating in his gut. He had taken a chance by touching her.

The night before, he had been unable to stop himself from comforting her. Her lips had caressed his skin in a soothing, gentle way which managed to dissolve all his resolutions with the heat of his need. Her palms on his chest had stirred the embers of his passion until they flared to a white hot fervor, and rational thought no longer controlled him. Just the memory of what they had shared during the night caused the embers of desire to smolder within him.

He swallowed as he glanced around the room, hoping to distract the renewed bud of warmth building between his legs.

The Inn's common room bustled with travelers who mingled with vendors. Some roamed from table to table, others sat on benches lined against the two side walls. Odors of cooked food and body scents, some good— some not so good, saturated the place. Laughter interspersed with conversations swept across the room. Feet shuffled under tables and across the room as the vendors vied with the locals for a space to sit or stand so they might break their morning fast. He ignored most of the noise, allowing the flow of activity in the inn help him keep his mind away from thoughts of the strange woman. When he looked around, several females blushed and twittered to each other behind their hands.

He frowned at the sight then lowered his focus to cutting another piece off the steak. The attention he garnered was the same everywhere he traveled. The women reacted like they had never seen someone like him. Yet, in his homeland, all of his clansmen were tall and light haired with light eyes. They were much like him. The dragon blood ran strong in his clan. What would these dark-haired, rounded women say if he told them that in his land, he was considered rather plain?

Wooden clogs clopped down the stairs, drawing his attention. The off-worlder had arrived. Dressed like a young male, her small frame went unobserved by the inhabitants of the room, but he noticed. His heart skipped a beat. Dainty, delicate, the soft lines of her heart-shaped face strengthened the seed of desire she planted inside him last night until it threatened to bud into a clinging vine, refusing to release him. He gritted his teeth and unintentionally clenched the handle of his tankard. No matter what, he had to maintain controlled in her presence. Never again would he allow weakness to rule his body. He mustn't allow a repetition of the previous evening. She made it clear she didn't want him.

She stopped on the last step and looked around the room. There, she glanced at his table, she turned away but her stare returned immediately. He witnessed her swallow, and then raise her chin to a higher degree. He tilted his head, smiled and motioned her to the table.

She stepped away from the stairs, merging with the many people roaming throughout the room. She was so small, fragile even when compared to the others in the room. The muscles in his back tightened, and he straightened in his chair. Dressed in breeches and a white rough linen shirt, she still stood out among the patrons. Her slender form served to refresh his memories of her body, naked, supple, and pressed against his while her soft cries entered his mouth when he slid…he tensed, slamming the images to the back of his mind.

"Good tidings." He rose from his seat and gave her a tight smile before holding out a chair. For the briefest moment, their eyes met. She murmured a thank you as she slid onto the seat.

Calis' eyes widened and his mouth dropped open. "Now, Cap'an, I'm not one to complain about yer preferences, but I draw the line at bedding children."

Paladin laughed out loud. The woman gasped, her eyes wide.

Not giving her time to respond, he slapped Calis on the shoulder and grinned. His tension slid away under Calis' comment. He would rather have her ire turned on him than his first mate. "Well, my friend, I happen to agree with you, but this is no child. A bit small, but she is indeed a grown female. This I can attest to."

She glared at him. Without remorse, he smiled wider.

Calis leaned over the table. He gave her a hard stare. "Why is her hair so short? She's not marked for a crime, is she?"

"No, she isn't marked. She was a gift to me from the

Cosmos. A shooting star brought her," Paladin replied, keeping his voice low.

Calis sat back, frowning at him. "Bah, ye and yer mysticism. It's enough to make me sick."

"Do you mind? I'm hungry," the woman said. Tension and perhaps fear more than any other emotion spoke through her clasped hands with the white knuckles and the tightened jaw. Paladin curled his fingers into a fist to keep from touching her in hopes of reassuring her.

"What's her name?" Calis asked, waving a serving wench over.

Paladin had neglected to ask her. At the time, it hadn't been important. While he stared at her, a strong premonition filled him. He'd caught a flicker of life within her, separate from her own force. His stomach threatened to empty into his throat. The sensation grew until he knew without a doubt the truth to it.

"I'm Seren." She held out her hand to Calis. His first mate cocked a brow at her hand. She pulled back, clasping hers together in her lap. "Never mind."

"Yer name is Seren Never mind?"

Struggling to keep the bile down, Paladin forced a chuckle past his lips. "No, her name is Seren. Nothing else. My sweet, this strapping gent is my first mate, Calis Mer. And of course, you know who I am."

Calis grunted. "Ye dern right she knows. Probably why she sniffed ye out. Any woman in her right mind would want bragging rights on bedding Captain Paladin Fulcan."

Paladin grinned and winked at Seren. She rolled her eyes, her lips twitching. *Well, she took that comment in fine form.*

With another grunt, Calis stood. "I suppose I'll leave

ye two for a bit. I'll tell Alice, that lazy wench, to bring a platter for the mite here. Remember, Sire, we don't have much time before we sail."

At Calis' slip of the tongue, Paladin stiffened. Calis dipped his head, pivoted on his heels, and hurried to the counter. Paladin stared at his retreating back, knowing his first mate realized his error by the slump of his broad shoulders.

Fool, what was he thinking to call him by his long-forsaken title? He'd given up his royal vestiges many years ago, yet Calis seemed to forget the fact. He glared at the man disappearing amid the occupants and tables. The woman cleared her throat, bringing his attention to her.

She laid her palms flat on the table, angling a look at him. "Do your men call you Sire very often?"

"You have discovered a secret. Not many know of it," he said, lifting his tankard and taking a sip. He watched her over the rim. Calis' misled loyalty might cause complications with her.

"So I screwed royalty last night." She closed her eyes, swallowed, and then faced him. "Look, I want to go home. I have friends, people I work with who'll worry about me if I don't contact them."

He set the tankard down, relieved that the fact he was of the royal line did not affect her. His interest caught on her smooth features. The soft curve of her lips tempted him to lean close enough to cover her mouth with his. She spoke again, forcing him to pay attention to her words.

"You said the dragons were the ones who opened the door. I need to see them. Can you tell me how?" She started then stopped with a shake of her head. "No, that's not right.

Can you take me to them?"

Her gaze sought his and she hesitated a moment before she continued. "If you go, maybe they'll listen to you more than me. Then they'll send me home. To Earth."

Had she practiced her words before she came to meet him? Tilting his chair toward the wall behind him, he draped an arm over the back. "No, I cannot. No one goes to see the dragons unannounced. A request must go out across Avaris to the great clan leaders. If they agree to meet with us, a gathering will then take place."

Silence passed between them for several moments. She opened her mouth then shut it. He watched her internal battle pass over her features. After a few moment of consideration, she found the strength to speak.

"Fine. Tell me how to send the requests. They have to listen to me."

He glanced at the rough surface of the table, trying to think of a way to make her understand. Taking a breath, he said, "No matter what you and I desire, I believe the dragons opened the portal for a reason. They want something from you, and possibly, me. I care little for their manipulations, but there is nothing I can do to fix this without their help."

Taking a chance, he covered her hands with his before continued. "I deeply regret bringing you here. For now, we will travel to the land of Bae to visit the other off-worlder. Perhaps there, we will learn of another way you might return home."

She released a shuddering sigh. Her body sagged as a small smile passed over her lips. "Thank you."

Under his palm, he felt what had to be relief surge

through her body, making the blood race in her veins. It spiraled to end at the base of her belly, reminding him, even verifying what he'd sensed earlier. He had never been a man to keep silent if another needed important information. She needed to know this, now, not later. Still, he hesitated for a moment before he spoke.

Paladin cleared his throat, turned away from her for a moment, glanced around the room, cleared his throat again, then turned back and met her eyes directly and spoke bluntly. "You carry my child."

She flinched at his words and shook her head in denial. He tightened his hold on her hand.

"You do. I could sense it when you came downstairs. The child's dragon blood cries out to his sire," he explained. With disbelief radiating from her eyes, she seemed unable to comprehend what he spoke of.

She slipped her hand from beneath his. Fisting it, she hid it on the other side of her body, her arm formed a protective barrier across her stomach. He focused on her abdomen. Yes, a slight flicker. He still sensed it there, growing stronger with each passing second.

She glared at him. "There isn't any way you can tell if I'm pregnant. It'll take weeks before my body will start showing signs."

He half-smiled. Her ignorance of his world made it difficult to explain things like this. "If the child was pure human, yes, but this babe carries the white dragon blood in its veins. A male child."

Seren opened her mouth to speak, but Alice appeared. She dropped a platter on the table.

"'ere ye go. Fresh cooked." Sliding the plate filled with fluffy eggs topped with plump sausages toward

Seren, she grinned and winked at Paladin before flouncing away.

Grateful for the interruption, Paladin lifted his tankard. He kept an eye on Seren. She gulped, took a deep breath, and then picked up the tine. She frowned at it, shrugged and stuck the two-pronged, metal implement into the eggs.

One small bite and she glanced at him. "Needs a little salt."

"Salt?"

"It's a seasoning," she said.

He tilted his head toward her. *A seasoning? Ah, to flavor foods.* "They have brine sticks. Some prefer to take a lick before each bite. I've never cared for them."

"It's okay. I'll pass," she murmured, ducking her head after another small bite.

He studied her, calculating the changes due to occur in her body from this babe she carried. Her rich human blood, untouched by magic, would affect the child's magic. In what manner, he dared not begin to imagine.

He narrowed his eyes, assessing her slender frame above the table, watching the vein pulse in her neck. Her blood carried no magic. He tried to understand why the dragons, knowing this, granted his wish. She had mentioned a white dragon. Lior, leader to his clan, was the only white dragon he knew of who possessed the ability and power to implant visions.

If Lior wanted to give him a child, why do it this way? The baby would battle against Seren in his effort to survive. Paladin stared into his tankard. Sorrow mixed with guilt over touching her.

For all Lior's help, the great white dragon chose the wrong female for his child's vessel. No matter her reasoning, Lior should have found a different woman, another dragonseed, to carry his child. Not a full-blooded human. He intended to assist Seren in her search to find a different way home, yet he dreaded the idea of having to approach the dragons to request help. The overlarge beasts were at the best of times temperamental. He never knew what to expect from them.

There was also the strong possibility of her miscarrying. This weighed heavy against her. To his memory, no woman without dragon blood had ever transfused their human blood for dragons in order to give birth, nor to his knowledge, had one carried a full-term dragonseed babe.

These other women had been born and lived on Avaris all their lives. Their blood soaked in the magic from the planet, but even this had little effect on the outcome of their terms. The babes had always died, taking the mother with them. Seren had human blood from Earth, a place where magic lay dormant under the inhabitants' disbeliefs. He cringed. Their child had little to no chance of survival.

Yet another son of his was destined to die. He had been careless. Last evening, with all the drink, he'd allowed his staunch guard to slip. He had needed a woman, any woman to fill the emptiness inside him. For just once, he had desired a woman to want him, not because of his ancestry, but because of him. Now, he'd have their deaths on his conscience.

She set her tankard on the table. The sound pulled him out of his morose thoughts. He smiled at her. Her eyes widened, and then she lowered her gaze to her plate.

When he saw she had eaten a sizable amount and showed no sign of partaking more, he stood, offering her his hand.

She looked at him, watching his every move.

His stare wandered over the fragile length of her neck to the sweet slope of her breasts where her shirt gaped. "I travel to the Black Dragon stronghold of Velhavin. We will detour to Dene and speak with Leo, the other off-worlder. He is a close friend with a powerful wizard there. Perhaps, we can discover from him another pathway to Earth. From there, we will decide what to do next."

A spark of hope flared in her eyes. She stared at him, chewing on her bottom lip. From the expression on her face, she considered reaching the other off-worlder. For now, that was fine. She had enough to worry about with her arrival on Avaris. He, however, had decided. Her future and his were tied to each other. He refused to let her slip away from him.

He slid his fingers under her arm, and helped her stand. "Come, we must be off. The winds are picking up. The time is best to depart while they are strong."

"I get sea sick easily," she blurted out a second before they reached the front door of the common room.

He chuckled, her innocent response on venturing into the unknown cast a bit of light on his darkened thoughts.

"Indeed, that would cause a problem if we traveled across the seas." Out of the corner of his eye, he caught the look she aimed at him, a frown marring her heart-shaped face. "You will see soon enough."

Still holding her arm, he moved through the door which led to the inn yard. Her pulse jumped under his fingertips. It annoyed him that her fear and nervousness increased with each step. He'd give anything to calm her fear.

Wide-eyed, she surveyed the locals scurrying throughout the yard. She gasped, coming to a complete stop. He glanced in the direction she stared. The Solrai moon floated white and full in the blue sky. Shadowing the pearly circle, the second moon appeared in crescent shape.

He leaned closer to better hear her soft words. Her hand trembled as she pointed toward the moons. "There's a design in the center. On the surface. How did it get there? It's a moon. That's impossible, isn't it?"

For a moment, he stared at the silvered disc in the sky. The dragon skull image covering the entire surface appeared normal and comforting to him.

"Why would it not be possible?" He'd never realized how different her world was from his. Books told the basic facts, of how each planet had a moon in orbit around it. He could not recall if Earth had one or two moons. Still, how different were these when compared to her world's moon? Her strange ideas intrigued him more with each second he spent in her company.

She frowned at him and lowered her hand. "They're in outer space. Thousands of miles away. You'd need a space ship to fly there along with several decades to do something of that magnitude."

He tilted his head, enjoying the wide-eyed surprise mingled with amazement etched on her features. "It may be impossible for your world but not ours. Great magic formed the dragon's skull which marks the Solrai moon. In turn, the moon guides our world."

"How? How does it guide you?" She pulled backward.

"In the ways of our lives." Paladin smiled, realizing he had confused her more. Without knowing how to explain the answer she needed, he released her arm. He started to walk once more, drawing away from her while he spoke. "The moons show us the seasons, planting crops, wars, all things, including the times of birth."

Seren's wooden clogs clopped over the cobblestones in the yard. He glanced at her out of the corner of his eye. Good, she followed. Silence reigned between them for several minutes while they moved away from the inn and onto the path leading into the main section of the port city. Each time she lagged, she came to a halt, staring at what he assumed was something exotic to her. Paladin slowed and waited, giving her time to assimilate the differences of their worlds.

Excitement raced through him like a dragonseed who'd just gained their wings and had taken flight for the first time. He couldn't understand why, but he wanted her to be pleased with his ship. Perhaps it was his guilt over knowing that he was responsible for her presence here, but reality told him it was more than that. He liked her, enjoyed being with her, and genuinely wanted her to be happy here. He was proud of his vessel, and he wanted her to think it spectacular.

A gift from his deceased father, he took great pride in the vessel. Sleek and swift, the air ship cut through the skies like his blade through the flesh of his enemies. He moved away from her, beginning the trek to the dock,

When too much distance formed between them, Seren called to him, "Wait up."

"Fear not, I will never leave you. My responsibilities are a duty I always tend to," he said over his shoulder.

Once she reached his side, she spoke, icy anger

47

lacing her words. "I am not your duty, nor your responsibility."

Paladin chuckled. "Are you not? How do you expect to survive without me to fulfill your needs and offer protection until you reach Dene?"

She remained silent for a few seconds, so he continued. "Do you realize how vulnerable you are? You have no knowledge of the customs of our world. How do you expect to survive if you leave my side?"

"Just shut up, will you?" she snapped.

Several feet in front of her, his back to her, he grinned, confident she wouldn't notice and become more irritated with him. Seren's fiery spirit held great promise for her ability to cope in this world. He sobered a second later. If she survived, that is.

The stone path leading from the inn to the docks overflowed with vendors and customers. He sidestepped a child that darted into his path. When he realized the child might collide with Seren, he reached out, snatching the young one by the collar, halting him.

"Not so fast. There is too many people here for your speed," he warned the boy. The youngster nodded, his attention on Paladin's face

The innocence in the child's eyes sparked the sorrow of his loss. A son to hold, to teach...to love. But now, Paladin had nothing except the black box which was sealed with magic and encased the remains of his wife and child. Even the child resting within Seren held little promise it would survive until birth.

The squirming boy slipped from his numb fingers. Paladin turned his face away lest Seren see the raw pain he experienced. The boy ran, dodged through the crowd and disappeared. Desire reared. It brushed against the searing pain of his loss. Need for a son from his body to race ahead of him, laughing and full of life was something he'd given up hope of ever gaining.

Seren placed a hand in the middle of his back, catching his attention. He didn't turn, just started walking forward, glad for the interruption.

Her voice, filled with curiosity, reached him above the rapid tap-tap of her clogs. "Why is everyone staring at you? Are you so different? Do they know who you are? Or are you an oddity here?"

Shaking off his melancholy, he welcomed her inquisitiveness. He assumed she meant the way he was formed and his features. "They stare because of my heritage. The white dragon clan is well known, but few have the opportunity to see one of my blood. My clan members do not travel across Avaris much. They prefer to trade closer to our homeland."

"So you're like a famous person?"

He stopped and shook his head. "By famous, do you mean high status of birth or placing?"

"Popularity."

"Ah." Of course, the world she came from judged each other in such a fashion. Was this why she never spoke of a special person waiting for her on Earth? Did her kinsmen view her unsuitable because she refused to have another child? If so, then her yearning to return to a world which didn't accept what she desired seemed odd to him. Few, even on Avaris, possessed the strength to stand against what society viewed to be right. Only the strong ones refused to allow the world's dictates to rule them.

"Hurry, Seren. Time is slipping by. My crew awaits us." He steeled his features and faced her, his hand extended before him to guide the way.

His steps lengthened, but his speed did not. The taptapity from her clogs told him she stayed with him. Paladin's hearing was keyed to the sound so when it stopped, he glanced over his shoulder. He suppressed the need to laugh out loud.

The look on her face seemed a cross between surprise and shock. Turning to the direction in which she stared, he saw what had stopped her. A group of Felerians, all females, washed and rinsed their brightly-colored clothing at a freshwater stone drain. Singing one of their native songs while they worked, the group failed to notice they'd captured Seren's attention. He tried to see them in the same manner she did.

Unable to comprehend why she found them so odd, he moved closer. He leaned down to study her. "Do you not have females like these in your world?"

"They're cats. Animals. But they're shaped like humans." Stormy gray eyes, glazed with amazement, rose to meet his. "I don't understand?"

"Then do not. Simply accept, because you will never fully understand the why," he remarked. "The Felerians have existed for thousands of years. They are a gentle, but mischievous clan."

Her eyes widened. "Clan?"

"Of course," he said, taking her by the arm and leading her away. "There are a few males aboard my ship. Perhaps if you speak to them you will become more accustomed."

When she raised her hand to brush across her forehead, he noticed it tremble. She spoke low, "I don't know if I can ever become accustomed. It's a little overwhelming. I don't feel good."

"In time, your distress will end. Look." He pointed toward the dock. "Just ahead. There's my ship."

Chapter Four

Seren's knees started to buckle. She locked them, struggling to remain standing. Paladin stood with his feet apart, pride evident on his face. How did he stand there so calm while her entire world threatened to splinter into a thousand pieces?

Sails clapped in the wind, catching her attention. She swung her gaze from the tall man next to her to where he looked.

His ship rose four stories from the bottom to the top of the center mast. Six sleek propellers extended on poles, rising above the sails and out from the sides of the ship, two upright from the deck along with two horizontals on either side. The beautiful natural tones and textures of the wood flowed beneath a coating of glossy sealant. Crisp white sails flapped in the brisk breeze coming from the seas beyond the cliffs. On the front of the ship, a carved figure of a white dragon perched, its wings open, its nose pointed to guide the way. The beauty amazed her, but her admiration disappeared when she noticed the vessel floated not on the water, but in the air next to the dock.

He turned to her, but she ignored him. Still in a state of shock from all the strange people and creatures moving around her, she stood frozen, staring with her mouth open. A lean finger pressed up on her chin.

Light glinted in his eyes. His excitement became evident with his wide smile and the eager sound in his voice when he asked, "Do you like it?"

A few quick nods turned into a few adamant shakes of her head. "It looks like a clipper ship from my world. Only there, they float on water and there aren't any propellers."

He chuckled. "This one can ride on both air and water, the same as the white dragon."

The strange heaviness she experienced the night before had never disappeared. With everything happening so fast, she'd managed to ignore how weighed down and slow she seemed to have become. No longer physically able to move, she looked at him and said, "I think I'm going to be sick."

At her whispered comment, he leaned closer, his head cocked while he listened. One hand slipped around her waist, bringing her body against his. He moved nearer to the gangplank. "Easy now. I'll take you aboard so you may rest."

She tried to pull away, the soles of her clogs skidding over the stones. One step and she would physically collapse. Everything she knew to be true was gone and her perception of the world around her threatened to overwhelm her. Seren feared that momentarily she would crumple into a sobbing heap on the cobblestones. Yes, she would, without a doubt. The sudden weakness in her legs verified it. The muscles in her thighs trembled. She shook her head, "No."

Paladin stopped to study her for a second, and then asked. "What do you fear?"

"I don't know where I am or even who I am anymore. Am I insane and this is the result?" Her eyes sought his, anxious to know the truth.

He shook his head. "I fear I have no answers to give you peace in this matter."

There, in his blue eyes, lay the truth to his words. Still, could she trust him? He was the dragon, the one who had haunted her every minute before he'd arrived and rescued her. Her knees, no longer able to hold her up, gave out. His strong arm, encircling her waist, tightened. He turned her toward the long, wide gangplank. Her feet missed the boards several times, but his strength helped hold her up. Once on deck, he released her.

The world spun. Lightheaded, she tried to remain focused, but doing so became more difficult. The sailors' shouts along with ropes pulled through pulleys, even Paladin's deep voice speaking to the man she'd met at the inn came to her like it was through a tube, distant and hollow.

Everything that had happened was too much for her to handle in such a small amount of time. She sagged and he grabbed her arm. With his touch, a stream of vibrating electricity raced up her arm to the nerve endings in her body.

More aware, she looked up at him in surprise. The moment of weakness passed. What had he done? She found no answer in his worried stare.

"Come, you're pale. You should rest a while," he murmured, and then swung her up into his arms. She should have struggled, but the effort didn't seem worth it. She buried her face in his neck, taking a deep breath. Spicy rich flavor saturated her senses.

"How are you?" he spoke low against her temple.

She couldn't answer. Her mind swirled with

awareness of him. He remained silent until he turned sideways to enter a door to go below. "A short rest will help."

Heat from where his body pressed against hers, his vibrant life force spoke, reminding her of their night. She decided to stay quiet, afraid she might say something she would later regret.

This man had rescued her. She had given her body to him the night before without a thought. Now, she found that she wanted him once more. Why? What quality did he possess which attracted her so much?

Down a set of narrow stairs, he moved across a dimly lit hallway to a door on the right. He twisted the knob and entered a large cabin. The bed, built into a wall on one side of the room, captured her attention. A white quilt embroidered with a blood red emblem in the center was spread over the bed. The crimson in the pattern brought forth a tide of revulsion in her.

Similar to a coat of arms, the shield of the decoration carried an unfamiliar design in the middle. The red in the pattern washed over her. Blood scent whirled through her head, sending sharp crisp memories of Mandy's death rushing to the front of her mind. Thick, sickening blood had slipped through her fingers. And she was useless, unable to capture it and draw back into her tiny daughter. Her stomach turned, temples pounding a steady tempo.

"Put me down," she cried, struggling in his arms. She flipped over, landing on her hands and knees. The rough wood grain on the floor dug into her skin. Bile filled her throat and spilled from her. Retching, she continued to gag until her stomach ached worse than her knees. Her head, but most of all, her heart turned numb.

A cool cloth passed over the back of her neck to her face.

He cleaned her up, calmly reassuring her with gentle words. Embarrassed, Seren heard the soothing tones, but they came from a distance, making it difficult for her to concentrate enough to understand the phrases. Her knees and palms ached from the fall. Exhaustion overrode all her senses. She slumped to one side, allowing darkness to take her away.

****

Paladin lifted her against his chest. He walked to the bed. For several seconds, he stared at the sleep cover his deceased wife had made just before her death. He changed directions. He went instead to the window seat at the rear of the room. With gentle care, he lowered Seren onto the thick white cushions.

Several minutes later, he had managed to remove her clothes. He used heated water to bathe her, and then tucked a thick, soft blanket around her. Sure she would rest easy, he cleaned the floor. Once finished, he stripped and folded the bed cover. One long glance at her reassured him that she rested well. He left the cabin, carrying the cover with him.

Thoughts churned in his mind as he went to the lower reaches of the ship. Seren's illness worried him. Because she was from Earth, she carried none of the innate magic most on Avaris possessed. Could this be what caused her sudden illness or had his child's blood already started poisoning her?

After walking through the maze of cargo, he'd gone half the length of the ship when he reached the depths of the ship. He approached the coffin which was sealed with magic. The lid was encrusted with the runes of both the Black and the White Dragon clans. He clenched his teeth and flung the spread over the casket containing his wife and child's bodies. A tug here and there straightened the cloth so the emblem centered on the elongated box. He rested his hand on the top for a second, seeking comfort, but then he shook his head and turned away. He would never find answers with the dead.

He'd sensed his new dragonseed's spark of anxiety over the spread. Had his tiny son recognized and then rejected his clan's emblem designed in the offensive crimson? If so, this would explain Seren's reaction.

For a moment, a streak of unease riffled through Paladin. He stumbled on the stairs leading to the upper level of the ship. His hands slapped the wall on either side of the stairs. He stopped to regain his balance. If the unborn infant was able to sense the insult to their clan, then his strength outmatched Paladin's. The babe would be considered a threat to his uncle, Rylen, the new king of the White Dragon clan. With no heir of his own, Rylen would fear a child of Paladin's, especially one with such strong magical ability.

Paladin took the stairs leading to the upper level two at a time. He pushed all the worrisome thoughts from his mind. Seren needed him. If their child had not caused her to be sickened by the crimson emblem then her body might be trying to end the pregnancy. Should that be the case, he needed to stay with her. He would not have another life lost because of his carelessness.

****

Seren felt the sun's heat on her face. She smiled, enjoying the warmth. For a second, she imagined she heard Mandy's soft voice calling her.

She cracked her eyelids open and glanced out a clear window pane. Blue skies dotted with cotton clouds filled her vision. Something fluttered in her abdomen. She covered the spot with her palm. There, she felt it again. Comfort touched her mind. She concentrated on the spot, soaking up the emotions coming to her.

Birds appeared on the outer edges of her vision. She shifted her gaze. She watched the wings moving, brilliant white down and bluish gray up. Their feathers along with their shapes reminded her of the herons she often saw in the bayous and marshes around New Orleans. She smiled. The reminder brought wonderful memories of growing up in the Crescent City.

Every summer her parents would take her to beach on Pontchartrain Lake. Water, sand, and sun had covered her from head to toe. She'd loved the summer months with picnics in the park. They'd feed the pigeons in Jackson Square. Then when she'd grown and had her child, she'd done the same for her. She smiled at the memories.

Soft footsteps approached her from behind. The touch of a warm palm on her neck soothed her. A second later, the cushion dipped from the person sitting.

Paladin's deep voice warmed her more than the sunlight. "You're awake. You must be much better if you can smile."

"What kind of birds are those? They look similar to ones on Earth," she asked, not ready to face him.

Silence answered her for several moments.

When he leaned above her, he cast a shadow over her shoulder and chest. "They are not birds. Those are dracs, fledgling dragons. They are from my clan's namesake."

Surprised, she shifted closer to the window, studying the flying beasts. Small, with slender bodies, the creatures showed little to no resemblance to the beast from her vision. "Those are the dragons?"

She glanced at him. What she saw melted away her surprise. Golden strands lay against the high cast of his cheeks. Seren reached up and glided a fingertip across his bottom lip. His smooth, almost silky lips parted. She lowered her hand, returning her gaze to the window.

She struggled to keep her desire under control. Need pounded between her legs. When she spoke, she kept her tone even. "I don't like the way you make me feel."

"In what manner do you speak?"

"Heat, lust…passion."

"Is that so terrible?" His voice had deepened.

She sighed. "For me, yes. I don't want to feel those emotions. I wanted the vision to end. Desiring you doesn't fit into the picture."

"Desire is not bad." He brushed the back of his hand over her cheek.

She studied him for a moment. All she had to do was agree, wrap her arms around his neck and pull him to her. He wanted her. Probably in the same intense fashion as she did him. She closed her eyes, savoring the gentle touch. "No, but I promised myself I wouldn't ever leave my heart open to anyone again. That includes casual affairs. I won't take a chance of having another baby. I wasn't able to see the danger to Mandy. Even with my special sight, I couldn't save her."

There, she'd said the words out loud. The very ones which ran through her mind every day like a constant cyclone, ripping and tearing her apart. Did he understand how she felt with the loss of his child? Had he held his baby against his breast while listening to each quiet breath? She had carried and given birth to Mandy, had watched her grow into a vibrant little girl. In the end, she'd buried her, leaving her with nothing but sorrow filled memories

"Will your ability save our child?" He slid his hand away from her cheek to place his palm over her flat belly. She felt a slight flutter in her abdomen.

She inhaled his scent. Powerful, intoxicating, she wanted to roll over and face him. It'd be so easy to reach up and cover his beautiful lips with hers. She bit the inside of her cheek, fighting the desire threatening to overcome her.

Once she had her need for this man shut behind a mental lock, she faced him. Her voice stayed strong as she said the words she dreaded speaking to him. "I don't want your child."

His eyes widened. The only sign of his reaction. He nodded once. "It is for the best. You are human, I am not. The dragon blood in my veins will overpower yours and you may die."

Seren held her gaze steady with his. "What do you mean?"

"Dragon and human blood must be magically fused so the combination of the two will not overpower one or the other."

"Sounds like oil and vinegar before you shake it."

He shrugged. "Once the blood is fused, the risks of the child destroying you are lessened."

"That's good to know. I don't want to die, especially not here."

A smile flittered across his lips. "Try not to worry. I swore I would keep you safe. Did I not tell you this when I found you?"

She wanted to kiss him, to feel the warmth of his

mouth on hers and the slick length of his tongue while he thrust inside her body, sending her over the edge. Steeling her mind, she responded in a cool tone, wanting to drive him away so she could gather her resolve alone. "I don't need you to protect me, just find a way for me to go home."

He eased back. With each passing second, the chasm between them widened. He took a deep breath, his chest expanding under the gray cloth. "Very well, I will find a way to fulfill your desire."

They were strangers to each other, yet he'd saved her. Even now, he seemed to want to help her escape from this world. "What happens if this child you claim I carry threatens my life? What will you do? Will you chose me or the baby?"

He didn't hesitate with his answer. "I will bring you to the mystic healer myself to take my child from your body before I allow you to die."

Chapter Five

Surprised, Seren studied him. She hadn't expected him to choose her. He stood and walked to the door. He glanced at her with his hand on the knob before he left. She stared at the door for a long time, unable to form a solid thought with him gone.

With a sigh, she faced the window. A drac flew nearer to the ship. This close, she saw the difference between it and the herons. Feathers hadn't reflected the light. No, it was the pearl-colored scales covering the beast. Instead of an elongated yellow or black beak, its narrow snout ended in a point. Long incisors overlapped its lips.

For a moment, the young dragon appeared to look at her with its slit-pupil, amber eyes. She sat up, unable to turn away while the beast, its wings moving up and down in a hypnotic rhythm, drew next to the window. Warmth increased in her abdomen. The fluttering she felt while Paladin was with her increased. The drac's wing brushed against the pane, it opened its mouth and emitted a low mewl.

Intense warmth erupted in her womb. She froze, unsure of what was happening to her. But pain soon raced through her body, eliciting a cry from her. She fell off the window seat, trying to draw in a breath. Confused, unsure what was happening, she fought against the rise of panic. She forced movement to her lethargic limbs to escape from the area around the window. The heat increased inside her body, so strong it seemed like it was going to engulf her. The drac cried out once more and her torment overcame her. She writhed in agony on the wooden floor.

****

Paladin stood on the bow of the ship. Blue water, capped with white tips, churned below him. He closed his eyes, inhaling the salty air. Four more days would see them in Dene. If the weather held. If Seren lived.

Her skin seemed paler to him and her body more fragile. This strange woman suffered because of him. He had planted his seed in her, now the effects of the pregnancy were occurring too fast.

A flock of dracs appeared in the left side of his line of vision, distracting him. He counted six.

Calis' heavy step approached from behind. His first mate's words confirmed what he suspected. "They're gathering. Too many sighted too close together. What do ye make of it?"

Paladin watched several more dracs cross the ship's path. "That you are correct. Have you heard any rumors coming from Xelerdin? Has Rylen caused more havoc to the neighboring realms?"

One young dragon glided up from the side of the ship, hawked at him, and then swung to meet the others. The drac's word, not a true language, but understood by all who carried dragon's blood in their veins slapped him in the face.

Sire.

He started to step forward, but stopped. His younger brother, Rylen, was King. Bask, the guardian wizard to the great white dragon, Lior, swore he had informed all of their blood the news of Paladin's abdication. Did the drac not know? Had he never received the news? Or had it refused his brother's right to the throne? If so, was it alone or were there others like this one?

"Ye should never have denied yer rightful place." Calis pointed toward another large flock following the same path of the first. "They gather for certain. Looks like war is coming, and I don't see anyone but ye able to stop it."

Paladin angled a look at his friend. "What has my brother done?"

Calis shifted from one foot to the other for a moment before he blurted, "He's widened his borders. A great deal from the word I received in Gilliesport. Didn't want to tell ye, what with yer recent loss and all."

Paladin closed his eyes, gritting his teeth. Why did Rylen desire more than what he already possessed? What was his purpose in expanding the White Dragon realm? Was it domination over the weak or annihilation of the lesser rulers? Paladin tried to understand, but no answer came to him.

Battling to control the anger growing inside, he pivoted toward the door leading below. He must do something, but what? How should he stop his brother? The timing was off. He had sworn to help Seren. He fully intended to keep his word.

When he neared the door, it slammed open. Seren fell onto the deck in a tangle of blanket and slender limbs.

Shocked, fear overpowered all else, he leapt forward. He wrapped his arms around her. Her skin burned like she was on fire from the inside out. The rancid smell of illness rose from her skin. Underneath the odor, the sharp scent of dragon increased. Grabbing her against his chest, he whispered spells to protect her internal organs, veins, and brain, hoping to block his child's dragon fire which raged within her. He hurried to his room. Calis' footstep rang out behind him.

Without looking at the other man, Paladin ordered, "Bring freeze water. Buckets of it. Now, before we lose her!"

Boots thudded on the wooden floor behind him while Calis shouted orders. Paladin ignored the distraction as he laid Seren on the bed. The blanket dampened. It soaked up the body fluids escaping from her pores. He tugged the covers from around her waist and placed his palms against her abdomen. He concentrated, drawing the growing heat through his hands. Her stomach muscles contracted. He hoped the child would pass. Only then would Seren have a better chance of survival.

A fluttering started under his palms. His eyes widened.

The babe, his son, shifted and worked to cool his own blood. Paladin, amazed at the strength coming from the babe, worked harder to help.

Calis settled his large hand on Paladin's shoulder. "Ready, Captain. I've got all we have here on board ready. Talen also works using an icy spell to make more. Switched course too. We're heading for the nearest town to restock, just in case."

Paladin stood and lifted Seren then swung around to his bathing tub. Calis passed him to grab the first bucket filled with more icy water. Chunks of ice floated in the slush. Paladin lowered Seren, still wrapped in the blanket, into the tub.

He took the bucket's handle from Calis, and poured the thick liquid onto Seren's abdomen. She screamed, jerking, fighting in her semiconscious state. Her cries tore at him. He caused her pain, her tears.

As the minutes flew by, the crew refilled the empty buckets until a constant stream raced between his quarters and storage area. Vaguely, the thud of running boots registered as he worked over Seren. He drained the tub and started all over again. He helped her swallow cold water while Calis kept the tub filled. Each time Paladin touched her abdomen, he hoped it had cooled, but the heat remained. She twisted under his palm, trying to escape his touch.

The day turned to darkness. Tremors trailed up and down his spine. He'd experienced worry in his lifetime, but nothing like this. The only outcome he saw was her death. Nothing he did worked. He couldn't see how she would pull through this. The freeze water melted on the first touch to the skin over her abdomen. Her body rejected the cold. What else could he do? Paladin rubbed a hand over his face. He'd never been so helpless before. The cool liquids she took in passed from her pores. It just wasn't working.

Stubborn, he refused to give up. Long into the rising, his mind and body exhausted, he worked nonstop on her, hoping, yet at the same time, he waited for her death. He continued to pull the heat from her through his touch while Calis poured the frozen liquid over her.

On the second rising, the ship docked. At the thud of the gangplank connecting to a dock, he glanced at Calis. His first mate's haggard gaze met his. Paladin, his back aching, nodded and said, "Send word to find a local mage."

Calis looked at the suffering woman. He nodded and departed. Paladin knelt next to the tub, leaning over the brim. His hands, blue from the cold liquid, touched Seren once more. His skin turned pink under the heat. A hopeless sob escaped as he removed his hand. She was going to die because of him. His selfish need to have her put her in this situation. He'd never forgive himself for this. He lifted her from the water and carried her to the bed. With efficient strokes, he dried her before he pulled a light sheet over her.

Tears burned his eyes. In the middle of the night, his son had stopped fighting. He sensed no movement, no life force from him at all, yet the heat continued within Seren. After effects? Had the babe given up or had his strength ebbed?

He studied the agony etched on Seren's pale face. He eased onto the bed beside her, pulling her into his arms. For the first time since she'd fallen onto the deck, her restless battle against the heat ceased. He tensed, waiting for her next breath. He counted each one, hoping she would survive.

The door swung open and his first mate approached the bed, alone. Paladin realized before his friend spoke what he would say.

"They have no mage here, Sire. The nearest one is a day's flight to the north. I've ordered our immediate departure."

Paladin curved tighter to Seren, holding her closer. She would not make it to another morning. Her body might live, but her mind would not.

"Very well," he muttered. His gut felt like he'd swallowed a hundred dragon stones. The heaviness wouldn't abate. The weight of this night sat on his shoulders and it became heavier as the guilt loomed closer. He could not escape it and did not try. Seren's condition was his responsibility alone. He was the one who'd brought her here. He should have had better control. What kind of monster was he to do this to her?

His damnable wish. He desired a son, but not at the cost of murdering the child's mother. He groaned. If he had not drunk so much, had not made his wish, the door would never have appeared. But he had, and now he must pay penance for his carelessness.

He laid his palm against her lower abdomen. A faint stirring came to him. He waited. There—a slight movement.

He tilted his head toward Calis. "Leave us."

The older man tripped over his feet in his hurry. Once the door shut, Paladin turned his attention to his son. He narrowed his eyes, his vision becoming all-seeing and magical, a gift born of his dragon flesh. Focusing on the spot, he saw past Seren's skin and muscles to where the babe lay attached to her womb. His son's diminutive form resembled more the namesake of his clan than anything human.

Paladin studied the fast beat of his tiny heart. The babe's head turned toward him. A pulse of supplication surged to Paladin. In one beat of his tiny heart, Paladin understood what the unborn child tried so desperately to do.

Without considering, Paladin centered his power to his small son. He sent him the strength he needed to erect a barrier between his dragonfire and Seren. The barrier thickened and became wider. The babe swirled in the vortex of magical dragon flames, but the fire remained contained within the shell of his birth sack.

After several minutes, Paladin sensed the babe dozing. The heat, which had flared nonstop in Seren, ebbed to normal. He allowed one sob to escape before he shifted to his human sight.

Exhausted, he rolled from the bed and called for Calis. When his friend arrived, they set about cleaning the room.

Once Calis departed with the tub, Paladin washed the sweat from Seren, hoping to make her more comfortable.

Under clean sheets, she lay still. Hands trembling, he tucked the edges against her. So pale, fragile, she had not wanted a child. Once more, guilt slapped against his conscience.

Calis returned, carrying a chair to the side of the bed. "Here ye go, Sire, sit. Rest. Ye deserve it."

Paladin suppressed an urge to laugh. Deserve a rest? No, not he. He deserved to suffer the same way Seren had for what he'd done. He sat in the chair and turned to look at Calis. "Head for Dene. I want this ship there in one day. Use all of the dragonstones if you must."

A quick nod and Calis was gone. Paladin shouted to his first mate as his footsteps faded, "And rest. That's an order."

Seren frowned, stirring, her eyelids fluttering. He straightened in the chair, regretting the shout. Her eyes opened, and she looked at him. Without saying a word, she shifted onto her side with a groan, curling into a fetal position. He remained silent, motionless. She drifted off. He sighed in relief. Now, he would wait to see if her mind survived the ordeal with the dragon's fire. He rested his head against the back of the chair and closed his eyes.

Chapter Six

Quiet footsteps approached the bed. Seren opened her eyes. Paladin stood over her, blocking the rest of room. The beauty of his face took her breath away. She stretched. Sensitive muscles screamed silent messages throughout her entire body, forcing a gasp to escape.

"Careful. You have been sore ill," he said, taking her hand.

She stared at him while she tried to bring the pain under control. "What happened to me?"

Before he could answer, memories of the drac at the window rushed forward—the burning agony, her flight from the room, her need to find him. He would help her. Only him.

"The babe," he murmured.

At his soft comment, a sharp flash of fear shot across her chest followed by a wave of grief. She frowned, her hands moving to cover her abdomen. "I lost it?"

"No, our son lives. He helped save your life."

She studied him for several moments, trying to understand what he meant. A slow dull pounding set up behind her eyes, against the back of her head and radiated down her neck. Right now, she didn't want to hear an in-depth discussion on the baby's abilities. She wanted to find out what put her flat on her back with so many aches she was afraid to move. "That beast—the dragon—did something to me when it came to the window. It cried out. I felt like a fire was cooking me from the inside out."

Paladin nodded and eased onto the bed next to her. "He called out to our son. In turn, the babe responded."

"By trying to kill his mother?"

"That was not his intention. If you die then he dies. No, instinct caused him to answer the drac's call." He leaned toward her, and his hand brushed across her brow. "I am thankful you are whole."

She stared at him for a long time. "Me too. I want to go home"

"I'll not have your death on my conscience."

She grunted and shook her head. "If carrying your child is going to cause me this much pain, then why did you touch me?"

A sad, mischievous smile flittered over his lips.

"Uncontrollable passion?"

Another grunt and shake of her head. "I'm to blame too."

He brushed a finger over her lower lip. "You came to me so I might help you. Why? That is the reason you went above when the pain began. To find me. You knew I would help you?" His eyes held a spark of wonder. The light dwindled after a moment. He continued, a gentle smile returning to his lips. "You do need me."

His soft words evoked a rush of heat up her neck to her face. How dare he insinuate she needed him? The constant agony in her head increased. She clenched her hands into fists to keep from slapping his cheek. She narrowed her eyes and glared at him. "I don't need anyone."

"If this is so, why did you seek me out?"

Seren sighed, unable to remain furious with his

quietly asked question. She lifted a hand to her pounding head. Even that small motion caused her pain. Every muscle in her body ached fiercely. She couldn't think. Her brain refused to come up with any other reason for her action other than the truth which she blurted out with her last bit of defiance. "You're my stability here. There, are you happy?"

Paladin didn't crack a smile. He didn't even look pleased "Is this all I am to you?"

She gritted her teeth, determined not to reveal how much she wanted him. Never again. The pain was too fresh in her mind. When she didn't answer him, he shifted away and stood.

"We dock in Dene in an hour. Your clothes are there," he said, pointing to the foot of the bed. "Once we arrive, I will come for you."

After he closed the door, she laid there for a long time, her body refusing to relax. This wasn't her world. Her life. Why was this happening to her?

Her entire body ached worse than when she'd had the flu a couple of years ago. He said she'd almost died. If she died, so would the child he claimed she carried. She placed her palm on her abdomen. The fluttering came again. She bit her lips and squeezed her eyes shut, trying to control the sudden rise of tears.

A surge of warmth mingling with a sense of peace raced through her. Her eyes shot open and she clasped her belly over the spot from where she sensed the emotions rising. Her vision blurred, blackening along the edges. The first physical sign of her psychic abilities. Her mind floated away, and then, just as fast, returned with a jolt.

She glanced around at the white marble walls and

columns lining the portico. Sunlight slanted between the columns to produce a ladder effect. Broad slants of shadows interspersed with light on the floor and the back wall. Pulse throbbing, she realized she stood inside a tomb. She touched the side wall. Upon contact, she jerked away. Smooth cold stone, solid and real, surrounded her.

Dream of a death meant news of a birth.

The old meaning appeared in her mind. But whose death? Why was this vision so real? She actually felt the solidness of her body. Was that wind coasting over her skin? She rubbed her hands over her bare arms, and took a step toward the entrance. The soft cloth of a simple white shift covered her body, leaving her arms and calves bare. She tingled at the gentle caress of the material against her skin.

"Why do you not want me?"

A bolt of fear zagged up her spine. Her skin erupted with goose bumps. She glanced over her shoulder and saw the bottom half of a tall stool in the far corner of the tomb. Boot heels hooked over the last rung. A man sat in the shadows, facing her. She saw nothing of his face except for where the light cut across his eyes, revealing the strangeness of two different eye colors, the left clear blue and the right a gray hue. The shock of color in the white place surprised her. She returned his stare, trying to comprehend who and what he was to her.

"Oh, God," she muttered, "I'm psycho. I just know I am."

Light-hearted laughter came from him. She shivered. The sound of his laughter reminded her of someone, but she couldn't quite place it. Years ago, Mandy's laughter always brought a smile to her face.

This strange man's joy made her want to smile too. But why? What was it about him that put her at ease when she should have been tense?

She wanted to leave this place, to return to the present, but as with all her visions, she had to stay until the end. With her fear lessening, curiosity sparked. Her hand slipped to her abdomen, tightening over the spot. Unsure what to do, yet unable to stop, she whispered. "Can you see me?"

"Yes."

She gasped, her eyes wide, at the clear voice ringing within the cold white walls. A touch of joy edged his answer.

Seren waited, hoping the vision would end soon. Clouds streamed by, casting sunlight followed by lighter shadows across the floor. After several minutes, she took a deep breath and asked, suspecting who the man was, but not wanting to know for sure. "Who are you?"

"Your son."

A laugh of disbelief escaped. Oh, yes, she had lost it. More so now than when she'd first arrived in this place. This wasn't possible. She had never had a vision so real before. She had always been the observer not the participant.

Helpless and unsure, she shook her head. "No."

"Why do you deny my existence?"

Seren balled up her fist, fury followed on the heels of helplessness. "What am I supposed to think? It's impossible for me to know I'm having a baby this soon, and it's impossible for you to talk to me in a vision. Someone is playing with my mind. I don't like it." Her words were laced with venom. She shook with her inability to regain control over her emotions.

Suddenly peace coursed through her, stronger than before. Wanting to fight against the calming influence, she panted for a second, and then cried out. "I don't want another child."

He never moved. His eyes remained calm, serene. "I am not your lost one."

Seren froze. His words struck a hard blow to her heart. She relaxed her hold on her lower belly and stood straighter, her muscles no longer tender. "I know that. There'll never be another like her."

"No, never. But I am not her. I am myself."

She tried to suppress a sob, but failed. Her mind refused to face what this young man demanded she accept. She didn't want to experience the torture of her loss any longer. "Don't do this to me. I loved her so much. The pain I went through when I lost her...I don't ever want to feel that way again."

"Do you fear you will love me more than her?"

His question surprised her. She frowned, considering, but failed to find an answer she wanted to admit. "I don't know."

"Yes. You do. You have nothing to fear. I will never leave you. You have been chosen by the seven great dragons to be the vessel for my creation."

Seren frowned in confusion. "What? I don't understand. How do you know this? How can you appear to me like this? This isn't possible on Earth. I would be declared insane if anyone knew I was speaking with my unborn child, and he, a full-grown man, was answering me."

His eyes crinkled at the corners with his unseen smile. They lit with an internal joy and acceptance. "I am who I am from the moment of creation, thus my spirit became instilled within this form which is my body. Through the magic of the dragons, I have been allowed to release my power sooner than a normal dragonseed, thus at this time, I can speak to you through your ability to see visions."

Seren frowned while she considered his answer. Speech in the form of coherent language needed time to learn. Was the magic he spoke of powerful enough that even an unborn babe had the knowledge needed to communicate with her? When she didn't respond, he continued.

"I am here for a purpose, just like you. The dragon's magic opened the door to this place for one purpose. My creation."

Seren remained silent for several minutes, mulling over this new information. "Why would the dragons want you created? Why are you so important to them?"

"They fear the coming times. With me, all dragons will unite. They will become one power. Without me, chaos will reign. This world will end in a firestorm of war and plague as in the past. History repeated."

"And your father—me? What will happen to us?"

"My father is expendable. You are not."

An image of Paladin bleeding, dying, came to her. A sharp stab of regret sliced through Seren's chest. She hadn't expected this reaction. Only a few days had passed since she arrived on Avaris. Had she grown to feel more for the tall captain than she'd realized? She shoved those thoughts away and caught hold of the last part of his comments.

She laughed, bitterness filling her. "What makes *me* so unique? My wonderful ability as a mother? I couldn't save my child. So why is he expendable and not me?"

"He is the White Dragon King. The one to bring the seven great and powerful dragons together, but I will rule over them. Their blood will be one in me, never in him."

Relief flowed through her for a brief second. His answer pleased her. For some reason, she didn't want to examine why she didn't want anything to happen to Paladin too closely. Not right now. "So he won't die anytime soon?"

"I cannot say. There are other forces plotting Avaris' future besides the dragons. If all goes the way the seven desire it to, my father will live to see me on my throne. I would have it no other way."

She nodded, satisfied. "You can talk to me, but can you read my mind?"

"I am a part of you."

"I don't want to love you...please, understand."

Silence passed between them while his eyes remained locked on hers, and then he looked down. Sadness edged his brow. He shook his head. "I understand many things, but this is one I do not—you are my mother."

She took a deep breath, squeezed her eyes closed, but the tears still managed to escape. "If I love you, I'll never want to lose you. If I do, I know it'll be a million times worse than with Mandy. That's what I fear the most."

When she finished speaking, thick blackness coated her vision. She jerked, and Paladin's quarters reappeared around her.

A wave of peace washed over her. Her tense muscles relaxed. He comforted her, sweet baby. Her son. She patted her lower abdomen and smiled through her tears.

****

The shoreline along the island of Bae stretched out from either side of the city of Dene. The white strips showed stark against the gray cast of the sky along with the dark green foliage further inland. Stone buildings stood in staggered heights along the slopes and ridges of the coast.

Paladin paced back and forth on the bow, gazing at the land. His tension increased with the ship's approach, coming in low to the churning bluish-green sea, to the pale wooden docks sticking out into the water.

Lightning illuminated the deep charcoal clouds racing across the sky. The bolts streaked toward the trees just beyond the city. Sparks shot out from the smoke rising from the spot. The wind increased, bringing a singed odor with it. Paladin waited for the cool downpour.

Seren worried him. Not her ordeal with their son's dragon fire or even her strange beliefs, but how she affected him. The memory of how she felt under him remained, teasing, tempting him. Every time he shut his eyes, he saw the passion on her face when she…

He clenched his jaw. No, he refused to dwell on the matter. She made her decision. Far be it for him to argue, but he wanted to. He wanted more from her than she seemed willing to give. With their departure and her illness, he put the memories of their night from his mind. Now, they rose up to haunt him.

The sky roiled, roaring for all to hear the news of the approaching storm. The turmoil in the air called to the baser side of him, the part controlled by the beast—his dragon blood. With the call, his blood warmed with the need for a woman, but not just any woman. He wanted

Seren, desired the soft curve of her hips, the plushness of her inner thighs, her lips and tongue driving him wild. He closed his eyes, remembering how she felt beneath him—her body, small and slender, cushioning his while her inner muscles clasped him.

He had not wanted to pull out of her. She had created an unquenchable thirst in him for her which was now multiplied by the fact that she carried his child.

He tried to understand what she was going through, but he failed to comprehend the depth of her pain, her fear. He had lost a child, yet he had no desire to isolate himself from the world. No matter how he looked at her situation, he was lost because she gave him no real reason behind her refusal to have another child.

"Cap'an." Calis spoke from behind him.

Paladin pivoted to his first mate. Calis stood with his hands clasped behind his back. The barrel-chested man nodded toward the door leading below deck. Paladin shifted his glance and saw Seren, dressed in her boy's clothes, leaning against the doorframe, looking around.

Unobserved, he studied her, watching for any signs of her recent ordeal. Her eyes rounded with curiosity. The noise and bustle picked up with several of the sailors calling greetings to her. She had said there were none like the Felerians in her world. Now, she surveyed the males with intensity. Jealousy reared in him.

He took a step toward her before he realized what he'd done. He stopped, hands balling into fists. She did not belong to him. They had shared one night with no resulting bond but their child between them. Seren was well within her rights to look at other males if she so desired. He clenched his jaw. She didn't have to do so in front of him.

"Fetch two cloaks," Paladin barked at Calis. He stiffened in frustration over his reaction to the off-worlder. He turned toward the shore, eyes focused on the wall of rain approaching the ship.

"Aye, Cap'an" Calis replied, and then his gruff voice softened. "Uh, should she be up so soon after her illness?"

Paladin refused to allow anyone, even his good friend, to hear any concern from him about Seren. He responded in a level tone, "She is fine, besides I do not believe she would listen should I order her to remain abed. Go now, the storm draws nearer."

Thunder boomed, silencing the thud of Calis' retreating footsteps. Lightning flashed, illuminating the white-tipped waves. Paladin waited, confident she would seek him out. The wind gusted, shoving the loose strands of his hair away from his face. He breathed deep, his eyelids drooping as the weather's power flowed around him.

"Is this the place where the man from Earth lives?"

The question caused him to close his eyes. She had raised her voice so he would hear her above the storm. Desire to turn and gather her into his arms threatened to overpower him, but he managed to stamp the need down. He spurned the thought of her knowing how much he craved her.

"It is. Dene, City of Storms. The climate here is unstable, but the land is rich. The ground fertile to crops. Those who live here have learned to adapt." He glanced over his shoulder toward the doorway leading below. Where was Calis? The rain wall, dark and thick with ascending moisture, moved forward at a fast pace.

His first mate stepped from the passageway. He

hurried toward them. When Calis handed the dark cloaks to him, Paladin nodded.

"Here ye go, Sire." Calis bobbed his head. Without another word, he spun on his heels and left them.

"Put this on. The rain here is thick enough to drown a human," Paladin said, ignoring Calis' slip, handing her one of the bell-sleeved, hooded coats. Silver threads woven into the black fabrics glinted in the dimming light.

Her eyes rounded and her mouth formed a very enticing little O, her surprise was extremely becoming. His body stirred, the tingling beginning of need making him uncomfortable not being able to touch her.

"Drown? Are you serious?" She slipped her arms into the long sleeves, pulling the sides together in the front. He cast an admiring gaze down her slender body. The material clung to her every curve.

"It has been known to happen." He slipped his own over his shoulders, keeping a close eye on her. He watched, transfixed by the graceful movements of her lifting the hood over her head and pulling the thin protective veil down across the opening.

Her hand brushed the material, a frown marring her smooth brow. "What's this made of? It's not velvet."

"Sea drac scales. The ones that do not survive to become dragoons wash ashore. The clans of Bae harvest them. They weave the scales together into a cloth. Their clothing is made of this."

Through the veil's dark tint, her cheeks held a small measure of dusky pink. He fisted his hands to keep from slipping one under the material and touching the satiny skin there. With his jaw clenched, he faced the shore in time for the rain.

The sharp sting of the water against his skin helped

take his mind off his raw desire for her. He hesitated to lift the protective hood. Once certain he controlled his actions, he flipped the hood forward.

She brushed her fingers over the cloth. Her voice rose above the rain and wind. "It's not even absorbing the water. I've never seen anything like this, except maybe plastic."

"Plastic?"

She grinned at him. "That's a man-made material. We don't have dragons on earth."

Surprised, he brought his focus to her shielded face. "No dragons? I could not begin to imagine a place without dragons. They are so much a part of Avaris, I do not see how we could survive without them."

"There are myths about them on Earth, but no one has ever seen one. There are large lizards scientists..." She stopped when he lifted a brow in question. "Learned men called biologists who analyze animals among other things. They call the reptile a dragon, but it doesn't have magic. It can't fly."

Paladin stared at her while he mulled over this strange information. Dragons which never flew. Amazing.

The ship coasted closer to the water. The waves slapped at the hull, forcing the vessel to tilt to the left. With the sudden movement, Seren stumbled. He caught her around the waist, steadying her against his side. Her body pressed against his sent a streak of need coursing through his blood.

He gritted his teeth and muttered, "We will soon dock. Perhaps you should go below. I will come for you when we are more secure."

She shook her head. "No, I'm fine. I came to ask you

something."

Unable to relax, he waited for her to continue.

Her usual confidence fled when she spoke. "Can you...I mean...do people with dragon blood...can they appear in visions. I mean appear in a physical manner?"

Chapter Seven

Paladin's mouth dropped open. Of all the questions she had asked, this was not one he expected. "Appear in visions?"

She looked at him, her eyes pleading for the truth. "Yes…can they have an out of body experience, but it would be real. Can the ones with sight touch things in their visions, not just see them?"

Her answer surprised him so much he released her. "No. Nor have I heard of anyone who could. Why?"

"No one? Not even pregnant women?"

A fearful thrill speared through him. The idea that his child communicated with her pleased him, but what she spoke of was impossible. Even on Avaris. He had never heard of such, especially females of dragon blood. He shook his head.

"Oh." Her shoulders slumped. "I didn't think so, but I had to ask."

"Did our son appear to you?"

She turned away. "No."

He didn't press her. Although he possessed no ability to read her mind, he sensed that she lied.

Through the dense downpour, several ship hands, each cloaked for protection, scurried around them, throwing lines. They shouted greetings to the men on the dock.

His thoughts raced through what she had revealed.

The babe had appeared to her. He spoke to her. Why had she lied? Was she afraid he would not believe her? He decided to bide his time. When she was ready to tell him, she would.

"We will go straight to Largin's home. Leo, the other off-worlder lives near him," he said, hoping to put her at ease.

"Who is Largin?" She stepped to the rail, her movements careful and slow on the rain-slicked deck. He had to strain to hear her question.

Paladin moved to her side. "A wizard of renowned powers. Perhaps he can explain why the door opened.

Perhaps he can even help us open a way for you to return to your home."

Before she responded, Calis appeared behind them. "The plank's going down. If ye ready to disembark, I'll send a couple of men to find dragoons for ye."

She glanced at Calis, a frown on her face.

"That would be fine. Let me know when they arrive." Paladin motioned for his second in command to leave them. After Calis moved away, Paladin answered the question in her eyes. "Dragoons are older than the dracs. They have survived to the age where they lose the ability to fly until they mature into adult dragons. Many clans use them to travel across the land."

"How?"

"By riding them. How do you travel on Earth?"

"We have mechanical vehicles. Automobiles, airplanes— years ago people traveled by horses, a large four-legged animal." She rubbed her temple. "This is so strange. I don't know what to think."

"Come, we will wait on the dock. You will see there is nothing to worry over in this place." He hoped to alleviate some of her stress. Each time she learned a piece of information uncommon to her, she seemed to have a difficult time understanding.

He tried to think of a way to help her adjust, but had not by the time they reached the wide wooden dock. Two Felerian males stood holding the reins of a couple of iridescent blue-green dragoons. High-backed saddles sat on the sloping backs of the beasts. The adolescent dragons lowered their heads to the ground. They emitted low, scratchy caws.

Stopping several feet from the dragoons, Paladin stared in amazement. Never had he witnessed any dragon, young or old, show signs of reverence for one of another dragon clan. These were of the sea dragon clan. No humans carried their blood in their veins. He shot a glance at Seren. Was she the one they did this for or— his gaze dropped to where his child rested. Unease grew in his mind.

Seren covered her abdomen with one hand and stepped nearer to the dragoons. The closest one squatted lower to the ground, its scales reflected the small amount of light within the dense rain.

She looked at Paladin and an unsure smile flickered over her lips. Understanding, he took her by the waist, holding her steady while he lifted and swung her onto the saddle.

A low gasp escaped her, followed by laughter. "It's just like sitting on a horse."

Surprised but pleased to hear her laugh for the first time since he had found her, he relaxed, chuckling in response. "I would not know."

The dragoon straightened, standing on its hind legs. Seren squealed, leaning forward, trying to wrap her arms around the thick, long neck, but she failed to gain a secure hold on the wet scales. Paladin laughed out loud at her scrambling.

He slid an arm about her waist once more. "Sit straight, you will not fall off."

She eyed him through the veil. Doubt lines furrowed between her brows. "Are you sure?"

"Indeed."

He sensed that she was still tense, but she straightened her back. Once upright, Paladin placed her hands on the pommel, and then stepped back. He chuckled at her delighted amazement before he leapt into the saddle on the other dragoon. He leaned over and told the nearest Felerian how to reach him in case the crew needed him. Once settled in his seat, he glanced at Seren.

The rain increased, obscuring the solid lines of her body. He switched to his dragon vision. A red outline formed on her arms and head. Satisfied, he nodded, taking her reins in his free hand. "Hold on. I will go slowly, but with the rain, the trail will be rough."

The wind carried her affirmative answer to him then tore it away just as swiftly. He reined his dragoon's head to the right, nudging its sides. The beast stepped forward, its footing steady and sure on the slick stone slab streets.

Seren screamed. She scrambled to wrap her arms around her dragoon's neck. "Wait. Can we walk instead?"

"No. Sit straight. Hang on and you'll become adjusted to the gait. Or if you like, I can carry you before me." Hope budded in his chest and migrated to the area between his legs. He would like her to agree. He wanted to feel her body pressed against his.

Her answer came quick, without hesitation. "No."

Paladin chuckled. They proceeded up the winding street through the city, passing the white-walled buildings with the palm leaf roofs, and into the dense jungle beyond Dene.

The wind howled through the canopy. The rain thinned out. The jungle's dense foliage prevented the pounding downpour from striking them as severely as when they were in the open streets.

He leaned back in the saddle, shouting over his shoulder.

"It is not far ahead."

Seren did not answer. He glanced in her direction. Her grip on the sinewy neck had loosened and she sat a little straighter.

Even with the protection of the trees, the rain struck heavy blows on Paladin's head and shoulders. After several minutes, he looked back at her. She slumped in the saddle, her head low and tilted to the right side. Worried, he leaned over, shouting above the rain. "Are you alright?" She nodded.

Concerned, he turned to the front. He should have stayed on board his ship until the storm had passed, but he wanted her to meet with the man from her Earth. With a hard thrust of his foot, he urged the muscled beast forward. The dragoon's wide, webbed feet with three-inch claws, clung to the slick clay silt on the path. Step after long step, they moved faster.

A throbbing fire set up in Paladin's shoulder. Holding Seren's reins, his arm was pulled back and bent at an odd angle. He squeezed his fingers around the leather, tugging, hoping the other mount would move closer to give him a small amount of relief. He didn't want his arm going numb, causing him to lose his hold on her reins.

Seren's dragoon obeyed. The greenish scaled beast placed its tapered nose against Paladin's knee and kept it there. From this distance, he needed only to reach out to touch Seren. A grim half-smile formed while he fought to suppress sudden protective instinct rising within him. She was female to his male. He quelled the urge to howl out his need for her. The rain would prevent her from hearing, even at this close range, anything lower than a booming shout.

The jungle path widened at the top of a high sloping ridge. Three lunges and the two dragoons broke over the top. Small, white twinkles appeared through the thick downpour. He sighed in relief. Excitement raced in his veins at the light up ahead. The dragoons sped up; Paladin frowned at the change of pace. Both beasts moved without any guidance, as if they knew this place. The only explanation was that Largin, the wizard they were going to see, had sent them. No wonder the Felerians had no trouble finding dragoons for them to ride. But how had the wizard known of their arrival?

A sprawling house came into view. One story on the nearest end, two on the other, the stone walls with the thatched roof beckoned him, offering refuge from the weather. Yellow flames flickered in covered sconces on either side of the solid wood entrance. A small window cut high in the door spilled light on the stone steps leading to the door.

Paladin's dragoon halted in front of the entrance and roared, its head thrown back, mouth open to reveal sharp, pointed teeth. He patted the elongated neck in thanks for the ride and slipped from the saddle. He hurried through the sticky mud to Seren's side.

The ride, though short, had worn down the little bit of strength she had left. With her eyes half closed, her face pale, she tilted toward him. He grabbed her and carried her to the door. He prepared to set her on her feet to bang on the wood, but before he could, the portal swung in.

Largin stood in the opening. With his chin raised, nostrils flaring, black eyes sparkling, and his white hair tangled about his shoulders, he barked, "I have been waiting for your arrival."

Fear shot through Paladin. His father's old teachings echoed through his mind. *'Dangerous business to keep a wizard waiting. Never do so.'*

He cocked a brow at Largin, hoping his unease remained hidden from the wizard's keen gaze. "Have you?"

Largin nodded, motioning for Paladin to enter. Once inside, Paladin bent, helping Seren to stand. She still leaned against his side, and he kept his arm around her waist, holding her steady. Largin stuck his head out the door. He glanced left then right for a moment before ordering the dragoons to their beds. With a nod, he slammed the door shut.

The wizard's dark breeches and navy shirt hung on his thin frame. He had declined since the last time Paladin had visited. Concerned for the elderly man, Paladin frowned. "What has happened to you?"

Largin opened his mouth to speak but stopped. He stared at Seren's veiled face for a moment then shifted lower to her abdomen. "So, it's true, the rumors I have heard in the last few days."

Paladin stiffened. Seren glanced at him, questions evident in her eyes. He shifted his arm to her shoulder, giving it a squeeze in hope of relieving her worry. "This is Seren. She is from the place Leo comes from—Earth."

"I am aware. The scrying stone revealed this to me three days ago." Largin nodded. He waited until they had removed their cloaks, and then he waved for them to move ahead of him. "Come. You know the way, Paladin. Warm yourselves before the fire. I will summon Leo before I bring food and drink for all of us."

Paladin took Seren's arm and led her down the dimly lit hallway. His thoughts grim, he realized the time had come for answers, for him and for her.

****

Seren stood with her back to the blazing fire in the hearth. Cozy, even homey, the room where Paladin had led her set her mind at ease. The four leather armchairs, seats worn and glossy in places, faced each other like they waited for someone to sit and enjoy the warmth coming from the fireplace. Bookcases, lining all the walls, overflowed onto the faded fabric of the area rug. Several large, glass-covered lamps gave the room a snug atmosphere, not too bright, but not dark either. Seren smiled. Just right.

Huge, colored stones sat on the hearth, the mantel, the bookcases, even the floor. Strange lights flickered in each one. Reds, yellows, blues, greens, purples, and blacks, the invisible auras expelled by them sent many different reactions through her when she gazed at them. The clear crystal ones attracted her the most. Her smile widened at the feeling of peace which flowed through her mind at the sight of this particular color.

She rubbed her warmed hands together and looked over at Paladin. He stood next to her, staring into the flames, hands braced on the mantel.

When he didn't react to her look, she moved to the nearest armchair to take a seat. She rested her head against the padded back and shut her eyes, savoring the gentle lull of the crackling fire. She inhaled the scent of wood smoke tingeing the air. Warmth coasted over the front of her body.

Paladin shifted. She opened her eyes to see him facing her. Deep and soft, his voice imbedded into the deepest reaches of her mind. "I asked if our child appeared to you. You said no. I am asking again. Did he? If so, you must tell me what he told you."

She met his gaze for a moment before she nodded. "This place is like a fairy tale only it's not. It's real, isn't it?"

He nodded. His expression was unreadable. "I do not know what a fairy tale is, but this is very real. It is no jest."

She looked away from him to the dancing flames in the hearth. Within the fire, she envisioned his reaction to her telling him the truth. He wouldn't believe her. He'd probably say she was crazy and he'd be half right. She was lost on this new world, not even sure it was reality. If he left her, she'd be an outcast on this planet where everything was so different from what she considered normal. He was the only person she felt safe with in this place. On the other hand, she feared not telling him. He could help her. If he chose to believe in her abilities, in what she'd seen, he could help her understand what was happening to her. There wasn't a choice, she had to trust him. "He said the seven dragons opened the door for me to come here so he could be created."

She placed a trembling hand over her stomach prior to meeting his steady stare again. "He said you were expendable, but he hoped that wouldn't happen."

A flicker of pain crossed his face before he asked, "Did he say why the dragons did this?"

"For him to be the one King over them."

His jaw clenched. The muscle ticked in his cheek. He nodded in response. She counted the seconds by the twitch until he spoke again—*one, two, three, four, five, six*... "I had hoped you could stay here while I traveled to return my wife's body—you would be more at ease with someone from your world, but it cannot be. I have to take you with me. It is the single way to keep you safe."

"Safe? From what?" She leaned forward, needing to know what he meant. "Explain to me why anyone would want to harm me or this child?"

He stepped to her, going down on one knee. He lifted her hand, holding it tight between his. A frown creased his brow. "There are those who would feel threatened by such an event as one King over the dragons. They may try to harm you, and through you, the child.

"Within the dragon's guts, they produce valuable stones with their magic. All of Avaris revolves around these dragonstones. To preserve peace in the lands, the dragon clan leaders formed a blood pact with humans. The stones are given free of any obligation by the dragons. They are a token of their trust in the human clans," he explained. "Many more adult dragons live on Avaris besides those leaders. They are exiled to the rogue lands because their magic is not strong enough to defeat a clan leader. This also keeps them away from the lands occupied by humans."

"Wait, you're confusing me. What do the other

dragons have to do with any of this if they are exiled?"

"Each rogue is related to a clan dragon. The dragonseed king of each clan can call the rogues to come forth to assist their clan in battle. Right now, even the dracs are gathering, which is a definite sign of pending war."

She studied him, glad he paused for a minute. "Won't the kings be able to stop war from happening?"

"Which king?" He raised a brow at her. When he continued, his voice hardened. "The ones our child will usurp after he is an adult? Or do you believe an unborn babe has the power to stop this war?"

Seren drew back. His words frightened her. "Why me? I asked him. He didn't answer me. He talked about you and the dragons. Nothing else."

"This is not just about you."

Frustrated, she glared at him. "I know that."

He stared hard at her. "Do you want my child?"

Seren returned his look for several seconds while she collected her thoughts and tried to calm her nerves. "Since you brought me here, I've felt lost. Even with you near me, I've still felt alone."

After a gentle squeeze, she tugged her hand free of his and stood. She moved around the room, studying one stone after another. "At first, when I had the vision of our son, I thought I'd lost it, but then he started asking me questions I didn't want to answer. About things I refused to even think of before."

A clear crystal sat in the center of an ornately carved square table. The stone, larger than any of the others, radiated a sparkling light within its center. The rays drew her closer. She ran a finger along the sharp edges, marveling at the beauty of it before she continued. "I thought I wanted my life to go back to normal, but in reality, I didn't know what normal was anymore. There wasn't anything left from my life before Mandy's death. After talking with him, I realized that just because I lost my child doesn't mean I have to live in vacuum."

Paladin, steps muffled by the rug, moved behind her. She closed her eyes, waiting. Anticipation amplified her slow, steady heartbeat. The weight of his warm hands on her shoulders comforted her. She shuddered. When his lips brushed against the side of her neck, need for what he offered forced her to turn toward him.

She smiled a little and whispered, "Yes. I want this baby. I'll be damned if I'll allow anyone to hurt him."

Chapter Eight

Raw desire burst to life in Paladin's eyes and Seren's desire increased in answer to his silent call. Heart racing, its beat matched the rhythm of the vein in his neck. Lowering her gaze, she focused on the smooth curve of his mouth. She passed her tongue over her lower lip, wanting to do the same to his.

Never had a man affected her the way he did. The junction between her legs ached, flooding with need. Her breasts tingled, insisting she brush them against his chest's solid strength. She fought the gnawing passion inside her, but when he shifted his head down, she rose to meet him.

One gentle sweep, skin brushing against skin, he tugged her closer, molding her against him. The second pass of his mouth sealed their lips. Fire, so unlike the kind Seren had suffered through before, licked over her skin. She opened her mouth to allow his tongue to slide in. She moaned.

The door swung wide with a groan. She pulled her lips free to see Largin enter, his back to them, gripping a tray with carved wooden handles in his hands. "Here you are. Hot telee. Will warm you to your bones."

She lowered her head, resting her brow on Paladin's shoulder. She tried to catch her breath. He gave her a light squeeze then released her, letting his hand glide down her arm. They laced their fingers together.

Paladin appeared to have trouble controlling his breathing also. She smiled, glad she wasn't alone with the torment of the smoldering chemistry between them.

By the time she glanced back at the older man, he had placed the tray on an empty table in the far corner. He filled four small cups, and then carried two to them. She nodded her thanks, inhaling the spicy aroma rising from the white porcelain looking dish.

Her mouth watered. A second later, her stomach rumbled in response. She thought back, realizing she hadn't eaten in days. One sip sent warmth through her. The hot drink reminded her of tea, so she took another small drink until she emptied the cup. When she finished, she met Paladin's gaze. The kindness and worry she saw there brought a wave of stinging tears to her eyes.

"I sent word to Leo. He should arrive at any moment," Largin commented, retrieving a cup for himself.

Gaining control over her unsteady emotions, she lifted her cup. "May I? It's good."

"Have as much as you like. I brought some food also. Eat, my dear, to regain your vitality." Largin stepped to the side.

Moving to the table, Seren studied the platters of meats, bread, and round slabs of what looked like cheese. In those few seconds, she realized Largin had avoided looking at her since he'd returned. Curious, she lifted an empty saucer, mulling over the wizard's strange behavior toward her while she filled it.

When she had made her choices, she turned, directing her question to the older man. "Do I bother you?"

Largin stared at the floor a little to the right of where

she stood. "You as a human woman, no—but you are not just a human. You are the bearer of the Dragon King…well, that is a different matter indeed."

Seren's heart rose to her throat. The man's comment verified the unease she had seen in Paladin earlier. How had Largin known about the baby? Was he alone in his knowledge or were others also aware?

"We came here to find out if there's another way I could go home. One without the help of the dragons." Now, she had to know, especially after finding out her child might be in danger.

"Nothing is done on Avaris without the dragons' consent. I am sorry, but they brought you here, and here you will stay until they allow you to return to your home." The old man stepped to the mantle. He set his tea on the wooden beam that ran the length of the hearth.

Shocked, Seren stared at him, taking in his words. "But they don't have the right to keep me here. I want to go home. Wouldn't it also be better for my baby if I went back to Earth?"

"I cannot say."

"There has to be a way."

"Do not give up hope. I will research the matter more. With luck, I will discover some useful information."

Before she had the opportunity to thank him for his help, footsteps came from the hall outside the room. Seren's gaze flew to the door. Standing there, framed within the opening was the reason for her coming to this island.

Sparkling white teeth flashed in an ebony face. Gray salted the wiry short hair. Seren's heart skipped a beat then pounded double time. Built like an aging linebacker, he filled the entire doorway.

Food forgotten, she set her plate down and stared at the tall stranger. She wanted to run across the room and throw her arms around the man's tapered waist just to make sure he was real. Out of the corner of her eye, she noticed Paladin grinning at the new arrival.

Heart in her throat, she stood there unable to move. "You're real. You're from Earth."

"Yes, ma'am."

She stopped a sob from escaping and stared at the face which reminded her of those she'd left behind on Earth. High cheek bones, long face, full lips, and his eyes, so gentle and the color of rich chocolate, brimmed with joy. "Come on, darlin', come sit. I know how upsetting this must be for you."

With a small nod, she allowed him to lead her to one of the arm chairs. Tears mixed with the need to laugh threatened to take control of her, but she managed to overcome them. She sat, never looking away from his face.

"How did you come to be here?" She closed her eyes, collecting her thoughts. "Oh, God, there's so much I want to ask you."

Leo patted her hands where she clasped them in her lap. "Take your time. I'm here for the duration."

From the doorway, Largin interrupted them. "Well, we'll leave you two to visit. Come, Captain, there is a matter I want to discuss with you."

The older man waited, and from his stance, Seren guessed he wouldn't allow Paladin to argue. She glanced over at where he stood. Eyes narrowed and focused on Largin, he seemed about to refuse. Tension swelled while she waited, holding her breath.

With a curt nod at the old man, he looked at her. "I will not be far. Call if you have need."

Nostrils flaring, she drew in a deep breath, holding it as she nodded. Seren was relieved he'd decided to go. She wanted to speak to Leo, but with Paladin in the room, she'd fail to devote her full attention to the questions she wanted to ask. The man distracted her far too much.

****

Aggravated he'd had to leave Seren, Paladin followed Largin down the hall to a room on the opposite side of the one they had just left. Overflowing with tables and astronomical instruments, the room stretched half the length of the house. Papers towered on the surfaces. Some of the papers were bright and crisp, nothing marring them, yet others were so coated with dust the writing laid obscured, preventing him from reading them.

He had wanted to remain with Seren, but the wizard left little room for him to argue. Now, he trailed behind the old man without the least bit of curiosity about why he wanted to speak to him. Instead, his thoughts were centered on her.

The warmth of her kiss drove him to complete and utter mindlessness. He wanted…no, needed her. An ache settled in his chest. His life would never be the same. The woman from Earth had seeped into the crevices in his heart created by his wife's betrayal and touched him like no other.

He strode past a low counter and slowed. Dragon skulls amid a multitude of other bones lay on the surface. A shiver crawled up his back.

"Not to worry, none of those are from your

bloodline. Rogues all, special ones at that." Largin commented over his shoulder. "Similar to the one which attacked Rylen when he was younger."

This bit of information caught Paladin's attention, diverting his thoughts. Memories of his brother's agony after the incident Largin spoke of came to life.

Younger than Paladin by ten years, Rylen had wandered away from the family during a holiday to the shore. Everyone in the party had searched most of the day for the young boy to no avail. Paladin had refused to give up. After hours combing the beach, he had found his brother unconscious in the sand. The boy had been severely wounded by the breath from a rogue dragon. Rylen had lived in a fevered, delirious state for several weeks before the mystic healers were able to pull him back to awareness. Paladin never forgot his brother's agony. Those memories brought forth a rush of newer ones.

An image of Seren writhing under his son's dragon fire flashed through his mind. He shut his eyes. The pain she had suffered because of his carelessness was inexcusable. He shouldn't have touched her. Even now he should leave her alone, but his need for her wouldn't let him go. He shoved these thoughts to the back of his mind, concentrating instead on his brother.

Every one of the great dragon guardian wizards had named the rogue that had attacked his brother Arcane. The dragon's strange coloring and bearing set him apart from the normal clans. His scales had reflected every color of the different dragons on a smoky charcoal background. A mystic dragon—a new breed. Even his magic differed from what the inhabitants on Avaris were accustomed to.

Paladin moved closer to Largin. "What do you mean? Similar? I thought none had lived from the clutch of eggs he came from. None but him."

"True, true…but these are from the joining of the gold and black dragon. Thus, they are similar, but not the same as when the white and black mated." Largin stopped at a longer table, riffling through several sheets of parchment. Not finding what he sought, he moved further down. He did the same with more stacks of the papers. "The great Lior should never have mated with that black demon, Sinimal. All the hatchlings revealed this to the guardian wizards. Too much unstable magic in the wee fledglings. All of the guardians and wizards involved counted the fledglings' deaths a true blessing."

Paladin stopped near Largin, watching the old wizard search. "I agree. But the rogue was driven away. Last I heard he occupied the lands to the farthest north."

"So he does…Aha…Here it is." Largin pulled a dusty, thick tome from the farthest stack. The papers on top flew and scattered across the table, knocking over several nearby piles. A cloud of dust rose, surrounding the wizard.

Waving a hand in front of his face, Paladin took several steps back to escape. Largin wheezed, then coughed.

Patience wearing thin, Paladin gritted his teeth. The thought of Seren even this far from him sent a sensation of a fist slamming into his chest over the spot where his heart beat. He had to see her, touch her, even if just for one second more. "You called me here to speak with me. If all you want to do is fumble amid dry parchments and speak of rogues which are not a danger to me then I'll return to Seren. I do not care to leave her too long."

"Ah, but that is exactly why I have asked you to join me," the wizard commented, brushing past him. "This way, the lighting is always best on the other side of the room."

With a shake of his head, Paladin moved behind Largin, following him across the room. Paladin grunted. Of course, the area was better lit. The small torches, burning in their holders, caught and held the glow of the many dragon stones strewn over the counters.

The wizard set the tome on an uncluttered table, "Here we are. Now let me find the place." He pulled the book open midway and glanced over the page. Several moments seemed to slow to a crawl. Paladin counted each one with an impatient tap of his toe. When the old man cried out, marking a place with his finger, Paladin leaned forward, looking over the wizard's shoulder. "Here it is. Avaris' prophecy."

Another cold shiver spiraled up Paladin's spine.

Largin shifted out of the way, motioning to his eyes. "Here, you read it to me. My old eyes…"

He glared at the wizard. Old eyes indeed. Largin saw better than he. The warning from his father sprang to life in his mind. He stepped closer to the tome. With one last scowl, he concentrated on the thin script. Elegant and narrow, the words were written in an ancient language. Difficult to read, he still managed to make out most of the letters.

"On thys day, Annual Fourteen, age of the Whyte Dragon, a human accepted the most magycal of blood from the great and glorious Lyor, thus opening the door for the upheaval whych wyll over tyme and space expand across the whole of Avaris. For from thys blood lyne, the one true Kyng wyll come."

A twinge of unease shot through his chest and stopped Paladin from reading further. He glanced at Largin. The wizard half-smiled and nodded toward the book. "Read all of it."

With a deep breath, Paladin focused once more. "He alone wyll hold Avaris' future wythyn the folds of hys wyngs."

He leaned on the edge of the table, unable to go on. The ever present grain of fear sprouted into a clinging vine within him and crept through his mind.

Largin touched his shoulder. The gentle weight helped to steady him.

"The child is the one. Your child—your bloodline."

He faced the wizard. Seren's answers to his questions verified what Largin said. He desired to deny every measure of the wizard's comments, but…

With a finger pointing to the page in the tome, Largin continued. "If you read further, the mother chosen to give birth to this babe is spoken of. A woman from the cosmos. The woman you have brought with you is from the cosmos, is she not? From Avaris' sister world— Earth."

Paladin, heart pounding, fury overriding his normal calm, gripped the front of Largin's shirt, lifting the smaller man off his feet. May the dragon's fires destroy his father's teachings.

"Stop playing with me. Speak openly and be quick about it."

"She will be in great danger once word spreads that she carries the prophesized king."

"She is under my protection. None, beast, dragon, nor human shall ever harm her. This I swear by all the magic of the dragons."

Largin's eyes widened and his mouth fell open. A sudden spark lit in the wizard's eyes. He sent quick glances around them. Paladin sensed his fear and in the sudden lowering of the other man's body heat. The older man pulled at his shirt. Paladin opened his fingers, releasing him. Let Largin and all who dared to harm what he held dear turn to ash under the never-ending stream of a dragon's fire. Calmness returned in slow measures as Paladin silently accepted that he would do all in his power to keep Seren and his unborn child safe.

When the wizard spoke, his words crackled with alarm. "Take back your oath, King of the White Dragon Clan." Determined, holding true to his desire to protect Seren,

Paladin retorted. "Never."

The wind slammed against the small, unseen windows situated high along the outside wall of the room. Their panes rattled. The storm, having ebbed of power earlier, had regained its strength. With it, Paladin's own spirit to fight for Seren and his child's safety built to a white-hot boil. He drew in a deep breath and shook his head, defying the growing heaviness in the room. "No, I will never take them back. This I have sworn and this I hold fast. My oath stands."

Lightning slipped through one window, splintering glass and wood. The bolt struck a dragonstone resting on top of a table not far from where they stood. Sparks amid chunks of stone hurled up, thrown out across the chamber. Flames flared in the center of the table. The entire room vibrated long after the thunderbolt had vanished.

"Oh, flying drac's liver," Largin muttered. He hurried to the spot, staring at the shattered remains of a large stone. "Now look what you have done, my fierce dragonseed."

Paladin, unrepentant, moved to his side. At the sight of the shattered white dragon stone, he tilted his chin higher. The dragons had sent their message to him. He wondered whether they supported him, or was this their way of letting him know his life was at an end. No matter, he would guarantee them a battle supreme if their plans involved harm to Seren and his child.

****

When the door closed behind Paladin, Seren released her pent-up breath. At the questioning expression on Leo's face, she grinned. "He affects me. A lot."

Leo nodded. "He's a good man."

Her stomach answered him with a rumble. Embarrassed, hot blood rose to her cheeks and she apologized.

"I interrupted your meal." He stood, returning a moment later with something for her to eat. He handed her a filled cup.

She murmured in appreciation, and placed the cup on the small oval table between the armchairs. The delicious aroma of the cooked meat teased her, making her hunger more acute. Her mouth watered.

Once Leo settled into his seat, he asked. "You eat while I talk, if that's all right?"

She nodded, bringing a slice of meat to her lips. The smell had done little justice to the taste. Seren closed her eyes, savoring the juicy, tender bite.

"I suppose you're wondering how I arrived on Avaris. Well, it's similar to how you came here. I made a wish on a shooting star. I was in Nam. The night I left

Earth, my entire platoon had been wiped out."

Leo stopped for a moment. As he stared into the fire, Seren studied him, wondering what he saw in his mind's eye. When he noticed her look, he smiled, sadness reflected in his kind, dark eyes.

"It was right after midnight. I remember 'cause I didn't know how I was going to stay alive for the rest of the night. My time was short. Charlie would attack at dawn. The waiting for the final assault made me insane with fear.

"All I wanted to do was live. Praying, I looked up and saw a shooting star. My Granny used to wish on stars, so I thought what could it hurt? I repeated the words she taught me when I was little."

He grinned at her, and then recited the children's rhyme. "'I wish I may, I wish I might, have the wish I wish tonight.'" After he finished, a deep laugh rumbled out of his chest. "Next thing I knew, the land around me lit up like fourth of July fireworks. At first, I thought it was a spotlight from a rescue chopper, but it wasn't. Weren't no noise. None of the plants had moved. Next, I thought I'd died. I went to the light, thinking it was what I was supposed to do. But once I walked through, I knew something had happened."

Seren nodded, finishing the last bit of food on her plate.

"What did you do?"

"I walked. I didn't stop, either, until I found this place. Master Largin was waiting for me. He told me he'd felt the door opening through the star. Didn't know what he was talking about, and didn't care at the time."

"Did you want to go home?" Seren placed her dish on the table. She settled against the chair's cushioned back, tucking her feet under her.

"Honestly?" Leo shook his head. "No, ma'am. Didn't have any family left. Most of my friends had died in the war. So coming here didn't bother me none. Over the years, I made a good home. Married, even had kids. My wife passed away a few years ago, but my children are settled with good spouses. They're happy, a real joy to me. They've given me grandkids. That's a lot more than what I might have had back home."

He grinned at her. "I wouldn't trade the last thirty seven years for even one day on Earth."

Amazed, Seren stared at him. "But it's so different. How did you adjust?"

This time his laugh came out full and rich. "There's no adjusting. I simply accepted their world for what it is," he said, leaning forward. "The inhabitants of this planet take their magic seriously."

"I noticed."

"Maybe, but I don't think you realize to what degree they take this stuff. On earth, magic was make-believe, here it's not."

Before he had a chance to explain, a resounding crash echoed through the house. Seren jerked to an upright position. She faced the door, listening, trying to figure out where the sound came from and what could have caused it

Leo jumped to his feet, heading to the door. "Oh, Lord, I hope Master Largin didn't turn the captain into a toad." Shocked, she untangled her legs and ran after him.

Chapter Nine

Leo stopped in front of a door down the hall. Seren, following close behind him, stumbled into his back. He pounded on the wooden panel, calling out, "Master, are you all right? Is the captain okay?"

Shuffling came from inside the room. "Yes, yes, Leo. Nothing to worry yourself with. Just a little disturbance from the storm."

Seren, fearing the truth behind Leo's earlier comment, ducked under his arm. "Paladin? Are you in there?"

His deep voice carried through the door. "All is well, Seren. Go, finish your visit. You needn't worry for me." Relieved, she twisted to glare at Leo, lowering her voice. "Don't scare me like that."

He tilted toward her, whispering, "Didn't mean to, but it's true. Those wizards do some of the strangest things."

"Even turn people into toads?"

"I've seen it happen."

Without another word, he took her arm and escorted her down the hall.

Once she was seated with another steamy cup of the tea like drink in her hands, Leo continued. "Wizards spit out incantations all around. Our fairy tales touch the mere surface of what they can do. The ones who care for the seven great dragons, well, they're the most powerful of them all.

They know how to do magic without spells."

Apprehension battled with her newfound ease in this place and won. "So, it's true. There are seven dragons ruling this planet?"

Leo sat forward, placing his forearms on his knees. "At one time there were seven, but right now, only six of 'em gather. The seventh hasn't been seen for a long time. Some think it died out." He glanced at her middle. "From what the master says, the ones remaining have something planned for this baby you're carrying. Largin claims they brought you here just to give birth."

Surprised he knew of her child, and more than a little shocked at the verification of the dragon's plans for her, she set her cup on the table. Staring at him, she crossed her arms over her abdomen, the need to protect her innocent child utmost in her mind. "How do you know about my baby?"

"Master saw it in the scrying stone. He swears the vision was fuzzy, but he saw the baby. Most of the time, he's right when he looks into that rock."

"Did he see him born?"

Leo shrugged. "Didn't tell me. Just that you were going to have a baby and the captain was the father. Said the dragons want one king to rule over them." A deep furrow formed between his brows. "I've never heard of a human giving birth to a mixed breed. They'll have to purify your blood."

Puzzled, she asked. "Purify? You mean like a transfusion?"

Leo shook his head. "The clan leaders have to gather to perform a purification of your blood."

"How?"

"Don't know. Never seen it or even heard how it's done."

Seren stared at him. The solemn line of his mouth struck a chord in her. This man should smile, but instead, he worried about her and the baby. She looked toward the fire, trying to absorb what he had told her.

She rested her head against the back of the chair. "Paladin will know."

"Yes ma'am, he should," Leo agreed with a nod.

Seren smiled. "Stop calling me ma'am. You make me feel old."

Leo shifted in his chair, sat back and stretched his legs out in front of him, crossing them at the ankles. "I wouldn't feel right being disrespectful to you."

She grunted. "You won't be. Earth has changed a lot since you left. Please, call me by my name. I'm Seren."

They sat in the silence. She sorted through what Leo had told her. Tired of trying to understand, she glanced at him. "I don't know what to think. When I first came here, I was so confused. I guess I'm still a little fuzzy."

"It's the gravity."

She lifted a brow in question.

Leo grinned. "From what I can figure, Avaris is larger than Earth, so the gravitational pull is a bit stronger. It'll take you a little while to get used to it."

"Great, not only do I have to worry over the fact that I'm having a baby dragon, I have to do it while I get used to the gravity." She rolled a look at the ceiling. How did these people expect her to believe all these new aspects without being skeptical?

"You'll feel better after a while."

"Well, by the time I give birth, I should be accustomed to the pull. Nine months is a long time." She started to say something else, but the surprised look Leo aimed at her stopped her.

"Didn't the captain tell you?"

"What?"

"You won't carry your baby nine months. The term for a dragonseed is four months at the most. A third of the time a normal human is carried. They develop faster."

Seren's mouth dropped open. "Four months?"

He nodded.

Eyes wide, adrenaline pumping, she sat straight. "So that's why I can feel him moving."

"It won't be long before you'll be showing too."

She met Leo's eyes. "What am I having? Will this baby come out looking like a dragon?"

Leo waved his hands. "No, no. He'll be normal. It's all the magic in their blood. From what I've gathered over the years, way back when humans first combined their blood with the dragons, they were almost extinct on this planet. They needed children. This helped them."

"Because they could have more children in less time." Amazed, she stared at him.

"That's right. Also, the children had fewer illnesses. A minority, if any, died."

A sharp thrill passed through Seren's stomach. She pressed her hand against her abdomen. If what Leo told her was true, as long as nothing happened to him, her baby, because of the magic in his blood, would live to adulthood.

****

After Seren and Leo's footsteps moved away from the door, Paladin glanced at Largin. Under the weight of the older man's stare, he shifted.

The wizard continued to watch him, even raising a hand to tap a finger on his chin in speculation. "You were always a difficult dragonseed. Never wanting to comply with what was expected of you. Captain of an airship, bah. What good does that do your clan?"

Paladin turned his back to Largin, picked up a piece of the shattered dragonstone, and studied the jagged ends. "It's none of your concern. My father approved of my choice."

"Even the abandonment of your throne? I think not. If your father had not died unexpectedly, he would have made sure the crown went to you."

"The royal advisors decided Rylen was better suited to rule. I agreed." He placed the stone on the table and took a step back, concentrating his magic on the destroyed crystal. Shards mixed with slivers of the stone trembled. They slid over the table top. The pieces which were flung wide in the explosion bounced on the floor then flew to the growing mass on the table.

Fusing to each other, the broken stone reformed into its original shape. When he finished, Paladin angled a glance at Largin. The wizard, silent during the magical reconstruction of the dragonstone, stood several feet away, observing him in return.

Largin shook his head, something akin to awe in his low words. "To possess such power and still refuse to rule."

Paladin grunted in agitation. "A good ruler doesn't need great power. My father agreed with me on this matter."

"Rylen doesn't. He resents your ability." Largin walked to the table, grasped the lower edges of the dragonstone, and moved it more to the center of the table.

"He harbors harsh feelings toward you. I saw his face the day Bask announced you had to wed Zuresa. He wanted her and the prestige she brought to the clan. It's not enough for him to have stolen your right as king. He covets all you have."

Several moments passed while Paladin considered what the wizard had said. For two years, he had suspected his brother wasn't pleased with the decision which tied the black dragon clan princess to him. He had ignored the constant warning his senses had pounded him with each time he had returned home from a journey to discover the growing closeness between his brother and his wife, Zuresa.

The remembered doubts served to make his head ache. Largin would never understand his relationship with his brother. "Perhaps, but my wife is dead. Rylen has nothing to gain from me. He is king. I am a simple airship captain. There is nothing for him to fear from me. I swore my allegiance to his rule."

A memory of a small boy, gold hair streaming behind him, racing at his side, laughter filling the space between them slipped through his mind. The boy, his brother, had loved him. Paladin fought the onslaught of pain over the loss of their close kinship. The loss of his brother haunted him, the pain a festering sore on his soul.

When Arcane had attacked Rylen, their fellowship as brothers had ended. The child's eyes, once so alive with joy mixed with mischief, had become hard and calculating with an obsessive glint. Rylen had changed. Paladin tried to care for him in the same manner as before, but his brother had made it difficult.

The silence in the room enfolded the two men. Paladin refused to say anything against his brother. No matter his faults, Rylen still carried their father's blood in his veins. For this reason alone, Paladin's honor bound him to his brother.

The wizard continued as though the silence had never existed. "There are rumors. I've heard Zuresa did not die a normal death. It's been said you had a part in her passing."

He held Largin's gaze with his own, resenting the accusation that he was behind the death of his wife. "Do you believe this?"

The wizard snorted and shook his head, a brow arched. "Does it matter what I believe? I traced the gossip to its roots. Rylen's court. If he cannot kill you, he will ruin your name."

Largin turned and walked to the shattered window. Rain dripped through the broken glass. "I was there the night of your birth. Bask stood at the foot of the bed. He told your father to have special care of you because you had been blessed by the dragon's magic."

Staring hard at him, Paladin tilted his head. He had never heard this before. "You were there also?"

Clasping his hands in front of him, Largin mumbled a spell. Three claps followed. The area around the window blurred then righted. The glass became solid once more and the wood returned to its previous shape. Largin waved his hands in a circle, reciting a different spell. Rain dried. The splintered pieces of glass and wood vanished. "There. All fixed."

He turned and looked at Paladin. "Now if we could do the same with Rylen."

"You did not answer my question. Were you there the night my mother died?"

"I was summoned by your father. Your mother,

dragon's breath hold her, had weakened with your birth. He sent for me to help her deliver," the old man replied. "No one else, save Bask, was allowed into the room."

Several moments later, Largin continued, his voice soft. "To remember that night still causes much grief for me. When Bask told your father about you, he had to choose which of you would live."

Paladin swallowed the bitterness this information stirred in him. "So, he chose me?"

Largin moved to Paladin's side and laid a hand on his shoulder. The older man squeezed for a second, in an attempt to offer comfort. "Not so much a choice. The dragons had decreed how this matter would end. Your father had to abide by their will. He loved her deeply and to lose her…well, he was never the same afterward."

Shaking the hand off, Paladin stepped away. His father had rarely spoken of his mother. How could he believe what Largin had said? The man Paladin remembered had been cold and haughty, abrupt with all around him, including his sons. How could a man like that have a deep devotion for someone? "Loved? Is that what you call it? He remarried within a year. Rylen's mother was held in high esteem by him for the rest of his life."

Shrugging, Largin said, "True, but he never cared for the woman. Not like your mother."

"Enough. I've heard enough," Paladin said, raising a hand to stop the wizard. "I am tired. If you have more to tell me, let it wait till morning."

]]][=He turned, moving to the door, eager to leave the room.

"Very well, but this evening, think long and hard on what to do with this woman from the cosmos. Rylen will seek her out, if not to kill her then to take her from you. Are you prepared for this to happen?"

Paladin ignored him, threw open the door and strode down the hall. The old man's words held a truth he didn't care to examine just yet.

Chapter Ten

A floorboard outside the door creaked. Seren glanced at the opening to find Paladin standing motionless. Her heart accelerated at the sight of him. Worry etched his features.

What happened with the wizard?

Leo rose to his feet, nodding in greeting. "Paladin."

He inclined his head in return. "It is late. Seren needs to rest and so do I. You may visit with each other over the next few days."

Surprised that he'd decided what was best for her, she narrowed her eyes and almost told him not to worry. She wasn't his concern, but there was a haunted look about him.

She found that she wanted to do what he asked.

What had the old wizard told him?

"Yes, sir. I'd imagine you are both exhausted from your journey," Leo agreed. He continued with a chuckle. "Master Largin prepared rooms a couple of days ago."

Seren slid to the edge of the chair and stood. Paladin held his hand out. She stared at the slender fingers and calloused palm for a moment. She moved to his side, laying her hand onto his. Heat spiraled up her arm from the contact. Lacing their fingers, he led the way into the hallway. She followed, determined to remain strong and not allow her passion for this man to override her common sense.

They walked further down the hallway until they reached a narrow staircase built into the side of the wall. He guided her up the steps and down another passageway which was bare of any decorations except for the wall lanterns. Midway, he stopped in front of a paneled door.

He faced her. "This is my room. I want you with me."

His deep voice vibrated off her nerve endings. She shivered. His blue eyes warmed with a spark of fire, reminding her of her desire for him. She passed her tongue over her lips.

Raising their clasped hands, she flattened her palm against his and straightened her fingers. He aligned his with hers. She stared, enjoying the friction of his skin against her sensitive fingertips. "Why do you want me to stay here with you?"

His other hand swept the hair off her left temple. Gently, he cupped her jaw. In the same manner as she'd done to him the first day on the ship, he brushed his thumb across her bottom lip.

"I want to keep you safe."

"Nothing more?"

His pupils dilated, and his answer came out in a breath, "Yes."

"Who's going to keep me safe from you?" She released a low, husky laugh. "Or should I say, you from me?"

"I have no need for protection from you."

"You want to make a bet?"

He half-smiled at her. "I would lose the wager without a care."

She laughed. The tension in her body ebbed. "I'll

sleep beside you, but I won't make love with you. I want to go home. This place is way too weird for me. If we make love again, I'd be tempted to stay."

He inclined his head. "As you say. I will honor your desire. Having you next to me will be enough. For now."

Paladin opened the door then waited for her to enter before he followed. Quaint, possessing very little furniture, the room seemed strange for someone like Paladin. She had imagined gilded picture frames and brass bed posts. Instead, an upright six drawer chest and a narrow bed with a threadworn spread were the only furniture pieces there.

Their steps echoed across the wooden floor. Another doorway was centered on the side wall and she wondered where it led.

"If you like, I will wait for you to dress for bed," he said from behind her.

She nodded without looking at him. When the door shut, she wrapped her arms around her waist, enjoying the quiet. Seren stood still. She noticed his satchel on the bed. Surprised, she wondered how it came to be there. Had one of his crew brought it?

Shrugging, she moved toward the bed. She unbuckled the straps and flipped the lid over. A different shirt, a creamy eggshell, folded this time, lay on top. The billowy sleeves and the gathered yoke would provide a little protection against her passion. She half-smiled. If her skin didn't touch his, maybe she'd find the strength to control her need.

She removed her clothes and slipped on the shirt. During those few seconds before the collar slid over her head, she was surrounded by his scent. Blood rushed to her head. Her focus narrowed to binocular vision. In the direct line of her vision, red- streaked darkness raced toward her.

A vision. One like the many others she'd had in the past. Nothing was solid like earlier today when her son spoke to her. She searched the darkness until an image materialized.

Paladin stood several feet away on the edge of a castle wall, his head back, his gaze searching the darkened skies. She wanted to scream for him to run, to escape the horrible impression of danger she experienced, but in her vision, she remained rooted to one spot, unable to speak or move.

Black clouds sped overhead. Lightning flashed red, streaming across the sky. Paladin slid his weapons free, the blades glinting in the crimson light. From the darkness, huge wings flapped back and forth then two black dragons broke through the clouds, angling their bodies toward him.

She opened her mouth to scream, but no sound came out. He couldn't see her. She didn't exist in this time and place.

The dragons drew nearer, their massive maws started to open, revealing sharpened teeth the length of her legs. Fire appeared in the back of their throats. In the next second, an inferno poured from their mouths. Blue-black flames were flung out toward Paladin, striking him, consuming him.

Arms came from behind, grabbing her. One tug and blinding light engulfed her mind.

The abrupt end to the vision sent Seren to her knees, gasping for breath. Her heart pounded in her chest. With her arms tangled in the sleeves, she fought to bring the shirt down, removing it from her face. Sweat dampened her body. An ache set up in her bruised knees. For a few seconds, she was blinded by her vision. Hands shaking, she swiped at her eyes, trying to rid them of the fuzzy haze. When she opened them, she focused on the worn spread covering the bed. The faded blues and greens sprang out at her.

Tears threatened to destroy her newfound strength. She had witnessed Paladin's death—a painful and dreadful death by dragon's fire. She lowered her cheek to the covers, hoping to cool the heat in her face.

A fragment of the vision lingered. She replayed it over and over in her mind. Behind and off to one side of where he had stood, a banner whipped in the wind brought on by the dragon's wings. The cloth carried the same strange emblem she had seen on the bed covers in Paladin's room on the airship the first day. The flag revealed the design clearer than the one on the bed covers. A dragon, head up, wings spread, held a spear against its body. Its tail was wrapped around the weapon's long handle. This time, instead of crimson, gold was embroidered on a white rectangle.

She didn't have to ask. The flag belonged to the white dragon clan. His clan. Paladin would die at his home.

Fear for Paladin left her trembling. She fought to calm her breathing. Closing her eyes, she focused on his smiling face and the joy he'd brought her today. After a few moments, she realized she had to prepare him for what might happen. She struggled to her feet and stumbled across the room. The need to see him, to verify he was alive and unharmed helped calm her down. With a twist of the knob, she pulled the door open.

He stood, leaning against the door jam. Seren

suppressed a relieved cry and moved forward, resting her back on the opposite side, staring at him.

He inclined his head, his eyes narrowing. He returned her scrutiny, his gaze scanning her face. "Are you all right?"

Not able to speak, she stepped to him, hugging his waist. She buried her nose at the spot where his shirt gaped and the deep tanned muscles of his chest met. His arms held her secure.

He was alive. She would do her best to keep him that way.

She turned her face and rubbed her cheek against his skin. "You can't go home."

His back stiffened. He touched her chin, bringing her face up. "Why?"

"I had a vision."

Those simple words seemed to convey her message. Danger lurked within the boundaries of his homeland. He seemed to understand and nodded.

Relief poured through her. She shut her eyes. "I want you to hold me."

He placed his hand on the back of her neck, pulling her close. "Come, we both need rest. After a peaceful night, you will be more at ease."

Without another word, he led her into the room and then closed the door behind them.

****

Tugging the extra pillow over, Seren buried her nose into the downy softness as sleep faded from her mind. Paladin's scent lingered, bringing a smile to her lips. The pillow still held a touch of warmth, revealing he'd left her only a short while ago.

God, she wanted to find a tub of hot water. To soak and relax without the pressure of the dragon vision weighing on her would be heaven. She laughed. Heaven indeed! Bliss with her golden angel beside her.

Closing her eyes, she imagined Paladin bathing with her, his hands covered with soap, sliding across her slick body. A moan escaped her. Her blood throbbed in her veins. Sharp pangs of desire shot up through her belly from the junction between her legs.

Lying in bed, desiring him, wouldn't bring him back to her side so she tossed the covers back, trying her best to ignore her body's need for him. Seren sat up, stretching. Lowering her hands into her lap, she glanced at her surroundings. Her gaze stopped on the door on the left side of the room. Ajar, the opening revealed another room.

She leaned to the left to see better. The curved rim of a large basin showed just past the door. An excited laugh escaped her. For the first time since she'd arrived on this strange planet, she wanted to dance with joy. Maybe, just maybe, she'd receive what she desired—a bath. Unable to resist the temptation, she slipped from the bed. The hem of Paladin's shirt fell over the tops of her thighs, tickling her legs.

With one hand, she pushed the door wider. Yes, a tub was there, waiting for her to use. With a grin, she pulled the shirt over her head. Naked, she studied the narrow chain hanging on the side of a water spout. She tugged it. Clear water poured out of the curved pipe. After a few seconds, steam rose from the water.

Seren touched the clear, gushing water. Her smile widened. The temperature, bordering on hot and promising relaxing comfort, called to her. She stepped into the tub then sat, leaning back, enjoying the feel of the water covering her.

Her mind wandered to the last time she had sat in a bath. At that time, she had wanted the horrible, oppressive vision of the white dragon to end. Now, all her thoughts centered on Paladin and her unborn baby. She rested her head against the tub's rim, considering everything that had happened since then.

Thinking of the first vision reminded her of what she'd witnessed last night, but she shook her head, she wouldn't think about the past. She stopped memories from filling her mind. Right now, she wanted to relax, not consider how what had happened to her in the past might affect the future. This peaceful time would slip away. There wasn't any way she'd mess up this moment. She wanted to enjoy it. Who knew what this day would bring?

After soaking then bathing with a bar of plain, unscented soap, Seren dressed and left the bedroom. She retraced hers and Paladins' footsteps from last night, descended the stairs, and walked to the room they had gone to when they first arrived. No one was there. Next, she went to the front entrance, hoping to find Paladin out there.

A luscious, vibrant world greeted her outside. Sweat popped out on her brow. The high humidity reminded her of southern Louisiana where steamy humidity was a way of life. Plants and trees grew along the perimeter of the cleared area before the house, revealing a green hothouse of life which reminded her of home. Patches of bright white clouds floated across the brilliant blue sky. The gentle breeze brought the heavy scent of sweet exotic flowers.

When she didn't see anyone, Seren went back inside. Frowning, not sure what to do or where to go, she tilted her head and listened, hoping for some sign to tell her everyone's location. She didn't want to wander around the wizard's home by herself too much. Largin might not like it.

Voices came from further down the hall. She moved to the closed door at the end and turned the knob. The room, the width of the house, was the kitchen.

Aromatic herbs hung from hooks on the ceiling. A black kettle extended on a hook in the hearth spewed steam from its spout. The strong scent of telee permeated the room.

"Ah, you're awake."

Her gaze swung away from the kettle to the far side of the room. Largin stood next to a doorway which gave a view of the backyard. Light spilled inside, brightening that side of the room.

The old man stepped away from the opening, motioning to her. "Come, Leo and Paladin are without, enjoying the warmth of the sun."

With a nod, she walked past him and into an overgrown world of glorious life. Deep green vines with leaves the size of elephant ears climbed the outer door frame. Bright blue trumpet flowers with dark orange pistons bloomed in staggered places on the vine.

Amazed, she looked closer. The petals appeared coated with a strange waxy substance.

Leo's voice carried across the vibrant garden. "They're similar to the hibiscus."

Seren swung around to the sound. Paladin stood next to the taller black man. He appeared smaller, weaker against Leo. Memories of her vision the night before returned. There had been nothing spineless in the way he had faced the attacking dragons. Pride along with strength had radiated from him.

She smiled, wanting him to see her joy in finding him. He grinned, a warm light reflected in his eyes. "Good morning," she called. As she approached them, she focused on Paladin.

"You look rested."

His smile melted her heart. "So do you."

Leo chuckled. "Are you hungry? I threw a batch of drop biscuits together. There's fresh butter. Jam, too, if you like, and hot telee. You drank it last night. It's sort of like tea."

He pointed to a table hidden from view by several planters filled with greenery. Her stomach growled. She reached up, covering her heated cheeks. "Sorry. I'm starving."

"Then eat. There's plenty."

Paladin moved ahead of her. He pulled a chair out. "I was discussing with Leo the possibility of taking a ride up the mountain. There is a meadow not far from here. The view of the sea is exquisite. I thought perhaps you might enjoy an outing."

"I'd love to," she replied, picking up and buttering a biscuit. When she broke the round, golden bread apart, steam escaped, carrying the delicious aroma to her taste buds. Her stomach muscles tightened. Her mouth watered.

"Good. I'll go and prepare the dragoons. You will be fine here." The deep tone of his voice added to the loveliness of the morning.

She nodded, taking a bite. The food was delicious. She'd found heaven. Closing her eyes, she savored the flavors of the biscuit with melted butter.

After a couple more bites, she glanced up to discover both men had disappeared. With a smile which turned into a laugh, she fixed another biscuit and poured a cup of telee.

Chapter Eleven

An hour later, Seren sat on the back of a dragoon, waiting for Leo to finish tying the straps around a straw basket on the rear of his saddle. Next to her, Paladin sat astride his own dragoon. He reached out, touching her arm. When she glanced at him, he pointed up.

Birds flew from the leafy foliage of a nearby tree. Their tails streamed behind them, showing off an array of bright pinks and purple feathers. They glided toward the rear of the house. Their deep caws rang out in the quiet of the clearing.

Enthralled, Seren watched them until they disappeared. She turned to Leo. "They looked like macaws."

"Yes, ma'am. There are a lot of animals, plants, and birds similar to ones on Earth."

Once Leo mounted, Paladin led the way past the wizard's home. The trail cut through the lush forest. Croaks along with chirps greeted their small caravan. Seren looked at the dense undergrowth and the tall trees. Remnants of moisture hung in the air.

"It's so beautiful here," she said. "Peaceful. Fresh."

Paladin smiled at her over his shoulder. "I come here often. It is a fine place for a man to think."

His words made her curious about what he thought now. He looked at her. Had he sensed her inquisitive thoughts? "We will not consider the future while we are here. There will be time for that later. Let us enjoy the peace instead."

With a nod, she agreed with him, but kept her focus on him more than the landscape. His body shifted and moved with the gait of the dragoon with a natural balance. A grin tugged at her mouth. She'd never watched men, but she could grow accustomed to studying him. Her eyes wandered over the width of his shoulders, moving down the curve of his back to his trim waist. Desire spiraled from the tips of her breast to her lower body.

"Look there," Leo called from behind her.

Glad for the interruption, she glanced in time to see a strange cat-like animal scurry across their path. Her mouth fell open. A surprised gasp escaped. Once on the opposite side of the trail, the grayish feline peeked from beneath leaves and hissed at them. Its body hunkered low to the ground. As they moved past, Seren saw the cat creature's legs were no longer than her fingers.

Amazed, she turned to Leo. "What is it?"

"Sorta like a cat, but more badger. They live in hollow trees." His eyes, alight with joy, crinkled in the corners.

They continued on, each silent except for the times some new animal would appear or a strange looking plant caught her eye. Leo explained each one to her and compared it to something familiar on Earth.

The slow ride helped her forget she no long traveled on Earth. The gentle swaying relaxed her. Each tree and the growing plants beneath them thrived in the hothouse atmosphere of the island. A thin mist floated close to the ground, coating the floor of the forest. If she pretended, this place might be the Amazon jungle or even the swamps in Louisiana.

"Why isn't it more muddy after all the rain last night?" She asked, staring at the ground beneath the broad hind feet of Paladin's dragoon. "Where are the puddles?"

Paladin glanced over his shoulder. "The plants drink the rain in through the roots. Do you see the thickness of the leaves?"

She looked in the direction he pointed. All the plants they passed were coated with the same shiny glaze like the one at Largin's back door.

"It is their protection against so much rain. They draw every drop into their roots. What they don't catch runs off into streams then the sea, or to the island's interior which empties into one of the many lakes."

"This place is like paradise."

A puzzled look crossed Paladin face.

Before she had the chance to answer, the dragoon crested a ridge. A large valley extended to towering mountains on the other side. Off to the left, at the bottom of the valley, a green meadow stretched to a drop in the land. Out past where the meadow ended, the ocean, with its white tipped waves, rolled toward land.

The beauty of the view took Seren's breath with its postcard perfection.

Paladin moved his mount to her side. "If you look there, on this side of the meadow, you'll see a Felerian village. We will stop for a visit."

This pristine land made her pulse race with excitement. Seren smiled and nodded, willing to discover more of this alien world. She thought about the explorers of the Americas. They had to have felt the same thrill she was experiencing.

After another hour of traveling, they reached the edge of the village. Round vertical huts nestled in a natural indent along a sloping hillside. Upright poles held the straw cone roofs in place. Each hut sat on stilts above the ground and wooden steps led to the small blanket covered doorways. The blankets, made from multi-colored threads, cast a cheery atmosphere.

Felerians, smiles splitting their long, narrow jaws, came forward. The women wore bright reds, blues, and yellow sarongs while the men had on natural toned shirts with leggings. Some of them had nothing on except deep blue loin clothes, leaving their muscled chests, arms, and thighs bare.

The villagers approached the new arrivals in a sea of color, calling out greetings. She marveled at these people with round, slit-pupil, feline eyes and pointed ears on the upper side of their heads. Their slender fingers with sharp claws on the tips joined with palms much like her own.

She looked out at the growing crowd and stopped on one young girl not far from the front. Her features were more human than cat, yet she still had the ears, dark tipped nose and rounded green eyes.

Unique, even beautiful, the strange feline eyes were focused on Paladin. A sharp, jealous pang shot through Seren's stomach. Who was this girl? What was her interest in Paladin?

A path opened in the middle of the gathered villagers. An aged male in a zagged design yellow sarong, wobbled forward, a tall, heavy staff in his hand. The feathers decorating his crown fluttered in the gentle breeze.

The reddish fur on the elder Felerian's face was

sprinkled with white hairs. He raised the staff and announced in a voice no different than a human's, "My Lord, your visit is a great blessing to our village. A feast we will serve as a welcome gift."

Paladin lifted a hand, shaking his head, "No, Muggoossa, it is not necessary. We cannot stay. The storms will come once more today. We must return to Master Largin's before they do so."

"Then you will break the mid-rise fast with us. This we offer you in welcome," Muggoossa responded. He glanced to his left then to the right nodding. Several females hurried away, giggling in excitement. Seren assumed to prepare the meal.

Paladin stepped from the saddle to stand beside the dragoon. He extended his left arm, clasping the Felerian leader's.

The girl Seren had noticed earlier moved forward and knelt at Paladin's feet, her head bowed, hands held pressed together above her. "My Lord, is it time now for me to leave my home. I have passed through to my adulthood. Will you take me with you this time?"

Surprised at the girl's actions and words, Seren's mouth fell open before she snapped it shut. She never considered jealousy a part of her emotions, but the possessive reaction she experienced at what had just happened seemed to be the only explanation. Years ago when she and her husband were still married, he'd flirted with other woman, but she'd never had heat crawl up her back like it did now. Just thinking of Paladin with another woman made Seren see green.

The sudden heated anger which rose inside her surprised her. Had she grown so attached to Paladin? She tried to understand what she felt for him. Not love, no, not that, but something else. He belonged to her. Right now, while she stayed on this planet, he was hers. In return, he possessed her, too.

She took a deep breath, trying to calm the raging desire to jump off the dragoon and pull Paladin away.

"Leala, it is good to see you have grown, but the time is not right. You must stay with your clan a bit longer." Paladin reached out and ruffled the top of the girl's head.

She lowered her arms to look up at him with bright, round eyes. "But, my Lord, I am older…"

Muggoossa cut her off. "Be still, it is true what Lord Paladin has said. The time is not now. Go now, child. Help with the meal."

Leala sighed and stood. Throwing a hopeful glance over her shoulder, she shuffled off in the same direction the other females had gone.

"She wants to travel so she might view Avaris' wonders. I too desire to do so with her, but these old bones will not allow it," the Felerian leader commented as he watched Leala make her way into one of the huts.

"It is best she remain here. There is much turmoil brewing in the world. I fear war is bearing down on us."

With an understanding nod, Muggoossa faced Seren. "Welcome to our humble village, my Lady. I am Muggoossa, village elder."

Seren smiled, her jealousy fading after their conversation. "I'm Seren."

"Ah, so you are the one who has come to Avaris from the stars. Even your name means star."

Eyes wide, Seren stared at him in amazement. "How do you know that?"

"Our mystic healer saw it in the smoke of the sacred

fire." He held out his arm. She clasped it the same way Paladin had. "Have no fear, my Lady, you will return to visit us once more."

Confused by his comment, Seren tried to keep her face empty of any emotion. She glanced over at Paladin to see if he understood, but he didn't meet her stare. Leo stepped from behind her to greet the leader. He looked over at her and shrugged.

Muggoossa led the way into the village, pointing out different lodges, one was set up for healing, another larger one for community assemblies, and last, his own home. He introduced her to many of the villagers. Every female smiled, reaching out to touch her hand. The males nodded, chins lifted in pride, arms crossed over their chests and legs braced apart. Their bright colored clothing stood out against the greens of the foliage surrounding the village. Their hair varied. Some had long, thick, curly hair while others wore theirs shorter, thinner and much straighter.

They stopped not far from the elder's lodge when Paladin spoke to the elder. "Muggoossa, I wish to show Seren the meadow. We thought to break our mid-fast there."

The elder nodded. "Very well, the morning is good. The walk is not far. So be it."

With a slow smile, Paladin placed his hand on her lower back. "We will go ahead and wait for you."

"Yes, yes. We will follow soon," Muggoossa agreed. "Leo, will you go also?"

"No, sir. I think I'll stay to walk with you."

Paladin's smile shifted into a grin. He winked at Leo before he took Seren's hand. With a tug, he hurried down a dirt path cutting through the tall, slender trees with the grayish-bark topped with light green leaves which bordered the village like official guardians, watching and protecting.

Smiling, Seren glanced over at him. "Why do I have the impression that you planned this?"

He answered over his shoulder. "And if I did? What harm is there? I desire to show you the meadow. Alone."

That's what worries me. She shook her head, letting let him guide her along the narrow dirt path. Winds pulled at the leaves with a rush, dancing over their tops and creating delightful music to add to the beauty of the place.

The trees ended, opening up into a meadow. Green grass carpeted the land broken by patches of yellow and red wild flowers that bloomed across the expanse. Seren gasped at the beauty before her. The sky, a deep azure, dotted with brilliant white clouds, hung above them. Breaking free of Paladin's hand, she raced through the ankle high grass. She twirled, savoring the fresh air along with all the vibrant life around her.

When she stopped, her gaze met his. He walked toward her and stood at her side. Curiosity drove her to ask. "Who is Leala?"

A gentle smile formed on his lips. His eyes softened around the edges. "Her father sailed with me. He died last annual. She feels she must complete his duty to me. I do not want this. She owes me nothing."

Seren reached out and ran a finger down the center of his chest where his shirt gaped, revealing the sleek golden skin. Her mouth watered. "She's infatuated with you."

He lifted his hands up, cupped her jaw, bringing her attention to his face. The deep melodious tone weakened her knees. "Do you know how difficult it was for me to lay by your side last evening and not touch you?"

Stepping back, she pulled away from his touch, and turned from him. "I'm sorry. I shouldn't have slept with you. It won't happen again."

"Seren…"

She whirled to him, placing one finger on his lips to stop his words. "Don't misunderstand me. I want to, but I can't. My time here is temporary. I don't want any attachments to you. It'll be too hard for me to leave if I allow anything to happen between us."

His tongue tasted her fingertip. Liquid heat gathered in the vee between her legs. She shook her head. The passion overwhelming her, she pulled away. "No. Please…"

He let her go. "And if you find you do not care to leave? Could you come to want me—Paladin—the man?"

After considering for a moment, she nodded. "From my time with you, I believe you're a man I could grow to love.

I'm just not sure I should."

"You do not believe in love at first sight then?"

With a gust of laughter, she shook her head. "Maybe lust at first sight. I do lust after you." He stared at her, his expression serious as he contemplated her. Her smile faded as her attempt to keep the conversation light failed. He was serious. "Why? Do you believe in it?"

"In the ability to look at a woman…" He tilted his head in acknowledgment, "or one man, and know in your heart this person is the one for you? The other side of your spirit? That your heart is lost to him or her?"

Yes, she could understand the concept, but was

unsure of where he was going with these questions. Deep inside, though, she wanted to know. Her heart raced in anticipation. She needed to discover if she was the one person for him.

"When at the moment their eyes first meet, to see a future bright with happiness and love for the rest of their lives? This happens in a flash, branding onto their minds for eternity. I believe this is very possible. Is it because you are from Earth you do not believe thus?"

Not ready to explain or even to look too close at how she felt for him, she asked, "Did you love your wife?"

His expression changed—hardened and his body stiffened. With his reaction to her question, she regretted asking. Lifting a hand, needing some kind of contact to help him understand she didn't mean to pry, she reached for him. He stepped back. A deep sense of loss came over her.

"No. I am only honor-bound to her. The marriage was arranged. No links with our souls were involved."

Seren studied him for a moment. His expression remained blank, unreadable. "Yet you made love to her. She became pregnant with your child."

Pain flickered in his eyes. It flashed for a second to disappear, leaving the blue unreadable. His grin was tight and false when he answered. "Two people need not love to create a child."

The painful reflection in his gaze gave her a vital piece of information. He had wanted to love his wife, but for some reason, the dead woman had rejected his feelings.

Paladin had remained at Seren's side the entire time since she had come to this planet. He didn't take his responsibilities lightly. "Are you honor-bound to me?"

He raised a hand and touched the tip of her hair. "No. I keep you close to me out of choice, not duty. Even before I knew of the child, I wanted you to remain near to me."

"Why?" She had to know his reasons. Had he experienced what he'd described? Toward her?

"I wanted you. From the first moment."

Relieved he hadn't fallen in love with her, she leaned into his palm. He slid his hand to her throat. He leaned nearer and whispered. "I do desire you."

Seren's heart accelerated. "I loved my husband. When my daughter died, the love ended. I often wondered if I even knew what love was. And now, with you, all I can think of is having you hold me, touch me...."

She shook her head and stepped back. "But it's not love though, it's lust. Not a good basis for a relationship."

"You affect me much more than in a physical way. You lightened my days. Brought laughter and joy into my life after I believed they had deserted me."

Her heart clenched. When had her ex-husband ever told her something so sweet? The answer was simple. Never. Now, this beautiful man, the one whose child she carried, touched her to the center of her heart with just his words.

She blinked away the sudden burning in her eyes. She wouldn't cry in front of him.

Chapter Twelve

She twirled away, hoping to hide how much he had affected her. "Then my work here is done. Come on. Let's enjoy this place without anyone else around."

Running ahead of him, she sent what she hoped was a come hither look over her shoulder. He grinned, following at a slower pace. Sunlight flowed over her while the breeze, coasting in from the ocean, caressed her face. Coming to stop along the edge of the bluff overlooking the water, she waited until he stood next to her.

"You never did tell me why you're not a king anymore."

"My brother took the throne in my place."

This caught her attention. "Why? Is he older than you?"

"No. The oracles declared he would rule, so the throne went to him upon my father's death."

She looked over at him. His face revealed nothing. "Are you okay with that?"

"We were both raised to rule."

"Is he a good king?"

"From what Largin has told me, he is acting in a fashion unsuitable for the throne." Paladin lifted his gaze to meet hers. "He would see you dead before our child is born. I will have to stop him. It is not a task I look forward to."

"I'm sorry. I've caused you so many problems." Her heart ached for him.

Voices came from the trail behind them. Several villagers appeared on the path through the trees. Many of them called out to Paladin. He took her hand and led her to the people. Seren smiled, concealing her confusion over the increased attraction for him in her heart.

****

The sun moved across the sky. Looking at the angle of the bright circle, she assumed midday had passed. An array of meats cooked over a fire pit, strange fruits and vegetables, some cooked, others left raw, sent her taste buds into ecstasy. Overstuffed from eating too much, suffering from the drowsy aftereffects, she leaned against the trunk of a tree, listening to the insects buzzing in the meadow. Birds cooed and chirped in the leaves above. Dappled shade covered the ground around her. Lids half-lowered with lassitude, she silently admired the golden-haired man stretched out on the grass not far from her. He'd pillowed his head with a bent arm. Dark lashes hid his eyes so she couldn't tell if he slept or just rested. She'd considered crawling to his side, but with her full stomach and sleep tugging at her to close her eyes, she'd decided to remain against the tree, satisfying her desire for him through her unwavering stare.

A few feet away, Felerian children sat in a circle and sang clan songs, clapping their hands. Their youthful voices brought a smile to her lips. She wanted to remember this day long after she returned to Earth, every second here in this place, keeping it locked deep within her heart. Never had she experienced such peace.

One moment, she basked in paradise, the next, Paladin leapt to his feet with his swords drawn and held ready before him. Her energy returned with a blood rush to her head.

He faced the meadow with his head back, his eyes on the sky. Flapping wings brought her focus to where he looked. From the sound, huge wings. Her vision of Paladin, the dragons attacking him, flashed through her mind. Fear rose inside her.

Two gigantic dragons glided over the rim of the bluff overlooking the water. They coasted for several yards. Bluegreen scales glinted in the sunlight. They extended their back legs, both heavy with muscles, and landed several yards away. The ground shook. The leaves bounced in the nearby trees. Birds took flight, squawking in fear.

Paladin stood like a physical barrier between Seren and them. He lifted his right hand, the sword glinting in the light. "Be gone, Biaotoc. Be gone from here."

Both dragons lowered their massive bodies to rest on their shorter arms. Long necks, the scales rippling with their movement, stretched to the side, their lime green eyes, the pupils slit, focused on her. An inner lens opened and closed then stopped.

Low mewls came from their gaped mouths. Those low grunts, growls, and mewls transformed into words. She glanced around to see if anyone else heard, but most of the Felerians, their bodies tense, faces lined with unease, watched from behind the trees edging the meadow. They seemed unaware of the dragons speaking.

"We have come to see the truth."

The words, slow and elongated, slid into her thoughts.

Paladin answered. Her attention caught on him. He understood what they'd said too. "What truth, Biaotoc?"

The second dragon, smaller than the other, leaned toward the left, its words softer, more feminine in tones. *"Our king."*

Biaotoc, the male with its much larger body, stretched its head nearer, its nostril flared with its inhalation. *"We have heard the King has been created."*

"It is no concern of yours."

A gust of sea-scented air shot toward Paladin as Biaotoc reared back. *"Human."* He twisted his head to the other dragon. *"A human carries the dragon king."*

Icy shards of fear lashed at Seren's insides, freezing her limbs. Someone touched her arm. She tore her gaze away from Paladin to where long, ebony fingers curled over her upper arm. She looked up, meeting Leo's eyes. He squatted next to her. "It's okay. They shouldn't attack."

"Oh, that's great," she mumbled. His reassurance did little to relieve her.

In the seconds it took Seren to look back at the huge creatures, the other dragon slipped her head forward. *"I can smell him. Oh...he sleeps in his human mother."*

"You will not call to him," Paladin ordered, taking a step toward them.

A white blur passed in front of the female's face. It landed with a dull thump in the grass before the beasts. Standing on its lanky hind legs, the lone white drac spread its wings. The miniature dragon cawed and flapped its wings at the two larger ones.

Biaotoc's nostrils widened, his eyes narrowed as he stared down his snout at the drac. *"You dare order me— leader of the sea dragons."*

The drac flapped harder. Frightened for the small beast, Seren jolted upright. The little reptile shooed the larger dragons away. She raised a hand and the words spilled out before she thought, "Please…don't hurt it."

The male dragon focused on her for a moment then looked at the drac. *"You have been magic-kissed bold one for your actions this day. We will leave you in peace."*

He nudged the female's neck with his nose. *"Come, Faelee."*

Paladin remained with his back to Seren, swords ready. The dragons rose, their wings stirring the grass along with the flowers. A moment later, they took flight.

The drac hopped in place a few times then wobbled to Seren. It flopped down onto the ground next to her, lying on its back. Rear legs stretched out, the front ones hung over its chest, leaving the smooth white belly unprotected.

Without giving any thought to the matter, Seren touched the drac's stomach. She marveled at the soft texture of the scales. "He's so pretty."

Glancing over his shoulder, Paladin grunted. "He is a she. Do not grow attached, they do not survive long. Few live to be dragons."

Surprised at his uncaring comment, Seren glared at him. "I don't know. She has a ton of courage. She'll live. Maybe even become *the* great white dragon."

The tension faded from his stance. He turned to her and slid his swords into their scabbards before he responded. "Perhaps. Her actions reveal strength."

Seren scratched at the corner of the young female dragon's jaw. Low, deep moans rolled from the drac's throat and one back leg bounced. Laughing, Seren passed a hand over the downy neck to pat her narrow chest.

Paladin squatted next to her, bringing her attention

to him. "We must depart. Come, the storms will return before long."

Disappointed, Seren nodded and stood, brushing the pieces of debris from her rear. The little drac rolled over and came to her feet, tilting her head toward Seren. With a laugh, Seren motioned with her head, speaking to the drac. "Come on, you can ride home with us."

They told the villagers goodbye and promised to return soon. Seren turned to walk down the path to the village. She'd miss this place and its peacefulness.

The pat-pat of the drac's feet came from behind her. Surprised the little beast had listened when she'd told her to come, she glanced at the drac. Her lips stretched over pointed teeth in what might be called a smile. Seren giggled. Turning to Paladin, she asked. "Can we keep her?"

He looked at the drac, shaking his head with a grin. "Dracs do not belong to anyone. They are free to come and go how they please. From the look of her though, it appears she might stay for a while. There must be a purpose for her appearance here. I for one do not want to anger fate by driving her away."

Seren took his arm with a grin. He cocked a brow in question. She touched her cheek against his shoulder and murmured, "Thanks."

They hurried to the village, where they mounted their well-tended dragoons. Seren turned in the saddle for one last look at the peaceful valley. She wanted to remember this wonderful day. The drac, sitting on her dragoon's rump mewled at her. She patted the soft white head, faced forward, and nudged her mount behind Paladin's.

Chapter Twelve

On the morning of the third day during their visit with Largin, the drac flew away. The white wings spread out against the blue sky as the drac caught an air draft. The winds carried the small creature out of sight. Seren looked on, trying to catch even a glimpse of the drac. The strange beast had captured Seren's heart and with its departure, sadness came over her, making the day less bright and cheery. A short time later, Paladin informed her that they were to leave the next morning. The winds had increased, and he needed to continue their journey. Concern with where their trip ended sent worry streaming through her mind, but she was eager to see and learn more about Avaris. Leo decided to travel with them. Early the next morning, they said their goodbyes to Largin and departed. Several hours later, far from Bae, she listened to Paladin inform Leo of their destination.

Hands on his hips, Leo stood on the ship's bow, a frown marking deep lines in his forehead. "Did your momma drop you on your head when you were born?"

Seren, standing at the rail listening, bit down on her bottom lip to keep from laughing out loud. Leo continued, his expression incredulous. "You have to be crazy if you think you can just sail into Velhaven and stay in one piece. They'll shoot you down with all those magical fireballs you people use."

The wind gusted over the deck. Blond strands

fluttered away from Paladin's face. He stood at the rail, looking at the horizon with his arms crossed over his chest and his feet braced apart. A smile tugged at the corner of his mouth.

"Damn it, this isn't funny." The anger and fear in Leo's tone caused Seren's back to stiffen.

No longer amused, Seren chewed on her bottom lip while she watched the two men.

Paladin shook his head. "I am not laughing."

"But you find humor in it?"

With a slow and steady motion, Paladin faced Leo and placed a hand on the older man's shoulder. "No, but I can do nothing else. My duty to my wife requires I return her body to her family. I cannot pass this duty to someone else."

Tucking his chin, Leo shook his head, his lips forming a tight line. "If you have to, fine, but drop Seren in a neutral port. You don't want her hurt 'cause you want to act noble."

"I had already decided to do so. We go to Durfalin first. If you will, stay and watch over her until my return," Paladin said. He lowered his hand and met Leo's eyes. "She will be closer to me there than if I had left her with Master Largin."

She had to stop from opening her mouth to argue with him. When had he decided this and without talking it over with her? Her heart beat faster. What was she supposed to do with him gone? Clenching her fist, she glared at him. Why hadn't he said something? She wasn't sure she wanted him to leave her. Her entire life revolved around him. This realization stopped her. When had he become so important to her? A smile pulled at her lips. From the moment he brought her to this world, that's when. She ignored the prickling of aggravation brought on by his neglecting to tell her and focused on their conversation again.

Leo agreed with Paladin. The conversation drifted to the running of the ship. Seren only half-listened. Her thoughts were on what would happen during her time away from Paladin. Even though it probably wouldn't be for long, the implied separation frightened her. She wasn't secure enough in this strange new place, yet at the same time, she understood the reasoning behind his decision.

The wind passed over her face, cooling her. She closed her eyes and drew in a deep breath, savoring the fresh sea breeze. The heaviness she experienced upon her arrival on Avaris seemed less. She found that if she lifted her hand, she didn't have to struggle to do so.

Sails clapped in the windy gusts. Dracs that mingled with a flock of birds passing nearby cawed. She glanced over the rail at the white tipped water below. Bluish-silver wings flashed in the sunlight as the birds dove into the sea for a minute or so. They erupted from the water in little geysers with small glistening fish wiggling in their beaks.

She turned and leaned back against the railing, her head tilted to see the sky. Clouds floated by while the sun kissed her face. The peace she experienced in that moment relaxed her. Deep in her heart, did she want to return to her old life? There wasn't anything tempting her to go home except for Mandy's grave. Paladin stood a few feet away, and she watched him unobtrusively.

After several minutes, Calis appeared. He challenged Leo to a board game. When they moved to another spot on the deck, Paladin's gaze met hers. She refused to lower hers first. Her reaction to the way he looked always struck her the same. She had difficulty catching her breath even as her pulse danced through her veins.

He walked to her side, the corner of his mouth lifted in a teasing fashion. "You look fetching today." She raised her brows. "Fetching?"

His smile widened. He leaned closer to whisper.

"Beautiful."

Speechless, she studied him. Sincerity echoed in his words and the open, honest look he leveled at her.

"I'm not sure I believe you." She waved a hand in front of her body, indicating her worn boy's clothes. "This doesn't flatter me."

"It's not the clothes I see, but the woman in them."

"Why do I have the feeling you're trying to seduce me?"

"Because I am."

He held her stare. For a brief moment, she suspected there was more to his teasing remark than he wanted her to know. Seren grinned, glancing away. "Won't work. I won't give in. I want to discover all your secrets."

"What secrets? I have none."

"We all have some in one way or another. I want to know what makes you tick. What makes you the man you are?" She spun on her heel and placed her forearms on the rail. Fighting the smile tugging at her lips, she stared out across the sky and sea. "Why didn't you fight for the throne?"

He placed a hand next to her arm, his fingers a mere inch away. A pang of desire danced across her stomach. The heat of his body radiated to her. She wanted to fall into his arms and devour him with her mouth. Instead, she waited for his answer.

"I believed to do so was a better decision than for me to rule. My younger brother was the better choice."

"Why?"

"Why not? He was taught to rule our country."

"So that makes him a better king?"

"You twist my words."

"Tell me, what do you mean? You believed at the time you made the right decision. You just said so—but the other day, you told me you had to stop him. What will it do to your relationship with each other? Destroy your kinship?"

He looked at the sky. An expression of doubt crossed his face for the space of a second, just long enough for Seren to see.

"I had hoped he would be a great king. Matters have changed."

"Me?"

"No. He's invaded neighboring countries, laying them to waste. I expect the downfall of my clan if I do not stop him."

Seren had a sense of foreboding. "How are you going to do it?"

"When I complete my duty to my late wife, I intend to return home."

"No." The word came out before she thought. The images of her vision flared to life. With them came the biting fear she would lose something special if he returned to his homeland. "I told you the other night. You can't go back, not now."

He nodded, slow, deliberate. "Yes, but you failed to say why I must not."

She wanted to open her mouth and admit what she'd

witnessed, but the words stuck in her throat. How could she tell him she'd seen his death through a vision? She looked away. Her mind went blank of anything to say.

He picked up her hand. Compelled to meet his eyes, she tried to keep her face expressionless in hopes of hiding her fear. A gentle smile graced his mouth. "You do not have to say the words. I know. It was a vision. If I am meant to die, there is nothing anyone can do to stop it. Do not carry the burden of keeping this from me. I will not allow you to suffer any guilt."

A sailor called out to him, ending their conversation. Paladin squeezed her hand and left. Somewhere along their journey, her watching, all her worrying about him had become a hobby. This gave her a focal point while she waited for the baby's birth. She smiled and patted the small bump in her abdomen.

Paladin stood next to one of the thick masts, looking up at the sails. He removed his coat, caught one of the ropes, and climbed, hand over hand, until he reached the yardarm.

For a second, the world wobbled before her eyes. Her legs weakened, refusing to hold her up any longer. She slumped on the deck with her back against the solid wood below the railing. She gasped for breath, fighting to drag each molecule of oxygen into her lungs. She closed her eyes.

A man's face appeared behind her lids. His head was bald—round, smooth, and silvered in the surrounding light— the stranger stared at her and smiled, his teeth flashing white. Her eyes flew open. Terror gnawed at her. In an instant, her vision righted. The sudden sickness passed. Heart pounding, she sent a glance up. She met Paladin's blue eyes. She reached deep inside her, managing to find the strength to smile so he wouldn't wonder.

Shaken, she stood. On unsteady feet, she walked to the door leading below. She needed to lie down. No, she needed to find out the man's identity in hopes of discovering why he'd appeared to her.

****

Early the next morning, Seren came above deck. Men, human and Felerian, worked tying lines, mopping the deck, and attending to other tasks. She searched the area for Paladin, but he wasn't there. Disappointment darkened her morning. She had wanted to thank him for the use of her room. She decided not to mention she'd spent a restless night, tossing on the narrow cot. She had missed the warmth of his body, but the continued temptation of having him so near at night bothered her. She refused to give in to her desires.

Leo, sitting on a small barrel on the other end of the deck, called out for her to join him. She smiled, waving in return. Shifting left and right around the sailors, she made her way to his side. He patted the top of another cask next to him. "Have a seat. Eilan just left to fetch some food. I thought it'd be nice to eat out here this morning."

They visited for a few minutes before the food arrived. After they had finished eating, Eilan, one of the Felerian sailors, approached her. Seren glanced up and saw him staring at her.

He bowed with a shy grin pulling his lips up to reveal long canines. "Your pardon, my lady, might I play a song for you?"

Surprised at the request, Seren nodded with a smile, pleased he wanted to do such a nice gesture.

Long incisors appeared on the outer edges of his grin. Seren waited until he returned with a long handled, four string instrument. The strangeness of watching and speaking with these amazing creatures no longer bothered her.

He captured her attention with the first strum. Her gaze met Leo's. He grinned, nodded, and nudged her. The fast tempo of the song affected even him. Soon, another sailor produced a long flute, his music joined with Eilan's. Before long, deep male voices rang out across the ship, the tune was cheerful. Listening to it brightened her morning.

Unable to resist, Seren laughed while she tapped her foot in time with the music. When the song ended, Eilan started a softer melody.

Paladin appeared at her side. Without a word, he held out a hand. She stared into the blueness of his eyes a moment before she placed her palm in his.

He tugged gently and she came into his arms. She positioned her other hand on his shoulder, allowing him to lead her into a dance similar to a waltz. He moved with lean grace, whirling around the deck. Ropes and casks disappeared from their path with the help of the men. The sailors laughed and cheered as they passed close to them.

Heaven had granted Seren another chance to live happily. In that moment, she decided to do her best to fill the years ahead with simple pleasures like dancing aboard a ship, or even just laughing out loud. Right now, she had reached her goal.

A shout from the lookout jarred her daydreams. Paladin stopped and squinted up to where the sailor called.

"Pirates."

Chills swept across Seren's back. She stiffened, her hand squeezing Paladin's. Repeating the word in surprise, she glanced at Paladin. His mouth straightened into a line.

"Go below. Stay there until I come for you." He gave her a little push in the direction of the door leading below.

Leo appeared at her side and took her arm. Every sailor aboard scurried across the deck, preparing in case the thieves attacked.

She shook her head, tugging her arm free. She turned in time to see Paladin grab a sail line that was tied off on the center mast below the lookout. He drew his shorter blade and cut the rope. The sand bag on the top dropped. With the sides of his coat flapping, he rode the other side up to the yardarm. Once there, he leapt onto the narrow piece of wood and walked to the center lookout post.

It felt as if her heart had stopped beating until he reached the round tub supposedly the lookout. Oh, God, what was he thinking? He was so high up. What if he fell? What would she do without him? She wrapped her arms about her waist, sending up a silent plea to whatever powers might hear to keep him safe. She'd given up on her belief in God with her child's death but if her request was granted, she might rediscover her faith.

Several grappling hooks flew out from a nearby misty cloud bank on the right. Metal thudded into wood as they hooked onto the ship's railing. Two lines wrapped around the yardarm where Paladin stood. More shouts rang out from the ship's crew. The ropes joining the two ships stretched taut. At the sudden jarring, Seren grabbed hold of a nearby barrel. The pirates winched their ship closer until wood scraped against wood with another teeth shaking jerk.

"Come on, the captain and the crew will take care of them," Leo muttered near her ear. He took her arm. Lost in a dazed shock, not believing this was happening, she allowed him to lead her to the door leading below. Just before they reached the hatch, three pirates, swords drawn, blades glinting in the sunlight, jumped on board not far from them.

One charged Leo, who in turn, pulled Seren behind him. Her feet tangled with each other. She fell with a whoosh, the breath knocked out of her. The ship tilted. She slid backward a few feet. Fighting to inhale, she looked at where she'd last seen Paladin. Out of the corner of her eye, she caught a glimpse of Leo ducking to avoid a downward sword swipe. He punched out with two quick jabs. Knuckles met the attacker's jaw with a dull thud. Blood trickled from the corner of the pirate's mouth.

Unable to find Paladin, she searched the deck, worried he'd fallen or worse, been knocked off the yardarm when the grapples caught hold of their ship. She glanced back to see the other two pirates avoid their unconscious shipmate's tumble and swerved past Leo, each angled at her. Trembling, she slid her legs beneath her, prepared to fight for her and her baby's life. She refused to let the attackers harm her child.

Someone shouted from above. She shot a glance up in time to see Paladin step off the yardarm. Seren froze, terror piercing her heart.

He fell, not twisting and fighting for a hold to stop his sudden drop, but more graceful, as if he dove on purpose. His right hand held the handle of his sheathed sword. When he reached a point of several feet above the deck, he slipped the blade free. The silvered length blurred with the speed of his movement. The two pirates faced him. His sword slashed out, slicing through stained, dingy white shirts to cut deep into their chests. Both men, their eyes wide, breaths gurgling, staggered back. They crumpled to the deck. Blood pooled on the wood beneath their bodies.

Paladin landed, feet first, but his knees gave way so he knelt with one knee touching the deck and the other bent, his foot flat. His head remained lowered for a second then he stood in the same slow manner she'd grown to love.

Unable to stop it, her mouth dropped open as her gaze bounced from the yardarm to him and back. How had he not crashed into the deck? Her vision wobbled a moment then cleared. The heavy scent of blood in the air turned her stomach. She tried to figure out how he'd fallen without being dead weight with the strength of the gravity on this planet, but she had nothing to compare this to on Earth. For the first time in several days, she experienced the familiar lost feeling—that of being alone with her confusion in this new world.

More scarred, armed pirates, howling, their weapons waving in the air, poured over the side of the ship. Many attacked the sailors, but the majority of them formed small packs. Their focus appeared aimed at Paladin.

Seren shook her head, scooting out of the way until the wooden side of the railing stopped her. She counted at least ten armed men advancing, their stances intimidating and heading for him. He couldn't fight all those men alone. Each of them held a hateful glimmer in their eyes. Her fear threatened to blow up into a full-blown panic.

A moment before the mass of sweating, reeking pirates reached Paladin, loud caws streamed from the sky above. White dracs, countless numbers of the small dragons, swooped down on the attackers. Sudden, wild fear flared in their attacker's eyes. All the pirates retreated. The dracs started to land, their mouths open to release gusts of heated air at the pirates still aboard. The entire band of bandits broke away, scrambling to return to their ship. All the lines were severed. The other ship sank into the white cottony cloud bank and disappeared from sight.

Hands trembling, Seren released a sigh of relief. She closed her eyes, resting her head against the wood behind her. When she opened them, several dracs landed. The small dragons stood facing her. Paladin, balanced on the balls of his feet, held his swords in a guarded position before his body.

"My thanks, but now you may leave," he ordered the white-scaled creatures. Small frills at the base of their heads fluttered with each call they made to him.

Six scurried closer, their throats working up and down. Once they stood within a few feet of him, they opened their mouths. Shining gems gushed from them to fall to the deck at his feet. He took a step back and shook his head.

Gasps and quiet whispers came from where the crew stood further along the deck. The gemstones caught the sunlight, sparkling with internal flames.

Leo tried to shift around the dracs. The ones closer to him twirled with a vicious cry, fangs bared. His eyes widened, and he held out his hands, shaking his head.

Paladin's voice boomed out above the cawing dracs. "Be gone, I say."

She jerked at the sudden volume of his tone. Honed sharpness added force to his words. He'd never reacted like this before. Even when the sea dragons had come the other day, he had been calm. All that was absent now. The dracs had to leave now that the danger from the pirates had disappeared, but instead the miniature dragons refused to budge even with his order.

A disembodied voice, musical in tone, floated in the air around Paladin. "Be gone? Come now, how dare you speak to your brothers in such a fashion. They wish only to save and serve you, my king."

Glimmering lights swirled around Paladin. These strange lights settled behind where the dracs had formed a semicircle before Paladin. Caws changed to excited squeals.

The brightness from the lights increased until the form of a man appeared. Long tattered white robes fluttered in the breeze over a pale shirt and pants. Bare feet floated several inches above the deck. Slender to the point of thinness, the strange man stared at her.

A slow smile curved his mouth to reveal white teeth. Like a warrior's helmet, a silvered skull cap covered his head. His blue-gray stare sent uneasiness through her. Recognition flared in her. The man from her vision of the other day. She glanced at Paladin.

"For shame, my boy, you have insulted your kin," the man murmured. He shook his arms out from his sides to spread them wide, encompassing all the glittering stones on the deck. "These valiant children have gifted you with great wealth."

Paladin's jaw tightened. "Bask."

The smile widened. "Lior has sent me. She yearns to see the mother. The time draws near. This blessed woman's blood must be purified."

"I will bring her."

"I think not. We will take her this day. You will not interfere."

"You dare defy me?"

Bask threw his head back, guffing out a laugh. Paladin's shoulders, already taut with tension, tightened more.

"You are the one who gave up his rights to rule. You are the one who rides the skies searching for what? Even you do not know what that something is. Yes, I dare. This and even more." Bask, hovering above the deck by several inches, glided to the right. His gaze met Seren's again.

She froze, hypnotized by the fires of strength burning in his eyes. He smiled, gentle yet knowing, and then nodded.

A muffled flap came from behind her. Five dracs, hidden from view by the railing and much larger than the ones on deck, rose from the side of the ship. Each grasped her limbs, and the fifth one caught hold of the waistband at the back of her pants. Lifted up, face down, Seren screamed, jerking, trying to escape. Strong and agile, they twirled around and returned the way they had come, her body mere inches from striking the rail.

Paladin whipped toward her and leapt the distance between them. His foot landed on the rail, his hand reaching. She struggled to stretch her arm to him. Time slowed, each second branded into her mind. She met his eyes, their gazes held, their fingers brushed then separated.

The moment froze in time. His forward motion continued. He tilted too far out. With nothing to stop him, he fell over the side of the airship. Several hundred feet separated him from the sea below.

Seren's scream trailed after him.

Chapter Thirteen

Nauseated at the horror of him falling off the ship, Seren struggled against the clawed talons that clutched her wrists and ankles. Tears blinded her. Sharp pains cut across her chest, pressing in on her. She screamed Paladin's name. No, he couldn't die, not now, not when she had just found him.

Her son's words echoed in her mind.

He is expendable.

"No, not here. It's not supposed to happen here. I won't lose him," she cried.

The dracs still aboard the ship dove over the sides whirling around him. Hope that they would help him brought her struggles to a brief halt. She cried out for them to help him, but they snapped and slashed their claws at him. His body jerked once. A glow started to emanate from his entire form. The dracs which had flown after him, separated and swept after the ones holding her.

Paladin stopped mid-air.

She watched, mesmerized at the sight of him stationery between the ship and the water. One fleeting second of amazement blinked in her thoughts.

The dracs holding her increased their speed, the beat of their wings vibrating through her body.

Paladin threw his arms out to his sides. Wings sprouted from his back.

The wings on Paladin's shoulder blades unfurled,

sweeping back and forth for a moment. In the next second, swords still held in his hands, he flew after her.

Seren giggled hysterically. She shook her head, trying to deny what she'd seen. Leo called to her, reassuring her. Help calm her down? What was Leo thinking? The father of her child, the one she believed was falling to his death just had wings pop out on his back. What wonderland had she landed in? She ignored Leo and started to struggle again, hoping to slow the creatures down.

Low mewls mixed with ringing caws cut through the air. The dracs increased their speed. The sharp gusts of the wind slid across her face. Her kidnappers dropped closer to the waves. Salty water sprayed over Seren's face. Sputtering and blinking to remove the drops from her eyes, she kept her eyes riveted on the shrinking ship behind her and the man flying after them.

Paladin drew nearer. His wings were much larger than the smaller ones on the dracs holding her. He came within several yards behind her. She looked in his direction. Cold determination etched his face.

She had wondered why his coat had such large slits, now she knew. So his wings could unfurl.

Wings. He had wings, like angels. Would he be her savior by rescuing her? Her breath escaped, going out of her body in short fast gasps. Her muscles ached and shook from her struggles. She'd never get away like this. Her wrists were bleeding from the small nicks from the dracs claws. It was up to Paladin. He had to save her.

Air swept past them while the day sped overhead. More dracs arrived from the direction they headed, joining the ones carrying her. She lowered her chin to her chest to look down the front of her body to see where they were taking her.

After checking for the hundredth time, a dark form appeared on the horizon. The setting sun glinted off the shape. An island soon loomed against the magenta and orange skyline. White stone cliffs leaned inward. Large eroded caves in the cliffs grew larger in size, becoming dark indents the closer they came. Waves crashed against the rocks, drowning out the cries of the dracs.

The creatures carrying her ducked into one of the narrow but tall caves, their speed still fast even with the solid stone walls on either side of them. Twisting and turning through the caverns, they erupted into an open area at the tiny island's interior. In the center, a rounded slab of melted stone with several curved columns rising above it supported a covered section situated on the rear side. The huge formation looked like a half-shell cover, reminding her of an amphitheater.

The dracs stopped, and with careful movements, lowered her to the slab. As wide as it was long, the white rock stretched several hundred feet on either side of her. Weak from fear and near hysteria, she managed to sit up, laying one hand flat on the cold stone and bracing herself.

She had lost sight of Paladin in the caverns. Sick to her stomach, she swallowed, trying to keep the bile down.

Paladin appeared in the opening she'd just exited. He stopped for a second. Behind her, a patter of small pebbles warned that she was no longer alone. Frightened to look, but unable to stop, she glanced over her shoulder.

A white dragon, larger by several feet and many tons heavier than the sea dragons from Bae, towered over her.

Shining, pearl like, lace-edged scales gleamed white in the sunlight. The same dragon from her vision, the one she'd heard Paladin mention during her time on Avaris— Lior, the white dragon clan leader.

Her heart plummeted to her stomach for a second, only to rise to her throat the next. The beast stared at her with its slit-pupil blue eyes. Lior's incisors overlapped her top and bottom lips, each equal in length and wider than Leo's legs. Trembling, Seren tried to scoot away, her terror giving her false strength. A massive clawed foot landed next to her. The slab shook, forcing a cry from Seren. She ducked, covering her head. Dust and salty moisture bounced around her.

Paladin shouted her name. She glanced up in time to see him attack Lior. The dragon roared, followed by a heated blast of breath aimed at him. He lifted his left arm, the one with the dragon tattoo, blocking the brunt of the oversized lizard's assault. Silvered flames flowed over his body to disappear behind him. With tight, swift movements, he swerved in a circle, swinging at Lior's head with his blade.

The dragon shifted away. At the last second, its tail swung, striking Paladin against his right side. His sword flew out of his hand, falling against the slab with a metallic clang, sliding until it came to a spinning stop, not far from where Seren sat huddled. Thrown across the open area, Paladin crashed into the cliff on the opposite side.

Not caring what the dragon did to her, Seren jumped to her feet. On unsteady legs, she staggered to the edge, reaching for him. He crumpled, his head hanging at an odd angle, eyes rolled back. Without uttering a sound, Paladin fell toward the water surrounding the slab.

All warmth drained from her. She tried to think, but emptiness filled her mind, her body, her soul. She dropped to her knees and slumped onto her side. He broke his neck. Hope diminished to nothing as she watched him drop to the water motionless. He wouldn't survive if he went under.

She'd lost him. Numbness took over her. This time his wings wouldn't save him.

Huge clawed feet landed behind her. Back stiff, muscles aching, she turned and stared up at the creature who had taken Paladin from her. Its jaws opened, teeth flashing in the fading sunlight. White glistening breath poured over Seren.

The force shoved her flat on her back. Blinded by the intensity of the flames, she wavered between consciousness and black darkness. Still the breath coated her. During rare lucid moments, she imagined Paladin's arms around her, lifting her, comforting her. Most of the time, she swirled in and out of blackness.

Once, she opened her eyes to find Lior leaning over her, the dragon's nostrils wide, smelling her. It grunted, straightened, and opened its mouth. More crystallized air blew from the gaped jaw. At the touch of her breath, Seren's clothes turned to dust. Her skin burned under the cold flames licking at her. She twisted her head back and forth, wanting to escape the torture, but unable to so.

Seren looked to where her hand lay on the cold surface. Palm flat against the stone, the flesh pushed against bones.

She opened her mouth to cry out, but no sound emerged. She had to live—for her baby. Exhausted, she gave in to the pain, allowing the darkness to swallow her.

****

Cool liquid splattered on her face. She stirred, a moan slipped out. Agony rippled through her. Lying on her right side, she managed to find the strength to crack open her eyes.

Rain poured over her, soothing the heat inside her. Light dimmed and blurred. She blinked. Not far from her, Paladin lay on his side, naked and facing her. His eyes, half opened, stared blankly at her. Dark purplish bruises covered the left side of his face and jaw, trailing down his neck and onto his shoulder. His head, still at an odd tilt, rested against the stone. More cuts overlaid deep purple bruises which covered his limp body. Slow rattling breaths escaped the tiny gap between his chapped lips.

One arm, stretched in her direction. Palm up and his fingers curled, his hand seemed to beckon her. Determined, she tried to touch him. Inch by slow inch, she moved her arm to his hand. Pain lanced through her body, but she refused to stop. Seconds slipped by, then the back of her fingers brushed his knuckles.

His eyelashes fluttered—once.

Heart thumping in rapid succession, a measure of hope bloomed within, warming her. He was aware, conscious of her at his side.

Satisfied, she relaxed, allowing sleep to ease her pain, her fingers barely touching his.

****

"Up with you, my fledgling."

Her eyelids flew open. The man from the ship, the one Paladin called Bask, slipped his hands under Paladin's arms from behind and lifted. Seren gasped, wanting to scream for him to leave Paladin alone, but her throat lacked moisture, the lining too tight to allow any sound to emerge.

Paladin's limbs flopped without any muscle control. His head dipped lower. It was still cocked to one side. A low moan came from his dry, cracked lips. She opened her mouth to once more shout at Bask to leave him alone.

Nothing came out except a rasping breath.

"Be still woman. This wayward dragonseed is fine. You will soon witness my love's power."

The words should have comforted Seren, but they didn't.

Once he'd lifted Paladin's limp body, Bask wrapped an arm around his waist, grasped the back of his head, and turned him toward where the silent dragon waited.

"I warned you, didn't I? You cannot think to defy my beloved Lior. She cares very little for rebellious children, my boy. No, no, she doesn't. Now then, are you ready? Consider this a great boon on her part to you. She should have left you to drown, you ungrateful whelp."

Bask smiled and called out to the dragon. "Your magic, Lior. Use your magic to heal this misguided son of yours. He has, indeed, learned not to interfere in your affairs. Come, my beloved dragon's heart."

The baby rolled in her belly. Without thinking, she touched the slight mound. Surprise flitted through her for a second at her ability to move. Sore and tight muscles ached, but she was able to shift her legs.

White breath flowed out of the dragon's maw onto the two men standing near her.

Bones cracked, muscles shifted, and the bruising vanished from Paladin's skin. Paladin's chest expanded then deflated with a deep breathy intake and exhalation. His eyes fluttered then closed. His feet found a solid hold on the ground. He slumped within Bask's grasp.

There had been very few moments in her life when she'd experienced undiluted joy. They were such rare and precious moments for her—Mandy's first steps, her excited squeals in her inflatable pool. Small memories, but ones which caused a flare of incredible and painful happiness within Seren. For the past two years, she'd wallowed in her own grief and fear of loss. She'd been given another chance on this planet with another child and the man who'd come to matter so much to her in such a short amount of time. She had to put the past behind her. Paladin was more important than she'd ever dreamed another person would be after losing both Mandy and her ex-husband.

He'd protected her, fought for her, and almost died in the process. She'd never had anyone care for her in such a way before. Her heart raced with joy. Tears blurred her vision.

Seeing Paladin healed, knowing he would live, sent these blissful echoes vibrating through her soul. Suppressing the need to sob and laugh at the same time, she sat still, blinking back the burning tears rimming her eyes.

"Excellent." The strange man cried. He helped Paladin sit then lay at her side. With a pat on Paladin's shoulder, Bask grinned. "All better?"

The sight of his throat working reassured her all the damaged was healed. Paladin glared at the man leaning over him before shutting his eyes. Bask's grin widened as he glanced in her direction.

"Tonight, woman, they will gather to bestow upon your child the true power he requires. He will take the blood of all the dragons, thus the beginning of the prophecy will be fulfilled." When he finished speaking,

Bask faded into the same twinkling light she had seen on the ship.

She shifted her legs.

Lior mewled.

Seren ignored her. Tense, sore muscles obeyed her mind's request, and her trembling legs slid on the cool stone. She scooted, slow and with care to Paladin's side. She touched him. Cold, a pale blue, his skin still carried a coating of Lior's breath.

She wrapped a leg and arm around him, pulling the full length of her body against his, trying to share some of her warmth. She shut her eyes and rested her head on his shoulder, waiting for their warmth to increase.

Rubbing her cheek against his breast, she swiped a tear away. His hand threaded through her hair, touching her scalp. She smiled, lifting her face to stare at him. "Why didn't you tell me about the wings?"

Voice weak, but still deep and melodious, he asked. "Or my magic?"

"I'm glad you have magic." She swallowed the lump in her throat. She didn't want to remember how she'd felt the moment she believed him lost. She smoothed her palms over his throat, seeking any damage. "Are you healed? Tell me the truth."

"Yes. My father, Remis, his father, and down through the ages, have carried the pure undiluted strand of white dragon blood. This is why I was chosen to sire this child."

She shook her head, but he stopped her by placing a finger against her lips. "Let me finish. I am what we on Avaris call a dragonseed, a mixture of both human and dragon. You have suffered much. All of it is my fault. Because of this, I desire to apologize for not telling you the truth of what and who I am. I just wanted you to…"

Grasping his hand, she tugged it away, shaking her head. "It doesn't matter. Not anymore. You told me once I needed to accept what I didn't understand. Well, I don't understand how you're alive, how you have wings, but you know what? Right now, this very second, I don't care. I just want you to be alive and safe."

The side of his mouth lifted in a half smile. "As I do you." He tilted nearer to her while his arms slid around her. She laid her palms flat on his chest, reassured with his increasing heat. His heart thudded under her cheek. She closed her eyes, savoring the fact that he lived. "I don't want you to die."

"We all must die at some point. Whether we desire to or not, the choice of when is one we have no option to decide." He brushed his palm over the crown of her head. "You mustn't grieve if my time comes and I leave you. Swear you will not."

Squeezing her eyes shut, she fought against the burning behind her eyes. With a shuddering breath, she mumbled,

"I'll try."

"Good. Rest. The night approaches."

A comfortable silence passed between them. She wanted to do what he asked, but worry intruded with questions needing answers.

"What did he mean by giving the baby the dragons' blood? What are they going to do to me?"

"I do not know." His teeth ground together. "I would take this upon my own body if they would let me, but this is something you must bear alone with our child. With hope, the babe will give you a measure of his strength."

With a nod, she ignored the increasing fear coursing through her with the approaching night. "Will it help keep the baby alive?"

His chin rubbed over her brow with his nod.

Satisfied, she closed her eyes, murmuring, "Hold me."

His arms tightened, and his strength sent a thrill through her, knowing they were both safe. At least, for now.

Chapter Fourteen

Black velvet clouds drifted over the Solrai moon with its shadowing twin. Paladin shifted on the hard rock, seeking a more comfortable spot. Dull pain radiated from his hip and shoulder where they pressed into the stone. Seren moaned. He tightened his hold on her, pulling her snug against his chest, wanting more than anything to take her pain.

She buried her face in the curve of his neck, whispering his name. Chills swept through him. He closed his eyes and savored her breath's light touch against his skin.

The sound of large wings flapping in the distance came to him. The six great dragons gathered on the columns of judgment. Soon they would take her from him. Powerless to stop them, he would have to watch them purify her. They would do so for the baby's sake. Seren's suffering would end.

If they didn't destroy her with their power.

He closed his eyes, inhaling her sweet scent. She must have her blood cleansed, otherwise, she would not carry the babe full term, and if she miscarried, her own death would follow.

He should never have touched her, but he couldn't change what had happened in the past. He had to move ahead and try to make this better for her.

Roars erupted in the night sky. He glanced over his

shoulder, seeking the source of the sound. The clouds drifted past, revealing two dragons, coasting on the upper wind currents, and twirling in front of the silver moons. Their noses pointed down, they dropped in a vertical dive in the direction of the white stone pillars.

He rubbed his cheek against Seren's head, her silky hair sliding against his skin. He battled his ever-growing fear that she would die under the dragon's fire.

Bask appeared, gliding over the smooth surface of the slab to stop at their side. He held two robes, one white, and the other deep blue. When he reached them, he dropped the clothes across their legs. "Up with the two of you. Dress and prepare. The time draws near. Blue for the human, Sire."

The silver skull cap on his head glinted in the moonlight. Ignoring the White Dragon Guardian Wizard, Paladin lifted the blue robe and roused Seren. He helped her slip the flowing garment over her head. His own robe took but a moment to pull on.

Unsteadily, Paladin started to rise, but when Bask held out his hand, he stopped. He stared at the hand, slender, delicate in a beautiful way, then shook his head and stood on his own. Paladin desired no help from Bask. In a way, the wizard had betrayed him. Paladin never intended to forget that fact.

A low laugh came from the wizard. He glared at Bask.

One brow rose and the wizard smiled unrepentantly at him. "Fear not, oh mighty king, my days are numbered, so you will not have to worry long over my punishment for stealing your lady."

Bask gone? This thought overrode all else. Paladin's resentment about the wizard's actions vanished. "No, do not say such a thing. It's not true."

"Ah, but true it is. Lior has told me. I am prepared for the event. Too long have I walked this world. I have been promised to look upon this child with my own eyes. This one wish, I so desire to be fulfilled."

The wizard turned, keeping his back to Paladin. He tilted his head back. "Five here, one left to arrive." He looked at Paladin, "When all is ready, I will return."

With those words, he faded into the glimmering lights which flickered around him.

"He talked like he's going to die. How would he know? Does he have the sight?" Seren stumbled to her feet, rubbing the sleep from her eyes.

"Lior has the ability to see into the future." Paladin squinted in the direction of the White Dragon's lair. Empty. He glanced up to the tops of the seven columns. He found Lior perched on one of them. Next to her, the Black Dragon stretched his neck in her direction.

He loves her. Paladin frowned. The black dragon, terror of the west, cared for nothing other than his clan. Yet, the soft grunts, flaring nostrils, even the half rise of his horned frill, revealed the dragon's fondness for Lior.

He studied the white dragon's response. A bubble of laughter rose. The female tilted her nose up, turned away from the male. She obviously wanted nothing to do with Sinimal.

Another dragon landed atop an empty column on the other side of Lior. The deep blue one, Karia, from southern Avaris. Paladin's heart pounded in his chest. He wrapped an arm around Seren's shoulders, holding her to his side. Soon, the ceremony would start.

With the threat of losing her wrapped around his neck, Paladin waited, holding Seren. Her trembling increased. He rubbed his hands over her shoulders and back.

When she spoke, her voice was so low, so soft that he had to lean closer to hear her question. "Will this hurt our baby?"

"No, not him. You though, I would that I could tell you no also, but I..." his words trailed off, leaving an unsettling silence between them.

She wrapped her arms about her waist, looking up at the dragons where they perched on the columns. "They're so huge. After seeing Biatoc, I imagined these would be about the same size."

He shook his head. "The ones gathering here are the great six, mightier than any other. At one time there were seven, but the golden dragon no longer exists. There is another beast prowling the land. He appears to have equal strength as any here. His name is Arcane. His parents are Lior and the black dragon, Sinimal."

He pointed to the two dragons on their stone seats.

"Arcane's powers are increasing every day."

"Will he be here tonight?"

"No, he is not one of the clan leaders. He is a rogue and must be watched. Should he overstep his bounds within the hierarchy of the dragons, these great ones will see to his chastisement, his sire in particular."

"They'll kill him?"

"It will depend on his crime."

The last dragon was accompanied by another. They rode a wind current and landed with resounding roars on the last two pedestals. The red dragon flapped its wings twice before settling them against its sides. The other dragon, though, captured Paladin's attention.

Golden scales shimmered in the light. Straightening,

Paladin stared in amazement. The very beast he had just spoken of now sat above them. Seren shivered. Paladin kissed her brow and gave her a little squeeze.

So the golden one was alive. Was his friend, Ren Murdock aware of this fact? Ren had been declared Guardian Wizard to the Golden Dragon, but had never been ordained by the beast. He had never been able to fulfill his duties. The absence of the beast made this difficult, inspiring the belief that the golden dragon no longer existed.

A low, nervous laugh escaped Seren, pulling his attention to her. "I guess you were wrong. It's still alive. Seeing it doesn't help me. I'm scared to death, but then I thought, if I was back on Earth, this would be nothing more than a dream. Once it reached the scary parts, I'd wake up. Right now, I want to be back home."

In the same twinkling light, Bask appeared. He glided to them. "They are gathered."

He extended his hand to Seren. She looked at it for a second then lifted her gaze to the wizard. "Swear to me that my baby won't be hurt."

Bask grinned and placed his hand over his heart. He said, "Upon my head will fall your ire should this child be harmed in any fashion. No, no, my lady, your babe will soon blossom into the one who is promised to save Avaris. He will gain such strength, none, dragon, beast, nor human, would dare oppose him."

"Will they send me home after they finish?"

"Perhaps, there is a possibility of such happening in the future. What is important now is for them to enable you to carry this child. Do you not want this?"

She didn't hesitate in her answer. "Yes."

"Then let us begin." Bask beckoned for her to take

his hand.

Paladin stared at her, memorizing every curve of her face. His stomach tightened, cramping like never before. He had trouble loosening his arms from around her. Glancing at him, she smiled. It was a sweet, soft flicker of her spirit. "I'll be fine. I didn't die in my bathtub. And I won't now. I want to see my baby, to hold him, and watch him grow up." He nodded.

She slipped from him, taking Bask's hand. Paladin let his arms fall like dead weights to his sides. Bask wrapped his free arm around Seren's waist. His wings materialized on his back, and he rose into the air with Seren pressed against him.

Her short hair fluttered in the increasing wind. The clouds grew thicker. The moons disappeared from view. Particles charged with magic floated in the air. Paladin's heart raced. He had trouble catching his breath.

When Bask reached the place in the pedestals' center, he hovered and started an incantation. The bare hint of the wizard's voice reached Paladin. The words he chanted were blown away with the rising wind.

The dragons leapt at the same time to fly in a circle above the pillars. Faster and faster, they created a vortex, swirling in a magnificent array of white, black, gold, red, blue, green, and purple until the aura surrounding them combined into a rainbow. They joined into one entity, diving toward the center, coming together, their wings angled, one up, one down. Their heads met, cheek to cheek. There they halted, suspended several hundred feet above where Bask held Seren.

The wizard passed a hand over her face then levitated her, releasing his hold. He descended, landing not far from where Paladin stood.

Once Bask's feet touched the slab, the dragons opened their mouths. From deep inside their chests, flames poured out, combining into one column of magical fire aimed at Seren.

"She will not feel any pain. I used a spell to send her into a deep slumber," Bask murmured.

Paladin swallowed. When the column struck Seren, she dropped several feet. He took two quick steps in her direction, building his inner magic to produce his wings.

Quiet and calm, Bask ordered, "Do not interfere."

Clenching his fists, Paladin fought the need to help Seren. He didn't want to lose her, not now. His heart pounded, and he chewed on his bottom lip until a strong metallic taste formed in his mouth. Bile rose to the back of his throat. He gritted his teeth to keep his mouth shut, but the need to shout at the dragons to stop nearly overwhelmed him. Lightning flashed across the darkened sky. Thunder cracked, vibrating the air. Dust along with small stones bounced on the slab at his feet. His dragon's blood boiled with the increased magic swirling in the air.

He tore his focus away from her to where Bask waited. Paladin yelled over the windy gusts. "Swear to me, she will live. Swear upon Lior's head."

Bask, face expressionless, cut his gaze to him. "Swear. There, done, final. Does this make you less frightened, oh mighty king of the White Dragon Clan?"

Paladin gritted his teeth in frustration. The wizard dared to mock him.

With his next words, Bask verified he did indeed mock him. "Words are words, thrown out so carelessly. Here, this very second, the dragons prove their worth. What they decree will be. You and no other on Avaris can stop them."

Taking a step toward him, Paladin raised a fist, prepared to pound the truth out of him.

"Be still, king. You bother me with your faithless self. Wait. Watch. And consider—do you truly believe they would harm the very vessel their king needs for his survival?"

The question stopped him. He looked up at the dragons and Seren. Within the column of fire, a golden aura encompassed her form. She glowed with the dragons' full magical power.

Rain splattered, blurring his vision. He swiped at his eyes, refusing to look away.

After what seemed an eternity, the blast ended. The dragons snapped their mouths shut as one creature. They took flight, roaring amid the wind and rain.

Seren descended, coming to rest on the slab, her eyes closed while her body remained limp. Peaceful and serene, she appeared to be sleeping.

The wizard reached her at the same time Paladin did. He checked the pulse in her neck, smiled then placed his hand over her abdomen. He shut his eyes, his brow lined with his concentration.

Paladin knelt at her shoulder. He brushed a trembling hand over her head, smoothing her hair back. Her skin was coated with the strange yellow dust from the combined fires of the dragons.

When Bask grasped his wrist and tugged, Paladin jumped in surprised. The wizard grinned, "Feel your son now, Sire."

He sensed the power of the baby without needing to touch Seren's rounded belly. Instead, he ignored Bask. He wrapped his arms around her, lifting her, pressing her body against his chest. He swayed lightly with his cheek pressed against the top of her head.

With a grunt, Bask left them. After several moments, Seren stirred, her eyelashes brushing across his neck. His eyes squeezed shut while he battled the tears burning behind his lids. She would live. So would the child. He would hold her close for a while, and he was thankful for the boon.

She moaned.

He tensed.

Raising his head, he tilted to one side so he could look into her eyes. She stared for a moment, recognition absent, then like the lightening flashing through the night skies awareness pooled in her gray depths.

"I'm alive," she murmured.

He smiled and passed the back of one hand over her cheek. "Very much so. How do you feel?"

She frowned, a puzzled expression crossing over her face.

"All right, I suppose. I don't feel different. Except…"

He leaned nearer. "Except what?

Lifting one hand, she studied it, the layer of gold glinted when she turned it one way then another. "Colors, they're brighter for some reason." She tilted her head in the direction along the edge of the slab. "And I swear I just heard a fish in the water."

Paladin grinned. "You're fine. You will soon become accustomed to these things."

"So, your senses are acuter than mine were? This is normal for you?"

He nodded.

A low laugh came from her. "I don't know if I care

for this. It's so different, weird even."

Shifting behind her, he helped her sit up. Footsteps approached from behind. He kept a hand on her back to keep her steady.

Bask had returned. "I sent word to your ship. They wait outside the boundaries of the island. In the morning, you may go. Here, take this, it will help you adjust."

He handed Seren a twisted torque with two stones on the front at the opening, one white and one black. Inside them, a mist swirled and moved as though a torrent wind blew.

Power emanated from the entire piece.

She glanced at Paladin, her eyes wide, uncertainty vivid in them. He took the torque from her and guided the open end over the back of her neck so the stones rested on the points where her collarbones met at the base of her throat.

Bask touched the stones. He looked into Seren's eyes. "Sleep, mother of our new king. Allow the magic of this place to soak into your body until none you meet will doubt the powers which hold you dear."

Eyes drooping, she leaned against Paladin, her body heavy, relaxed. He moved her into a more comfortable position so he might settle in for the night to pass. So caught up in watching each breath Seren took, he never noticed when Bask had left them.

Chapter Fifteen

Water crashed over stone, rousing Seren from the depths of sleep. She came awake in slow degrees until she opened her eyes, inhaling the salty, moist air. Sunlight glimmered over the white rocks. The brilliant glow fell on Paladin's golden head where it was bent over her. She smiled, and touched a stray lock, enjoying the fine texture between her fingers.

She sensed more than saw him open his eyes. When she looked up, she became lost in the blue irises. He bent to her. Her tongue slipped over her bottom lip a second before his covered hers. With tender warmth and sweet attention, he laved her lips with gentle care, almost like she was a precious object he meant to cherish. She reveled in the moment, but soon she wanted more. Much more. She pressed her tongue into his open mouth, exploring his secrets.

She found heat. Passion battled in their tongues' dance. When his slipped past to enter her guarded depths, she sucked, drawing him deeper. He groaned, grasping her hard to him. Uncontrolled need flowed in her veins.

Breaking the kiss off, he tugged her arms free of his neck, forcing a cry from her. "Not here, not now. We will have time once we're aboard the ship. I'll not have any, man nor dragon, privy to what we do any more than need be."

She panted and dropped her forehead on his chest,

trying to gain control over her raging desire. Overhead, huge wings flapped. A moment later, they stilled. Great heaves of breath echoed around them. The dragons had stayed during the night.

Soft grunts and mewls reached her. Fire heated her face. She didn't care that these giant creatures could sense her emotions regarding Paladin. They liked the fact that she wanted him and he wanted her in return. Surprised at these new realizations, she found Lior sitting on one of the columns. Was the oversized dragon smiling at her?

The abrupt halt of their kiss along with the dragons surveying their movements forced some of her need away. Slow, with difficulty, she loosened her grip on his shoulders. Amazed at the intensity of her passion, she couldn't meet his gaze. If he didn't already know the depth of her desire, he would the moment he looked into her eyes.

He pressed a kiss to the top of her head. The simplicity of this one small gesture released the tension in her body and helped her relax.

With his hands on her upper arms, he pulled away and looked into her eyes. "I warn you now, tonight, on board my ship, there will be no barriers between us. You belong to me as I to you."

Her need for him simmered in anticipation. She agreed with a silent nod. His arms slid from her. She glanced around, hoping to find a distraction from the throbbing between her legs.

Through the gaps in the stone pedestals, the glittering blue-green water met the deep azure sky in the distance. White sails fluttering in the distance appeared in the corner of her vision. Facing the gap in the stone, her heart raced at the sight of the ship hovering just beyond the island.

"How are we going to reach them?" She nodded at the ship, keeping her attention on the polished vessel.

"I'll fly, unless you are frightened."

Astonished he would make such a comment, she shook her head. "I already know you can fly. I don't think you can amaze me much more."

He grinned at her, cocking a brow. In that grin, she found the quiet promise of many more stunning abilities he possessed.

Several of the dragons roared, their mouths pointed toward the sky. Seren started, her gaze darting from one to the next, wondering why they did so.

"They too desire to rejoice in the morning."

"Can we leave? I hate to admit it, but they make me nervous. I keep remembering a movie I watched years ago about a dinosaur eating a man in a bathroom. I'd hate something similar to happen to us."

A look of complete bemusement crossed his features. She shot him a quick smile, no intention of explaining, and scrambled to her feet. "Come on, let's go."

"You go without a farewell."

Paladin, on his feet, stiffened at Bask's comment. Seren bent a little to look around Paladin at the wizard's magical glide over the stone slab to reach them. The man awed her with his strange behavior and capabilities. "You said we could go."

The smug half-smile on Bask's narrow face irritated Seren. "And you may. Good day to you, my Lady. Also, to you, King of the White Dragon Clan."

Without a word, Paladin whipped around. He

grabbed the wizard by the front of his robes. "I am not the king. My brother has taken over the reign of my clan. You will never refer to me in this manner again."

Bask inclined his head, eyes shadowed by his lashes. "As you say…Sire."

"Wizard or no, I will take your head from your shoulders."

Laughter from deep in his chest sprang forth from Bask. It soon turned to guffaws. The thin man struggled to catch his breath. "You are a good man, Paladin. Take my head…your visits are always a pleasurable treat."

Before Paladin could react, the wizard dissolved in a sparkling mist. Paladin muttered a low curse that was filled with suppressed anger. Seren, having never heard him use foul language, stared at him wide eyed. Deciding she needn't add fuel to his anger, she kept her mouth shut, tucking her lips so she wouldn't be tempted to comment.

He faced her, his features smoothed over, his anger seemingly ended. "Ready?"

She nodded, eager to leave the island. A hot bath sounded great. When he wrapped his arms around her and lifted, his wings sprang from his back. They spread wide. Slowly, they moved back and forth. "Are you frightened?"

"No," she said, confidence ringing in her voice. She encircled his neck with her arms. "Not anymore. Not with you."

He walked to the edge of the slab and stepped off. They dropped for a second then lifted to the sky, rising above the pillars. The dragons, their roars filling the air surrounding them, took flight. They twirled above them. The wind whooshed on either side of them.

Seren watched the magnificent beasts for several minutes, and then raised her gaze to Paladin's wings. They were just like the dracs except his were longer and wider. Thick, wrist sized bones connected the folds of scaled flesh and muscle. Smaller bones attached to the joints of the larger ones angled down so each wing was divided into three separate parts.

A thought occurred to her. "Do I have wings now?"

With a half-smile and a shrug, he said. "I cannot say. Would you like me to drop you and see if they appear?"

He loosened his grip while she tightened her arms about his neck. "Don't you dare!"

His chuckle vibrated against her chest. "I would never drop you on purpose, now loosen your hold before you strangle me and we both fall." They drew closer to the ship. The dragons circled once more above them then separated, flying in different directions. "They go to their own lands. For now, their duty is finished."

She looked at the ship. Leo and Calis paced, each crossing next to the other, their gazes searching the cliffs. Leo froze, eyes wide, while Calis, grinning, slapped him on the back. The second Paladin's bare feet touched the deck, the tall black man rushed to meet them.

"Don't ever do this again. We've been worried sick, wondering what happened to the two of you," he ranted. "You could have let us know you were all right."

Paladin set Seren on her feet before turning to the frantic man. "We were tied up."

"We were." Seren agreed with a brisk nod. Memories of the bruises along with the broken bones Paladin had suffered appeared in her mind. She took Paladin's hand and gave it a squeeze, thankful he was whole.

Infuriated, Leo placed his hands on his hips. "Too busy to let us know you were alive? We've been flying around this island for a week now, and then all those dragons started arriving. That magical fireworks display last night could have scared the boogie man."

Seren glanced at Paladin. "A week? That's impossible. It seemed like we were there for a day, maybe two."

"Oh, no, ma'am. Nothing is done slow when those dragons do it. They took you nine days ago. We followed right behind you." Leo passed his hands over his face. "I was scared thinking about what might be happening."

"Leo, my friend, we are tired and filthy. It'd be best to discuss this later." Paladin turned to Calis. "Bring a heated bath to my cabin."

When the man turned to leave, he added. "And food."

"Aye, aye, Cap'an," Calis called over his shoulder. He pointed to a couple of men near him. "Come on with ye, the cap'an's back. He's placed his order. Step to it, me lads."

Seren moved to a small cask and sat. She touched the curve of her belly. A solid mound pooched out. The baby had started to show. "Leo, there's seven days in a week, but you said nine. If we were gone nine days, that's longer than a week."

Leo stepped to her side. He went down on one knee. "Not on Avaris. The time on this planet is longer than on Earth. The days have more hours and the weeks two extra days."

"Wait, I'm lost. Okay, I arrived here four days before we reached Master Largin's, right? We stayed there three and traveled for three more. Now you're say nine have passed since I was taken. So it's been nineteen days since I first arrived," she said. The strangeness of this world continued to baffle her.

"Sure enough. On Earth, it'd be a longer amount of time. There's twenty-four hours in a day, but here there's thirty. The planet revolves on its axis at a slower rate." Leo patted the back of her hands where she clasped them in her lap.

Paladin, the wind ruffling the hem of his robe and tossing his hair away from his face, moved to her other side. "Come, you must bathe, eat, and rest. You will have time to discuss these differences once we reach Durfalin."

She brought her gaze up to meet his. He brushed the back of his fingers over her cheek. She melted under the warmth of his eyes and touch, unable to draw in a deep breath.

Clearing his throat, Leo said. "You two go on below. I bet Calis has the tub ready. Paladin's right, we'll talk later. I'll explain everything to you."

She nodded while Paladin helped her to her feet. He kept his hand at the base of her back all the way to his cabin, adding a layer of comfort. The tempo of her heart almost doubled the closer they came to his room

He opened the door and allowed her to enter first. She glanced around for a second, taking in the neutral, soothing tones of wood on the floor, walls, and furniture before she moved to the window seat. She reclined against the cushions, tucking her feet under her. She faced the glass, taking in the glistening water and cloud-dotted skies.

Seconds merged into minutes. Ears attuned to the sounds behind her, she heard the exact moment when

Calis along with a couple of sailors finished preparing the bath. Wisps of heated moisture floated in the air. Warmed sandalwood, rich and fragrant, rushed through her body with each breath.

The door clicked shut behind the men, leaving Seren and Paladin alone. Skin tingling, she closed her eyes, waiting for him to move closer. He had to come. She didn't believe she had the strength to turn and rise to meet him. Anticipation of what would happen between them grew in her with every heartbeat.

His footsteps approached the windows. When he stopped next to her, a minute of silent peacefulness passed between them. He touched her shoulder. She turned to look at him.

"Come, I'll help you bathe." His gentle offer brought a smile to her lips.

Allowing him to help her stand, she moved to the tub which sat on the opposite side of the room from the bed. Steam rose from the water. The rich aroma of sandalwood increased. She smiled. The scent would always remind her of him.

He reached from behind her and loosened the ties on the robe she wore. He slipped one side over her shoulder. His lips followed, brushing against her skin. Goosebumps erupted over her body. Her muscles liquefied. Eyes drifting shut, she rested the back of her head on his shoulder. She drew in slow, careful breaths. Heart racing, body throbbing with a delicious, passionate beat, she anticipated his next move.

At the feel of his lips gliding over her bare skin to the curve where her neck joined with her shoulder, she clenched her hands in the robe's folds to keep from turning and grasping him. She wanted to savor his lovemaking. To taste, feel, and brand the spiraling pleasure he gave into her memory forever.

His palms slid over the bare skin at her waist. He stopped. "You carry a dragon mark also."

Through the haze in her mind, his words registered. She glanced at the spot near her belly button. Tanned, lean fingers feathered along the edge of a raised tattoo. Surprised, she touched the strange mark.

She lifted her gaze to him. "What is this?"

"It is proof you have been blessed by the dragons. I've never seen such like this one nor in this place before." Leaning against her shoulder, he studied the way the image of a slender dragon circled her waist, its head and tail disappearing into her belly button. "The colors appear to meld with each other, changing and rippling with your movements."

Heated breath flowed against the top curve of her breast in short gusts, distracting her amazement from the band encircling her waist. His mouth was so close to the spot where she wanted him. She twisted in his arms and arched her back, offering her body to him. The need inside her grew stronger, more controlling with each second.

A deep chuckle answered her change of position. He slid one hand under her butt, and tugged her closer to where his own need pulsed. She whimpered at the answering throbbing between her legs.

"Easy, my sweet, we have all night," he murmured, and then ran the tip of his tongue over her nipple.

A gasp escaped before she could stop it. "I don't know if I can. I've never wanted someone like I do you."

He took the tip into his mouth. A second later, he sucked, drawing a moan from deep inside her. Her head fell back, leaving her neck open and vulnerable. Panting, she marveled over how his simple touch could leave her feeling boneless. He nibbled her breast and soon buried his face in the curve where her shoulder joined her neck. She shuddered, her body moving of its own accord against his.

His hands clasped her waist as he lifted her off the floor and into the tub. "I'll bathe you if you return the favor," he whispered.

All she could do was moan and nod.

He removed his robe before he stepped into the warm water after her, guiding her down to kneel in front of him. Eyes half-closed, she watched him take a cloth and pour shimmering liquid onto it. Paladin rubbed the two ends together until a white sudsy foam appeared. He placed the cloth on her shoulder, massaging the soap onto her skin.

She leaned closer, kissing the edge of his jaw, her lips parted to draw in his flavor. The tension between her legs tightened, throbbing slow and long. The cloth moved over and around her breasts, pulling at the hard tips, sending sharp tingles through her belly.

"You're tormenting me," she ground out.

He chuckled, deep in his chest, before he dipped the cloth between her open legs. At the first contact of material against her, she cried while shockwaves flowed from the swollen flesh between her legs. Hands gripping his shoulders, holding on, she bucked her hips in time with his hand's motion. Striving to maintain control, she relaxed when he slipped the cloth over the rest of her body.

Each touch added to her passion, demanding more. He gave it. Once he finished passing the soap over her and rinsing her off, she glanced at the cloth, panting. She took it from his hand. "Payback time," she said with a lazy smile.

From the very first moment she had seen him, she'd thought he was beautiful. The very first night, she'd made love with him, but it had been almost an animalistic mating, both seeking some type of fulfillment for the emptiness inside them. Now, she savored each touch to his body.

His hard, lean abdomen quivered under her hand as she in turn leaned into him, taking the tip of his breast into her mouth. He released a breath through clenched teeth. She smiled. Applying pressure to his middle, she eased him back so that he sat, his knees spread, allowing her to stay kneeling between them.

She grazed her palm over his tattoo, admiring the lines shifting with his muscles. The grayish-white design rippled under her touch. She slipped her hand up to his collar bone, running her fingertips over the hard bone before continuing down the center of his chest to his belly button. His teeth ground together. She shifted lower to grasp the hard length below.

He groaned, clenching the tub's rim, knuckles whitening.

She straightened, shifting her legs to fit on the outer side of his hips, her body stroking up over his, ending with the pulsating core between her legs opening over his tip. The pressure within increased with her slow descent over him and wrung a moan from her.

Wrapped around him, she was complete. She'd come home without even realizing it. He shifted closer and she murmured his name. She moved on him, starting a slow, mind-numbing rhythm. He slipped his palms under her hips, guiding her, helping her.

His strength filled her with the one piece of her soul which had been missing for so long. All the new sensations along with the deepening emotions riffling inside amazed her. Lights, dim before, brightened. The air permeated with rich sandalwood; his aroma, the one she would remember as belonging to him.

Throbbing around him, she continued to move, striving to reach the glowing splendor he'd given her the first time they'd made love. Heat built, muscles tightened then exploded in white hot layers between her legs, sending numbing fire throughout her body. His body stiffened then jerked, spewing his life force into hers, branding her.

She lay, pressed against his chest, her cheek against his neck, waiting for her pulse to slow. A low, rumbling chuckle vibrated under her.

Smiling, she pressed a kiss over the beating vein in his neck. "What's so funny?"

"Not funny, just happy. Content." He massaged her scalp with both hands. "You've made me complete."

"Me too." She nuzzled his neck.

He tightened his arms around her and stood. Lifting her, he stepped from the tub, set her on her feet, and then moved back, separating from her. She wanted to cry out at the loss of his closeness, but he was already reaching for a towel. He dried her with the plush white cloth, his hands massaging her body, making the fires re-ignite in her. She moaned, moving closer to him.

When he'd finished, he lifted her again and carried her to the bed. Tucking her in, he dried off. She studied him, admiring the taut skin covering hard muscles. She could never tire of staring at him. He met her look. She patted the mattress at her side.

He slipped under the covers.

"Hold me close," she murmured, moving nearer to him.

He encircled her with his arms, and tucked her against him.

"Forever," he promised, his lips brushing her hair.

She closed her eyes, snuggling alongside him, trying to shove all worry aside, but one sad thought kept appearing in her thoughts.

His forever would end once she returned to Earth.

Chapter Sixteen

Paladin stretched, enjoying the texture of the clean sheets against his skin. The musky scent from their recent lovemaking rose from disturbed covers. In an instant, heated desire pooled between his legs. He throbbed, painfully. Without opening his eyes, he rolled toward Seren and pulled her close.

He positioned her head so when he opened his eyes, her features would be the first sight he'd see. Such a beautiful face with a light line of freckles coating her nose. Her skin carried a slight tan from her time aboard his ship. Her lips tilted up at the edges.

Seren was so different from his dead wife, who'd had pale skin, black hair and eyes. She had been beautiful in a cold, untouchable manner. He'd tried to open his heart and love her, but she made it impossible. Not at all like the warmth coming from Seren.

When Seren spoke, laughter laced her voice. "Do you like what you see?"

"Very much."

She opened her eyes, the pale gray sparkling with joy. "You're not so bad yourself."

He bent and kissed her, basking in the fervor of their passion. The slickness of her tongue over his urged him to rise up and ease on top of her. She opened under him and allowed him to slide inside her. Wet, hot, and slick, her body welcomed him.

She matched him stroke for stroke, urging him on until he could hold back no longer. His blood pounding completion took his breath. He laid there for several moments before he found the strength to move off her. She moaned, her hands pressing him closer.

"I'm too heavy," he mumbled, settling at her side.

"I don't mind," she answered.

He chuckled, "You do not, but I believe our son will have some complaints if I stay."

She smiled against his shoulder. The tender peace which radiated between them made him desire to stay there in bed and never leave, but Avaris beckoned with its bright sol light.

A heavy fist pounding on his door was followed by the announcement that land had been sighted on the horizon. They had arrived in Durfalin. And as his crew demanded his attention, so did the world.

He swallowed, dreading how little time remained for them to spend together before his departure to Velhaven. Would he survive the trip to return to her? He desired a future with Seren more than his life, but Denol, his father by marriage, might want him to suffer. If so, he would be hard pressed to survive. The unknown reeled in front of him.

"A penny for your thoughts," Seren whispered, her hand cupping his jaw, bringing his gaze to hers.

Puzzled at the unfamiliar phrase, he asked, "What?"

"Nevermind, it's just a silly old saying on my planet."

"No. I think it is special, just like you."

She flushed a lovely rosy tint. "I'm not special. I'm just me."

"Stay like you are. I like it."

The blush on her cheeks increased, erasing some of his worry. He grinned. "Come, it is time to see my world with your blessed blood. Let us enjoy what it offers together. We might not have an opportunity to do so again for some time."

She shot him a knee weakening, bright smile. Without waiting for him, she crawled from the bed and pulled on her clothes. The sight of so much bare skin had Paladin's mouth watering. He wanted to reach out and grab her, hold her tight against him while he devoured her lips. The curve of her hips disappeared, hidden by the pants she tugged on. He sighed and stood, finding fresh clothes then started to dress.

Once clothed, they went on deck. There, they found the crew preparing to dock the ship. A wall built from pale, creamy-beige stone towered around the city, completely encircling it. A broad walkway atop the wall spanned the diameter of the city. Soldiers in formal blue and purple uniforms paced in their positions along the walkway. Each man carried a long pike with blue and purple ribbons tied to them.

"Is it dangerous here?" she asked.

"Not anymore. Many years ago, this city lay amid the neutral lands between the white and black dragon clans. They fought many battles on this land." Paladin took her arm to guide her to where Leo stood on the bow. "Look there, the docks."

Durfalin's docks sat a few feet lower than the top of the wall. Wooden wharfs projected from the side of the wall with wide stone ramps leading through archways and into the town. Nothing supported the wharfs from below. Seren's eyes widened in surprise.

Paladin grinned at her reaction. He pointed at the

nearest wharf. "Magic is used to keep them in place. Durfalin has the greatest wizard's academy in all of Avaris. Many prominent families aspire to send their children here to learn. They often practice their abilities to create new and better ways to improve the city. This is one of them."

"Does the magic ever fail?"

"No, the docks remain in place during the day, but are lowered in the evening. If an attack is launched after dark, the invaders cannot use them as a means to enter the city," he explained.

He changed the direction of where he pointed to the ground below each of the three wharfs. "See there, those are the containers which hold the dock structures. The cases magically protect the wood. With them sealed away, an attacker cannot utilize the wood to build their own war devices or set the city on fire."

Seren studied the large rectangular units situated underneath each of the docks along the outer walls. They did sit directly beneath each dock. Double doors lay open, waiting for the wharfs to fit inside so they could be closed. Each case was made from a swirling coppery-like metal.

When she looked back at the spot their ship glided toward, she noticed several men and a few women who roamed amid casks, barrels, and large wooden crates. Inhabitants of Durfalin, merchants, and travelers milled along the wharf. Small tented booths were pitched along the outer edges, closer to the archways leading onto the wide top of the wall. The voices of customers along with vendors rang across the dwindling distance between the ship and city, growing louder the nearer they came.

She glanced at Paladin. He winked at her, his body

relaxed. Without thinking, she wrapped an arm around his waist.

"Do you suppose I can get some decent clothes? I hate to say it because I'm grateful for the ones I have on, but I'm getting a little sick of wearing clothes that don't fit me." Her gaze dropped to the oversized pants held up with a leather strip and one of Paladin's gray shirts.

"You may have anything you desire," he replied. "There are many shops here. You will be able find something which suits you."

She glanced at him and smiled, slow and sexy. Memories of their recent lovemaking rushed to his mind. Just the thought of how she felt under him made him desire her again. His sex hardened, pressing against the front of his pants. Tightened to the point of pain, he debated whether or not they had enough time to return below.

With his body tilted toward her, blocking her face from curious eyes, he warned, his voice gruff from his desire. "Do not look at me like that Seren."

Her eyes widened in what he could only call innocence. "Sorry, I was just thinking of soft silky, see-through underwear back on Earth. I wonder if they have anything similar here."

He hadn't thought it possible for his body to react any stronger, but it did. Deep throbs pulsated through the length, the ache increasing. "Why don't we step below for a moment to discuss this?"

She ran a finger across his chest where his shirt gaped open. "Anticipation, Paladin. Buildup of tension makes what you do so much better."

His knees weakened, and he placed a hand on the rail to keep from falling at her feet. "Does it?"

She lifted a brow at him, daring him to argue with her. Without saying another word, her finger gliding a bit lower before she turned away. She moved, her hips swaying with each step, to join Leo and Calis further along the railing where they watched the approach of Durfalin.

He remained where she'd left him for several moments, hoping that once he went to meet the others, the evidence of his need for her would have lessened. How had she become so important to him in such a short amount of time? He admitted the baby brought forth his need to protect her, but this strange emotion that came to life whenever she was near—he couldn't explain it. She had become a delight. Every moment they spent together strengthened her hold on his heart. Was this love?

He'd believed he had cared for his wife. When he was under better control and had moved to their side, the ship had maneuvered to an empty berth. The off ramps were put into place.

Once the ship was tied off, he laid a hand at the base of Seren's back and escorted her down the ramp and onto the dock. Humans, Felerians, dragonseeds, and many more rushed in the bustle around them. Shouts of greeting to his men, nods of respect to him, and curious glances at Seren flowed over them as they moved past one group to the next until they reached the archway.

Seren stopped and tilted her head back. Her body swayed. "Wow, it didn't look so big from the distance."

"Each one has a name. This one is called Justice. It is considered a blessing from the dragons to enter here. To receive justice for all things is fortunate. The one there is opportunity. Most who arrive desire to enter through that gate, but not all are lucky enough to do so."

While he explained, she looked on either side of her much the same way she had the first day in Gilliesport. But instead of the uncomfortable insecurity, the surprise and shock, all evident on her features back then, she now stared with wonder and pleasure.

She pointed at so many objects, animals and places, comparing them to many similarities on Earth. Halfway to the residence of his merchant friend and wizard, Ren Murdock, she stopped. "Oh, that looks just like a monkey."

The 'monkey' she referred to was a lemur, it's white and black coat shining in the sol light. Round, wide brown eyes studied them from the awning over a street booth. A long tail curled on a corner post.

"It is a flying lemur."

She shot a glance at him, excitement edging her words. "We have those on Earth…only, I don't think they fly."

"These do."

"Cool."

He lifted a brow. "Are you cold?"

She laughed and shook her head. "No, it's just an expression."

Understanding dawned on him. He tugged her past the lemur to continue down the bricked street. "I have a friend who lives deep in the city. He is well placed in power and wealth, a renowned wizard. With these behind him, he is very capable of seeing to your protection until I return from Velhaven. His name is Ren Murdock."

When she remained silent in response, he glanced at her. A slight frown marred her brow. "You are not pleased."

"I don't want you to leave me here."

"It's for your safety."

"I want to go with you." She stopped and faced him. "I'll worry about you. Velhaven doesn't sound like it'll welcome you with open arms."

He shook his head. "No. I do not suppose it will, but it is my duty to return my wife. I cannot ask anyone to do so in my place."

Frustration radiated from her tense body. She nodded. "I know...I just want to go with you."

Facing her, he stared, the noise of the crowded street fading in his awareness as he fell into the depths of her gray eyes. Sweat and spices mingled with aromas of cooked meats and vegetables, but her scent rose to him, overwhelming all else. He shifted nearer, seeing her driving need in the sincere expression on her face and echoed deep in her eyes.

He cupped her chin, his thumbs brushing the rise of her cheeks. "I would that I could, but..."

Her shoulders slumped. "I know. You don't have to say it. I have to stay here because we don't know how they're going to react."

She wrapped her arms around his waist, resting her cheek against his heart. "Doesn't make me feel better."

"I will return to you as swiftly as I can. Believe this in your heart, Seren, I will not be separated from you for long unless some force prevents me from returning." Her head moved and the friction of her skin over his drove his mental need for her deeper than before. "Come, we must go. The sooner I depart, the swifter I will return to you."

She smiled, the movement sweet to him. "So you're going to dump me and haul it, huh, bub?"

He chuckled, fully understanding what her strange

phrases meant, and gave her a tight squeeze before releasing her. He lifted her face to his. "No, I fully intend to leave you something to tide you over until we meet once more."

She rolled her eyes and twirled away. "Promises, promises, you had better keep 'em."

"Always," he murmured, following behind.

****

Seren stood in the doorway opening out onto the terrace. Her room—no, she shook her head, a smile tugging at her lips—their room was adjacent to the terrace overlooking the walled gardens below.

With her body still humming from their latest round of lovemaking, she waited for Paladin to rejoin her. He'd gone below to speak with several of his crew members about their departure in the morning. She didn't want him to leave her but who was she to stop him.

She moaned and rubbed her temples. How the hell had she become so involved with him? She hadn't meant for it to happen this way. Even though she wanted to deny it, she couldn't. Paladin had become a very important part of her life and not just for the sex. Yet, what did she really know about him? Not much, but before he left her, she intended to change that fact.

The bedroom door opened and the object of her thoughts walked in, closing the door behind him. She watched him over her shoulder, trying to decide what she did feel about him. Was it love? He moved toward her, a slight smile on his lips. Her legs grew weak and threatened to give out on her. If it wasn't love then it was awfully close.

"It's chilly tonight," he said once he reached her side. He wrapped an arm around her shoulders and pulled her to his side.

"I suppose. It's pleasant."

She listened to the quiet of his breathing and enjoyed the secure feeling she got from having him so close.

He gave her a little squeeze. "What was your saying? Penny for your thoughts?"

A laugh escaped her. "You don't want to know."

"Yes, I do. You seem troubled by something."

Releasing a sigh, she turned away. The absence of his arm reminded her of how really alone she was in this world.

Without him, she would be lost, unable to assimilate the way she'd need to with the cultures on this planet. She looked back at him.

A gentle breeze stirred the sheer curtains on either side of where he stood framed in the doorway. She didn't believe she would ever tire of looking at him.

"Come join me," she said, holding a hand out. "We need to talk. Tonight, before you leave."

He took her hand and allowed her to lead him to the rumpled bed. As they sat side-by-side, he asked, "What are we talking about?" He touched her face.

She ignored the gentle sweep of his fingertips along her jaw. "Why did your wife do what she did?" The very thought of saying the words he had said the morning after she arrived bothered her. How could a mother kill their child? But his wife had, and Seren wanted to understand why. The reason wasn't Paladin. She was positive about that.

For a second, his entire body went stiff. Even his features hardened into a grim façade. He drew in a deep breath, and when he released it, some of the tension loosened. "Why do you want to know?"

"Do you know the reason why? I believe you do. I have to know; to be sure I have nothing to worry about with this baby."

"Our child is well." He stopped and swallowed once before he continued. Was it this hard for him to speak about? Her heart ached because she knew exactly what it felt like to lose someone close.

"My dead wife never cared for me. She desired my brother. I am sure she destroyed our child as a way to prove to my brother how much she cared for him. Besides, she never wanted the child."

Seren sat in silence. Her own words came back to haunt her. She had told him almost the same thing that morning so long ago. His child was not what she wanted. But fear of losing the child lay behind her reasons, not desire for another man.

"And your brother? What do you believe he thinks about what she did? "

Paladin shrugged. "I do not believe he thinks much on it. He never cared for her. She was simply a means to strike a blow at me. Or so Master Largin thinks."

This piece of news surprised her. "Largin knew what was happening? But how?"

"Wizards have their ways. It is common for them to discuss the coming and goings of royalty. My family is included in the conversations. The rumors are that I murdered my wife." He stared at her. "I give you my word on my honor I had nothing to do with her death."

She waved away his explanation. "I'd sooner believe pigs fly than that you murdered your wife."

His eyebrows rose. "Pigs flying? You have those on Earth also?"

Unable to stop the laughter from spilling out, she

leaned against his chest while she giggled. "Please tell me that's a joke."

"But they do fly near the southern end of Avaris. Do they not on Earth?"

"No, not at all."

Several moments went by without either of them speaking. Seren thought about what he'd told her. It helped her understand why Paladin was so defensive when asked about his dead wife. Her heart ached for what he must have suffered when he heard she'd died.

He put a finger under her chin and raised her face so she could meet his gaze. "Why were you never able to let go of your lost child?"

Crap. She fought hard to remain relaxed, but the familiar defensive tension came over her. She thought about telling him none of this was his business. No, she wouldn't do that to him. He'd opened up to her about his wife. How could she not do the same for him?

"I lived for two years alone after my daughter died. I wanted to be alone to wallow in my own self-pity. Isn't it strange that I can see this now? If someone back then were to tell me to move on, to be thankful for my life, I probably would have despised them and told them to mind their own business. My grief belonged to me. I wanted to suffer because of the guilt I felt in not being able to save her." She trembled and he wrapped his arms about her.

"Her death was not your fault."

She laughed shakily. "Oh, I know that." She touched the spot over her heart. "Here, I know that here. It's my head that wouldn't accept it."

"And now, with our child, do you still believe you were at fault?"

"No, not really. After the conversation with our son, it's like my pain vanished. I wanted it to come back but it was gone. All I found was the happy times with Mandy. I will always miss her, but I have to move forward for our baby."

"And this is a good thing to you?"

She grinned at him. "Yes, a very good thing. Oh, I forgot tell you. I decided on a name for the baby." His right brow went up in question.

"What do you think of Legion?"

"Legion?"

"Yes. He has the power of seven dragons in him. I thought it'd be appropriate."

"If that is your desire, then so be it. I will not argue."

She frowned. "You don't like."

He gave her a quick squeeze, dipped his head and pressed a gentle kiss on her mouth.

"I like it." She said and started to argue her reasoning behind the name, but he cut her off with a longer pass of his lips over hers.

Another giggle escaped her. "Are you trying to distract me?"

"Never," he murmured against her lips as he pressed her onto her back. "I just think there are other things we might be doing rather than discussing Legion's name."

With those words, Seren forgot all about his reaction to the name she'd chosen for their son.

Chapter Seventeen

Two days later, Seren huddled under the soft comforter on the canopied bed, her arms wrapped around her drawn up knees. She stared out the terrace doors overlooking a walled garden. Paladin had been gone for a whole day and she missed him so much all she wanted to do was to give in to her tears.

Memories of the night before he left arose in her mind. He'd made love to her with a fierce possessiveness meant, she was sure, to relieve her fears, but instead, she experienced even more anxiety.

Goodbye, that's what it had felt like—a final ending to their relationship. Had he deserted her here? Had he satisfied his desire with her body and then decided he didn't need her anymore? No, he didn't seem the love 'em and leave 'em type. She had to stop this constant internal battle. Denying her doubts about whether he would or even could return for her wasn't helping. From what she'd understood, his life meant very little to the people of the country he traveled to, and even now, he might be lying dead far away from her. Throbbing set up in her temples. She had to stop the constant worrying about him.

With a deep sigh, she threw the covers back and rose from the bed. The soft gown she wore floated around her legs then fluttered against her ankles. She lifted her arms above her head and stretched, hoping to loosen tense muscles. Even though this place was peaceful, she still yearned for the familiar surroundings of her home. A wave of homesickness came over her. She had to return home. Paladin would come back for her—he had to. He'd sworn to her he'd find a way to send her home.

Even with her emotions in such turmoil, she still had to function. She dreaded having to dress to go below to meet Leo and Calis, both of whom Paladin had left to protect her. She didn't know Calis very well. Paladin had insisted on leaving several of his sailors to watch the perimeter of the property. He'd said all of them were capable of guarding the house. She didn't even recognize any of these men from the ship. Her gaze wandered over the light blue area rug to where the doors, opened to the sea breezes, let in the brilliant sunlight. Day had arrived. She should have made Bask open a way for her to return home. On Earth, she wouldn't have all these worries. She could return to her normal routine.

A small foot kicked her. She rubbed the spot and smiled, silently thrilled that her baby was moving.

Knowing that moping around all day was no real excuse to stay in bed, she moved to the tall wardrobe at the back of the room. An array of colorful clothing waited for her there. Each one was a reminder of Paladin's generosity to her. They'd gone shopping yesterday before he'd departed, and he had given his approval for all the clothes.

Not in the mood for brightness, she chose the dullest, an olive-green pant set. She couldn't seem to shake the listlessness. The way she felt must be because of the way the baby was growing so fast. She wasn't sure she liked it. With a shake of her head, she dressed and then ran her hands over the smooth front of the tunic.

Thin with a silky feel, the long slit-sided shirt was thicker at the chest, but gaped in the back by one long opening from neck to waist. Panels of seethrough cloth hung in the front and back of the shirt, split from the waist to hem on the sides. They stopped below her knees. The pants hung loose on her body and allowed her to remain cool in Durfalin's dry, hot climate.

Once ready, she wrapped a dull gold sash around her head to hide her short hair. The long ends of the sash dangled down her back to her waist. Leo had cautioned her that the people here might take offense at seeing a woman with her glory removed. Seren had frowned at him, but he explained the women here never cut their hair unless convicted of a crime. She hadn't argued with him afterward.

The other sash, the same color and texture of the first, she twined around her thickening waist.

For a moment, she wondered what Paladin would think of the way she looked dressed in these strange clothes. Would he find her exotic, even beautiful? A rush of need to have him with her almost forced her back to the bed. For the first time in a long time, she wanted her psychic ability to work long enough for her to see if Paladin was all right. But what if he wasn't? She moaned at the possibility that he might, even at this moment, be dead somewhere. Tears burned the back of her eyes.

Once more, her son reminded her of his presence with a harder kick.

She patted the spot on the increasing mound. Her baby grew. Much faster than what she was accustomed to. She liked it, too. His activity amazed her, but also sent thrills of joy through her heart. She no longer feared his death. Since her pregnancy with this child, the gnawing emptiness inside her had filled with the knowledge of a new child growing inside her. Leo's reassurances of the strength of dragonseed children helped alleviate much of her fear so that it dwindled to only an occasional worry. She had a new chance for a child of her own, one sure to survive and outlive her.

A knock on her bedroom door brought her attention to the white portal.

Leo spoke quietly through the closed barrier. "Ms. Seren, breakfast is ready. Come on and eat."

"I'm almost finished dressing. I'll be down in a bit."

God, he didn't understand what she felt like. She wanted to see Paladin, touch him, and make love to him. A wave of worried fatigue came over her. She sat on the edge of the mattress, wanting so much to crawl beneath the covers and not come out again until Paladin returned for her.

She squeezed her eyes shut. More tears stung behind her lids. She didn't want to need him this much. It'd leave her open to heartache which was the one thing she'd had too much of in the past; first with Mandy's death, and then with her ex-husband filing for divorce. If she was truly honest, the latter had been mostly her fault. She'd grown cold and empty, unable to come to terms with her grief. Dealing with a husband who didn't seem severely affected by the death had made her pull further away from him. Strange that now she was expecting another child, those past memories returned with such clarity. She hadn't expected to realize them and in the end accept them as truth.

When she opened her eyes, a ray of strength grew inside her. He wouldn't want her to react like this. Seren searched her mind for something to keep herself busy while she waited for Paladin's return. What were the other psychics here on Avaris like? Did they see into the future? If so, maybe she could find one and discover if Paladin was all right.

She forced her body to move off the bed and march across the room. Her hand trembled as she lifted it to turn the door handle. She gritted her teeth, jerked the handle down to tug the wooden portal open.

Leo stood on the other side, waiting for her. She yelped and took a step back, not expecting to see him still there. She lifted a brow. "Did he tell you to watchdog me like you've been doing?"

Ivory teeth flashed. Leo's deep chuckle echoed in the empty hallway. "Now, why on earth would you think such a thing?"

She shook her head and moved past him. "You're getting on my nerves."

He continued to laugh while he followed behind her. Further along the wide hallway, she came to a broad, curved marble staircase. Below, an atrium spread wide, overflowing with an abundance of flowering plants. The scent of sweet perfume filled the air. Seren closed her eyes, savoring the aroma. "You know what, Leo?"

"What's that?"

She started down the stairs, speaking over her shoulder.

"I want to find something to keep me busy so I won't worry."

The tall black man moved to her side. "What do you have in mind?"

"I'm a psychic on Earth. A lot of people used to come and want me to read their fortunes. Do the people of Avaris have something similar here?"

Leo stopped. When Seren reached the atrium, she turned to look up at him. His Adam's apple bobbed. "Uh, I don't think it'd be a good idea."

Puzzled, she asked. "Why not? I'm a great medium. That's what everyone told me."

He shook his head and hurried to join her, hands stretched toward her. "These folks take their soothsaying seriously, just like they do their magic. You don't want to go messing around with something that has so much power."

She started to argue, but he grasped her hand and gave it a little squeeze. "I'm telling you the truth. Think of something else to do. Anything short of diving head first off a cliff."

"Now you've made me curious. Take me to one—a local medium."

He stared hard at her. "I don't know."

"If you don't take me, I'll find a way of going on my own." She grinned and tapped him on the chest. "Come on, what could it hurt? I can find out firsthand how powerful they are."

Reluctant, Leo nodded. "Let's feed you first, and then we'll head out."

Seren rushed through her meal of fruit and a tall glass of milk. She couldn't seem to get enough of the pale cream liquid. It tasted like regular milk, but was sweeter, a little thicker, sort of like eggnog. She'd asked Leo about it and he'd grinned, saying it had dragon's milk added to it. She'd eyed the first of many glasses she'd consumed with wariness. Now, she drank several during each day, preferring it over the telee.

Once she finished, her excitement over wandering through the city had increased. She was excited about looking at exotic sights and unique people. She needed this distraction, anything to help keep her thoughts away from Paladin.

They departed the house, heading down the bricked walkway which led across a walled front garden. Once through the gates, Leo guided her into the maze of adobe buildings.

The stone houses were built in a staggered fashion from the center of the city to the wall surrounding the entire place. Stairs along with ladders led from the narrow streets to the entrance doors. Terraced gardens overflowed over walls, adding splashes of brilliant greens, reds, yellows, and purples to the smoothly finished, dull beige buildings.

Everywhere she looked, she spied smiling faces, along with new and strange clothing. Here and there, she noticed animals that were similar to those on Earth, but different in one way or another here.

Some of the people she passed stopped and stared at her, some even bowed in reverence. Self-consciousness flashed through her, but she held her head high and continued on her way. She didn't understand why they were doing this unless they sensed a greater level of power about her. Did they know she carried the dragon king inside her?

A little further ahead, Leo touched her arm. She came to a stop. He met her look with a small smile and said, "Wait here. I'll be right back."

He disappeared through the front door of a shop. Seren clasped her hands behind her back and glanced around. Across the way, a fruit vendor with a melodious tenor voice sang out with the news of a unique berry, sure to cure any illness. She snickered at the absurdity of the announcement. Not many people even looked in the vender's direction.

At the sound of Leo footsteps, Seren faced him. He frowned as he spoke. "I found a place. It's not too far either. Come on, this way."

He took her arm and steered her down the walkway. They came upon the entrance to a narrow alleyway which branched off to the right. Leo nodded to it, and they entered. The alley's narrowness forced him to walk behind her.

"Straight ahead, last door on the left. There's an old woman who reads fortunes from the cards."

"The cards?"

He kept his voice so low she had to strain to hear him. "There's only one type of seer cards on Avaris. All fortune tellers use this deck for their business."

After several moments of walking around barrels and stepping over buckets, they came to a bare plank door. Leo reached around Seren to tap on the wood.

No one answered. Seren glanced over her shoulder at Leo. He shrugged and knocked harder. A few seconds later, they heard shuffling from inside just before the door cracked open.

Wiry black hair escaped from a crimson turban. Course strands stuck out around the edges of the woman's pale, wrinkled face. Her watery blue gaze flickered over Seren then Leo. "What do you want?"

Confident, Seren answered, "My fortune told."

"Cannot do."

Seren lifted a brow. She looked at Leo. "Are you sure this is the place?"

He shrugged. "That's what the shop keeper told me. Said her name was Luci."

She faced the woman once more. "Do you tell fortunes? Are you Luci?"

"I do and aye, I am."

Surprised, Seren asked, "Then why won't you tell mine."

"Dragons."

Before Seren could respond, the woman continued. "Now if ye wanna tell mine, I would be honored."

Understanding came over Seren. "You knew I would come here."

"Sure, read it in the cards this morning."

Seren shifted her weight to her rear foot. She studied the woman, trying to decide what to do. She wanted so much to believe this strange woman had the true ability to read fortunes, but she knew how the game worked. Of course, here on this planet nothing was the same as it had been on Earth. Coming to a decision, she nodded. Luci swung the door wider to allow them to enter.

A rush of cinnamon aroma flowed over Seren. She stopped, closed her eyes and inhaled, enjoying the scent. When she opened her eyes, she watched the woman wobble to a lone wooden table in the center of the small room. Two chairs, opposite each other, waited for them. On the table's roughened wood surface, a stack of cards was placed in the center.

Doubts sprang in Seren's mind and rushed through her abdomen. What was she doing here? She had only wanted a distraction from her worries. Leo's words sprang to her mind, and she wasn't sure she wanted to follow through with this.

"Sit, my Lady," the woman motioned to one of the empty chairs. "Come now, this is yer desire."

Seren, who wanted nothing more than to turn and

flee the way they had come, moved to the chair. With a large amount of trepidation, she sat down, wondering if she was right to be here. Did she want to see Paladin hurt or dead? Maybe he was standing on his ship, on his way to meet her here. Leo leaned against the wall inside the doorway. What had she gotten herself in to by insisting on coming here? She glanced at him, not comforted by the worried frown pasted on his face.

Once the woman sat in the other chair, Seren looked at the deck of cards. A simple pink diamond pattern covered the back of the top card. No different than the decks of playing cards Seren had owned on Earth. She touched the cards, half expecting a surge of power to flow into her from the soothsaying tool, but nothing happened.

"Ye know the way. Three cards, past, present, and future. This is what I desire to know." The woman rested her back against the chair. She studied Seren from under half-lowered lids. Eyes focused on the cards, Seren swallowed, battling the growing uneasiness inside her. She lifted the cards and shuffled. When she had finished, she laid three cards face down on the table. She glanced at the woman. A slight smile shifted the wrinkled lips up at the corners.

Refusing to consider why this woman wanted Seren to tell her fortune, Seren flipped the first card over.

Past.

A bright kaleidoscope of colors swirled over the face of the card. Instead of a six of wands or high priestess, no solid figure graced the face. Caught by the hypnotic whirls, Seren stared, concentrating. Pictures formed in her mind.

A much younger, carefree Luci sashayed down

crowded, unknown streets, laughing at the many men who followed her. Mental thoughts touched Seren's mind and she spoke.

"Past, you wanted to live free, unattached. You desired to succeed in your powers of soothsaying, not caring who you hurt along the way."

"Aye, aye, that is correct." The woman leaned closer to the table, excitement brightened her eyes. "Verra good, my Lady."

Seren turned the middle card.

Present.

She waited for the message from the cards. When she received the meaning, she hesitated to speak. She met the old woman's eyes and waited until she nodded for her to continue. "Present. You have regrets. Many regrets. Foremost is the one of leaving your family—your lover and children. You feel they are lost to you forever."

The woman's lips formed a straight line. Her head wobbled up then down. "There is more. One card to go." Hoping this card revealed the woman would reunite with her loved ones, Seren flipped the last one over.

Future.

Caught in the circling colors, she bent closer, trying to see clearer.

Roars erupted in her mind. The sky, blackened by smoke and ash, stretched out above her. Screams, along with terrified pleas, echoed across the city. She hurried, half-running, half-waddling, down the street, seeking refuge, even escape. The beat of mighty wings drawing nearer brought her gaze over her shoulder. Slit pupil eyes, flaring red in the light of the flames eating at the buildings, stared at her. The dragon opened it jaws and released its breath.

Terrified, Seren jerked away, her chair falling back from the table. She managed to twist and catch a solid footing so she landed on one knee. She gasped, sucking in deep breaths, trying to calm her frantic heart. Leo knelt beside her. She looked up at him. He opened his mouth to say something, but she shook her head.

She had witnessed the woman's death.

Death by dragon fire.

The woman's raspy words came to her. "So, ye know my fate."

Leo's gentle hand wrapped around Seren's arm. He helped her stand. "Told you not to come here. This ain't play like it is on Earth."

Pulling away, Seren faced the woman. "Is it definite or just what may happen?"

Wiry hair shook as the woman tilted her head. "May happen? The cards dunna lie. What they foresee will be."

A resigned expression flickered across her face, revealing the unseen hope things could change.

This was enough for Seren to continue. "Has anyone ever defied the cards? Tried to change the outcome. On Earth, it is only what may happen, not what will happen. Humans decide what their fate will be."

The woman's eyes widened. "Earth? You choose...so it is true what I see in my crystal. You are from the cosmos."

"That doesn't matter. Tell me, is your family here, in this city?"

Luci tilted her head. "No. They be far to the south."

Relieved, Seren nodded. "Good. I want you to leave. Today. Go and join them. The vision I saw happened here. Maybe if you leave, your future will be different.

Do you have the funds to travel?"

With a shake of her head, the woman stood. "No. So you see this will not be."

"Oh, yes, it will." Seren looked at Leo. "We'll give her the money to go. Paladin won't mind. I want to see her aboard an outgoing ship before the day is over."

Leo, his face shining with a thin coat of perspiration, nodded. He glanced at the woman. "Gather what you want to bring. We'll take you to the docks."

For the first time since Seren had stepped into this small dwelling, a flare of true hope appeared in the woman's eyes. She glanced around her, and then went to a curtain-covered doorway at the back of the room. Several minutes later, she returned with a small bulging sack.

"This is all I'll take," she murmured, stopping at the table. Her gaze fell on the stack of cards. "I bless ye with these. May truth and wisdom reveal to ye the paths ye must take."

Seren eyed the deck. She didn't want the cards, but the woman was sincere in her gift so she picked up the deck.

A fragile aged hand rested on hers for a brief second. Small, perfect shaped teeth appeared in the woman's smile. "I thank ye, my Lady. Ye give me hope for the first time in ages. One day, I will return to ye this mighty boon."

Lifting a hand, Seren shook her head. "No, don't worry about it. I just want to help you."

Together, the three left the room single file and made their way to the dock. Seren waited with the old woman, each silent while Leo purchased the fare for her journey. When he returned, he handed Luci the papers to board the ship and extra cash to aid her during her trip.

Standing on the wall next to the dock, Seren watched the ship depart. The baby rolled in her stomach. She ran a gentle hand over the mound, hoping to calm him. On board the ship, Luci leaned against the rail, her gaze locked with Seren's. The elderly woman lifted her hand and waved. A smile bloomed on the winkled face and remained until Seren could no longer make out her features.

Once the ship disappeared in the distance, Leo took Seren's arm. He escorted her through the city to the house where they stayed. Exhausted, she went upstairs to her room and eased down onto the cool covers of her bed. Closing her eyes, a clear image of Paladin appeared. Tears sprang to life in her eyes. Exhaustion pulled at her more each day. She rolled over, buried her face in her pillow, and allowed her fears to escape through her sobs.

Chapter Eighteen

Velhaven castle's black spires appeared on the gray horizon. Paladin waited on the bow of his ship, watching for any sign of attack while his vessel drew nearer to the open docks at the base of the foreboding stronghold. Tension touched every muscle in his body, tightening them. Forcing his jaw to unclench, he glanced at his helmsman.

"Order the flags up so they may be aware of the reason for our arrival," he ordered.

The man motioned to the signaler. Flags fluttered in the breeze as the sailor relayed the message to the dock keeper.

The return answer came within moments. Permission to dock granted.

His heart rose to his throat. He tried to swallow past the knot but failed. He hoped to carry out this duty without any problems, but with a grieving king and father to deal with, the possibility of him escaping unscathed narrowed.

Soldiers rushed out onto the dock. They lined up in formation, their banners flapping in the breeze. Honored guards, elite fighters, all would die for their king and clan. Paladin squeezed his eyes shut for a moment, steeled his will for the needed strength to leave his ship and greet his deceased wife's father.

The ship's walkways clanked into place. Paladin

jerked, startled by the jarring motion along with the loud noise. He curled his hands into fists, determined to remain strong no matter what occurred.

Six sailors came from the ship's hole; three on either side of the casket holding the remains of his wife and child. Paladin lifted a hand, halting them. He took his place in front of the sailors and preceded them off the ship.

They came onto the dock without a surge of soldiers attacking them.

A large, broad-chested man, stood across the wide berth under the two-story high archway marking the entrance into Velhaven city. His rich apparel and commanding stance with the haughty tilt of his head spoke of his power.

Denol, King of the Black Dragon Clan.

Proud and defiant, Denol lifted his chin higher. He strode toward Paladin. A sharp flicker of trepidation weakened Paladin's thigh muscles. He stopped and waited for the King to reach him.

The older man, royal to his bones, halted in front of Paladin. Over-bright eyes stared into Paladin's. He reached out, gripped him by the upper arms, and jerked him into a tight embrace.

"You have been a good husband. Pity my daughter never realized this during her lifetime." Denol's quiet words sent relief through Paladin.

He relaxed. He tried to pull back, but Denol tightened his hold, his voice low and urgent. "Be still. Listen to me, this is the only time and place I have which will suffice to tell you what I must. Mind you, there are spies everywhere.

"Your brother plotted with my daughter to kill you.

When she discovered that she carried your child, she committed the unspeakable act of murdering the babe. They knew the true Dragon King would come from you, so they had to destroy you and all of your lineage."

Paladin's heart pounded in his chest. He stared, unseeing, straight ahead. How did the King know these things? Could he trust him? Here on the Black Dragon lands, he didn't have much of a choice except to listen. Hoping Denol had more information, he gambled on the integrity of the older man. "Yet, they failed. Both of them."

"Have they? Even now Rylen bites at my borders. He has brought rogues with him. All of the outlying villages are lost." Denol shook his head. "He is determined to gain control of many realms before the new King is born."

So, he was right. The old man did know more. Paladin tried to keep his voice level, maintaining a bit of calm. "He knows of the babe."

Denol squeezed his shoulders. "Everyone knows. I would much rather serve under the true king than one such as Rylen. He cares nothing for anyone or anyplace. He desires only to conquer and destroy."

"I would speak with him, persuade him to stop…"

Drawing back, Denol stared hard at Paladin, interrupting him. Several moments ticked by before the older man said, "Your words will do no good. He is crazed, my son. There is only one way to stop him. It is for the true king to be born. Then, by the graces of the cosmos, the dragons will be honor bound to obey him."

"It will take time. You cannot expect a small babe to rule over the beasts immediately."

"We have *no* time. Do you not understand? He is

coming even as we speak. My daughter, who loved him with an obsession, will not have been interred for long before he destroys her grave."

Stiffening, Paladin pulled free from the older man's grip. "I will never allow him to do so."

"How can you stop him? Even Sinimal, the great black one, will be hard pressed to halt the attack."

At the mention of the black dragon, the flapping of gigantic wings carried by the wind reached them. Paladin glanced over his shoulder in time to see the dragon Denol spoke of sail close to the spires before he angled at the dock. The giant dragon landed not far from where they stood. When the massive clawed feet hit the stone, the ground shook.

The soldiers scrambled out of the way, some cried out in fear as they tried to avoid the wide taloned feet skidding on the stones. Deep guttural grunts came from the dragon, its scales flickering like ebony crystals in the dusky light. Steam gusted from his nostrils at the same time his words took shape in Paladin's mind.

"Return you from whence you came, Lior's king. Return now. For much will be lost if you tarry too long."

Scant moments before, he had trembled with fear of coming face-to-face with his late wife's father. Naught but a tremble when compared to the images the black dragon's words painted in his mind. He'd never experienced such a reaction to where his legs threatened to give out on him and cold sweat beaded his brow. What had happened? She'd been glowing with happiness at the prospect of the impending birth of their child. A chill swept through him. Had his brother—damn his soul— done something to harm Seren and the baby? By the dragons…

"Return now. I cannot follow, but Lior is aware. She flies with hopes to stop him."

Paladin panted as he strode to the walkway leading aboard his ship. His heart threatened to beat out of his chest. All he could think of was to depart. What if Lior didn't arrive in time? What if something befell Seren and their unborn child? He tried to stop the onslaught of his worries but they grew stronger with each heartbeat. Denol, shouted orders to bring dragonstones and food stores for the journey then hurried after Paladin. "Restock first. You cannot leave here with depleted resources. What good will you do the offworlder or the babe if you must stop along the way?"

He nodded, never missing a step up the boarding ramp.

"Have them fill the bins then we must depart."

He stopped, pivoted on his heel to face his father-by-marriage. "I would stay to see to them properly placed in their resting carne, but I cannot."

"Even though she was my daughter, I do not blame you. She made wrong decisions. She paid for them with her life. Do not let this worry eat at you. I will see that their final place befits both of their stations in life."

Satisfied Denol would not treat his daughter like a traitor and an adulteress, Paladin nodded. The older man clasped his arm in farewell and departed. Denol strode across the dock and through the gate. Paladin hoped his clan fared well against Rylen's impending attacks.

The loading of supplies frayed his patience. He paced the deck until the preparations were complete. Once done, the ship took flight. He stood at the rail offering supplications to the dragons for Seren's safety.

****

Screams and shouted orders echoed through the balcony window, waking Seren. She tossed the light sheet off, jumped from the bed, and hurried to the terrace doors. She shoved them open in time to witness a huge dragon, a shade lighter than the night sky, blast one of the archway entrances to fine thick dust.

Memories of the tarot cards she had read for Luci lanced through her mind. Her future vision had come true. But Luci had departed and Seren remained. Whirling back into her room, she ran to the wardrobe and grabbed some clothes. She wasted no time in dressing. The dragon's cries mixed with ear piercing explosions came nearer. The room vibrated with aftershocks.

Leo banged on her door. "Seren! Wake up! We have to leave now."

She jerked the door open and tumbled out, tripping over her feet. Leo caught her arm, hauling her up. "The dragon's taking out the entire city. He's a rogue."

"Where's Calis?"

"He's gone to help the soldiers distract the beast. Hopefully, it'll give us all time to escape."

Horrified, Seren pulled back. "He'll be killed. Doesn't he know that?"

Leo turned and stared into her eyes. "True courage is when someone is willing to give their life to protect another. Learned that a long time ago in Nam. Calis is willing to die to make sure you're safe. Are you going to allow him to give his life in vain?"

Confused and terrified, Seren shook her head. "I don't want him to die."

"He wants us to leave. Now!"

Tightening his hold on her arm, Leo tugged her after him. He wouldn't allow her to stay. Because of Calis and what he tried to do, she had to go. They raced down the stairs and across the foyer. Leo led her to one of the front sitting rooms, through the terrace doors, and into the garden. A small opening in the shrubs revealed a gate in the stone wall surrounding the house.

Once past the gate, Leo ran, Seren followed, stumbling now and then, down the street. The city's residents surged in streets, many screaming. Their horrified cries tore at Seren's heart. Terror drove the inhabitants of the city in frantic motions and different directions. Fires flared with each explosion. The thundering booms became deafening within the walled city. Seren, having never witness such violence, glanced around, her own panic pounded against her chest. Nausea roiled in her stomach. She searched for a way to escape, survival prominent in her mind.

All these gentle people looked at death and reacted in the same way those on Earth would have. Some took charge and were shouting orders, mothers and fathers held tight to their children, soldiers cut through the crowds, heading for the hot spots in the city. All wanting one thing—to live.

Several minutes later, Leo had dragged her down a number of streets, all the while heading deeper into the heart of the city. She didn't understand his reasoning. Why go deeper into the city? The stately towers of the wizard's academy came into view. Many of the masters stood atop them, casting magical attack spells at the dragon. The entire building glowed a bluish white. So, Leo meant to take them there.

Dragon fire bounced off the spelled walls. Hope stirred in Seren's heart.

Several people bumped into her. Leo's grip slipped.

A wave of human flesh shoved them apart. Leo shouted her name, but the sound grew less and less until she couldn't detect his voice any longer. Body shaking with fear, she slipped to the right side, out of the sweeping multitude of sweating, fear-laden flesh, and leaned against a garden wall.

Heart pounding, she looked around, trying to find Leo or some way to escape without being trampled by the massive flow of people. One hand caressed the mound of her baby. Just a few feet away, she noticed a gate entrance into a private garden. She sidled along the wall and eased through the wrought-iron gate. The sudden stillness in the place helped sooth her rattled nerves.

Trembling, drawing in calming, deep breaths, she moved further among the shrubs and trees, looking for a place to sit so she could rest a moment before she tried to tackle the terrified mobs in the streets. She rested her palm over the bulge of her belly. The baby banged against her inner wall, inspiring a smile. The reassurance he was all right helped calm her.

When she'd gone some distance into the garden, she came to a clearing. The fires from the dragon lit the night skies. The beast's cries had stopped a short while ago. She tilted her head, trying to hear the beat of its wings. The screams and shouts of the city's inhabitants tore at her heart.

Maybe the attacker had left…

Flapping wings rang out from her right.

She cringed.

Well, maybe it hadn't.

She rubbed her hands together, trying to warm the icy coldness in her fingers. With one blink of her eyes, the dragon landed in front of her. Air pushed out from the beast's wings and rushed over her face. The ground shook under its weight. She shrieked, but clamped a hand over her mouth while she stumbled back into the cover of the dark foliage along the edge of the clearing. Unable to move, she held her breath, standing still, hoping it wouldn't notice her in the dim light.

Iridescent light reflected off the dark scales covering its body. Wide nostrils flared and the beast lowered its head in the direction she hid, staring into dark shadows. The slit-pupil eyes never blinked. It came no closer. She blinked as realization came to her that no matter how much power this dragon possessed, he lacked one major factor. If he had been serious about destroying her, he would have already done it.

She straightened, the fear for her child decreasing. She spoke, hoping what she believed was true. If so then she'd found a bargaining weapon against him. "You can't harm me."

A low rumble came from the long neck. *"That may be so, but I can hurt the ones you care for. Do you desire that?"*

Her heart thudded then sped to a frantic pace. "What do you want from me?"

"Human, get on my back. The lesser king demands you come to him. He wishes to see this One Dragon King you carry."

Renewed fear for her child crawled over her back. Seren lifted her chin, determined not to allow her terror to show. "And if I refuse, you will continue killing the people here. Destroying their peaceful city."

"I care not what happens to these weak creatures."

A slight flicker appeared in the dragon's eyes. Did

he lie? "But your master is human. Don't you care about him?"

The dragon shifted its head back several inches, blinked and mewled. *"It pleases me to follow his dictates for now."*

"And when you are finished with him, he'll be destroyed too?"

The giant beast whipped its neck so it looked down the line of its nose at her, haughty, untouchable for someone low on the food chain like her. Its roar thundered in the enclosed gardens. *"I am Arcane. One day, I will reign over all rogue dragons. No human, wizard, or dragon will dictate over me. Even now, this lesser king deludes himself into thinking he controls my actions."*

Seren blinked, her mind rushing with the realization that this beast was the one Paladin had told her about. He'd called him a rogue beast. She called upon what little bravery she found inside and asked. "Then why? Why are you doing this?"

"I gain great power each time I use my magic on lesser dragons. Once vanquished, their magic belongs to me. After a time, none will defeat me. Avaris will then know the dragons' true strength. Not as protectors, but as the true rulers over the planet. The strongest will lead."

"It won't happen. Paladin will stop you from hurting anyone else. You are a wicked beast. Only pain and suffering will come to you."

"Silence." The roar rebounded off the walls of the garden. Seren jerked, a flash of renewed fear rushing in her veins.

When Arcane grunted again, his tone came out low

and calm. *"Do you not know what I have suffered from the hands of both humans and dragons? I was not to be. I was hunted, captured, tortured, and intentionally wounded so I would die. But I did not. I fought to live."*

Seren frowned. "Who did this to you?"

"The ones who feared what I and my fellow hatchlings would become."

She waited for him to go on, but he just stared at her. Empathy for him made her look at him with a little more understanding. Still, his actions were wrong. His pain didn't justify the death and destruction. He wanted revenge. He was selfish.

"So, you're proving them right by the way you're acting. Is that satisfaction enough for you?"

The long neck curved in a loop. Eyes narrowed, his nostrils widened. *"Enough of your logic. Climb on my neck."*

"If I do, will you swear not to harm this city?"

Low rumbling laughter came from his throat. He tilted his head. The long line of his lips curled up. *"But of course. It is such a simple matter to swear."*

She had no choice. If leaving with him guaranteed the good people in this city would live, she would go. Seren stepped nearer. A clawed front hand reached out and grasped her around her waist. He lifted her to the top of his neck. She straddled the width and laid her hands flat.

"I won't fall off, will I?"

"Will it matter if you do?"

Bravado came out in her words. "No, I guess it won't matter. After all, I can fly now."

Another deep chuckle escaped the beast. *"Of course, you can."*

His wings spread. They moved great gusts of air around the garden. Trees limbs swayed outward. Grass bent over and leaves lifted off the ground, carried by the unnatural wind currents.

When the beast took off, Seren caught the sound of her name shouted. She glanced in the direction of the gate she'd entered to see Leo and Calis rushing from the protective tree line. Calis came to a stop. He dropped to one knee, a large bow stretched in his hands, ready to fire an arrow with what appeared to be a harpoon tip.

Seren screamed, hoping he'd hear above the beat of wings. He had to stop. The weapon was useless against this dragon. "Don't do it. I'm leaving of my own free will."

Leo leapt at Calis, hands stretched out to grab him. "No! You'll hurt Seren."

With one blink of her eyes, the arrow shot free at the same time Arcane swung his tail. The long tail swept over the ground, taking bushes, flowers, and a couple of trees out before crashing into the two men, sending them flying several feet off the ground to land on the edge of the open area. The arrow grazed against the dragon's cheek, slicing a furrow below his eye.

Under her hands, tension increased in Arcane's neck. He drew in a deep breath, prepared to release his dragon fire. She lay flat against his neck and shouted to him. "You swore. Don't break your promise. If you do, I'll jump off. I'll allow my son's power to protect me and this city."

She didn't truly believe what she said. But he had to accept it. Nothing else mattered. If he left with her, chances for survival of all the inhabitants in the city, Leo and Calis included, increased.

The dragon straightened into a rigid, upright position. He stayed silent, unmoving for several moments. Seren waited as her gaze searched the garden below. She found the two men, their bodies crumpled and unmoving, a good distance from where the tail had struck them.

"Very well, human." Arcane muttered. His wings moved faster. His body leveled out, and he lifted away into the night sky. Seren, a single tear rolling down her cheek, kept her focus on Leo and Calis until she could no longer see them. She decided then that this beast, along with the king, he spoke of would pay.

Chapter Nineteen

Exhausted from trying to stay balanced on the broad neck of the rogue dragon, Seren struggled to keep her eyes open. The further from Durfalin the dragon flew, the more hope of escaping and finding Paladin dwindled. Paladin would never allow harm to come to her or their son. She yearned to see him, hear his voice, and touch his warm skin. Fighting panic born from fearful exhaustion, she focused on the gentle movements in her stomach.

The air currents grew colder. The sea below turned into frozen peaks of rocks and wide stretches of tundra. In the distance, a towering white castle stretched sleek and majestic to the sky. Outlined by the dark night, the dim light revealed the seclusion of the place. Protected by the surrounding cliffs covered in fir trees, the only entrance was a road which twisted and turned up steep inclines until it ended at the gates. At least ten turrets rose from the stone walls of the octagon double curtain walls.

Arcane swooped down. He glided to a wide veranda on one of the upper towers. Blue flame torches, set in holders, bracketed the wide archway into the tower. The flames fluttered in the cold breeze. Clutching the balcony's edge with his clawed back feet, Arcane lowered his head so Seren could slide off.

All those hours on Arcane's neck had left her legs numb. They refused to hold her up when her feet hit the stone and she fell back. She landed on her rear unable to move her legs right away. The chilly stone of the balcony went through her clothes and seeped into her skin. She shivered. Tingling set up in her muscles and she gasped.

Soft, deep laughter came from the opening to the tower. "Well done, my friend. Soon my brother will follow, and I will have my ultimate revenge. His head."

The words ended with a low chuckle. Seren stared at the darkened opening. A slender young man, dressed in a flowing white robe over his pants and shirt, stepped into the bluish light. Seren gasped. Prettier, thinner, and his hair a whiter hue than Paladin's, this man couldn't be anyone but his brother. Their features resembled each other too much to be a coincidence.

He reached her side. Seren stared wide-eyed and openmouthed at him.

"Come, my dear, surely my brother spoke of me to you." He held out a hand. She glanced at the slender fingers. She shook her head.

"No? Pity. He should have."

"Don't touch me." She slid her numbed legs under her and stood. Trembling with fatigue, she glanced at him. He met her stare. She sucked in a breath at the strange aura darkening his eyes. A purplish black rimmed the outer edge of the whites with a dusky veil coating them.

The baby moved. His eyes shifted to her waistline.

"So my nephew is aware of me, is he?"

"Not really. He's just waking up."

A slow, half-smile formed on his lips. "I am Rylen, Paladin's brother, King of the White Dragon clan. And you are?"

"Don't placate me. You know who I am."

The smile broadened. He was a pretty man, but she saw nothing but emptiness in his eyes. She found no trace of compassion in them. Seren, for the first time since arriving, feared for her child. "What do want with me?"

He raised his right hand and flicked a lock of her hair. "Why your life, of course."

Seren stepped back. "That's not funny."

"You stand in my way. You and the child."

The iciness of his voice and cold look terrified her, but the way he spoke, his actions, infuriated her. How dare he believe he would take the one thing she wanted most in life? "Do we? Well, that's too bad, isn't it?"

He chuckled, not bothered by her pretension. His eyes shifted to where Arcane waited. "She has strength. You did not expect that, did you?"

The huge dragon grunted low, the sound forming words to Seren. *"Matters not. She and the child will die."*

Her anger rose at the audacity of the two. Seren pivoted and glared at the dragon. "Dream on. You, along with you," she pointed from Arcane to Rylen, "will never harm my child. I'll see you both dead first. Now if you don't mind, I'm tired."

Rylen smirked at her. He reached out, his hand open to strike her. Several inches from her cheek, he stopped. The smirk disappeared. He pushed against the air separating them, but couldn't draw any closer. For a moment, Seren didn't understand, and then she saw a barrier, full of golden magical particles encompassing her entire body.

The time had arrived for her to gloat. "Not as easy as you figured, eh?"

He drew back. "For now, I will abide by your desires, but soon, the protection will not be enough to save you. This I say, this I swear," he muttered, an evil expression twisting his face. In the next moment, icy control cleared his features. He held out his arm in the direction of the entrance to the castle.

"If you please, my lady, I will escort you to your quarters."

She inclined her head and followed him. When she stood in the doorway, she glanced over her shoulder at the rogue dragon. His stare cut through her. Hatred and bitterness reflected in his cold eyes.

She sent a silent plea to Paladin. She desperately needed him.

****

The odor of burned wood mingled with the stench of rotting bodies was carried by the wind. The scent reached Paladin long before the city came into view. Need to leap from the ship and fly the remaining distance ate at him, but he waited. The unknown lay ahead of him. Better he and his crew approached with care, prepared for the unexpected.

Seren's face, alight with laughter, flashed in his mind. A searing pain shot through his gut. He gritted his teeth to keep from crying out. He had to maintain control until he discovered what had happened during his absence.

The lookout shouted from the top center mast. Paladin leaned against the ship's rail. He blinked to set his dragon vision to see across the distance to the city.

The deep blue outline of land grew darker along the western horizon. Thin black smoke columns drifted up and across the sky above Durfalin. As the ship drew closer to the city, the sight of the fire marks on the walls and upper levels of the buildings forced a shocked gasp from him. The pale stone was soaked in the soot and smoke, changing the color to a blackish brown. Armed, weary soldiers lined the walls. The docks lay splintered on top of their corresponding cases. Huge chucks and splintered wood were scattered across the raised land surrounding the city.

He ordered the ship to descend not far from the land gate on the western side. Ren's home sat not far from the entrance. From this spot, he'd reach Seren sooner.

Hovering five feet from the rocky soil, the ship came to a stop along the outer wall. Rope ladders rolled from the rails, attached by secured hooks. Paladin grasped the railing and leapt over the side, foregoing using the ladders. He sprinted the distance to the massive gates of the city.

The gate swung open. The guards on duty averted their gazes when he entered. Dread swirled in his heart. He hurried, his heart pounding against his ribs, until he reached the house where he had left Seren and his friends. The outer wall about the gardens remained. Breathless with disbelief, he stood, shoulders slumped, staring at the mound of rubble and scorched wood.

Sickening odor filled his nostrils. A pile of rotting corpses stacked one on top of another at the street corner sent the stench into the air. He couldn't look too close for fear he'd spy Seren or one of the two friends he'd left behind.

His dragon's blood boiled with the need to roar his frustrations, but he fought against it. Just because the building lay destroyed did not mean they were lost to him. He looked both ways down the street.

Several men dressed in tattered robes scurried behind him. He reached out and grabbed one.

"What happened to the people staying in this place?" He motioned toward the shell of the building with his head.

The man whimpered. "I do not know, my lord."

"Then tell me who would know"

"The mayor perhaps. He's assigned scribes to list the survivors and the dead." The man informed him. "They've set up a place near his home, over yonder."

Paladin released him. With renewed hope, he stared in the direction the man suggested he go. He strode down the street, focusing on one step at a time until he found the building. From the smell, it had been set aside to hold the dead.

People waited in lines outside the doors. Every little while, men and women would depart, their shoulders shaking, grief evident with the tears and sorrow etched deep on their faces. Others were allowed in.

Gritting his teeth, he shouldered his way past the waiting people. The guard at the door lifted his dragonstone lance in warning. Paladin ignored him, fixing the soldier with a look which forced the other man to back down.

"I would speak with the mayor."

The soldier swallowed, eyed the swords strapped to Paladin's waist. After a quick nod, he led the way inside and up a flight of marbled stairs to the left of the entrance. They went straight down the hallway to the end. Two more guards stood at attention on either side of a set of double doors. The soldier guiding Paladin whispered to one of the guards. The uniformed man slipped through the door. He returned a moment later. With a nod to Paladin, he opened the door.

Silus Moreia, governing mayor to Durfalin, sat behind a large ornate desk across the room. He held one hand over his brow, staring at several sheets of paper scattered over the desk's surface. His silver hair stood on end, and shadows darkened the skin beneath his eyes. Thin to the point of gauntness, the man appeared sick or injured. Silus lifted his gaze and met Paladin's.

Paladin walked across the room and stopped before him. He leaned across the desk, bracing his hands flat on the surface. "Who did this? Was it the white dragon clan?"

The older man shook his head. "Accounts from the soldiers claim these were rogues, led by an adult dragon. An iridescent one."

Arcane.

Fury at the beast threatened to overcome Paladin. Years before, the same beast attacked his brother. Yet, from what Bask claimed, Rylen controlled Arcane's actions. "What of the ones staying in Murdock's home?"

Shaking his head, Silus frowned. "All surviving the attack from Murdock's home were moved to his desert compound several leagues outside the walls. I'm not sure. They might be there."

"My thanks. My crew will be here to give assistance." He pivoted and departed without waiting for the older man to respond. He returned to his ship, informing his men to help wherever they were needed. He went below, hurrying to pack some supplies in a shoulder bag. Weapons and provisions prepared, he raced to the top of the eastern wall. He stood on the edge and called upon his inner magic. Innate power surged to his shoulders, sending licking flames over his skin. His wings broke free from his shoulders. Their full lengths unfurled. People spying him from below, cried out and ran. He ignored them, stepped off the edge and flew east into the desert.

Paladin had been to Ren Murdock's desert home once. Years had dimmed the memory of its location. Sensing any human life forms helped guide him. After a few hours, he spied a lush oasis springing from the sand dunes. A flat roof two-story house along with several outer buildings comprised the compound. Relieved, he grinned. He'd found it.

Ren Murdock made his living searching and successfully recovering ancient artifacts in the area surrounding his home. Rumors abounded concerning the wizard making forays into the rogue lands east of the desert. Murdock's techniques in acquiring the precious relics and gems were honorable except when he dealt with thieves. There, he was considered a formidable foe.

A shout brought Paladin's attention to the largest most ornate building in the compound. Several people moved from under the covered terrace in front of the two-story adobe structure. Tall and solid, his black skin glistening in the light, Leo rushed across the compound to meet him. Relief flooded Paladin. Leo was alive, and if he was here, Seren and Calis were also. They had to be alive.

Landing not far from the man, Paladin searched the area behind Leo for any other familiar face.

"We expected your return yesterday."

His breath caught in his chest. "I came at once after I became aware of the trouble. Where is she?"

Stopping several feet from him, Leo shook his head.

"That dragon, the one Master Largin told you about. He attacked the city and took Seren."

Heart pounding, his knees threatened to collapse. Darkness edged his vision for several moments. He dragged in deep breaths, trying to calm down. If Arcane captured Seren then she was with his brother. The spot of his chest where his heart beat tightened with sharp pangs. His emotions were torn between the two people he cared the most for in this world. He stood, silent, staring unseeing at Leo.

Leo placed a hand on his shoulder. "I know it's bad, but we can't let this stop us. We have to go after her."

He focused and lifted his gaze to meet Leo's dark eyes. Paladin swallowed and nodded. "You are right, my friend." He looked at the house behind them, searching for Murdock. "Where is the wizard?"

Sand and small stones scattered under Leo's large feet. The off-worlder wouldn't meet his look. "You should have warned him about Seren. He's upset. Very upset. Right now, I'd hate to be you. Knowing Murdock, he's aware that you've arrived. You don't want to keep him waiting."

Another problem he'd have to overcome before he could go to Seren. Paladin gritted his teeth. His frustration continued to build. He didn't need the added distraction of dealing with an irate wizard. Paladin trailed behind Leo, who headed for the largest compound building.

Several desert dwellers, swathed in layers of thin beige cloth, sat or stood under the wide veranda near the entrance. Only their eyes and the tips of their fingers showed in the fading light. Paladin nodded in greeting at them.

He entered the building. Deep mahogany panels lined each side of the hallway. The shaded effect cooled the inside by several degrees. Polished stone slab floors gave Murdock's home a cave-like atmosphere. Elegant carved chairs with high backs and cushioned seats were placed along the walls, waiting for their next occupant. Leo inclined his head down the length of the wide center hallway.

Paladin strode at Leo's side down the hallway. The off-worlder stopped at a set of closed double doors and shot him a glance, followed by a quick white grin.

Not sure if Leo was trying to reassure him or just making light of a deadly situation, Paladin stopped next to him. Leo's next comment verified it was neither. "Whatever you do, don't make him any angrier. He's already in a bad mood. You know his reputation. He has a habit of reacting before he thinks. So, try to stay calm. I managed to survive the dragon's attack. I don't want to die at the hands of an irate wizard."

Paladin agreed with a jerk of his head. Leo opened the door. Feet rooted to the floor for a brief moment, Paladin stared at the swirling design on the area carpet just over the threshold. Determined to find out what Ren knew, he stepped into the room. Tension permeated within the walls, and was made physical by the strong odor of incense. Paladin's back stiffened with unease.

Ren Murdock sat across the room at his desk, his back to them. His broad shoulders stiffened under the fine lawn shirt he wore. Ren glanced over his shoulder at them. Dark hair fell across his strong brow. His black stare carved through flesh and bone. The man seemed to search straight to the pith of Paladin's being.

Precise with his lethal spells, Ren could destroy him

in a heartbeat. Paladin clenched his fists. No one would prevent him from saving Seren. He steeled his courage and asked, his voice harsher than he'd intended. "Where did Arcane take her?"

With Ren's continued look dissecting him, he shifted, refusing to break eye contact. After several tense moments, his frustration at the breaking point, Paladin took a step to the wizard. "Where…"

Ren's quiet order overrode him. "Silence. Sit."

Not wanting to push the wizard to more anger, Paladin complied.

"Why did you not inform me of this woman's identity?"

Meeting Ren's hard gaze, Paladin asked again, "Where is she?"

A dark brow quirked. "So, she means a great measure to you?"

"Yes."

"Because of the child?"

"No."

Surprised flickered in Ren's eyes for a moment before he shifted his attention to the floor, his brow creased in a frown. "Are you ready to fight for her, then? Even to…die for her?"

"I'll destroy any who dares to stop me."

"Including your brother?"

The wizard's question stopped Paladin. Did he desire his brother's blood on his hands? He mulled the many aspects. Coming to an answer, he raised his gaze, locking onto Ren's. "I would that this matter be different, but if he stands in my way, yes, I will destroy him."

Ren grunted. "You have only the white dragon supporting you at present, whereas Rylen has a multitude of rogues in his company. How do you expect to win against such great odds?"

Angry over the wizard's questions, Paladin stood and spoke with quiet assurance. "I have no plan, but that will not stop me. Now, where is Seren so that I might go to her?"

A slow, cocky smile formed on Ren's face. "In the north, with your brother."

Pain of betrayal and jealousy flashed through Paladin.

Just as he suspected, Arcane had brought Seren to Rylen.

The wizard released a low chuckle.

Paladin glared at him. "Fool, you think this is laughable?"

He turned on his heel, intent on departing. Many leagues separated him from Seren. He had to leave now, needed to find her and hold her safe in his arms. Ren's next comment halted his progress to the door.

"And how do you expect to steal her from him?"

"I will find a way. She belongs with me."

"So you say, but until you rescue her, she will remain in mortal danger. Did you know that even while we speak, Rylen has a horde of wizards working on a way to break through the protective barrier the dragons have placed on your woman and unborn child. Time is running short for your loved ones."

Paladin took another step to the door before Ren spoke again. "Five thousand years ago, there was a horrific war between the dragons and humans."

Next to him, Leo muttered under his breath. "Why do you have to be so hard-headed? Listen to him."

Anger heated the blood pumping through his veins.

Paladin shot a wicked glance at the older man, who in turn lifted a brow. Leo shrugged and said, "Won't hurt to have as much useful information as we can to win Seren back."

"What does an ancient war have to with the present?" Paladin asked through gritted teeth.

"You learn from history, my friend. Guess who won the final battle?"

"Humans?"

The wizard pushed the chair away from the desk. He stood, long legs unfolding, and walked across the room. He passed Paladin, grabbed a navy cape lined with crimson from a peg near the door, swung it over his shoulders, and strode to the door. Leo's eyes widened as the wizard passed him and exited the room. Paladin followed, with Leo the last to leave the room.

Once out of the house, the wizard continued until he stood on the edge of the compound in a spot where the oasis and western desert met. The sun's descent cast a soft glow over the sands. The scalding heat from the day lessened. Hot winds tugged at Ren's short dark hair while he stood with his chin angled to the west.

Paladin stopped next to him. This time, he would allow Ren to have his say. No matter that he desired to leave and find Seren, if his friend possessed information beneficial in helping with the task, he would strive to hold his patience in line.

Ren lifted his left arm and pointed. "Do you see all this before us?"

He turned his gaze in the direction Ren referred to. "It's nothing. Only desert."

"Now it is, but five thousand years ago, this land flourished. Abundant in plant life, animals, and humans.

The last battle in the dragon wars was fought here. This is the result of it."

Surprised, Paladin scanned the area. White dunes rose and fell across the landscape. "How do you know this?"

"Research." Ren shrugged. "It's strange what you can find when you're searching for answers to your own questions. Mine had nothing to do with the battle, yet all I found was more and more artifacts pertaining to that last fight."

"Again, I ask you, what does this have to do with Seren?"

"Patience. You really must learn a little of it or you will end up getting killed."

Paladin grunted.

"This battle ended with the creation of the first dragonseed." Ren stopped speaking. He looked straight at him, his brow raised in speculation. "Your line of the dragons."

Curious where Ren was going with this, Paladin waited.

"The great white dragon and the mighty human warrior who defeated her agreed to form a pact where they could live in peace. She breathed her fires on the man, thus turning him into a dragonseed." Ren studied Paladin for a moment, and then nodded. "The warrior returned home and sired a child to carry on his blood line. He had a problem though. The babe and the mother did not live past the first few weeks. He returned, demanding to know why the white beast had tricked him. She, in turn, ordered him to bring ten couples, all of his blood, and she would do the same with them that she had with him. He complied, and so the women were able to carry children with white dragon blood.

"The warrior took another wife from this group. They in turn had children of their own. Years went by and a strange thing happened. The warrior did not age. His wife grew old and died, so did his children." Ren turned and strode off, heading for one of the out-buildings in the compound, his steps light over the shifting sands. His voice carried over his shoulder to reach Paladin. "Come, my friend, I have a gift which should help in your quest."

The two-story rectangular sandstone structure had a single door situated at the front corner. As Ren drew near, he waved his hand at the doorknob and a lock clicked. The wood panel swung open.

He walked through the darkened opening, Paladin close at his heels. What else could he do? He was willing to accept any information that would help him save Seren.

With a snap of his fingers, Ren lit the dragon stones in the metal brackets on the walls. The instant light revealed crates stacked between narrow pathways. Paladin stayed near the wizard, weaving through the storehouse. Soon, they came to a single square room. The room, dusty from the desert environment, brought an end to the path. More boxes stacked on crates lined the walls, but for the most part, the center of the room was bare except for a square table and a few wooden chairs.

Paladin looked around, seeing nothing out of the ordinary. "And? You want to show me something here?"

"I found a safekeeping place in the desert. An outcrop of rock hidden by the sand for many generations. The cavern within the rock formation was one of the many such places humans sought during the dragon wars. I have discovered some others during my search for the golden dragon clan leader, Saxilon. The first white dragonseed lived in the one I speak of now." The wizard pointed to a chest in the far corner. "Go, look there. You'll find what you will need to fight and win against any dragon who dares attack you."

Without another word, Paladin strode to the chest. He flipped the lid up. The hinges fell apart. The top hit the wall, and then slid down, coming to rest on its side. Inside, a tattered cloth hid the contents. Paladin ripped the rag away. Armor glinted in the torchlight. Silver and white, he could still sense the magic coating the metal. He lifted the top piece.

Formed to fit the upper body and arms in a snug yet supple casing, the white metal trimmed with silver flexed under his touch. He looked over his shoulder. "Is this still powerful enough to withstand dragon's breath?"

The wizard shot a smirking look at Leo, who in turn, lifted a brow in question. "This armor was worn by your ancestor. He defeated the most powerful of the dragons while wearing it. Do you, by any chance, know his name?"

With a shake of his head, Paladin turned back to the chest. He found gauntlets, helm, and leg armor along with a pair of lace-up boots. All the pieces appeared like they would fit him. "I do not care to know his name."

"You should."

Ren's quiet comment brought Paladin's attention to him once more. "What do you mean?"

Dark hair glinted in the light as the wizard shrugged. "Five thousand years ago, many great dragons lost to this warrior. During the war, a young white dragon, the new clan leader, witnessed the prowess of the warrior. She fell in love with him. But she was a dragon. Dragons and humans could never have a life together. They despised each other, yet this white dragon loved a human."

"Do you expect me to believe what you say? I have studied extensively, and this is the first I have ever heard any of what you say." Paladin, thoughts of the armor along with rescuing Seren pushing to the front of his mind, wanted to leave.

"This was five thousand years ago, some tales are lost with time. When I found the newly revealed haven, I discovered the journals of the men and women who lived there. These were left behind after peace came to the land. All of what I've told you is written in these books. Even this warrior wrote of his experiences with the dragons."

"But history…"

Ren frowned and shook his head. "History sometimes does not tell the entire truth. The humans want to forget that at one time the dragons almost destroyed them. When the dragons made the pact with the humans and bestowed their blood on certain ones, the human memories retained those, but not of what happened before. Thus, the history taught to you." Before Paladin could respond, Ren continued. "The white dragon's name was Lior."

No. Impossible. Once again Ren captured Paladin's attention. The wizard had to be wrong. Lior, love a human? Never! Paladin stared at Ren. He swallowed, smoothing the sudden dryness in his throat to make way for his question. "My clan's Lior?"

Ren inclined his head. "She made a wish to transform into a woman's shape. Her wish came true, so at certain times of the annual, she would turn into a woman so she might be with the warrior. He, not knowing her true form, came to love her in the same fashion.

"When the warrior discovered the truth, he was appalled, devastated. He had fallen in love with one of his mortal enemies. Not long afterward, the war ended. The dragon's blood was bestowed by Lior upon the warrior. He returned home and married. After many years, he realized something was wrong with him. He stayed young, watching his wives and children, even his grandchildren grow old and die, all the while he remained the same."

Lifting a brow, Paladin, curious now, asked, "This is in the journals?"

"He bestowed the throne on one of his great grandsons. He departed and arrived here. For a short time, he tarried in hopes of discovering what was wrong with him. Thus, more journals. Unable to find any help, he went to Lior, determined to force her to tell him the truth."

"What did he find?"

The wizard grinned, "That Lior was very crafty in the binding of her blood. This warrior would remain as he is until the day she no longer exists"

Amazed, Paladin starred at him, Ren's words echoing inside him. "She's still alive. Did he discover a way to break the spell, or…" He glared at Ren, realizing the wizard had craftily led him on the path he desired. Ren lifted one side of his mouth in a half smile while he waited. "What is his name?"

"Bask."

Legs weakened at the mention of the wizard, Paladin fought to remain steady on his feet. Bask, the guardian wizard who watched and tended to the great white dragon, Lior? The same long-ago warrior, lost with the passage of time? "How can that be? He'd have to be..."

"Over five thousand years old?"

Nodding, Paladin looked at the armor.

"Because of a dragon's love, he exists. They are happy."

Shocked at this information, Paladin stood silent for several moments. Thoughts twirled in his mind while he tried to accept what Ren told him. He glanced at the wizard. "Are you suggesting I go to Bask for help?"

A black brow arched over Ren's left eye. "Not suggesting. It is to your advantage to have the knowledge he possesses to fight and defeat your enemy. Dragons have buried deep in their hearts a need to destroy and conquer, most of this is aimed at humans. Arcane has thrived over the years on this desire.

"Lior had only one egg laying shortly before she fell in love with Bask. Arcane is one of those hatchlings. The others were all tracked down and destroyed."

The information was not new to Paladin. Largin said much the same during their stay in Bae. Paladin nodded. "So Arcane knows of the war between the humans and the dragons."

"He was alive when this was happening. Yes. He's learned from the dragon's mistakes. In turn, you will learn from Bask's mistakes and victories. This will give the one true dragon king time to be born and grow. The dragons bestowed their magic and wisdom upon your child. We now have to give the babe the time he needs to mature so he may take control."

With a grunt of disgust, Paladin gathered up the armor. "Meanwhile, we have to fight the rogues to keep the peace." Ren shifted and stared at Paladin. "We can assume that Arcane has waited, watching during the last five thousand years. He's had time to witness the humans and dragons living in peace, side-by-side. His anger must be immense enough for him to hunger for revenge. Humans no longer feared the power of dragons would be used against them. What better time to attack than at that moment to reveal Arcane's true might?"

"He planned this?"

With a shrug, Ren continued, "Lior has the ability to see the future. I have little doubt that she witnessed the harm this son of hers would cause, so she spoke freely to the other great dragons about what to do. They, too, remember the battles and losses of the war. They do not desire to return to those times. However, the exiled rogue dragons listen only to what Arcane tells them. Many do not remember the battles, but some do and their resentment is strong. Arcane is using this to his advantage. More and more rogues are choosing him as their leader.

"Lior must have seen the birth of your son, the one true dragon king. The guardian wizard to the blue dragon informed me that she told the others what would occur. They joined together to find the right vessel for the king and they succeeded. The off-worlder suited their purposes."

"I don't care to be manipulated in this fashion," Paladin said, heart pounding against his chest. He ran a finger over the smooth lip of the armor's neck.

"Manipulated? No, my friend, assisted is a more appropriate word. The great clan leaders want peace to continue. So do you. Your child will be powerful, but he will also know the true hearts of the dragons, the evil, and the good. His wisdom will benefit all the inhabitants of Avaris."

Ren stepped to Paladin's side and handed him a cloth sack. The soft material slid over Paladin's finger tips. He pulled the drawstring mouth open and put the armor inside. After he finished, he tugged the strings tight.

He lifted his gaze to meet the wizard's. "I want the journals. I don't have the time to return to Bask and learn his secrets. Seren needs me."

"They're in my library. You are welcome to them. After all, they are part of your heritage."

Without hesitating, Paladin turned toward the door. Eager to not only leave the compound, but to begin his journey, he strode out of the room, a driving need to see and hold Seren pressing on his heart.

Once they returned to the house, Paladin stopped in the doorway of the study. "What of Calis?"

Ren's shoulders straightened. He looked over the top of his left shoulder to where Leo stood in the hallway. "Calis is an idiot. This one had sense to know he would be spotted if he followed, but the other one charged after them. He was wounded during the attack. He did not even wait for his wounds to heal, so I know not if he lives or is dead. Ungrateful wretch."

"How did he leave?"

"I suppose on a merchant ship similar to your own. Many stop here and then go on to the White Dragon realm."

Without a word, glad Calis lived, Paladin waited while Ren collected the ancient books. When they were bound in a cloth sack, Paladin looked at Ren. "I thank you for this. With hope, everything you've given me will bring success to what I must do."

The wizard reached into his pocket and removed two palm-sized polished stones. He held one in each hand while he said an incantation, his lips moving in silence. Once he finished, he handed the stones to Paladin, explaining. "Take these and place one in the center of your ship. Keep the other with you at all times. They are cloaking stones. No one will be able to search and find your location once they are in place. When you reach your kingdom, you will need this to hide you."

Without another word, Paladin clasped Ren and Leo's forearms in farewell. He departed the compound, determination to rescue Seren overriding all else in his mind. He'd caused all her suffering on this planet, and he swore he would put an end to it. He'd promised to keep her safe. He always kept his oaths.

Chapter Twenty

The white dragon realm, with its icy snowdrifts amid staggering frozen peaks, drew nearer with each passing second. After giving an order not to be disturbed, Paladin shut his cabin door and became immersed in the journals. The words, written in ancient script, sprang to life from the pages. Many times, he had to rise from his seat and go to the deck above to calm his racing heart.

The hundreds of battles written of on the yellowed sheets left devastation and ruined lives in all areas of Avaris. The cries of those ancient souls rang out from the books. They tore at him. During those days, dragons tormented and devoured every human they came into contact with. Paladin breathed a thankful sigh he had not been born at that time.

When he had completed all the unknown authors' thin books, and only Bask's journals remained, he locked his door. He called upon his courage and opened one of the many journals his ancestor had penned. From the first moment, Bask's anger along with his unquenchable thirst for revenge permeated each page. His entire family had been murdered by the mighty white dragon, Ziane, Lior's father. Bask swore vengeance against the beast.

Throughout each of the books, Bask detailed instructions on the ambush and defeat of many lower-level dragons, but Paladin found nothing explaining how to defeat a dragon leader within the power spectrum of

Arcane. Then in the fifth journal, Paladin discovered what he searched for—the battle between Bask and Lior's father.

Dark smears marred the edges of these papers. He passed a finger over one. Blotches of blood. Bask's blood. The defeat had caused Bask grievous wounds, but had not taken from his overall joy of obtaining his revenge.

The wizard wrote that he had defeated Lior's father at the dimming of the day. The sol sinking on the horizon and before the Solrai moons ascended, he had delivered the killing wound. Earlier, when Paladin had scanned through the other journals, he had noticed that the men and women living during those turbulent times had mentioned the same thing. He had found a pattern. One man repeated many times that the best time to attack an adult was at their magic's weakest moment of the day.

Paladin leaned back in his chair. He concentrated on his own teachings and what he had discovered in these books. Magic was at its weakest with the setting and rising of the sol, and the ascending and declining of the moons. With a slow grin, he scraped his chair back and rose.

Moments later, he stood on the deck of his ship, staring at the Solrai moons. In a few days, the moons would disappear behind the sol's shadow. At this time, only a small sliver of the second moon would be seen. Magic across the planet would grow quiet at the risings and settings. It'd happened in the past.

He grinned, excitement building in his mind. He turned to his helmsman. "Burn more dragon stones. Leave only enough for the return trip to Durfalin. I want to make landfall to the north of Xelerdin before two settings have passed."

He faced northeast and stared. His need to be with Seren, to touch her, to hold her against his heart increased. Paladin squeezed his eyes shut. His spine tingled and blood boiled. Traces of hope waned as each second passed. His gut clenched at the thought of losing Seren. What was happening to her? His thoughts tumbled around in his mind like rocks crashing against a shore, battering its coast hard, leaving him with an aching head like never before. When he opened his eyes, he swore that once he held her in his arms again, he would never release her.

****

Xelerdin's jagged fjords crept into the sea at the base of a fir-laden mountain range. Craggy, staggered peaks cascaded behind, covering the icy land. Sharp, the frigid air sliced through clothing. Darkness swept over the land, broken here and there by the reflection of the moon's slight crescent and starlight.

Cloudy vapors enveloped Paladin's head as the ship glided low over the glassy surface of the water to the secluded dock sitting in a virtually unknown section of the white dragon kingdom. Once the ship neared, the crew lowered the docking plank. The dull thud pulsed through his body. Paladin, a bulging pack strapped to his back, strode down the wide beam to step on the wooden dock. Ice coating the dock crunched and cracked under his weight. The sailors pulled the plank back aboard. The ship departed with instructions to return to Ren Murdock.

Two aged men, dressed alike in matching pale blue robes, the hems pooling around their feet, approached from the cedars growing along the edges of the small clearing surrounding the dock. Only their sleeveless over tunics differed. The man on the right wore red while the other wore navy. Each carried a staff tipped with a pure white stone. Weather-beaten faces remained expressionless while their frigid blue eyes focused on him. Silvered hair, long and pulled back on the crowns of their heads, hung in an intricate weave of braids down their backs.

The Carilon twins, Cie and Rie moved closer. Powerful wizards and longtime friends to his father, their appearance sparked Paladin's curiosity. He assumed they were part of the royal court, serving his brother.

Out of respect, he touched the first two fingers of each hand together and gave them a stiff, low bow in the manner expected from a younger member of their clan.

The first of the two, Cie, inclined his head in acknowledgment. "You have returned."

Paladin straightened. "I come seeking what was stolen from me."

The second man's mouth tightened into a straight line. Rie spoke in the same slow, precise tone as his twin. "Your brother will not be pleased. He has placed a bounty on your head. He wants you returned, preferably dead."

The first moved nearer, holding out a cloak draped over his arm. "Matters not to us what his desires are, he is not our rightful king."

Accepting the cloak, Paladin stared at its outer white material and fur lining. The cloth swished in the frozen quiet of the inlet. Water lapped against the pilings beneath his feet, and the smell of the cold sea mingled with the fresh scent of cedar rose from the cloth. Removing his pack and slipping on the cloak, he looked at the twins. "And soon he will be your king no more. This I swear."

The two men glanced at each other and nodded. They turned to Paladin, their heads lowered. "Your words please us greatly, Sire. Now give us your command so we might fulfill your desire."

"Where is my brother?"

"He resides at Heart's Thorn Castle. There, he keeps what you seek. The mystic dragon awaits also, hoping to devour your soul."

With a slight tilt of his head, Paladin released a low chuckle. "Arcane may hunger for it, but he will find it a bit too tough to chew."

Rie raised his gaze and grinned, the full set of white teeth belied his age. "You have finally found your father's spirit. This is more than we have expected."

Rie's pleased tone echoed in the clear, cold air. For a moment, Paladin studied the two men. Both had lived long in these lower reaches of the kingdom. Preferring seclusion over the intrigue of the royal court, Cie and Rie came from this long-forgotten location within the kingdom. The two men, though old, still possessed vast magical abilities. At the moment, Paladin needed their skills. When the time arrived, and he took Seren back, these two would benefit him more than his ship's crew.

"Do you hunger, Sire?"

He shook his head. Seren's face appeared in his mind. No, he didn't hunger for food, but for Seren's sweet kiss. "I will eat later. I want to speak of your impending tasks."

Both men inclined their heads, and parted to allow Paladin to lead the way. He picked up his pack and walked to the path hidden by the trees. They followed behind. He remembered the way. He and his family had often visited this place during his growing years. The twins' secluded home lay not far away. The icy ground crunched under their boots.

The small wooden building, tucked into the side of a rising cliff, was sheltered at its back by the solid earth. Towering firs guarded the place on the three outer sides.

Mist from each breath they took trailed behind the men. They reached the door. Cie stepped in front of Paladin and shoved it wide.

Warmth rushed out, a shock in the freezing air. Paladin stepped over the threshold, thankful to be out of the chill. No more than a step into the structure, he staggered to a halt. A hearth with stones covering the entire wall opposite the door, held dancing flames. Sitting in an overstuffed chair in front of the fire, a woman tilted her head in his direction. Bask stood behind her, his hand resting on the top edge of the chair.

Without taking his gaze off the couple, Paladin shifted a foot to the right. He stared at the lengths of white hair flowing about the woman's shoulders. Her skin, even with the flames so near, gleamed pearly white, translucent with bluish veins visible beneath. Clothed in a thin, pastel blue gown, she shifted her stare back to the fire. Her hands, graceful and delicate, lay still in her lap.

Unsure of the identity of the woman, Paladin waited. Bask, his usual grin absent, stared at him through narrowed eyes. The silver skull cap reflected the reddish orange flames.

Cloth swished behind him, bringing Paladin's attention around. The twins knelt with their hands held together at their chests in supplication, their heads lowered in respect. His gaze moved back to the woman.

She looked at him. His breath caught in his chest and refused to leave. His knees weakened. Unable to stop, he staggered in her direction, a little to the left. A sudden, uncontrollable loss of strength weakened his muscles.

Bask, his voice low but hard, ordered. "Kneel, you fool."

The woman lifted a hand. Paladin regained the ability to stand. "Leave him be. He's never seen or even imagined me in this form. He cannot be held accountable for his disrespect."

Realization flooded Paladin. He stared from the top of her head to the softly rounded tips of her toes which peeked from under the edge of her gown.

Lior.

The great white dragon.

He forced words past his lips. "This is your human form."

She nodded. Unable to tear his gaze from the pure blueness of her eyes, Paladin stood awed by the powerful aura emanating from the woman.

His mind whirled through this information, but didn't allow fear to control him. He moved on to more important matters. "Why are you here?"

Seren's image appeared in his mind. His belly burned with the pain from her under his brother's control. Was she still alive? Was this why Lior and Bask had come? To tell him she and his unborn child had died? "Seren? Is she…?"

Lior shook her head. "She is well. For now."

Tension seeped from his shoulders with his relieved sigh. Her words eased his mind a little.

A gentle but knowing smile graced Lior's lips. "I came to tell you that when you go to her, the seven will have gathered once more. We will be ready to send your lady to safety. All you need is to make a wish."

"Safety? Where in all of Avaris is this safety?"

"Did I say it was on Avaris? No. She will return from whence she came. There, our king will be born and allowed to grow in strength. After a suitable time, we will bring him home."

He let her words soak into his mind. He would lose Seren if he returned her home. "And Seren? Will she return also?"

Bask laughed softly. "You are smitten with the off-worlder?"

Lifting a hand, Lior brushed the back of her fingers against Bask's arm where it lay on the top of the chair. Her glance met the wizard's. Paladin sensed the depth of their devotion to one another in their eyes. "It is good that he is."

She returned her attention to Paladin. "Avaris's future holds many paths. We can only hope that with the help of you and Seren, the one which is chosen will be the most beneficial."

The word choice sparked some hope in him. "Then we do have a choice in what will happen."

"You have always had a choice. We have only guided you to the right ones," Lior said. She rose from her seat and glided nearer to him. The scent of spring flowers came with her. "I go now, my king, to prepare for the moment you will need us. The man you have misplaced is hiding in the forest outside Heart's Thorn. I will send word for him to meet you at the castle."

Caught by her clear gaze, Paladin nodded, relieved to discover Calis' whereabouts. Seemingly satisfied with what she saw in his eyes, Lior sighed and glanced at

Bask. "Come, my beloved."

For a moment, Bask stared at him. He moved until he reached Lior's side. "Remember, Sire, love will guide your path."

The two then stepped out the door. Paladin continued looking at the opening long after they had disappeared into the darkness. Thoughts rolled around in his head, bumping and shoving against each other. Exhaustion shut the door on some while others brightened to awareness.

Bask loved Lior. For five thousand years. Paladin considered whether what he felt for Seren could survive so long. Her image formed in his mind. A slow smile pulled at his mouth. Yes, he believed so, but first, he had to retrieve her from his brother.

He glanced at Cie and Rie. "Shall we begin our rescue plan?"

Standing on either side the door, the elderly twins grinned at each other.

Two days later, Paladin sat on the back of a white dragoon. Dressed in Bask's ancient armor, he waited at the edge of the secluded tunnel entrance. Rylen had made his entrance into Heart's Thorn simple by hosting a costume ball. His brother expected him to arrive soon.

With his hair tied at the back of his neck, the helm fit over his head, concealing his face. He rotated his neck, trying to relieve the bothersome itch at the base of his skull. Unaccustomed to having a cover over his head, the helm pulled at the strands of hair, aggravating him. He needed no distractions tonight.

In less than two hours, daylight would arrive. The magic on Avaris would decrease. He took a chance the magic of his armor would decline also with the sol rising, but he had to take the risk. Seren's life hung on the brink of oblivion.

Movement on his right pulled his thoughts to the present. Simultaneously, Cie and Rie swung down from their mounts.

Rie spoke first. "Would that you allow us to accompany you?"

Several seconds passed while Paladin considered then shook his head. "You serve me better on the outside to help with the escape. Your magic is strong enough to hold the guards back. This is what I require of you."

They nodded in unison. With a deep breath, Paladin swung off his dragoon's back and entered the tunnel. Damp darkness along with the slow drip of water enveloped him.

He shut his eyes, switching to his dragon vision. When he reopened them, the darkness had dissipated a great measure. Water ran down the stone walls into the middle channel where it drained to the land beyond the opening.

Mist escaped from under his helm with each breath he exhaled. Hurrying, he made his way to the cellars. He soon reached a narrow opening in the wall. He slid through the crack into the room on the other side of the tunnel. Vaulted ceilings disappeared in the pitch blackness above. Tall racks and huge barrels lined the walls of the cellar.

He grabbed a dragonstone torch off an iron bracket on his way across the center space to a slight gape between two of the older wine barrels. Secluded behind the one to his right, a doorway concealed the entrance to the secret passageways running throughout the castle. His father had revealed the entrance to him many years ago. He hoped Rylen didn't know of them. With time racing, his plan depended on no detours. Having to dispose of any guards posted in the passageways would delay him from reaching Seren.

With his hand on the wall, he shook his head. Even if his brother decided to post sentries in the passages, there were many other ways to reach the upper library. There he would enter the castle and make his way to the ball. Instruments playing a fast song mingled with voices above him. The ball had begun. From the information Cie and Rie had given him, most if not all of the nobles within the kingdom were in attendance. If so, it made his task to disappear amid the revelry easier. The twins had even told him that many of the nobles had decided to wear antique white dragon armor. Hopefully, his brother wouldn't notice one extra guest attired in such a fashion.

The musty odor of disuse and age filled the passage. He held up the dragonstone to light the way. The damp walls glistened in the light. Cobwebs and debris cluttered the corridor.

Paladin climbed four flights of stone steps, eased through narrow walkways until he reached the third-floor library. He forced the cover off a peephole and surveyed the room on the other side. Walls of books, two stories high, met his gaze. A fire burned in the central hearth. No one occupied the room. Relieved, he released a pent-up breath. With extra care, he opened the secret door, shoving the sheltering bookshelf out from the wall. He slipped through and replaced the shelf.

Music filtered through the closed double doors. He strode across the room in the opposite direction of the doors. He would enter the ballroom through the balcony. He wanted to study the layout and locate Seren—if

Rylen had allowed her to attend. If not, his next move meant finding her.

The moment he stepped through the balcony doors, the icy cold of the northern regions slipped through the openings on the helm. His eyes watered at the instant change from heat to cold. He waited for the cold to chill the armor. It didn't. The magic induced spells kept the metal warm in the cold.

He grinned behind the face shield. He liked this armor, deciding that no matter what, he would keep it.

Slipping from shadow to shadow along the wide terrace, he reached the ballroom balcony undetected. Satisfied, he stood outside the multi-paned doors, and looked out over the room. Built to hold over five hundred attendees, the room overflowed with disguised guests.

The orchestra played in an alcove overlooking the ballroom. Half of the room comprised space for the guests to rest from dancing and visit at the tables lined with chairs placed there. The dance floor took the other half. Dancers twirled and glided across the area, faces bright in the dragonstone light that radiated from the brackets along the walls. Behind the tables, on a raised platform, Rylen slouched on a golden throne, surveying the entire affair. Next to him, a dark-haired woman, dressed in a sleeveless, gauzy crimson gown, sat, her legs crossed at the knee.

Paladin's breath caught in his throat. Her short hair had grown a bit since the last time he'd seen her. From this distance, her eyes appeared too bright in the light. Had Rylen drugged her to force her compliance to attend the ball?

He gritted his teeth. No matter what, he intended to make his brother pay for his crimes. If not tonight, soon.

Seren was his woman. His brother had no right to take her from him.

With Seren so close to Rylen, Paladin resigned himself to wait until either she retired or his brother left her side. All he needed was a moment to grab her and escape. Just one second.

Seren leaned closer to Rylen. At her movement, streaks of jealousy cut through him. He gritted his teeth and clenched his fists. His brother studied her under half-lowered lids. Seconds clicked by before Rylen inclined his head in response to what she'd said. She lifted the edge of her skirt and rose to her feet with queenly grace. Head held high, she glided down the steps leading from the dais. Relief surged through Paladin at the sight of her eyes rolling once her back turned to Rylen. She hadn't fallen under his brother's spell like his deceased wife had done.

He grinned behind the face shield. His chance to save her had arrived.

She slipped through the congregating groups, moving across the room to one of the tables covered with food dishes and drink. Once there, she picked up a white porcelain cup and raised it to her lips.

He shifted back onto the terrace. Careful to stay in the shadows, he moved to the next doorway leading to the balcony. He would enter here, closer to where she stood.

Making sure he remained hidden by the heavy drapery, he eased the door open. He peered through a gap between the stone wall and the thick cloth. Several groups of costumed guests crowded the area. Assured he would go unnoticed, he came out behind a large group of laughing people. Slipping past the drapes, he stood among them for a moment before stepping to Seren.

Chapter Twenty-One

Seren's gaze searched the room for a way to escape the madness she'd found in this place. She kept her back to the dais, knowing Rylen watched her every move. She would love for him to disappear, but realized the possibility would never occur. He hadn't mistreated her unless she counted the narrowed-eyed stares at the place where her child rested as a form of silent torture.

She took a sip of the cool punch but didn't taste it.

"Excuse me, beautiful lady, but I sincerely beseech you for one small grace."

Believing the owner of the deep voice spoke to someone else, Seren turned, curious. The soft tones reminded her of Paladin and caused pinpricks of need to crawl down her back. A man, head bowed, stood in front of her. His face, hidden behind a visor connected to a helm, added to the mystery of his identity. The man was dressed in tight-fitting white armor which vibrated with a power of its own. He straightened and held out a gloved hand.

"A dance, my lady?" he asked. "So that I might crow to the morning light the wondrous news that I partnered with the one true beauty of the ball."

Seren's heart accelerated. "Pal…" she started, but stopped. She kept her eyes glued to the armored man, making sure she did not look at Rylen. She half-smiled, tremors vibrated in her body. Seren nodded in agreement.

The leather-covered hand took hers. He led her onto the polished dance floor. Lights twinkled around them from the many dragonstones in their sconces along the walls and across the ceiling. Magical motes dotted the air throughout the hall.

He pulled her closer and placed his hand on her waist. The orchestra started a melody much like a waltz. The disguised man led her through the steps similar to that dance, but not exactly the same.

Her face turned from the dial, she whispered, "You came for me."

"I will always be here for you," he murmured.

She kept a fake smile pasted on her mouth, and didn't move her lips as they glided along the edges of the dance floor. "He's nuts. Insane. You have to get me out of here."

"In a moment, after the next round of the floor, I will take you onto the balcony. Be ready." He swirled her twice and leaned a fraction closer. "Did you miss me?"

"Uncontrollably. I was scared to death you were hurt or worse," she mumbled. "I don't want to lose you. I want our child to know his father."

"And so he shall. Another moment and then we're through the doors. Be prepared."

She hoped she kept all emotions off her face. One slip up and Rylen would suspect something was off. Her heart thudded with fear mixed with joy. Paladin came for her. Soon she would gain freedom from his brother's oppressive control. Before she could respond, Paladin swept her through the open balcony doors and out onto the terrace. Releasing her waist, he tugged her through the cold to the wall on the side of doorway. The icy chill cut through the thin material of the dress. Goosebumps erupted on her bare skin.

"Grab my neck. We'll go up and across. Once we reach the turret, we'll reenter the castle and go through the secret passageways." He placed a booted foot on a protruding stone. He waited for her to wrap her arms around his neck, and when she did, his armor heated the front of her body.

"Just hurry. He'll come after us. He watches me like a hawk."

"Since I don't know what a hawk is, I'll assume it's bad, so here we go." He scaled the wall, easily finding hand and footholds. Shouts came from the far balcony door. She glanced over in time to see Rylen step outside. Paladin's brother looked up and down the terrace. The deep shadows along the building gave them a little protection, but that wouldn't last long. They raced against time.

Seconds seemed to slow with each of her breaths. Rylen's gaze found them. Her heart pounded with fear. He pointed and shouted an order, but no soldiers answered the call. Flapping from huge wings rang out in the quiet cold.

Fear turned to near panic. She squirmed against Paladin. "Move it. Faster. He's called that monster, and I don't care to face him again."

Paladin answered with a grunt. He grabbed the edge of the wall. In a surge of strength which surprised Seren, he swung his legs to the side and leapt. Icy air flew up her dress. Chills swept down her body.

She squealed at the cold touch and the sudden emptiness surrounding them. The next moment, Paladin's feet touched solid stone. He landed, knees bent, hands flat on the stone with her still attached to his back. With very little spare movement, he gripped her wrist, twisted in the opposite direction and took off in a sprint in the direction of the tower on their right. She managed to grab enough material of the dress to keep from falling flat on her face while she tried to keep up with him.

The flapping wings grew with the beat of her own heart. Panting, fear for Paladin and her unborn child threatened to overcome her. The door leading into the tower opened. Calis, wrapped in a white, hooded cape appeared.

"Run, Sire. Run, the dragon's almost here."

Halfway there, her heart felt like it rose to her throat. More steps and hope blossomed that maybe they would make it.

Calis' eyes grew round and his mouth dropped open.

Seren glanced over her shoulder. Terror gripped her, forcing out a scream.

Arcane hung poised behind them with his mouth agape for the first onslaught of dragon fire. The very air surrounding him sizzled as if it too waited in anticipation.

Paladin turned to face the beast, twirling Seren so his body shielded her. "Stay behind me."

He slid his silvered blades from their sheaves.

Remembering her vision, Seren grasped his upper arm. "Don't. You can't defeat him."

Without answering her, he jerked away. He held his left arm, the one with the dragon tattoo, like a shield. Calis reached her. He wrapped an arm over her shoulders, positioning his body close to protect her back. Arcane released his breath, and pure purplish power surged over them. The air heated. The stones surrounding them glowed with an unnatural heat. Smoke rose from the icy surface of the wall. The armor Paladin wore deflected the dragon's breath on either side and protected them from the full force of Arcane's first blast.

Footsteps pounding across the ice-coated stone from their rear came loud after the magical fire ended. Armed soldiers poured from the doorway Calis had just vacated, cutting off their escape path.

Seren's gut-twisted. Her spine tingled and her mind raced. What were they going to do? They were trapped. Paladin would die just like in her vision. The babe rolled over and over inside her. She laid a palm over the curve of her stomach. Her skin heated with the intensity of her son's dragon fire. A terrified moan escaped her throat.

Paladin whipped the helm off. He stared at the dragon, his fist high in the air, the sword glinting in the torch light. He shouted above the noise of both the dragon and the soldiers. "I will never allow you to harm Seren or my son. I will keep them safe in my arms for eternity." Her gaze flew to the back of his head.

Rylen's laughter echoed in the cold. He strolled from the doorway at the opposite end of the walkway. He stood directly below the spot where Arcane hovered. Framed between the beating wings, he continued to laugh. The sound sent shivers through Seren's body.

"Admit defeat, Brother. Surrender and I might consider leniency." Cool, collective as always, Rylen lifted a brow in question. Madness sparked in the blue of his eyes. His tone carried a soft, persuasive note, deadly intent spread across the area separating them, saturating the air with hatred.

Seren pressed against Paladin's back and whispered,

"Don't believe him. He won't let you live. Arcane has complete control over him."

He didn't respond. Instead, he brought his arm down in a straight line. A fast buzzing started, approaching from either side of the wall. Two flocks of white dracs, each larger than any she'd seen on Avaris so far, flew over the sides of the walls. Their numbers so great, they appeared blended into one unit, joining their heads, bodies, and tails together. Two men, identical in dress and face flew from the darkened sky above. They halted, suspended in the air. Several feet separated them from Arcane. Simultaneously, they fired a magical blast into the dragon's eyes.

Seren barely had time to witness this, before the dracs, flying from the bailey, grabbed her, Paladin, and Calis by their shoulders. One moment they stood on the wall, the next they dropped over the outer edge, straight for the rocks and trees bordering the castle far below them.

At the sudden drop, a scream ripped from Seren's throat. An electrical sizzling started in the air above them and ended in an explosion. The force of the powerful charge sent shockwaves rippling over the rocks. Treetops waved back and forth with the wind caused by the magical blast.

Arcane roared. Was that pain mixed with fury in the sound? She didn't want to find out.

Frigid air plastered Seren's thin gown to her body. Chills, more from fear than the cold, shook her body to the core. The drac holding her stretched its body over the length of hers and wrapped its clawed hind feet over the sides of her thighs. Lifted, held secure by the beast, she blinked away the tears clouding her vision. Not far from the huge stones at the base of the castle wall, the drac veered. It traveled horizontal with the ground.

She glanced ahead, making out Paladin's form, carried by another drac in a similar way. Unaccustomed to the cyclone type speed, the little bit of juice she'd consumed earlier gurgled to the rear of her throat. She grimaced and shook her head, determined not to be sick in front of him ever again. Dragon fire blasted the trees next to them. Fir limbs toppled on the right. The dracs veered to the left, away from the falling timber.

Many minutes raced by. The deep silence of the forest enveloped them. Arcane's raging screams could no longer be heard. The dracs slowed and came to a stop. They lowered their human cargo to their feet and released their hold.

Seren slumped to a sitting position on the frozen ground, her legs still weak from the lightning fast ride. Her stomach rolled once. She swallowed, closing her eyes, striving to settle it back to normal. The young white dragons moved to the side. They stood up on their back legs. Their blue, slit-pupil eyes watched the sky.

A couple of feet away, Paladin knelt on one knee. He looked at the sky, his head cocked to one side as he listened. Seren waited, hearing tuned to the slightest sign of Arcane's location. He would follow them.

Paladin' gaze captured hers. "Hold hands. We have to stay in contact for this to work. Hold tight."

With a nod, she touched the gloved palm and his fingers curled over hers. For a brief moment, their gazes met and held, more secure than their grip. New warmth, a softer glint appeared in his eyes and her heart responded. She loved him. Dearly, irrevocably.

"Search the sky. Shout out when you spy a shooting

star," he said. His gaze left hers, his head tilted to the deep purple ceiling above the tree tops.

She focused on the sky. A few moments later, the figure of a lone dragon glided across. Just behind it, a shooting star curved toward the planet. She pointed at the spot. The soft pad of footsteps came from behind them. The two identical men who had helped them escape arrived.

Paladin glanced at them. "Take hold. We leave now."

With those words, he closed his eyes. Blinding light burst in the forest. In the center, a dark paneled door formed. Paladin twisted the handle, and fell through the opening, tugging her with him. The others followed close behind. The door slammed shut after them.

Silence and warmth welcomed them in the darkened room. A snap of fingers coming together rang out in the room. The entire area lit with many dragonstones in metal brackets situated on the walls. A dark-haired man, nude with a frown drawing his brows down over his eyes, stood next to a rumpled bed.

Seren stared wide-eyed, shocked at the sight. So much bare skin, gleaming in the bright light, and him, unashamed, made no move to hide his nudity. Tall, slender, his muscles tense, and his fingers still positioned from where he snapped them. The lines bracketing his mouth deepened. He glared at the human jumble on his floor, "Tell me I'm dreaming."

Heat rose to Seren's cheeks. She glanced away. Her gaze landed on Paladin. A grin spread across his face. He shook his head at the stranger.

"No dream, my friend. We've come for a little visit."

"You could have knocked first."

"True, but we were in a hurry. I needed a refuge. You were the first one I thought of." Paladin stood and held a hand to help her up. Warm, his palm and fingers, solid under hers verified she lived. Legs trembling, she managed to stand, smoothing the silky dress down.

Calis along with the two older men, legs and arms tangled, lay sprawled closer to the room's entrance. Seren eyed the door, afraid Arcane was on the other side. Grunts and a couple of moans later, Calis came to his feet. He helped one of other men to stand.

The naked man, unashamed of his lack of clothes, moved to a nearby chair and picked up a pair of navy pants. He pulled them on.

Paladin motioned to the stranger. "Seren, this is Ren Murdock, my old friend whose home you stayed at in Durfalin."

Dark hair shining, lean, chiseled features expressionless, Ren met her eyes. He nodded and pulled a white shirt over his head. "Now, what are you doing here? I can see you rescued her, but why here?"

"Where can I take Seren so she can be safe from Arcane and my brother? A place where she can give birth without worry over the ones trying to hurt her."

"What did Lior say?"

Paladin stiffened at Ren's question. "The seven would open the door for us to escape."

Dark eyes locked on blue ones. Seren sensed the silent battle between the two men. Why, she didn't understand.

Neither one spoke for several moments, and then Paladin asked, "Is there a place we can go?"

With a deep sigh, Ren turned away, shoulders

slumped. "The caverns, I suppose. They were the safe keeping place during the wars."

"Safe keeping?" Seren glanced from one to the other.

"No dragon ever penetrated the magical shield erected over the caverns. Even now it is difficult for dragonseeds to enter if an opening hasn't been prepared." Ren glared at Paladin. "This might endanger your lady."

"But you can open it? For us? There is a way." Paladin stepped to his friend.

Ren nodded curtly. "It is possible. Dangerous, but it can be done."

"Very well, we'll need supplies. I have messages I need to send. Lior and the others will know where we are, but I need to discover their intentions."

"I will inform my staff." Slipping on a pair of scuffed black boots, Ren departed. Calis motioned for the two older men to follow him.

Alone, Seren stared at Paladin. She took a step closer, lifted a hand and brushed a finger over his bottom lip. "You changed my vision. I thought you were going to die on that wall tonight."

"I did not."

A gentle smile tugged at her mouth. "No. I'm glad."

He wrapped his arms around her and pulled her against his chest. He buried his face into the side of her neck, whispering, "I have yearned for you."

She nodded and snuggled against him. "Me, too. I was so worried about you. Rylen wants you dead. He's crazy."

"No, he's controlled by Arcane. The beast must die. Avaris will never be at peace if he lives."

She nodded. The mystic dragon threatened everything. All living creatures Avaris held dear. Still, the determined glint in Paladin's eye worried her. She wasn't sure she wanted him to put his life in danger.

"You can't defeat him alone."

He grinned. "I have no intention of fighting him by myself. I will send messages requesting the aid of some powerful warriors and wizards. They will come." He sounded so sure, but Seren worried about his intentions. A small group of humans would never defeat Arcane and all the rogue dragons following him. She didn't hide her concern quickly enough. Paladin's gaze softened. He pulled her closer, kissing her, a gentle brushing of skin.

"You need not worry so. Concentrate on our child. Keep him safe inside you. This danger will pass. I swear we will live in peace."

She agreed, hoping to push the negative feelings aside, but a sense of dread stayed with her.

Someone knocked on the door.

"Cap'an? That wizard requests your presence below. He opened his scrying stone."

Her hand grasped in his warm palm, Seren followed Paladin to the door and out into the hall. Calis stood waiting. "He wanted to contact Durfalin to prepare for a possible assault. Before he could though, images appeared. He insisted I come for ye."

Uneasy with the summons, they trailed behind Calis. He led them downstairs to a room with bookcases lining the walls. On the far side, Ren stood at a small oval table. A black basin rested in the center of the shining, dark wooden surface. He bent at the waist, his focus centered on the glassy surface of the liquid in the basin.

They moved to stand on either side of him.

He glanced at Paladin, and then shifted his gaze to Seren. "The rogue dragons are on the move. They are flying into the human lands, attacking villages and towns, heading north to Arcane."

Paladin responded with a slow nod. "I expected this would happen. Arcane is determined to destroy what he can before he focuses his attention on us."

The wizard returned his attention to the smooth surface of the liquid in the basin. "Perhaps. Their movements are erratic. I can only assume the White Dragon clan's wizards are helping Rylen discover your lady's location. Once it's learned, the dragons will converge here."

"So, what do we do when that happens? Will this barrier you talked about hold?" Seren looked from the wizard to Paladin and back. Lines of worry creased between their brows while they stared into the basin.

Curious, she glanced down, her hands gripping the edges of the table. The surface remained smooth and flat. The longer she stared, images started to flow within the dark water, shapes of long, slender dragons, flying, entangling with each other. Teeth gnashed and unholy cries echoed in her mind. Her world narrowed to the center of the bowl and the swirling mass within.

Her legs weakened. She started to fall forward, but strong hands wrapped around her upper arms, holding her up. Dazed, she lifted her gaze and met dark eyes. Ren Murdock's midnight blue eyes met hers. They were so dark they appeared black. His dark hair framed a handsome, tanned face that was marred with a concerned frown.

Darkness clouded her sight. A vision flared inside her. Shiny golden scales glinted in a thick mist.

Sorrowful and fearful slit-pupil golden eyes searched. From Seren's left came the strong beat of footsteps moving across a stone floor, splashing through a thin layer of water she couldn't see. She turned to the sound. Ren, a cape flapping about his shoulders and long staff with an amber dragon stone on the tip, appeared.

The vision ended. She once more stared into Ren's eyes. "You search. So does the dragon. You are surrounded by fog. You can't find each other. You must find each other. And soon or all will be lost for you and her."

The wizard released her with a little shove. She stumbled away, but Paladin grasped her, keeping her from falling. The shocked and foreboding scowl on the wizard's face kept her from speaking. She looked up at Paladin. He glared at his friend, but his features softened when he too took in the expression on the wizard's face.

Seren pressed Paladin's hand, catching his attention. She shook her head. He seemed to understand her silent message to leave the other man alone.

"Perhaps, you should rest for a little while. I will prepare the necessary supplies and items needed during your stay in the caverns." Ren motioned at the door.

At first Seren considered arguing, but her body decided otherwise. Fatigue set into her muscles. She tried to stifle a yawn, but failed. She needed the rest. With what she'd seen in the bowl, and the vision afterward, fatigue dictated she retire. The baby grew more every day. This added to her exhaustion, too, wearing on her. She squeezed Paladin's hand again. "Come for me if there's any change. Oh, can you find me something else to wear. I hate red."

Curiosity gleamed in his eyes. "Then why are you

wearing it? Did Rylen force you?"

A low laugh slipped out. "No, I wore it to make him mad. He kept going on and on about the White Dragon kingdom this and that so I decided to put on something other than white."

Ren's dark brows quirked up. Paladin laughed.

She turned away, leaving the two men. She walked to the foyer where a servant met her. He led her upstairs down the dimly lit hall to another bedroom. There, the turbaned servant informed her that some clothes would arrive soon. She murmured thanks and he left.

The soft, muted green and burgundy striped cover on the bed matched the solid green lounging chaise and armchair across the room. She smiled in anticipation of much needed rest. Slipping out of her dress, she was glad to be free of the flashy material. She slid naked between the sheets to rest her head on the pillow. Just a little nap to refresh her and she would be ready for whatever the men decided. She released a satisfied sigh. A moment later, she fell asleep.

Chapter Twenty-Two

The morning sun domed above the sand dunes behind Seren. Wrapped in a hooded cloak, she squinted over her shoulder to the glowing horizon. Light filtered across the waves of sand in a checkerboard pattern. Cold still permeated the air, but with the slow rise of the sun, the sharp bite slackened enough for her to feel comfortable within the cloak's thin gauze material over the even thinner sarong the wizard's housekeeper loaned her.

Their party, consisting of her, Paladin, Ren, several of his servants, along with Calis worked their way across the dunes, heading in a westerly direction of Gimal Zabara. The true name of the safekeeping caverns deep within the desert.

During the night, the two identical men who'd helped in her rescue, Cie and Rie, departed for Durfalin. Their purpose, stressed by Ren and Paladin was to warn the city's leaders. The brothers would help erect a barrier around the surrounding walls and land.

She looked over at where Ren stood on a dune's crest, waiting for the slower members of the little caravan to catch up. Ever since the evening before, after she'd witness the vision about him, the wizard had avoided her. The vision remained clear in her mind. She assumed her ability to see things bothered the man.

"How are you?" Paladin asked from close behind

her.

Shivers of need passed through her. She turned, facing him. "I'm fine, ready to arrive. That's all."

He nodded. "It's only a little farther. I can feel the pressure from the barrier. Can you not sense it also?"

She stopped and stared into his eyes, uncertain what he meant. She tilted her head, concentrating. She didn't know what the barrier consisted of, she assumed magic, but nothing came to her. "No, not really."

"Perhaps once we are nearer you will."

"Maybe." She clasped her hands and took a deep breath, needing to ask him why the dragons hadn't sent her back to Earth after her rescue. She'd woken up this morning with a nagging need to find out something important. It'd bothered her, constantly nudging at her mind. Thinking it best to come out and ask, she looked over at him. "If I was back on Earth, would Arcane still attack?"

He stiffened, his hair fluttering in the soft breeze. "That, I do not know."

Staring at him, she sensed a sudden change in him. He wouldn't meet her look. Again, the impression that he withheld some piece of information from her sprang to the forward in her thoughts. Not sure how to proceed, she turned and stepped away. "I was just wondering."

"We can talk more once we reach the caverns."

A measure of relief came over her. She nodded with a contented smile, confident he'd assuage her worry. More eager to arrive at their destination than when they first left the compound, she walked at his side.

The heat increased, bearing down on her. She was thankful for the clothes on her back. She glanced around. The others members in the group appeared unaffected by the scorching air while others like Paladin suffered, sweat pouring from their bodies, soaking their clothes.

In the distance, a deep blue shape formed on the horizon. Heat waves shifted over the sand, and prevented her from distinguishing any details. With each step, the dark spot cleared, forming an outcrop of limestone jutting from desert. She sighed, relieved, ready to reach some type of shelter from the sun.

Overhead, dark forms moved across the sky. She recognized some of the distant shapes as dragons while others coasted too high for her to tell their identity. Three of the dragons flew toward the party. With their approach, their large, muscled bodies rippled in the sunlight, larger than dracs. Flying in a triangular formation, the beasts descended on a current, circling around to pass over their small caravan. Seren's stomach quivered with unease.

"What do they want?" she asked Paladin. He, too, studied them, his eyes narrowed in speculation.

"Let us hope they don't intend to stop. Those are adult lesser dragons from the rogue lands." He explained, tightening his grasp on her arm and increasing his pace. "We have one good factor on our side. Ren."

"What clan do they come from, black?"

"No, they are from the blue. I'm surprised to see them this far north. Their clan leader lives in Avaris' southern regions."

At his observation, a spiraling intuition struck Seren— they'd been sent to find her. Did Arcane's reach extend so far? She touched the rounded curve of her belly. They wouldn't harm her child, she wouldn't let them.

The trio swooped around them once more, spiraled

lower before landing in a spray of sand. One in front and another at an angle on the right. The third beast touched down on the sand several yards to Seren's left, well out of Paladin and Ren's attack range. Ren, sideways to the dragons, held his staff across his chest, the stone in its tip aimed at the beast in front of them. Paladin drew both his swords, prepared should the dragons attack.

This close, their scales glistened and rippled over their elongated bodies. Their legs, shorter, stockier than Lior's, shifted in the sand. A flowing frill started at the crown on their heads. It ran down the back of their necks to end at their shoulders. The frill moved up and down.

Ren held the front dragon off. Paladin did the same with the one on the right.

No one moved.

Time slowed.

Heated air carried by the wind passed over the group, coating them with a light sandy layer. Seren curved her arm over the top of her abdomen, determined to protect her unborn child.

Three sets of cold black eyes stared at them. Instinct warned her that they focused on her. The sand beneath her feet slipped a little, and one foot lowered with the shifting ground.

The frills on their neck stood straight. The two in front of Ren and Paladin snapped their long necks down, mouths gaped, revealing razor sharp teeth.

Magic flew from the stone on Ren's staff, sending shafts of glittering light shards at the dragon. At the same time, Paladin sprang at the beast before him, swinging his blades at the second one. Neither made a solid hit. Drawn away from her, they continued with their attack while the two beasts retreated.

Movement came at her from the left. She glanced in time to see the third dragon, who'd stood watching the others but now raced over the sand on its hind legs, clawed fingers reaching for her.

With more gentleness than she believed possible, it plucked her several feet off the ground. The momentum of the charge kept them going for a good distance. The deep blue beast shoved her away. She flew back, landing in the side of a dune, sand avalanching over her from above.

She fanned the dusty cloud swirling in front of her face, struggling to breathe, all the time trying to keep the dragon in her line of vision. He stayed in front of her, its neck straight with its jaw flattened against his throat. The frill on its spine stood erect.

The other two dragons leapt away from the two men and joined their ally. She anchored her feet to stand without sliding in the loosened sand. Heart beating, heat searing her lungs, sand scratching her eyes each time she blinked, she hid her fear, tilting her chin high. She tightened her hands over her abdomen.

They would never harm her child, though how she intended to stop creatures the size of a semi-truck, she didn't know.

Seconds ticked by. In the distance, Paladin and Ren struggled to reach her. Paladin shouted her name, worry and fear evident in his voice. Hot winds curled over the dune behind her, sending fine glistening particles down over her. Instead of falling at her feet, the floating dust twirled in front of her stomach with more rising from the ground. The dust shifted and deepened, forming the shape of a man.

Long strands of hair blew over a cloaked back.

Booted feet floated above the ground, levitating the form created from wind and sand. The image carried the deep earth tones created by the desert. Skin, hair, and clothes materialized without any other hues.

Seren scooted to the right, stopping at an angle to see his face, one she recognized, yet never viewed. In the vision from so long ago, she'd seen only his eyes and body. Now, looking up at the lean features, her heart tightened and tears washed the fine grains from her eyes. He reminded her of Paladin, though much younger.

The dragons' heads lowered. The one in front growled deep in its throat.

The image of the young man spoke, his voice soft, threatening. "You dare touch my mother."

A powerful magical charge surged at the beast. With the impact, it sank several inches into the sand.

"My mother." This time, the words came out stronger, almost a shout, the force behind them struck the dragon again, shoving it deeper into the desert floor. The two beasts on either side of the one who'd threatened Seren, slithered several feet away, their heads dipped in submission, touching the rippling ground.

Deep grunts came from the beast before him. *"Arcane instructed us to find this woman and bring her to him."*

A breeze fluttered over her son's image, lifting and moving the illusion of clothes and hair. "Arcane? You think he is so strong he will stand against me? You would follow death, my brother?"

"Humans have long sought to destroy our kind. Do you, human that you are, seek to carry through with their desire?"

"Dare you question me?"

Magic circled her son's form, visible to the eye with tiny particles of power. Each one glinted in the hot sun. Another magical blast struck the beast, but instead of forcing it lower, it drew the dragon closer. "My mother has named me. Do you desire to know that which is bestowed on me? It is appropriate for who I am.

"I am Legion. Many in one. An unstoppable force to rule over Avaris with a mighty fist, conjoining the clans. In my veins, there flows even the blood of your clan leader, Karia. Think you, she would approve of your actions this day?"

For the first time, the beast wavered in its angry resolve. Its gaze flickered, and then the thickly lashed lids closed.

A low laugh came from Legion. "I think not. Your actions of this day, the one against my beloved mother alone, have sealed your fate."

The air around the dragon shimmered like the heat waves across the desert. The beast opened its mouth in a soundless scream. Its body, starting at its nose, dissolved into a black mist. Sparkling light flickered among the vapor and separated from it, sucked in by her son.

Sudden pressure built in Seren's abdomen. Power flowed into her from her son's image. The baby rolled, kicked, and struck against his confines, drawing in the dragon's magic. The remains of the dragon disappeared. Having trouble pulling a deep breath, shocked by the dragon's death, she glanced at her son.

He stared at the second beast which cowered a short distance away.

"Be gone. Hie yourselves to Arcane. When he moves, you will send word, even at the cost of your lives. Go. Now!"

Both remaining beasts answered the order by leaping into the air. Neither looked back from their path leading northeast. Legion's form, held together by his magic, fell apart before Seren's eyes. She cried out, one hand reaching for her son. He disappeared.

A sob escaped from Seren. Paladin reached her and she faced him. He wrapped his arms around her, holding her tight against him. She buried her face in his chest and whispered, "I didn't want him to go."

"I know, love, but his time will come. And soon. Have no fear of that." He placed a hand on the back of her head, stroking her hair. "Come, we must hurry before any others decide to join us. It is only a little ways more."

She sniffed and nodded, struggling with need to see her son again. Paladin steadied her. With her feet planted firm in the sand, she glanced over at Ren. The wizard studied her, his eyes narrowed in speculation.

He met her gaze and asked. "Has he ever displayed his might like that in the past?"

"No. I've seen him only one time in a vision, but never in such a way."

"It's good he manifested to the dragons. Word will spread through the clans and beyond of his power. This will cause many to reconsider going against him."

"I suppose. I'm still scared even though he protected me."

Ren grunted in response. He pivoted and started walking in the direction of the rock formation again as though nothing had happened. "Come, it's best to reach the place before the sol descends."

Paladin kept an arm wrapped around her shoulders, giving her strength. Without a word, they followed Ren.

The sun moved toward the horizon. Perspiration

coated Seren's face. She swiped it with the sleeve on her cloak. She tried to swallow, but the dryness in her mouth stopped her. Her lips cracked in fine lines. Paladin passed her a water pouch several times, stopping, and letting her drink a little to restore the moisture she sweated out.

Legion's actions against the dragon played out in her mind. He'd physically sucked the life from the beast until nothing remained.

So, Arcane's comment held truth. He'd gained power by drawing the magic from others. She glanced at Paladin, needing to question him, but deep in her heart she feared what he would tell her. Was this how the dragons increased their magic, by devouring the very essence of weaker ones? She found no other explanation for the sudden increase of strength in her body and womb after the dragon evaporated.

Up ahead, Ren reached the formation. He stopped not far from it. The small party trailed behind him. So near, Seren sensed what Paladin had spoken of earlier. Energy surged around the huge slabs protruding from the desert, coating the stones with a glistening layer.

"Wait here. I will open a way," Ren told them, moving closer to the barrier. Streaks resembling colored electricity ran through the air before him. A multitude of colors, reds, blues yellows and greens, mingled together to manifest into a rainbow effect.

The wizard stopped. Winds coasting along the desert increased, lifting his cloak away from his body, flashing crimson on the inside and the deep navy on the outer side in the waning light. Ren raised his arms, his staff, tipped with the yellow dragon stone, held tight in his right hand. He chanted—the words unclear and carried away with the breeze.

Seren's heart accelerated with the magic generated in the domed barrier. Electricity spiraled in the air, sending tingles through her body. She reached out and slipped her fingers into Paladin's hand, seeking security in his touch.

He pressed against her fingers, tightening his arm about her shoulders, pulling her closer to his side. "Do not be concerned. He will open a path. We will be safe for a time."

"Hope so. My chest is starting to hurt, like there's a heavy weight on it," she said, leaning against his side.

"This will pass once he secures an opening. Watch, love, he will soon move to the cavern's mouth."

The easy way he spoke the endearment brought a smile to her lips. He appeared assured with Ren's actions. Sucking back a fear-laden laugh, she hoped Ren Murdock didn't do anything to blow them away.

Several minutes went by, the sun slipped further over the horizon's edge. Ren, hair tossed about on his head, took a slow step forward. Seren straightened and stared, amazed at the man's power. Another step and another until he stopped some feet from where he'd started.

Paladin squeezed her lightly. "He's done it. A gate is open to the safekeeping."

"Good, I'll feel better knowing there's something to slow Arcane when he decides to attack." She gave him a quick one-sided hug. She moved from under his protective hold and stepped to the gateway through the barrier.

"It will stop him dead."

She glanced at him. "Dead? Don't we wish?"

"Shh, do not ever say that word. It is forbidden."

Surprised at the strength in his quiet comment, she studied him. The way his brows drew together, and the tight brackets on either side of his mouth revealed he believed this. She shrugged, hoping to put him at ease. "It slipped out. Sorry, but the word is no big deal on Earth."

"Big deal?"

"Not important."

"Ah, I see. Here, the dragons hear through magic what each person, human, dragonseed, even Felerians say. With dragonseeds, the connection also goes to their thoughts." He moved nearer and took her hand. "The night I found you, I made one simple wish. They heard and responded. Because of this, your life and mine have been irrevocably changed."

She smiled, draping her arms around his neck. "For the better I hope. One thing we do know, this will come to an end and I will go home. To Earth."

The same strange shuttered expression from earlier crossed over his features, renewing the question inside her. He hid something from her. She felt it clear to her bones. "Paladin...?"

He stopped her with a brief passing of his lips over hers. "Come, we must move on. I'm not sure how long Ren can maintain the opening for us."

Deciding to let the matter sit until they had time to work it out, she nodded and let him guide her through the gateway. She eyed the wizard when they moved past him. He frowned, concentration evident on his features. Once everyone in their party entered, he moved past the spot he stood and in the direction of the entrance to the cavern. The barrier slipped into place, leaving no exit for the dragonseeds within unless Ren opened another passage for them.

This did little to relieve her though. Doubts concerning the barrier and Arcane's power to break through stayed with her. She glanced over at Paladin. He appeared so calm. Was he? Again, the doubts about his reasoning in coming to this place rose. She wanted to believe in him, but too many questions popped into her thoughts, making her question his reasoning.

Trying to shove the negativity aside, she followed him to the triangular shaped entrance into the cavern. Paladin stopped. She came to a halt behind him, and Ren joined them. At her side, the wizard raised a brow at her. "Welcome to your new home."

Paladin shook his head and glanced over his shoulder, a slight smile on his lips. "Only for the moment."

"If you wait here, I will continue to the living area and clear out the dust and debris." Ren offered.

"I'd rather we go with you. You're going to use your spells to do the cleaning, right?" Seren questioned, glancing at the wizard.

"But of course, it is the only way to keep everything organized and in its proper place." Ren grinned at her. She smiled in return. It pleased her that he appeared more at ease in her company. His good looks came alive with the smile.

"If we go with you, we won't be in the way?"

"Not at all. Come, mother to our unborn king. Let me see if you care for my cleaning methods." He proceeded to stroll down the darkened corridor leading underneath the flowing dunes of the desert.

Once inside, the blackness closed in around them,

thick and impenetrable. Ren's footsteps, crunching the sand on the stone floor echoed in the high-ceilinged passageway. A flash streaked in front of her followed by a flood of luminous light from the yellow dragonstone on Ren's staff. The eerie circle of light from the stone carried across the space between and several feet about them. On the walls on either side, engraved designs flowed over the surfaces, etched by human hands.

Seren moved closer to the wall on her right. She studied the pictures carved there. Dragons amassed in the skies above fleeing humans. A thrill surged to life in her veins.

"This is why they made this place?" she asked, reaching up to lay her palm on the wall.

"Do not touch," Ren's order came too late.

Images and sounds entered Seren's body through the pictures. Humans screamed in terror, their clothes, hair, even their very flesh burned under the dragons' flames. Compassion for the lost lives released her from the vision. She slid her hand down and away, balling her hands into fists.

"The marks were magically encrypted so their descendants would never forget the tribulation they suffered." The wizard stepped to her side. "This place was the sanctuary of the golden dragon so the magic in the walls is more intense."

Both she and Paladin faced Ren, shocked at the wizard's answer. Paladin stepped closer to the wizard. "Is it safe for us to come within its boundaries?"

The wizard frowned at them. "The beast no longer exists except for its bones and scales. I've been here many times. I have never seen any signs of a live golden one. Nor have I sensed its presence."

More than a little surprised, Seren stared at him. She'd seen the dragon at her purification. Paladin had too. "That's not true." She motioned to Paladin. "We saw one."

Ren shook his head and motioned with his head, "So he has said, but until the time I can see with these eyes of mine, I will continue to believe it is a hopeless cause. Mind you, I will never cease my search, but I admit freely it is a useless one. Come, we're almost there."

Confused by Ren's attitude, she nodded. She reached and took Paladin's hand. The touch gave her strength to continue after the wizard.

Ren moved deeper into the cave. The faint sound of water dripping further into the cavern echoed, and soon, mingled with their steps. The wizard halted. He tilted his head, appearing to listen for something while he waited. Seren's heart picked up speed.

"What? Is there danger?" Paladin let go of Seren's hand and slid his hands over his sword handles.

The wizard turned and faced the wall on his right. He lifted the staff so the dragonstone's light extended to reveal the bottom half of the wall.

Reddish brown worms, their many hairy legs swishing back and forth, poured from a crevice in the stone.

She swallowed, wrinkling her face in disgust. She moved closer to the two men so she stood between them. "I hate worms."

A frown flashed across Ren's face as he glanced at her. "Don't we all?" Without waiting for her to answer, he began walking again.

The path descended then rose to curve one way then the other. At the end, stone steps rose to such a height they disappeared into the outer edges of the light from the dragonstone.

They climbed the steps and came over the last one. The rounded rock stretched out a good distance across. An intricate design covered the entire surface. It reminded Seren of a strange type of a pentagram. Then a thought came to her. Years ago, she'd seen circles with marks similar to this in a magazine article about alchemy. She glanced at Ren. Did wizards here use a form of alchemy?

Dust-coated debris lay scattered over the surface. Ren kicked a petrified board out of his way as he walked to the center of the circle. Once there, he knelt, digging the sand out of a groove. Once he appeared satisfied with his efforts, he stood and placed the end of his staff into the slot.

He glanced at their small group. "Everyone, step back onto the stairs. Stay against the walls. This will only take a moment to finish."

Doing what he asked, Seren caught Paladin's gaze. She lifted a brow in question. He grinned and nodded at Ren. "Watch. You'll see. It's a simple spell."

Releasing the staff, Ren brought his hands together in front of his face. He closed his eyes and a look of total concentration crossed over his features. A vortex of air encircled the staff, widening until it streaked outside the circle's boundaries. The wind picked up every bit of debris in the area. With a rush of air, it traveled to the shaft leading out of the caverns.

When the current disappeared, Ren relaxed, bringing his hands down to his sides. He grinned. "There now, we'll be able to stay in a relatively clean place."

He snapped his fingers. Dormant dragonstones in

their wooden holders flared to life. The entire cavern illuminated with white light. Two stories high, the ceiling, smooth like polished glass but without the reflection, domed above them. Stairs, curving against and with the walls, climbed on both sides of the entrance, leading to rooms on a second level.

Ren understated his cleaning ability. Seren studied the spotless stone beneath her feet. She'd be able to eat off the rock.

"I repaired the furniture in many of the rooms. It's plain but serviceable." The wizard commented, removing his staff. "There's a larger room in the center, there on the bottom level. We'll use it to hold meetings to discuss this situation Paladin has put us in."

She chewed on her bottom lip, shooting a glance at Paladin. He stood, glaring at the wizard. "How is this my fault? It's written of in the ancient texts."

Ren grinned at him and turned toward the room he spoke about using for a meeting room. "Well, if you'd kept your pants up, none of this would have happened." The man stopped, looked over at Seren and winked. "Of course, I can certainly understand why you did what you did."

The glare cooled to an iceberg. Seren reached out and touched Paladin's arm. "He's teasing."

"That is not a subject to jest about." He clenched his teeth, and then said, "He shouldn't have flirted with you either."

Ren's jovial laugh followed after him, echoing in the open area.

"Fool." Paladin took her hand and trailed behind.

"But a dear one. Don't let his teasing bother you. You're the one I'm attracted to, not him." She smiled up at him.

He pulled her into his arms. "That pleases me to hear."

Staring into his eyes, she ran a finger across his jaw. "Can you doubt it?"

"Tonight, I'll hold you in my arms. I've dreamed of this moment for such a long time." Moving his head, he placed a kiss on her palm. Her heart warmed at his words.

Ren called to them and the moment ended. They both smiled, comfortable with the wait. Paladin, with an arm over her shoulders, led her to where the wizard waited.

Tonight, he'd said. Contentment flowed through her. Just a little while longer and they'd be together.

Chapter Twenty-Three

More supplies arrived within the hour with turbaned men and women carrying baskets. Some even rode on strange wind powered sleds. There was one large center sail and two smaller ones on each side of a catamaran type vessel.

Seren nudged Ren in the arm. "Why didn't we use one of those?"

"They sicken me when I ride them." He shrugged, looking down his nose at her. "Besides a little walk is healthy for you and the babe."

She rolled her eyes. "Walk in the desert with the heat and all the sand? No, I don't think so."

He chuckled before he left her, striding off to direct some of the newly arrived people to where they should go.

"You know, I can understand why he's your friend," she told Paladin, looking over at him where he stood at her side.

Curiosity lit the gaze he turned on her. "And why is that?"

"You're like salt and pepper, blending to make a perfect combination," she explained.

"Pepper?"

"It's a seasoning spice just like salt. You remember the brine sticks?"

"Ah, I see. We complement each other." He nodded in understanding.

The last of the day's sun, low on the horizon, cast a reddish glow across the landscape, softening his features. The reds mingled with the golds in his hair, burnishing them. Soft air currents passed over them, ruffling his hair. Impatient for the time they would be alone, she shifted closer and encircled his waist under his coat with one arm.

"Yeah. I like your choice of friends." She placed her cheek against his chest.

They stood quietly, his hand caressing the crown of her head as they watched more people arrive.

Dust blew up on the horizon. Seren straightened against him. A strange cloud spiraled in their direction. "What is that? A dust devil?"

"A what?"

"That's what we call a small vortex in the sand or dirt on Earth."

He grunted and stepped away from her, his gaze narrowed. He, too, watched the sand cloud racing closer. Ren came up behind them.

"Seems we have company."

The three of them stood inside the barrier. Seren felt safe from whatever approached. The cloud drew nearer. She searched for the cause of it, but nothing other than calm sand and sky surrounded it. When the dust hit the barrier, the magical wall parted. The form of a man took shape, moving through it. Once on this side, his bare feet hit the sand. He continued toward them, his momentum leading him straight to Paladin.

Bask.

There was no mistaking the wizard. The silvered

skull cap glinted reddish orange with the sun's waning light. He reached out, grasped Paladin by his coat and lifted him off the ground.

"Fool. What did Lior instruct you to do?"

Paladin's face became a mask of fury. He clasped Bask's wrists and squeezed. "Release me."

"Return the woman to Earth. Were those not her words?"

Seren's knees weakened. Her attention moved to Paladin's face.

"The choice was mine, and I chose to keep her close."

"To watch her die?"

"What makes you believe she would return? Just the loss of one clan leader and the door would be closed, not to be opened until another grew in power to do so. I refused to take the chance."

Mouth dry, Seren tried to take in what the two men argued about. Bask had to be wrong. Paladin knew how much she wanted to go home. He wouldn't have kept her here without telling her first. Would he?

"Paladin?" She lifted a hand and took a step to him. "Is it true?"

Bask shoved him away, releasing his hold. He turned to her. "'Tis true, little mother. With his foolish actions, he has risked your life along with the child's."

"Lior said the decision was mine to make."

The wizard slashed down with one hand. "She never thought you would do this."

Seren shook her head, not wanting to believe. Hurt welled up in her heart to overflow through her tears. With another shake of her head, she pivoted and walked into Ren's chest.

The wizard's right arm lifted, the staff extended in front of him. "Stay away. I believe she needs time to understand what has happened."

"Seren." Paladin's voice softened only to harden with his next words. "Remove your staff or I'll carve it into kindling."

"No, not another word. I don't want to see you right now. You knew how badly I wanted to go home. You didn't care." She hated the sorrowful note in her words. She had to leave. Had to find someplace where she would have quiet to understand why he had done this to her. Realization came to her. This answered her question. The one bothering her, the one Paladin evaded so aptly earlier today.

The scarlet side of Ren's cloak flashed as he wrapped an arm over her shoulders, concealing her from onlookers. "I'll take you to your room. You can rest there and maybe eat a little."

Unable to concentrate, she allowed him to lead her. They reached the room set aside for her. He guided her to the narrow cot and helped her sit.

"Why did he do it? Is it true? The door can't be opened again if something happens to one of the seven?" She clasped her hands in her lap.

"It's true, though, if need be, I'm sure a conjunction of a few of the more experienced wizards, me included, could manage to open it. I doubt he even considered that." Ren moved to stand inside the open door. "You must remember your escape from Xelerdin happened so fast. Mayhap, he had no time to contemplate the matter in depth."

"What was there to think about? Bask said Lior told him to open the door to Earth. He refused. I can't believe he did this to me. I could be back home, safe from any real danger." She shook her head, palms laid on the curve of her stomach.

"Our baby would be safe."

Reaching for the door latch, Ren nodded. "Rest, little mother, and remember there is not much which occurs on Avaris that those great beasts do not have influence over. Perhaps, it was their desire for you not return to your home. Paladin merely followed through with their wish."

His words lingered after he closed the door. All the noise from the larger room past the wooden barrier ceased. Shoulders slumping, she sat trying to understand. Unable to find an answer, she lay on her back, placing an arm over her eyes. She drifted into a swirling dark mass. Dreams assaulted her. She struggled to escape, but every way she turned, more blackness greeted her. Through the misty convolution, Arcane slid toward her, his body scraping against the stone ground. She tried to run, but the beast mesmerized her with his cold gaze.

I have found you.

Eyelids snapping open, panting, heart racing, Seren struggled to calm down. She rolled onto her side and stared at nothing in particular. In her heart, she cried out for Paladin. She needed him the most right now, but her wounded trust prevented her from opening her mouth and calling him.

****

The last of Ren's workers arrived. Paladin sat on the ground outside the cavern's entrance, listening to their jovial bickering over who carried the heavier load until it faded when they moved deeper into the cavern. With his back pressed against the rock surface, he watched the wind glide over the moonlit dunes, erasing the marks their passage had left in the sand.

With them, came a message from the Wizard's Academy. They affixed a magical barrier to surround the city. They even sent instructors across the planet to do the same for every city and sizable village.

The news relieved Paladin. After the incident with Seren, he needed some good news. He would have loved to take his anger out on Bask, but the man departed not long after Seren went below with Ren. Right now, he wanted nothing more than to wrap his hands around Bask's neck and squeeze. Still, it would not solve his problem with Seren.

He'd violated her trust, something he valued in others. His selfishness stood in the way of her wellbeing.

Rocks scattered over the ground. He glanced toward the entrance. Ren strode through the opening, and caught sight of him. The wizard walked to his side and squatted, studying him with a keen gaze. The dark-haired man grunted. "Are you finished sulking?"

"I do not sulk. My problem goes deeper than a childish reaction."

"Truly." Ren nodded. He slipped down beside Paladin. "Yet while you sit out here, she is within, heart aching for what you neglected to tell her."

"Please, no lecture." Paladin rubbed his brow. "My own guilt is enough to remind me of what I have done."

"And you don't desire to go to her?"

"To do what? Beg her forgiveness? If I believed she would listen, I would be there in an instant." Paladin shook his head. "No, not the Seren I know. She will take her time in deciding whether or not to forgive me."

"You do realize we will most likely die here? Yet

still, you wallow in your pride, refusing to go to her." Ren used the end of his staff to draw a rough sketch of a dragon in the sand and rocks at his feet. "You, my friend, amaze me."

Amazed him? Paladin's gaze shifted to his friend. "Would you have me go, pleading with her to forgive me for doing the very thing which may cause my death. I would much rather fight for her and live to prove I made the right choice. Better than begging her for forgiveness and then die."

A dark brow quirked at Paladin's comment. "I'll tell you what I would do. Not that I think you ever would, but I'd go to her, even if it was just to hold her. She is lost, same as you. She also doesn't have anyone on this entire planet she is close with, not like she is to you." Without waiting for Paladin to reply, Ren stood, shook the dust off his cloak, and reentered cavern.

The cold desert night chilled Paladin. He brought the collar of his coat up around his throat. He considered rising and going to Seren, but instead, he remained seated. How could he expect her to forgive him? He'd cut her deep with his actions. So, he sat long into the night, watching the wind dance over the dunes while he considered what to do about the woman he loved.

****

Several days swept past in a blur for Seren. She tried to cope without having Paladin near her, but seeing him across the larger cavern, yet never going to meet him tore at her. She wanted to, but pride stood in the way. His gaze, haunted with dark shadows under his eyes, focused on her every time she looked in his direction.

His haggard appearance verified his own suffering.

Even seeing this, she still had a hard time forgiving him.

Leo and Largin arrived a week after they had. They rode in on the backs of two lesser sea dragons. Poor beasts hopped from one foot to another, trying to avoid direct contact with the hot sand. Largin's dragon jumped just when the old man slid over its side. The old wizard flew above the dragon's back to land in a cloud of dust at the beast's taloned feet. The half-surprised, half-aggravated expression on the poor man's face caused a surprised laugh to well up from Seren.

Hair standing on end, clothes rumpled, Largin stood, brushed a hand over his body, and glared at his ride. "You could have warned me."

The dragon crooned low in its throat, a long-forked tongue slid from scaled lips and flicked at Largin.

"Oh, be off with you. Return to Bae. Keep well hidden. Don't come here again until called for by your clan leader." Largin patted the long neck. "I fully expect you to fight well during the approaching battle."

Green scales rippled over the dragon's body, its lips pulled back, revealing large pointed teeth. With another low mew, it sprang straight up, followed by the other. They flew toward the southeast. Dust billowed around Largin. He waved at the departing dragons before turning and scurrying through the barrier to where she and the others waited.

Amazed they could walk through the invisible wall, Seren looked over at Ren. He didn't appear surprised at all. She'd ask Leo about it later. Maybe it didn't affect humans.

The white-haired wizard stopped in front of her, his gaze wandering over her rounding body. "Well, young mother, you appear hale."

She smiled, tilting her head in acknowledgment. "I am. And you, sir, how have you been?"

"Fine, fine. Though I have to say, all this uproar is rather exhausting. Such a headache. Ah, Paladin, there you are." When Largin stepped to him, Seren sidled over to Leo.

She wrapped her arms around his waist, drawing comfort from the simple touch. He embraced her, one hand patting her back. Her face buried in the center of his broad chest, she spoke, her words coming through muffled. "I'm so glad you're safe. I was so worried, not sure if his blow killed you."

"No, I'm good." He leaned back, his head dipping to take in her features. "You look tired? The baby's doing this or did something happen we don't know about?"

With a shake of her head, she spoke low. "I'll tell you later."

He nodded in response. She moved with him so he could greet Ren and Paladin. For a few minutes, they stood in a circle discussing the increase in dragon activity over the desert. Largin expressed his concern that this sudden influx from the rogue lands showed signs of an upcoming attack.

White hair still sticking up in spots, the older man looked at each of them. "We must be prepared for that moment."

"Preparations are almost complete," Ren reassured him.

"Are they? I received word from Valhaven this morning. A village along its northern border took a full force attack. The dragonseed soldiers managed to evacuate the people. They remained and fought valiantly, but the masses overtook them. All would have been lost had that great black beast, Sinimal, not arrived and drove the rogues away," Largin informed them, a concerned frown on his face.

The news tore at Seren's heart. "Is this the only attack you've heard about?"

Lines of worry bracketed the older wizard's mouth. "The rogues are uniting under Arcane's authority. With this attack, it appears he is having difficulty controlling them. As for other attacks, there are none that I'm aware of, but this does not mean outlying villages have survived."

"All of it could have been avoided if I'd gone home." Without meaning to, her gaze met Paladin's. He stiffened at her comment.

"Not necessarily." Ren moved closer. "If anything, your staying has held Arcane back."

Surprised at his comment, she tried to understand what he meant.

He continued explaining. "Arcane wants to destroy you, but he learned when he took you, he cannot do any physical harm to the child while he is inside you. He's biding his time until you give birth. The babe will be at his weakest, unable to fully use his powers. Nothing more than a helpless newborn."

Horror at what Ren suggested replaced her surprise and sent streams of fear for her baby through her body. "Then he'll attack."

"There would be no better time. Arcane cares little what the lesser dragons do to occupy their time during the wait. If you had returned to your home, he would have started the reign of destruction immediately," Ren said.

Turning away, he faced the entrance to the cavern and started to move to it. "We need not worry for your safety for now. It's only after the child is here that the true battle will begin."

Watching the dark-haired man stride away from their group did little to relieve Seren. She jumped as a strong arm wrapped over her shoulders. She lifted her gaze and met Paladin's. Unable to stop, she wrapped her arms around his waist. "So, it really is better I remained here?"

"I do not know."

"I haven't forgiven you," she muttered against his chest.

"Nor would I expect you to." His hand passed over her hair, fingers dipping to massage her scalp. His sandalwood scent enfolded her, soothing her rattled nerves. Knees weak, she slumped against him.

"I just want to make sure our baby is safe."

She needed him to understand nothing else mattered as long as their baby had a chance to survive.

"And so, it will be. This I swear on my very blood. Our child will live to be King."

His answer seemed final, almost like a warning of his eminent death. She stiffened and stepped away. The very thought, even angry at him, of losing Paladin, never seeing, touching, and sharing precious time with him, brought more anguish. The baby rolled inside her.

Together, they walked to the caverns. She'd been honest with him. She still hadn't forgiven him, but right now even that wasn't important. They had to work together to fight against Arcane and his army. If they didn't, none of the humans on Avaris would survive.

Chapter Twenty-Four

For the next few days, the tension within the safe haven increased. News arrived every day of more attacks. Obviously, Ren Murdock knew what he spoke of when he told them the night Largin and Leo arrived that Arcane was waiting until the baby's birth to launch his major assault. The closer her delivery came, the more the rogues vented their hatred for humans.

Heart aching, Seren stopped listening to the reports. Often, Seren went and sat on the roof of the caverns, staring off into the distance across the dunes. Leo found her there. Almost two weeks had passed since he and Largin arrived. She was thankful he'd given her time to stew some before searching her out. Still confused and defensive, the added days had helped calm her.

From the corner of her eye, she saw him approach and sit next to her on the smooth limestone.

"Well, what happened?"

She half-smiled, knowing what he meant. She'd avoided telling him anything of her relationship with Paladin. It still hurt too much to believe the man she loved hadn't trusted her. "He made a wish."

"He's making a habit of that."

With a low laugh, she nodded. "He doesn't seem to have good luck with his wishes. First, me, and now me again."

Leo frowned at her. "That doesn't seem like a bad

thing."

"No, but he didn't give me a choice either time. This time though, he decided to keep me here without asking me what I wanted to do." She slumped against the rock behind her, staring at the rough stone ground. "It wouldn't hurt so badly if I didn't have feelings for him."

"You love him." His words came out as more of a statement than a question. She looked at him.

He shrugged. "A blind man can see it."

She released a breathy laugh. "It's that obvious?"

"The others didn't see you after he'd left to go to Valhaven. I did. I know how much you missed him."

"I still miss him, but I can't forgive him yet. I can't trust him either. Not so soon." She looked out over the dunes flowing across the horizon. "He should have talked to me before he did it."

"Did you have time to talk? When he rescued you?" Leo quirked a brow at her.

"You're deliberately trying to make me feel worse, aren't you?"

"Not really. Just thinking maybe you're being a little unreasonable."

She shook her head. Leave it to Leo to come up with a feasible excuse. "Just like a man. How am I unreasonable when he's the one who decided my future for me?"

"Did he wish for something both of you didn't want at the time? Hell, you two still want it. Just because you're from Earth and he's from here doesn't mean the two of you can't be together."

Was this true? Yes, she'd needed Paladin with a desperate desire, wanted him so much. Had he picked up on her what she wanted and combined them with his own to make his decision? She'd never asked him. Now it seemed too late. How could she go to him to find out?

"Do I belong here, Leo? Really belong?" She sighed and shook her head. "I don't know. I want to be with Paladin, but then I'm scared to stay here. Nothing is normal, not like what I'm accustomed to on Earth."

"It's strange you put it that way."

She looked at him, frowning over the way he made the comment, as if what she'd said amazed him.

He shrugged and continued. "I never once thought like that when I arrived on Avaris. You have to keep in mind that I knew I was going to die if I stayed where I was, so there wasn't a choice of me hurrying back to Earth."

When he continued, he studied her. "You were different.

There wasn't a threat to you. Or was there? Were you happy on Earth or were you just going through life, waiting to die?"

His question took her by surprise. "Not fair. You're not the psychic, I am."

"Hit a raw spot?"

She blinked, glancing away, hoping to hide the burning tears in her eyes. "Sort of."

"Do you love him?"

Swallowing the rise of tears clogging her throat, she whispered. "Yes."

"Then what's the problem?"

"He didn't trust me."

"He does. He wants you here."

She shook his reasoning aside. "He's never once told me he loves me." She stopped as a thought occurred. Paladin mentioned love before, but was it the same here like it was on Earth? "Does everyone on Avaris even know what love is? You know, the same way we do?"

A laugh started in Leo's belly, low and full of mirth. "I hope so, or my wife lied to me all the years we were together."

She smiled in response. "I suppose it's one emotion that's universal."

"Hate is too."

A sudden wave of exhaustion clouded her mind. She struggled to keep her eyes open and pay attention. She had to repeat his answer twice before the words registered. With a nod, she pushed off the ground with her hands and stood. "I supposed all emotions are. Sorry to cut this short, but I'm going in, for some reason, I'm tired all of a sudden."

He stood, offering her a hand. "Sure, honey. Do me a favor? Give Paladin a chance. He does care for you. A lot."

"We'll see. I used to think that, but after this, I'm not sure anymore." She said, taking a few steps in the direction of the stairwell. The third step, a spurt of liquid hit the ground between her feet. Surprised, she stopped and stared at the small puddle.

"Uh, Seren, are you all right?"

Embarrassed, she hoped she hadn't released her bladder. Checking for any signs of pain from the baby, she found nothing wrong. Had her water broken? Everything felt fine. No more liquid came out. Cheeks heated, she looked over her shoulder at Leo, shaking her head, her hands clasping her rounded stomach. "I can't believe I did that."

He grunted, a considering frown creasing his brow. "You go on down. Clean up and we'll see."

She agreed and started down the stairs leading to the caverns. Midway, heat spiraled from the center of her lower back and shot around to the front. She gasped, coming to a stop on the steep stone cut steps. Eyes wide, she counted the seconds her belly tightened.

When the tension released, she met Leo's worried eyes. "I don't think I wet myself."

Panic flashed across his face. "Oh, Lord, Lord, Lord. Come on, you need to get to your room now."

She didn't argue. This labor was so different from when she'd had Mandy. One thing, her labor with her daughter had been induced. The flood of pain-filled memories poured through her mind, sending strands of panic through her. Another flare of heat started in her back at the bottom of the steps.

"This isn't good. I must be in hard labor. The contractions are irregular. They're coming too quick." She tried to sound normal, but the pain came sharper than the last one.

"Don't talk, walk. Once you're in your room, I'll find Largin and Paladin. Master Largin'll know what to do."

She giggled, for some reason the idea of the elderly wizard assisting her in having the baby sounded ridiculous. "I know what to do, but if it'll make you feel better, bring the old man."

Concentrating on breathing through the increasing pains, she glanced up to see Paladin walking in the long-legged, slow way she'd grown to love toward the entrance. Without thinking, she called to him. He stopped, found her with his gaze, and changed directions, weaving through the multitude of people moving around the room.

When he drew nearer, she smiled. "Ready for a baby?"

His eyes widened with surprise. The next moment, he scooped her up into his arms. "Why are you walking?"

"I had to go to my room." She wrapped one arm over his shoulders and massaged her belly.

Leo hurried away from them in search of Largin. She still couldn't figure out why Leo wanted him there. Was he the equivalent to a doctor here on Avaris? She should have asked Leo about it.

Moments later, Paladin entered her room and set her on the small cot. She pointed to the chest at the foot. "Grab my robe. I need to change out of these wet things."

He retrieved her long white robe and handing it to her. His hands trembled. She glanced up at him, surprised. "Are you all right?"

One corner of his mouth lifted. Even in this state of disarray, she brought happiness to him. "My first child is about to be born and you have to ask?"

She started to laugh, but another heated pain swept across her abdomen, turning the sound into a groan. The pain this time was much sharper. Nausea bubbled in her stomach. Taking deep slow breaths, she waited until it ended before responding to him.

"Sorry, I forgot. I've been through this once so I know what's going to happen," she muttered, unwrapping the sash around her waist. He moved her hands away and loosened her clothes so she could slide them off. Warmth climbed up her neck. He hadn't seen her nude in weeks. With his gaze on her cumbersome body, heated embarrassment flooded her face.

She tensed as his hands passed over the skin on her

shoulders. "Wait, I can do this...please."

He stopped and stared at her. She waited. He shifted back, stood, and turned away from her.

"Are you in a great amount of pain?" he asked, his voice soft, gentleness flowing across the distance separating them.

Hurrying to remove her tunic and pants, she shook her head, forgetting he couldn't see her. When she realized it, she'd slipped the robe on and sat on the bed. "Not yet. I expect it'll be worse. You can turn around. I'm done."

He faced her, and she took in his haggard features.

Hoping to relieve his worries, she said, "I was in labor with Mandy for thirty-six hours. The doctor talked about doing a C section on me, but he didn't have to. She came out fine."

Before he could say anything, a knock came from the doorway. Leo entered followed by Largin and Ren.

She eyed them in curiosity. "Uh, Leo is there any reason why they have to be here?"

"They're wizards. They can help."

"With what? I am perfectly capable of giving birth." She scooted until her back was against the wall behind the cot. Trying to relax between pains, she studied the four men. "Isn't there some women here who know what to do? Or isn't that how it's done on this planet?"

"You would do well to let them help you." Paladin knelt by the side of the cot. He reached for her hand.

She pulled it out of the way, glaring at him. "Why? Did you forget to tell me something else?"

"No."

Another pain started to migrate and she asked through clenched teeth. "Then why are they needed?"

The elder wizard stepped closer. "Dragonseed babies have a habit of releasing their magic at birth to the detriment of the person helping to deliver the child. It would be best if Ren and I were here to prevent any harm to you or the child."

Ah, so this explained why. Poor Paladin, he probably thought she was becoming a shrew with this pregnancy. "My baby is not going to do that."

Determination lighting his eyes, Paladin clasped her hand and pulled it to him. "Seren, this baby has been blessed with all of the seven great dragons' magic. We don't know for sure that he will not blow the caverns apart. With them here, they can prevent this from happening."

Between pants she managed to answer, "All right, just be quiet. I'm trying to concentrate here. The pains are coming faster than when I had Mandy. They're not as severe, but they're beginning to hurt." She angled another glare at Paladin. "Bad, too."

There, she'd answered his question from earlier. Still hurt and angry at him with his deception, right now it seemed unimportant with the baby coming.

He raised a brow, stood up, and sat at the head of the bed. "Come, lean against me."

Wanting to reject his offer, but knowing it would be petty of her, she moved so she sat flush between his spread legs, resting against his body. He placed his hands on her ballooned stomach and spread his fingers over each side.

She sighed and tried to relax. The two wizards stood facing each other across the room. The length of the bed plus some feet separated them. They placed their hands, palms against each other at chest height and muttered some type of spell she couldn't hear. A diagram appeared on the stone floor, another circle like the one Ren used to clean the cavern. This one held more lines, strange shapes, and odd writing inside of it. The lines gleamed with golden hue. The light dissipated, leaving black marks imprinted on the floor.

After they finished, Leo and Ren came to the cot, one at the head, and the other at the foot. Paladin eased from behind her and helped them lift the bed. They carried and positioned it in the center of the circle.

When Largin spoke, he stared at Paladin. "Perhaps you should wait outside."

Despite her anger at Paladin, a wave of panic built inside her at the thought of him not being there with her. She started to argue, but Paladin interrupted her.

"I will be here when our son is born."

She sagged in relief. "Thanks."

He met her look, his gentle and caring. "I won't leave you. You will be safe in my arms."

Tears burned the backs of her eyes. He returned to his position behind her. She wanted to embrace him, but another pain, harsher than the other ones, cut from her back around to her lower belly. She panted, agony rendering her speechless.

The wizards moved to their previous positions at the edge of the circle and knelt, their hands flat within the diagram. Again, they spoke in lowered tones, snatches of words coming to her here and there. "Power...bound...subdue...protect..." All the words between were too obscured for her to make out.

Lights radiated from the marks, surrounding them. An invisible, heavy weight came down and the very air thickened, pressing on her. Paladin gasped, and concerned, she struggled to look up at him. His eyes dilated to the point where very little blue showed.

She opened her mouth to say his name, but another pang sliced into her. She cried out, clutching her stomach. Her son pushed all thoughts from her mind. Bare seconds separated the pains.

The contraction ended, and she managed to snap at Largin. "This won't hurt my baby?"

"Not at all. It only ensures the child's power will be repressed enough to allow it to be born. Nothing more. You and Paladin, of course, will feel the effects as well. Not to worry, little mother. They're simply safe guards. We have never had a dragonseed born who has been blessed with all the clan leader's powers. I can only hope it is an uncomplicated matter."

Uncomplicated? Seren snorted in response. Since her arrival on Avaris, complications sprouted around her like weeds.

Her world centered on her pain. Nothing else mattered but Paladin's arms around her along with his encouraging whispers close to her ear. A woman—one of Ren's servants, she wasn't sure–arrived and checked her. She grinned quickly at Seren. She scurried off to return moments later with folded white clothes and a basin of steaming water.

Seren eyed the basin. "That's not too hot for my baby, is it?"

Bowing, the woman shook her head. She set the basin on the table across the room. "No, my lady, not at all. It is a dragonseed after all."

Another sharp pain shot deep within her womb, forcing a moan to escape. The need to push came over her. She struggled to sit up, but the weakness in her limbs made it difficult.

The rich aroma of spice floated in the room. She sucked in lungs full of air and choked. Coughing, she pushed against Paladin, still fighting to straighten.

Panting, sweat pouring from her, she grunted, "I have to push."

The room spun around her. Paladin moved from behind and stepped to where her bent knees spread. The pain crested. A surge of fluid came from her, wetting her hips and the blankets beneath. She gasped at the sudden heat. Light radiated from between her legs. She concentrated on the illumination. Her body took over, stomach tightening then releasing. The birth took her control away.

The luminosity grew in brilliance until it exploded with power. The force shoved her flat on her back. Staring up at the stone ceiling, she gathered her strength, struggling to draw in air. A low mewl came from the end of the bed, followed by a howl. Tears welled in her eyes, blinding her. She managed to half rise to see. Held in his father's hands, their red-faced son vented his fury to the world. Matted with blood and mucus, he squirmed, batting his plump arms and legs at whatever he believed caused his discomfort.

Sobbing with joy, she watched when the woman came and took her child to bathe him. When she'd finished, she wrapped him in a blanket and carried him to Seren. With gentle care, the woman placed him in Seren's arms. Smiling down at her son, Seren tried, but found no words to describe how happy this moment made her. She lifted her gaze and met Paladin's. He stared at their son.

"He is healthy."

She laughed. "Very much so. Look at his hair. It's two colors."

The thin wisps covering the baby's head were ebony mixed with some white blond. Random sections resembled a zigzag across his head with the black on bottom.

"I wonder if it'll stay like this? Do any of your family have hair similar to this?" She looked up at Paladin.

He shrugged. "I've never seen such. Have you decided on a name?"

She nodded. "He said his name the other day. Legion."

"Look, his eyes are open."

Their child relaxed his scrunched lids, revealing two different colored eyes. One was blue like his father, the other gray like hers. His cupid bow mouth shifted in an open smile aimed at them. Her heart melted.

She held her son. Wrapped tight, he looked at her with such knowing eyes. They had to succeed in keeping him alive. No matter what. Sending up silent, sincere pleas, she hoped Avaris' problems disappeared and they would remain safe.

Chapter Twenty-Five

Seven days after Legion's birth, news arrived concerning the clan leaders flying toward the caverns. Seren asked Ren why. He'd looked at her in his stoic manner and walked away without answering. She stared after him, the first rays of fear shattering the peaceful fairytale world she enjoyed with her son.

She searched for Leo and Paladin, finding them in the small room they shared. Leo held a front panel to the armor Paladin wore during his rescue of her. His swords lay across one of the beds. They both turned to look at her. The fear burst inside her. She stood in the doorway, unable to speak or move.

Eyes vacant, Paladin stared at her. With his stare, no words were necessary. The answer lay there for her to see.

Arcane and his army approached.

She clasped her hands together. Her teeth ached from clenching them so hard. He seemed so calm, standing there. Didn't he realize their doom drew closer? He turned away to finish dressing. She whispered his name.

"Do not, Seren." He angled a hard glare at her. "This is war, and with war, battles must ensue. We cannot stop it. They want to destroy us. In turn, we desire to stop them."

"But—"

He lifted a hand, stopping what she'd intended to say. "Be still. I will not go to fight with the memory of your fear in my thoughts. Be strong for me and for our son."

She took a deep breath, struggling to shove her growing terror aside. Next to Leo, even in the armor, he appeared small and thin. Too thin. Their forced separation had affected him.

His deep voice broke through her muddled thoughts. "Where is Legion?"

"He's sleeping. I asked one of the girls to watch him for me. I'd wanted some fresh air but now…" She bit her tongue to keep from crying. Tears burned her eyes and her vision blurred. She reached out to touch his arm, trying to find the words to keep him close. Instead, she curled her fingers into her palms. No, she wouldn't do it.

The last clasp fastened under his fingers, and the helm placed on his head. He picked up his sword belt. With fast efficient movements, he buckled it around his slender waist. He walked to her side, slow and with ease in his movements. Would she ever see his walk—God, she loved his walk— again?

His fingers, lean and beautiful, brushed a lock of her hair from her brow. "I cannot stand by and watch them fight. I have to help."

With a nod, she moved out of the doorway. Paladin stepped through it, his gaze never leaving hers. "I will return."

Seren, suddenly chilled, wrapped her arms about her waist. Her words after Bask's visit returned. She wanted to tell him she forgave him, and that she loved him, but not now. She forced an answer past her lips. "I know."

He left the room to trail behind several other

warriors moving to the passageway leading to the entrance.

She followed, her legs weak with fear. Once above ground, he continued through the gap in the barrier Ren held open for the ones intending to fight.

At the sight of the desert surrounding the entrance, her eyes widened. The six clan leaders waited. Not alone, either.

Heart racing, she gazed over the area outside the barrier.

Dragons, too many to count and of all sizes, colors, and shapes, surrounded the limestone entry way. They waited on either side of the cavern's opening on the outer edges of the barrier. She stood, mouth open, staring at them.

The reality of what was about to happen bit deep in her heart. She started to cry out for him to stop, but his wings burst out from his back. He whipped around, flying toward the spot where Lior waited with other white dragon clan beasts still loyal to her. They spread out behind her, their white scales catching the light around them.

Trembling, Seren stood stiff, pain rippled through her chest. The ache increased over not telling him how much she cared.

Leo came to her side and placed an arm across her shoulders. "Come inside. We'll go to the top. The barrier should hold against an attack. You'll be able to see the battle from there."

She nodded, jaw aching from clenching her teeth to keep from screaming at Paladin to stay with her. The calm way Leo spoke did little to soothe her nerves. This impending battle would result in a life and death struggle, not a fireworks display on July fourth. Didn't he realize it? Paladin left. He might not come back. The thought ripped a hole in her heart.

Unable to vent at her friend, she followed him through the cavern to the spiral stone stairs leading to the top. They came out on the flat ledge.

The sky darkened. Dragons, too many to number, waited for the rogues' arrival. To the northeast, a black line formed on the horizon. So many had come to destroy them. Uncertainty entered her mind.

She drew in a shuddering breath and glanced at Leo. "Will he be all right?"

"We just have to hope. Trust in our strength. They know what they're doing."

Though he spoke words of assurance, doubts about how much they both truly believed his words remained with her.

****

The magic swirling in the air thickened the closer Paladin came to Lior and the other clan leaders. He landed nearby, his gaze taking in the lines of dragoons. On their backs, dragonseed soldiers waited for the order to charge. All the leading clans, their banners slapping in the gusts blowing over the desert, cried out of the unity of the black, red, blue, green, and purple dragon clans. Dracs pranced alongside their older relatives, cawing and blasting magic from their elongated throats.

Bask glided from Lior's neck to land next to him.

The silvered skullcap glowed with a white brilliance. "Are you prepared to die, Sire?"

Gritting his teeth, he glared at the ageless wizard. "I am ready to live. So should you be."

A low chuckle came from Bask. "Ah, but I have

lived far too long. The thought of death no longer brings fear to my heart."

"Nor to mine. I have no intention of dying this day."

"Take care, mighty White Dragon King, there will be many desiring your head." With this morbid warning, the wizard returned to wait atop Lior's shoulder. Paladin studied them. What did the two speak of while the enemy came closer? The gentle way Bask caressed Lior's neck revealed his affection. The sight brought a regretful twinge shooting through Paladin's gut. He should have mended matters with Seren. At least showed her his love.

Screeches rang overhead. He raised his eyes and stared in awe at where the lesser dragons of every clan glided above on the air currents. Magic glinted in the sky around the winged beasts, sending streams of sparkling dust trailing behind each.

Legless forest dragons with vertical striped green and yellow scales running the length of their bodies with long trailing feathers weaved through the flying ranks of their distant kin. Roars erupted below them to echo across the dunes. Sand whirled around the dragoons and whipped up to the flyers.

Along the northern horizon, black clouds roiled closer, powerful magical waves propelling in the direction of their waiting forces. He narrowed his eyes at the approaching army. Through the grayness, Arcane flew in front of the mass of writhing dragons.

"Well, old friend, our guests will soon be upon us."

He shifted his gaze to the left. He'd never noticed Ren's arrival. "So it seems."

A wicked grin flashed across the wizard's face. "Best method to relieve tension. Fighting and sex. Two ways to a man's heart."

His comment, so strange coming from the serious man, brought a laugh from Paladin. "For once, I have to agree with you."

"So, shall we go and greet them in the manner most fitting for their visit."

Responding with a like grin, Paladin nodded. He called upon his innate magic to unfurl his wings. The wizard leapt on the shoulders of a nearby lesser white dragon. Sand billowed with the fanning of their wings as they lifted into the sky and headed for the encroaching enemy. Many of the other lesser dragons fell in line behind them.

****

Worry clouded Seren's mind. Her concern increased with the many dracs taking flight above them. Waves upon waves of dragons ascended to the sky above the cavern.

Seconds later, the first swell of rogues arrived with Arcane in the lead. The converging magnitude shot straight for the seven dragon clan leaders. The dracs which were closer to the caverns, swished through their larger kin. They flicked with huge teeth and claws to leave bloody slashes on the enemy rogues that fought under Arcane's orders.

She held her breath at the sight of the mystic beast diving for Lior. The white female flew at the desert floor, reversed direction to rise straight up, aiming for Arcane's underbelly.

Arcane dodged. He slashed toward the white dragon's head.

Seren's heart rose to her throat.

Lior swerved out of the way at the last moment. In her place, Bask blasted Arcane with rays of pure magical energy. The beast passed through the bright beams, seeming unaffected. In Arcane's place, some twenty lesser dragons surrounded Bask while driving Lior farther away.

Arcane circled, coming closer to the protective barrier, and the spot where she stood. She kept track of his movements, feeling uneasy with the way he eyed the magical wall separating them.

"Leo?"

He grunted in response.

"Are you sure he can't break through?"

The black man shifted, a frown on his face. "Pretty sure. Why?"

She continued to observe the hypnotic rise and fall of Arcane's wings. "I want you to go below. Get ready to run with Legion. Just to be on the safe side."

"Seren?"

"Please, do what I ask. I want to make sure my baby is safe," she whispered.

He nodded, pivoted on his heel, and hurried toward the stairs leading to the caverns.

Magic exploded behind her. She sent a quick glance over her shoulder to see two huge beasts blasting each other with fire. When she faced forward again, Arcane hovered even with her, leering.

Terror froze her to stone.

Chapter Twenty-Six

His skin itched. The dragon mark on Paladin's left arm twitched, the beast struggling for freedom. Rage at the injustice of Arcane's actions boiled over into his fighting. High above the center of the cavern, Paladin sliced through the armored underbelly of a lesser black dragon. His father's words filled his mind.

"Slice with the scales. A clean cut, no jerking. The blade will go deep, the kill swifter."

Dark blood, entrails, and dragonstones burst from the opening. On contact with the air, the flesh and internal organs evaporated into shimmering dust. The beast howled while it fell, writhing with its death. Paladin concentrated on keeping out of reach from most of the rogues' breath, and all of their clawed slashes. Lessons from years ago vibrated through his mind.

"Draw in the magic, it will give you strength whereas the breath will take it from you. Avoid, duck, roll, flip out of the way then drive for the kill."

To his right, Ren managed to avoid a massive swing from another black rogue's clawed hand. The wizard leapt from the beast he rode, flipping over once to land on his feet, balanced between the wings of another white dragon.

The dark-haired man raised his staff to send a powerful spell at his attacker, but a jarring strike to the underbelly of his new ride knocked him off-balance. The blow sent Ren sliding to the right.

Fear for his friend had Paladin angling in his direction.

Behind Ren, a massive billow of air, sand mingled with glittering magical motes formed into the shape of a fanged, six-horned dragon. Rimmed with gold, the sandy figure roared in fury. Ren turned his head as he fell, eyes wide at the sight.

Hoping to reach Ren before he tumbled off the white dragon, Paladin whipped closer. Ren remained unmoving, his gaze locked on the beast behind him. The form streaked past the wizard. It struck the dragon attacking him, blasting a fissure the size of Paladin's body through its chest.

The wizard tumbled and started the long descent to the desert floor, his cape slapping against his body. He'd dropped a few yards. More currents of magically charged air mingled into four gold-edged dragons. Two caught the wizard. They carried him to the ground. The others created a buffer between Ren and any attacking enemy.

Concerned for his friend, Paladin landed next to him. Ren waved a hand at him, demonstrating he needed no aid. Paladin, even more determined to finish this fight, took flight into the fray.

He lifted into the air, relieved Ren had suffered no harm. After two successful strikes on a red and green rogue, a force hit Paladin on the right side. Knocked off balance, he flipped once, dull pain radiating from his hip. He glanced to his left. Rylen, his wings unfurled, straightened and turned back to him. The younger man, armored in white, motioned to him.

"Come brother, fight me. Alone. It is I that you desire to destroy, is it not?" Rylen smirked, his gaze coated with a misty darkness.

"Below then." Paladin motioned to a sandstone slab coated with magical dust a good distance from the entrance to the caverns. "We will finish this."

They landed on the smooth sandstone. Their wings disappeared. Rylen slid both his swords free, one long, the other shorter by half the length. The longer weapon, similar to the one Paladin used, glinted in the twinkling sparkles dotting the air around them.

With a grimace, Paladin nodded to the blade. "You would defile our father's sword in this manner?"

Rylen lifted a brow and sneered, "Defile? You foul the very air I breathe."

He charged at Paladin.

****

Seething hatred poured from the glance Arcane sent Seren. Uncaring, she gritted her teeth and paced along the edge of the stone overhang. She clenched and unclenched her hands while she waited for him to make a move.

From the right, Lior rammed against his side, sinking her pearl-scaled claws deep into his back and underbelly, holding tight. Her mouth opened. The massive white dragon bit into his arm, incisors slicing deep. Bones snapped, the sound loud amid the battle. The mystic dragon's arm hung limp against his side.

Arcane roared, pain and fury evident in the cry. .

He swung around, shoving and pushing against the white dragon, trying to dislodge her hold. He slammed her into several approaching rogues. Releasing his black fiery breath, he struck her in the upper body. Lior screamed, ending with fire spiraling from her mouth. The streams of flames raced toward Arcane.

While mother and son battled, Seren searched for any sign of Paladin. The air thickened with a hazy mist. Worry tightened her chest so fiercely that pain cut into her with each breath. She sent up a silent plea for his safety.

****

On the defensive, Paladin planted his feet on the stone, his long sword held horizontal across his chest, his shorter one at his side. Rylen leapt up, his blade over his head. For a moment, time stopped. The image burned in Paladin's mind. His father's words came to haunt him.

"You are the future King of the White Dragon Clan. My heir. Be proud, be strong, and never allow your enemy to defeat you."

His brother's white-gold hair gleamed with the swirling motes floating in the air around them. Fierce determination sparkled in his mist-shrouded eyes. The next second, Rylen swung down with all his strength. The impact of metal against metal drove Paladin back, his feet sliding on the stone. Blue sparks lit the blades' edges grating over each other. Sandstone dust floated up beneath their feet, choking Paladin.

With a grunt, face-to-face across the blades, Rylen complimented him with a grin on his face. "Well, done, but not good enough."

He shoved harder. Paladin broke to the left. Rylen swiped back and forth, driving him toward the edge of the slab one step after another. Their weapons connected over and over. Amazed at his younger brother's fighting skills combined with his power, Paladin realized Arcane instilled these abilities in Rylen.

After Arcane's assault on him in his youth, Rylen cared little for any type of fighting with weapons or not.

Before that incident, he had acted like a normal young prince, interested in every aspect of his teachings, in particular fighting. The dragon's black breath had fouled him. Paladin tried to recall the last time he'd seen his brother pick up a blade, but could not, yet now he fought with an expertise beyond his capabilities.

Arcane caused Rylen to act in the manner the rogue believed all humans behaved. Arcane bestowed on his brother this new fighting ability with the same magic used to control him. Paladin shot a quick glance up in an effort to see how the battle flowed. The lesser dragons, along with their younger kin flew above him. Arcane and the seven great ones fought elsewhere.

Distracted, he still managed to avoid a slice from the right. The gust of air passing by his head spurred his father's voice to return from his memories.

"Pay attention. Your death is sealed if you lose your concentration."

He lifted his weapon to block, and succeeded in stopping the blow, but not in time to halt the next one.

"Too slow," Rylen mocked, his eyes alight with malicious intentions.

The shorter sword, turned with the handle aimed at Paladin's abdomen. The strike broke through Paladin's defense to hit him in the belly. The air whooshed out of his lungs. Rylen shoved him with a shoulder in his chest, sending him backward several feet. He hit the edge of a protruding boulder and slumped. He tried to catch his breath, but Rylen followed him, leaving him no time.

He rolled to the right in an effort to avoid a thrust. On his feet, he resumed his stance, weapons held in defense. Sweat dripped from his forehead, slipping into his eyes, mingling with the dust to sting them. Rylen growled. Annoyance replaced the intense glint in his eyes.

"Fight me," he muttered. "Never."

"Are you such a coward?"

"No. You are my brother. Blood of my blood. My love for you is stronger even than the hate I have for all Arcane has made you do."

"Fool—idiot." Rylen charged, frustration disappearing under his anger. Both his blades cut left and then right in a flurry. Paladin blocked each one, adding to Rylen's growing fury.

Breaking from this new onslaught, Paladin slid away to leave a broad gap between the two of them. He took deep cleansing breaths, trying to remain calm under his brother's onslaughts. "Soon, the mystic dragon will be gone. We will defeat him. He will die. Do you truly believe I would harm you knowing this?"

Mimicking his words in a high nasal tone, Rylen swiped his sword down from left to right. "We will defeat him. Ha, more like Arcane will devour all of you. Do not underestimate the strength of that one."

"Neither should you believe so strongly that Arcane is the better. We fight for our very lives. I swore to protect the woman and child I love. I will be victorious."

For the first time since the battle commenced between them, Paladin surged at his brother. His sword connected with Rylen's again and again. Powdery sand coated his tongue. His breath rattled with each short pant of air he drew between his teeth.

A dragon's scream of anguish distracted him. Rylen took advantage of his quick glance at the sky. His brother swung wide, missing him, but followed with a thrust of his shoulder. Paladin took the full force of the shove against his left side. He stumbled and went down on one knee. Rylen corrected his direction. His brother raised his weapon above his head, crazed laughter ringing out in the sudden silence of the battle around them.

Exhausted, Paladin tried to regain his stance, but his legs, weak from the battle, trembled, the muscles exhausted. His brother angled his blade down, aiming for Paladin's head.

****

So lost in her search for Paladin, Seren didn't notice Arcane break free of Lior. The iridescent scales on the mystic dragon's body flickered with his pass in front of her. She stiffened and stepped back, her focus returned to the beast.

He circled and headed straight at her. Opening his mouth, he blasted the barrier with black flames. The barrier shifted, rays of lightening streaking from where the breath hit. Without stopping, he rammed his head against the magical protection.

More electrical streaks raced from the area impacted by his head. The barrier cracked. Air whooshed over her, bringing the scents of burned flesh and blood—human and dragon–along with an array of other odors she couldn't identify. The sudden impact of the wind through the hole shoved her back a step. She clasped her hands at her waist, her gaze riveted on the beast before her.

"You thought to hold me with this pitiful excuse of a barrier? You presumed too much, human."

His nose, followed by his jaw, squeezed through the opening, disrupting the magic in the barrier. He forced his head further inside the protective shell.

Calm came over her. Her mind vaguely registering him at all. Instead, memories of the days before Mandy's death danced through her mind. The laughter, sharing hugs and kisses, the playground, teaching her to ride her bike, all her love given to the little girl, her child, her life, then…

Her skin heated from the inside out with the memories of her lifeless child bright in her mind. The laughter and joy ended for eternity, all her love buried with her daughter. Or was it?

Legion's gently rounded head, his clear dual colored eyes, one blue, one gray, the milk-sloppy smile Paladin swore came from gas, shoved her painful memories aside. The fire under her skin increased. Sharp pain cut into her shoulder blades. She cried out. Taking deep breaths to ease the pressure, she reached back and felt…Her finger traced over soft feathers. She gaped in amazement. Wings came from the inner section of her shoulder blades. The soft feathers glided beneath her fingers.

"Wings will not help you, human."

She lifted her gaze to Arcane. Fear no longer controlled her, only the need of a mother to protect and guard against encroaching evil.

"Do you know your weakness against me?"

The dragon's brow creased. *"I have no weakness."*

Moving one step closer to him, she nodded, a smile playing across her lips. "Yes, you do."

She held out her hands, stretching her fingers wide. Another step brought her in front of him. "You assumed because I am human, I have no strength, but you're wrong. My strength lies in the love I have for my child. My love for those who have worked so hard to keep me safe from you."

"Therein lays your weakness. Love is weak.

Useless." He narrowed his eyes, unmoving.

She touched the outer edges of his mouth, placing her hands flush to his scales. "Because I am human, I have the ability to feel greater emotions, to know truer power simply by believing. You don't, and because of this you will fail."

She finished speaking. The glow surrounding her body migrated to her hands and exploded, shaking the stone beneath her feet. Arcane, eyes wide with what could only be called surprise, gaped at her. He pulled free from the split in the barrier, but not soon enough. A sizable portion of his left bottom jaw turned to dust under her attack. The light streaked up the sides of his face, slicing deep into his left eye. Howling, he swept a hand at Seren. He missed. Lior, Sinimal, and Karia pinned him from three sides. They blasted him with fiery breaths. Huge chucks of flesh and muscle flew off his body.

The sudden onslaught from the three dragon clan leaders drove him away from the cavern. Bask appeared in his path, assailing him with wave upon wave of fire balls. The mystic dragon drew near to the man. He slashed at the wizard, catching him across the chest, cleaving him open. With one last swipe of his tail, Arcane struck Bask on the shoulder, the tail sliding over his head, dislodging the skull cap.

Lior's scream echoed above the battle.

Unable to help, Seren, heart pounding in horror, saw the wizard pummeled to the ground. Lior followed, landing not far from him, hovering over him, protecting him. The dust in the air billowed around them, clouding her sight.

Chapter Twenty-Seven

An inch from hitting Paladin's head, Rylen stopped, a confused frown marring his face. He squeezed his eyes shut and shook his head. He opened them again. At once, Paladin noticed the dark tinge to his eyes had disappeared. Joy leapt in his heart. The absence of the coloring meant defeat of the rogue beast, Arcane. If not death the beast had been beaten or weakened to such a degree he no longer maintained control over Rylen.

He lowered his weapon, the point angled at the stone beneath his feet. "Rylen?"

After several moments, his brother nodded. His gaze searched his surroundings. "What am I doing here?"

Paladin stood, slid his swords into their sheaves. Without a word, he moved to his brother and wrapped his arms around him. He embraced him for the first time in years. At his touch, Rylen stiffened, but soon relaxed.

"Do you not remember anything?" Paladin asked.

A groan, followed by sudden tension of his body, came from Rylen. "What have I done?"

Shifting his hands to Rylen's shoulders, Paladin drew back to stare into his brother's pain-filled blue gaze. "Not you. Arcane. Come, this battle is not over yet. The remaining rogues must be driven away."

Worried about the battle's course, Paladin moved away, unfurled his wings. He leapt up and glanced at the desert along with the skies still filled with rogue fighters.

Dragons, adult and young, swooped, their bodies moving in an acrobatic dance of war. The crowded skies echoed with the beat of their wings and cries. After he cleared the top of the protective barrier to the caverns, screeches coming from below reached him. He looked down. The sight below halted his forward flight. Pangs lanced through his gut.

Small flocks of dracs hovered or danced on the rocks protruding from the desert near the other side of the barrier.

Their attention focused on the huge white dragon and her fallen guardian.

Magical motes swirled around Lior, her form changing to the shape of a woman. Long pale hair floated about her head as she knelt next to the fallen man. She lifted his head onto her lap, passing a hand over his cheek, closing her eyes, pain etched in deep lines across her face.

Paladin swept down. He landed next to them.

Lior's words sent streams of fear through him. "My love, don't leave me."

The white dragon's eyes flickered open, her eyes pinpointing Paladin, stopping his approach to where she sat. Rylen's feet touched the ground a second later. A cry of sorrow came from him.

Breathless, the low sob seemed strange coming from the ethereal woman. "Dragonseeds, my dragonseeds."

Hand trembling, Bask smoothed his knuckles down her cheek, bringing her gaze to him. "Shhh, my love, be still. It is time."

She gasped, tears brimming in her eyes.

Speaking slowly, Bask's voice was edged with agony evident from the jagged wound tracking across his chest, he whispered, "Release me, love."

His words from Lior's island sprang forth to slam with harsh realization against Paladin's mind.

I am not long on this world.

The strength left Paladin's legs. He struggled not to collapse next to Lior and beg Bask to stay.

"My beloved. This dragon's heart has always belonged to you. You are right, the time has come. We will depart together. Are you ready?"

The pain-filled worry lines bracketing the wizard's mouth eased. With a gentle smile, he nodded. "I will go where you are. For eternity if need be." Lior glanced at Paladin.

The horrible gaping wound still oozed blood. A huge, blue-black bruise covered the side of the wizard's face. The familiar skull cap rested on its side several feet away, leaving his head bare. Paladin took a step back, shaking his head, shouting in his mind for them to stay, but the words refused to pass his lips.

"Dragonseed, you are the rightful king. Your place is set. Go. Rule in the manner I know you are capable of." Her sorrowful blue gaze swerved to Rylen. "You there, younger brother. You must find what you have lost, for until then, you will never be able to move from this time. Remember well though, my heart has forgiven all you have done. Now, you must learn to forgive yourself."

A drac, white pearl tinted scales glinting in the dim light, landed not far from Lior's head. Bask coughed. He blinked to focus on Paladin. "Be strong, my son. Avaris needs your strength now more than ever. So will your new clan leader."

Lior ordered with a nod toward Paladin. "Leave us.

Fly to your lady and take him with you. What happens here will be much too powerful for even a dragonseed to withstand."

Understanding, Paladin touched his brother's shoulder. Rylen looked at him. Anguish and guilt burned in his eyes. Paladin's heart twisted at the sight. Rylen shook his head, but Paladin insisted. "There is nothing we can do. Come."

They took flight, Rylen trailing behind him. Paladin glanced back at his brother. Rylen's gaze stayed locked on the scene unfolding below them. Paladin slowed to allow the younger man to reach his side. He took his brother's wrist and tugged him forward.

For him, the sight of Lior and Bask departing Avaris cut deep. He would not watch them die. He tried to imagine the white dragon clan with a new leader but failed. Lior would remain their one true clan leader.

A muffled cry escaped from Rylen. Paladin closed his eyes against the sudden surge of magic behind him. He kept flying in the direction of the cavern, but unable to resist, he cut a look over his shoulder.

Dust mingled with magical motes surrounded Lior and Bask. Bask lay in her arms. They stared into each other's eyes, oblivious to the smaller drac not far from them.

The miniature beast straightened onto its hind legs. Magic glowed and materialized between its front two clawed hands. A pale glowing circle appeared with streaks of bluish rays circling within. The power vortexed around the three figures. The ball increased in size. Lior and Bask dimmed. Several moments later, their flesh and bones crumbled. The dust, all that remained of the two powerful beings, was carried away in the breeze, leaving only the silvered skull cap laying on the stones and sand.

Rylen pulled against Paladin's hold on his arm.

He screamed, tears streaming down his cheeks. "*Lior!*"

Paladin cut off his own anguished cry. He blinked against the tears burning his eyes.

The power continued to build between the smaller beast's claws. She lifted her head and roared. The magic entered her chest. In the swirling blink, the drac transformed into an adult dragon, larger, a more massive beast than Lior.

Lacy scales gleamed like a thousand pearls in the glistening bluish light. Muscles flexed and rippled across its body. Amber eyes blazed with an internal flame as her gaze circled the area around her. She lowered her front legs to stand on all four while her tail swished over the desert floor. Many dracs, dead from the battle, lay smashed on the rocks. Each touch of her tail passing over the corpses dissolved them into dust leaving only the creamy bones. Their lesser powers surged to her, absorbed into her body.

"Guide us well," he murmured.

The tail stopped. Her slit-pupil eyes focused on him. Reptilian lips pulled up in the corners, one eye winked at him. Paladin lifted his sword to his helm in a salute and grinned in return.

Her aura radiated to all the lesser beasts near her. Many roared. Paladin, unsure if they mourned Lior's passing or rejoiced in the creation of a new, younger leader, listened, his heart aching.

A choked sob came from Rylen.

Torn by this surprising event, Paladin tugged at

Rylen's arm. "There is nothing we can do. Come, brother."

He turned to leave, desiring to assist with driving the remaining rogues away. He searched for the mystic dragon. Had the great ones destroyed the monster? The sand roiled to the right of him, a good distance from the cavern. He stared at the place. A flock of white dracs cut a line up from the desert. They flew in front of him, fleeing from the spot.

They extended their back legs at Rylen and him, driving straight for their chests.

Paladin gasped. He lifted his left arm to protect his chest and face, but the dracs caught hold of his limbs. They flew in the direction of the cavern. Several yards behind them, the dunes exploded with a tower of golden power. The magic blasted everything in the near vicinity, dissolving everything in its path into dust and glass.

The dracs holding Paladin and Rylen zipped faster. The moment they reached the caverns, the new white dragon leader appeared from behind them. She swooped, her huge wings surrounded them, protecting them. Another explosion followed.

Sand, smoke, and debris struck the new leader, driving her toward the barrier. Paladin clasped her talon where it wrapped around his chest.

Sensing the danger of them drawing so near to the barrier, he shouted at her. "Stop. Now."

Not sure she heard him, he waited, trying to see how close they came to the protective shield over the cavern. Breath caught in his throat, his vision blocked by her body, he struggled to break away from her. She managed to dig her taloned feet into the slippery ground and lean forward so she lay almost flat, huddled over them.

"Be still, Sire, you are safe, and safe you will stay." Her words came into his mind, sending waves of comfort through him. Next to him, Rylen released a choppy sob.

"What is happening?" Paladin sank his feet into the sand, twisting and shoved up, hoping to see.

"Sinimal is driving the mystic beast away. Fury is ruling him. Never have I witnessed such." Rolling to her side, she loosened the protection of her wings a bit so he might have a better view of the scene.

Dust, stirred by the wind and generated from the dragons' wings, gusted, dancing up to the sky. Gaps in the dusky clouds revealed Arcane hovering below Sinimal. The great black dragon sent fiery streams down on the rogue, ripping holes in his wings and opening wider the slashes covering Arcane's body.

"See, Sinimal drives him away. Do not fear, Arcane along with his minions are finished." The husky comment vibrated through his body.

Her words repeated what he witnessed. Arcane, injured, hopefully with mortal wounds, fled south from his own father. The massive mystic dragon flew close to the ground. His agonized cries echoed above the continuing battle.

Paladin glanced at the white dragon, holding him safe. He sent silent thanks to her for her aide. He waited for joy to come to him for their victory against such horrific odds, but only sorrow for the loss of so many pooled in his mind. Seren's sweet face appeared in his mind, sending a need to see her spiraling through him.

"Release me."

"As you say." She set him on his feet beside her. *"Go then to your female. She is safe. Take with you this brother. He too is done with this fight."*

Stepping away, intending to fly to the caverns, he stopped, faced her and bowed low. "My thanks to you."

A low rumble came from deep in her throat. *"None are needed. We have fought for our mutual survival here."*

"Still, you saved both Rylen and myself. That debt I can never repay." He straightened, lifting his eyes to meet hers. "Tell me your name. It will be written for all to know the greatness of the new White Dragon Clan leader."

"Melina, my king. Now go, your lady yearns for news of your safety."

He nodded, turning to the entrance. After he'd taken a few steps, Ren materialized from a cloud of dust to his right. The wizard, leaning heavy on his staff, stopped when he caught sight of him.

Blood oozed from a deep slash on the top of Ren's right leg. Paladin hurried to his side. He pulled Ren's arm over his shoulders.

"You were careless, I see."

"Nonsense. A mere scratch." Ren grinned at him.

"Then you don't need my help?"

"I would not go so far as to say that, but it is not as bad as it looks." Ren chuckled. "I suppose I am becoming much too old to prance around on backs of dragons in flight."

"You need wings."

"Once I find where Saxilon is hiding, I will have my true powers. I won't need them then."

A shout rang out. "Sire."

Two white dragon clan soldiers rushed to them. The battle weary men fell to their knees before Rylen. His brother stared at them then glanced at him, confusion evident in his frown.

The man closer to Rylen spoke, his voice breathless, filled with pain from the many wounds on his body and face. His white armor showed deep gouges streaked with black burn marks. "Our forces are being driven back. We need your command, Sire."

Rylen shook his head, his bottom lip trembling.

Without considering, Paladin barked at the men. "Rally your troops and fall back toward the caverns. The white dragon king has surrendered our father's sword to me."

Eyes wide, the man's soot-coated head swung around. He gaped at Paladin. His open mouth, his stuttering speech revealed his surprise. "But…"

Not uttering a sound, Rylen pulled free his sword. Hilt first, he handed the blade to Paladin. "Do as he says. He is the rightful king. We would do well to follow his lead."

Nodding, the two men raced off to where they came from.

Holding Ren steady with one hand and clasping the sword with the other, Paladin managed to steer the three of them to the entrance. Soon, they reached the barrier. Ren spoke the spell to open a pathway. Just as they entered, a startled cry came from behind them. Looking over his shoulder, Paladin witnessed Largin's tumbling dismount. The elder wizard half-fell, half-slid from the back of his mount, eliciting snickers from Ren.

A bark of laughter spurted from him at the sight of Largin hanging upside down by one foot. "Rylen, go, help him." He glanced at Ren and grinned. "There's another who needs to stay safe within when there is fighting."

The laughter helped alleviate some of his tension, but the torturous day along with the constant fighting had taken its toll. Exhausted, Paladin shuffled through the gap. He'd taken a few steps into the cavern before Seren appeared in front of him. Feathers fluttered on the wings protruding from her back.

She stopped her headlong dash, coming to a sliding halt steps from them. Breathless, she stared at him. "You're safe."

He nodded to reassure her. His gaze wandered to the wings and he asked. "How?"

She reached up and back, touching them. "Oh…they came out. I don't know how to make them go away."

"Ah," he smiled, understanding her dilemma. "Come, let us tend to Ren then I will show you the way to dispel them."

"What about Bask? I saw him fall."

The mention of the fallen wizard's name brought a return of his pain over losing the man and Lior. He shook his head.

"He is gone. As is Lior."

She gasped, a hand going to her mouth. "No. Oh, no. He died because of me."

Her comment sent anger coursing through his veins. Not so much because of her self blame, but she believed this battle her fault. He imagined the turmoil in her thoughts. If she had remained on Earth then none of this would have occurred. "Don't. He died defending our way of life. Do not assume this battle was solely because of you and Legion."

"How can you say it isn't?" Tears sparkled in her eyes. He wanted to reach out and smooth them away, but wasn't sure she would accept his comfort.

"Arcane has been planning to annihilate the humans and dragonseeds for thousands of years. You are a tiny part of this. Whether you were here or not, he still would have tried to destroy all the humans on Avaris. Do not place the blame on yourself. It doesn't belong there."

Without waiting for her to answer, he moved past her. They started down the steep incline into the tunnel. Ren remained silent during the conversation and continued to do so.

A shocked cry came from Seren. He looked over his shoulder. She stood, staring at his brother.

"What are you doing here?" She placed her hands on hips, glaring at the younger man.

Throat working, Rylen looked at him.

"Seren, he's here with me. Arcane's shadow no longer falls on him. It is not our place to judge him." He started to say more, but Ren interrupted him.

"I am going to bleed to death if this leg is not seen to. Seren, leave him and come with us. I helped with Legion's birth, now it is time to return the favor." The wizard nodded at the inner tunnel. He tilted his head closer and murmured low so she wouldn't hear. "Hurry, before she realizes I have distracted her."

They proceeded without waiting for any of the others to follow. Paladin took Ren to his quarters where the wizard stripped off his pants. Paladin helped him recline on the cot and covered his hips with a blanket. When he finished, he looked up to find Seren standing in the doorway.

"I ordered hot water to clean it. Who's going to stitch him up?" She moved nearer, eyeing the deep cut. Swallowing, she glanced at him. "Don't expect me to. I don't know how to sew."

"Sew?" Paladin frowned at her. Her strange ways amazed yet confused him at the same time.

Ren repeated the word. "No one is going to sew me up. Why would you think that?"

She shrugged. "That's what we do on Earth. We stitch severe cuts with sutures. How is it done here?"

The wizard chuckled, an expression of relief passing over his face. "We use magic. Only magic. The wound will be healed from the inside out. This, sometimes, takes several days to complete. Largin will take care of it. I'm sure he'll be very busy over the next few weeks."

"That's a relief, I was beginning to worry you wanted me to do it. I'm sorry, I like you, but I'd end up hurting you worse." She smiled down at Ren. "Do you want some water or maybe something stronger for the pain?"

He waved her away. "No. Paladin, take her away. Show her how to dispel those wings. She's leaving feathers on my floor."

Neither argued with Ren. She followed Paladin out of the small room into the larger central cavern. He took her arm and led her a short distance away to a quiet, sheltered alcove.

Facing her, he placed his hands on her shoulders. "Concentrate on your wings."

She closed her eyes. Her face screwed up into a thoughtful frown.

"In your mind see yourself with the wings. Now think of what you look like without them. That is all you have to do," he said, watching her face for any sign of confusion.

After a few seconds, a whitish aura radiated from her.

The wings dissolved from her back, some of the feathers falling at their feet.

She reached to feel. Her eyes lit with excitement. "They're gone."

"It is a simple matter to call them and then dispel them. You'll become adjusted to it." As soon as the words came out, he regretted them. She would never grow accustomed. She intended to leave Avaris. He had no idea whether the magic in her blood would work on Earth.

"Thanks." The sweet smile he loved to see slipped over her lips. Her gray eyes rose to meet his stare. "Are you all right? Truly all right?"

"I took no wounds. There will be many arriving who are injured. I need you to help tend them, Largin will show you how. I have to return to the battle to make sure all ends the way it should."

"What do you mean?"

"The white dragon clan must know I have accepted Rylen's surrender. I have to make sure all of them are aware. If not, more innocent lives will be taken and I refuse to carry that burden." He touched her brow. "I will return."

She licked her lips, the skin glistening, and nodded. "I don't want you to go, but I understand. Just make sure you come back."

"I give you my word."

He strode away from her, determined to remain strong, and never allow her to see how he had hardened his heart in preparation for her departure from Avaris.

Chapter Twenty-Eight

The heat from the palm-size green crystal pressed between her hands built to a tolerable degree. Seren swept it over the open gash on a black dragon clan soldier's head, holding the stone an inch above the cut. The poor man's face carried a deep purple bruise on the left side. He groaned.

Thankful Largin took the time to show her how to heal the wounded humans and dragonseeds, she concentrated on healing the man. The process astonished her. Energy in the emerald stone passed into the injury, restoring health to the flesh. How many people on Earth would benefit from one stone with this type of magic in it? Illness, even severe injuries would fade into healthy bodies. Many lives would be saved. But Paladin mentioned the dragons who traveled to Earth had died, unable to survive because of the lack of magic there.

She finished healing the soldier, straightened, and glanced around. So many men and women lay injured. Most of the serious had been taken to the city. The wizards at the academy used more powerful methods to tend them. The worst cases, the ones not able to travel the distance, remained for Largin to take care with her assistance.

Standing, she stretched and scanned the room. Paladin hadn't returned. They would have told her if something happened to him. Or would they? Her head started to throb, the painful pulses banged against her brow. She rubbed her temples. Eyes half-closed, her gaze caught on the spot where Rylen sat on the floor across the cavern from her. He'd helped with the healing earlier, but now he sat, knees drawn to his chest, his arms draped over them. His head rested on his arms.

Still upset with him, she thought about Paladin. Rylen was his brother. This reason made it difficult for her to ignore him. Moving with slow steps, she walked to the young man, zig-zagging through the wounded stretched out on the floor. He'd threatened her life and Legion's. Memories of her time with him worked their way through her mind to taunt her. She should turn her back and not bother with him.

Putting her emotions aside, allowing her resolve to harden, she reached the spot and eased down next to him, resting her shoulders against the wall. The muscles in her back twinged with exhaustion. She shifted to find a better position. He lifted his head and looked at her. She met his gaze. He averted his eyes.

Good sign there. Guilt ate at him over his actions.

The silence between them outweighed the moans and quiet comforting voices echoing throughout the cavern. She tried to think of something to say, but nothing came to mind so she waited, wondering if and when he would speak.

The serving woman she left to watch over Legion appeared in the doorway to her room, carrying a blanket wrapped bundle. Even though she saw Seren and who sat next to her, the woman headed straight for her. Seren wanted to scream at her to stop. The man had threatened Legion's life. Didn't the woman realize this?

Yet, Seren waited, keeping silent, to see how Rylen

reacted. This test would prove Arcane's influence no longer controlled him.

The dark-skinned woman halted before them, leaned over and handed Legion to her. "Pardon, my lady, but he is fretting."

Clasping her child against her breast, Seren lifted the blanket from Legion's face. The scrunched features surprised a laugh from her. She murmured thanks to the woman and glanced over at Rylen.

He stared at Legion, an expression of wonder on his face. He lifted a finger to the baby, but stopped. His throat worked and he looked away.

When he spoke, his voice, so similar to Paladin's, cracked with unshed tears. "You will never forgive me. I do not blame you."

Uncomfortable and unsure, she blurted out. "It'll take a lot of proving on your part for me to trust you."

"I understand."

The meekness in his answer fanned her ire. "Understand? Yeah, right. You don't understand anything. You tried to kill me and my baby—your own nephew. He's your blood relative. Explain that to me."

He shook his head, averting his eyes. "I do not truly remember a time when I wasn't under Arcane's spell. I was seven when he attacked and placed his spell on me. Afterward, I only recall bitterness and hatred for Paladin, the brother I had always loved with all my essence."

"Why didn't you fight against the spell?"

Resting his brow on his arms which were still folded over his knee, he hid his face. "How was I to fight against an adult dragon's dark magic? I had not yet grown into my wings."

"What does that have to do with anything?"

He rolled his forehead across his arm. "My wings would have given me more power to repel his attack. As it was, I fell to him."

"What now? Are you going to fall to another dragon if it decides to make the world a wasteland like Arcane? Do you have the ability to stop it?" She had to make sure.

His response came low and quiet. "I do not know."

Legion laughed. The sound surprised her so she looked away and smiled down at her son. He actually laughed loud for only five days old. She glanced at Rylen. He lifted his head and stared at his nephew, amazement evident on his face.

Taking a chance, hoping she wasn't wrong, she said, "Well, he seems to think you do."

Rylen met her gaze and crumpled. Tears filled blue eyes a shade lighter than Paladin's. He tried to speak, but just a breathy gust escaped. After several attempts, he managed to speak, his voice no higher than a whisper. "I'm sorry, so sorry. I never meant…"

"Hush, it's over with. Paladin believes you're back to normal. I'm not comfortable with that, but I trust him. Why, I don't know. He wasn't honest with me either." She reached out and smoothed a hand over the back of his head. "You're his brother. I can't change that."

Not sure how it happened, whether he tilted or she pulled him, but he ended up with his head against her shoulder, sobs breaking free from his chest in deep heart-rending gasps.

Tears sprang to her eyes. Quiet forgiveness entered her heart. She offered him no words, just gentle pats and low comforting murmurs. Voices, louder than earlier, came from the entry to the large cavern. She glanced over to see what'd happened. Paladin stood several feet inside the room. His gaze centered on her and his brother. For him, she soothed Rylen. For him, and him alone.

****

The sight of his brother sobbing against Seren's shoulder forced Paladin to stop. Warmth bloomed in his chest. His love for Seren grew to a higher level than he'd believed possible. She put her anger aside and opened her heart to his brother.

He drew in a deep breath, steeling his mind for what he must do. Requesting this boon from her would sever all her ties to him. She would despise him. He moved in their direction, halting once he reached them.

She said Rylen's name. His brother lifted his head, swinging around to meet Paladin's look.

She shifted Legion in her arms, worry clouding her eyes.

"Is it over? Are they gone?"

"No." Frightened, torn by what he must do, he knelt on the other side of her. "The rogues refuse to surrender. Legion is the only one they will obey."

Her eyes widened with comprehension. She shook her head. "No. I'm not sending him out there. He's a baby. What can he do?"

Clenching his teeth, Paladin rubbed his brow. "Seren, even though he is an infant, he is still the one dragon king. They must obey him."

"And if they don't? What then? Will they kill him?" Terror edged her words, her body trembled. Her hair shook even though she stiffened.

He met her gaze and held it. "I would die protecting him. He will not be taken from you. I have given my sworn oath. I will stand by it with my last breath."

She shook her head, over and over, tears welling in her eyes.

He reached for his son, slipping his hands under the tiny body.

Legion cooed, blowing bubbles.

She tightened her hold.

Paladin gritted his teeth and closed his eyes, searching for the strength and wisdom to make her understand. "If he is not shown to the rogues, they will overrun the world. We will return to the way it was five thousand years ago. You did not come to this world for that purpose, and Legion was not born to destroy, but to preserve. Please, let your faith in me return once more. I swear I will keep him safe in my arms."

She sniffed, sucking in shaky breaths. With gentle care, he took Legion from her. Her hands covered her face, shielding her pain from him, but her sobs stole through, shredding his heart.

Unable to witness her despair, he stood and turned, striding to the entrance. Resolve melting under grief, he hurried, seeking distance to strengthen his mind for what he must do.

Light footsteps followed by heavier ones, trailed behind him. He glanced over his shoulder. She came, tears streaming down her face with Rylen fast on her heels.

Paladin reached the mouth to the cavern. Largin waited ahead to open the barrier. He nodded at the old wizard who spouted the spell. The gap appeared. Paladin went through. Heat, dust and sparkling motes met him on the other side.

Continuing across the desert, he came to an abrupt halt. The six clan leaders landed, surrounding him. He turned in a circle staring at each one, studying them, waiting for their guidance, hoping if any within this battle would keep him and Legion safe then they would.

****

Unable to drag in a deep breath, Seren wrapped her arms around her waist. She wanted to join Paladin, stand at his side, but Rylen took her arm and held her back.

She glanced where he stood a step behind her. He, too, stared at his brother, worry bracketing his mouth and wrinkling his brow.

"Will he be safe? Will my son?" She had to know. He lived with Arcane, witnessed his evil. He might have an idea of whether the rogues would accept or reject Legion. *Please, don't let them destroy my son.*

He shook his head, moved to her side, and wrapped an arm over her shoulders. A sob broke through and she slumped, trying to blink the tears away. No one, not Paladin, his brother, or anyone here understood how her fear for her child grew within her. She experienced such joy, pure bliss with his birth, and hope he would outlive her, sharing his own happiness with her.

Instead, she stood watching her tiny baby brought out to the very creatures determined to annihilate all humans. She'd witnessed Mandy's death. Was she now destined to watch another child of her heart die? Her strength left and Rylen helped her remain on her feet. She kept her gaze riveted on the man and child she loved.

Next to the six clan leaders, Paladin appeared minute, no more than a fragile child's toy. One swipe from their clawed hands, and he, along with his precious bundle, would die.

Sending out silent pleas for their protection, she fell to her knees, rubbing, twisting, clenching her fingers, anything to stop the numbness from taking over her mind. Sand bubbled from below Paladin's feet. She stilled, unable to pull her attention away.

Earth-toned grains swirled inside a cylinder shape. A column came from the desert beneath his feet, lifting him until he rose above the clan leaders' heads. Over the wind and roars from the battle continuing to flow over the desert floor, a low mewling reached her. A baby's call to its mother. Her baby. Heart clenching, she focused on the one thread connecting her to her child. Legion, her treasure, was crying and she was not there for him.

The sand shimmered around Paladin. It surrounded him, hiding him from her. She lifted a hand, wanting to help, but she knelt, useless to them. The sand took on details the same way it had when Legion had appeared to the dragons attacking them in the desert at their arrival to the caverns. The figure resembled the adult Legion, yet this time, wings furled out from the body, swishing back and forth. Complete now, the form separated from Paladin, towering above him.

Slender magical tendrils reached out from the form's flowing hair, extending toward the dragon clan leaders. The strands matched the color of the corresponding dragon. Each beast pivoted, facing outward from where the incarnate figure of Legion floated above Paladin.

A roar came from Legion, racing across the battlefield in physical waves, roiling over dunes and beasts. The last echo ended, he spoke, his voice carrying over the desert. "Hear me, dragons of Avaris. I am Legion, Dragon King. Bow to me or die."

Every movement, every cry ceased.

Seren, shocked by his ultimatum, waited for a

response.

The dragons, most battling for their lives against their enemies, faced him. All stared, eyes unblinking, bodies held motionless.

Legion lifted his arms.

Another wave, this time pure magical power, raced away from him across the open dunes, sending sand spewing up and away before it.

Upon contact, the beasts cowered, pulling apart from their combatants, bodies lowering to the ground.

All the dragon leaders roared, showing their support for him.

A thrill swept up Seren's back. Wide-eyed, she waited for the rogues' reaction. Seconds passed. Quiet and low at first, soon a multitude of words filtered from the roars along with the underlying softer grunts and mewls of the attacking beasts. From forest to sea dragons to the ones who lived in the highest peaks of unknown mountains, they questioned, demanding answers.

"Will you seek revenge?"

"The humans will grow in numbers and attack, destroying our homes."

"These despicable creatures hold nothing sacred."

"What will you do with them?"

Legion's sand form thickened. A fine sheen formed on it. Each grain, ignited by his power, bonded with the next, turning the figure into liquid glass. Shifting and undulating as though alive, Legion's dragon form turned full circle, taking in all the rogues and even his allies.

"Your concerns are well met, my kin. I have been created for one purpose. To be your King. But I am human also and with that, I will be King over The White Dragon Clan. This enables me to make changes with how humans affect this planet also. We all must seek the same course. Avaris is our home, dragon and human. Together we must strive for peace. If not, our world will be no more."

Several larger beasts along the perimeter, shifted through the dunes, moving closer to Legion. One peeled back his lips, responding. *"Can we trust you? You are half human."*

Another from the opposite side roared. *"Will you send forces into our lands and attack us?"*

The glass dragon's clawed hands clenched. "Will you test me?"

The defiant creatures halted their movements.

"Are you strong enough to defeat me? I am giving you a choice to live in peace. If you desire to fight me then my choice will be final. *For you!* Which do you prefer?" A glass-eyed stare, flicked over the tense battle field.

Gradually, one by one, all the dragons across the sand dunes lowered their heads in deference to Legion. Most stared at the Dragon King with a mixture of resentment and pride in their gazes, but none refuted his claim over them. Others appeared to have smiles curling their lips, happy to have Legion as their King.

"Return you to your clans. Should I have need of you or you of me, come, I will listen to your needs."

Roars rolled across the fields, praise for the new King.

The rogues took flight. The desert erupted with a chorus of roars, squawks, and wings flapping.

Seren shifted to the barrier, waiting, muscles tense until they departed, leaving the land empty of all but the allied forces. The glass dragon shattered into a shower of glistening sand. The clan leaders took to the skies, each soaring in the direction of their own homes. Through the dust, Paladin appeared, Legion held against his chest.

His gaze met hers and she managed a small smile. Rylen's strong hand helped her stand. Largin opened the passage through the barrier, but she waited. He came to her, his walk slow and easy. Damp streaks marked his face. She covered her mouth with one hand. He stopped in front of her, staring into her eyes. She wrapped her other arm around his waist and embraced both him and their son.

Chapter Twenty-Nine

Cool breezes fluttered the white gauze curtains inside the open terrace doors. Seren stretched out across the bright covers on her bed, enjoying the peaceful afternoon. During the short time they'd remained in the safekeeping caverns after the battle, Ren returned to Durfalin. She didn't understand how he'd done it, but in those few days, he restored his home to its former splendor. She asked Leo about it. He'd quirked a brow at her, and muttered something along the lines of the magic on Avaris.

She grinned at the memory, passing a hand over the soft fluffy hair on Legion's rounded head. Though she tried, the image of Ren standing watch while workers repaired his home didn't work for her. Leo commented that there hadn't been any workers, just wizards, making the repairs to the destroyed home.

"I suppose it doesn't really matter, does it?" she murmured to Legion. His bright blue-gray eyes focused on her face and he cooed.

A week. One very long week. She missed Paladin. He'd stayed at the cavern after almost everyone else departed. From there, Largin informed her, he'd gone to the White Dragon Kingdom to straighten out some of Rylen's messes. Cie and Rie traveled with him to give support should any question his right to the throne.

Someone knocked on the closed door. Curious about

who would be disturbing her, she called for them to enter. Everyone in the house knew this time of day she stayed in her room with Legion. Normally, Legion took a nap, but for some reason he wanted to play today. His awareness grew more and more each day.

The door opened to reveal a servant. The turbaned, darkskinned man informed her Master Ren and His Royal Highness, Paladin Fulcan requested her presence in the study. Coldness swept over Seren. She thanked the servant and he left.

Paladin had arrived? Why hadn't he come to her? With the trouble gone, didn't he want to see her? Uneasiness crept into her mind, making her tense for the moment she would see him.

Hurrying, she stood, lifted Legion and went below. She stopped outside the closed door of the study. Taking a deep breath, she clasped the handle, opening the door.

He stood across the room from her with his back to the mantle. His clothes, white trimmed with gold, made him stand out against the dark wood tones. Rylen had worn a similar style during his reign. Matters must have gone smoothly for him at home.

Their gazes caught, and for a brief second a spark ignited in his. Another moment and the joy she witnessed lay hidden behind the veil of his lashes. She glanced at where Ren reclined in a large armchair. He stared morosely into the tankard clasped between his hands. He offered no help so she returned her gaze to Paladin.

"What's up? The dragons aren't causing problems, are they?"

"No. I met with the clan leaders. They have agreed to open the portal so you may return home. To Earth."

Her heart froze in her chest. That's all. Nothing

about him missing her and his son. He stood there, so stiff, his tone cold and non-committal. Even after all they'd been through? His words registered. The dragons agreed to send her home. She'd leave this world behind. She narrowed her eyes, studying him. Would he miss her?

She didn't comment, so he continued.

"We leave today, in an hour. If there is anything you desire to bring, you must do so now. My ship is waiting."

The coldness radiating from him rivaled the icy tundra of his homeland.

The close bond they'd developed for so long had vanished. A towering stone wall separated them. Her mind scrambled to find a way to reach him. A week ago, nothing would have stopped him from coming and embracing her. He'd have kissed her with passion. But not this man. The King of the White Dragon stood there and acted the part perfectly. Numbed by the news, and the tremendous change in the man she loved, she nodded, spun on her heel, and hurried from the room.

She reached her room and waited for the tears, the anger—for some way to react. Instead, memories of his gentle touch, his caring words, and his oath to keep her safe rushed through her mind. What changed him? Had he lied when he acted like he cared for her? He'd never told her he loved her. Yet, his actions had shouted he did. Had he lied? Again?

Laying Legion on the bed, she stared at him. He returned the look, his wide eyes unblinking. Every time the baby acted this way, she expected him to open his mouth and speak. He never did, but the impression that he wanted to lingered.

"Well," she glanced about the room, "it's been fun

while it lasted. He's right. I've harped on wanting to go home the entire time I've been here. Now it's happening. I should be happy."

She packed a few things, keepsakes from her time here. The cards Luci gave her, a few clothes, and the sock toy Leo put together for Legion to chew on. Touching the ugly sock, with its red triangle tongue and its round black thread eyes brought the sting of tears. He'd done each thread with love. She'd miss him.

Taking a deep breath, she fought back the sorrow of leaving a friend and tucked her treasures into a small cloth bag. On top of all these, she placed the baby's things.

Hanging the bag from its strap over her shoulder, she lifted Legion and returned downstairs. When she came through the doorway, the men stood. She stopped several feet from them and said. "I'm ready."

With a nod, Paladin turned to Ren. "Do you travel with us?"

"Of course. It is only fitting I bid my farewells to the One Dragon King and his mother."

Seren stiffened at the sarcastic tone of Ren's answer. Her gaze went from one man to the other. The slight tightness bracketing Paladin's mouth revealed the tension between the friends. What had happened? She'd been so excited to see Paladin, followed by numbness with his standoffish attitude; she'd never noticed anything wrong with them.

Fear kept her from discovering the answer. She needed to remain strong, so she stayed quiet.

Paladin walked to her in his lazy, easy stride. Her memories of his smiles, his laughter, his touch, and his passion flared to life. Fighting the growing weakness at his nearness, she looked over at Ren, hoping to divert her thoughts from the man she loved.

"May I carry him?" Paladin asked.

She closed her eyes and took a deep breath, trying to calm her racing heartbeat. Smiling past the increasing heartache within, she placed Legion in his arms. Those same arms which held her, protected her, and carried her. In silence, she fought against the growing fear of losing the one constant on this planet—Paladin's tenderness. He walked to the door, and she followed him out the room.

****

Flocks of dracs, rainbow streams, flew in tight bunches on either side of the ship. They hawked, shrilled and danced over the strong air currents. She held Legion to see them. He batted his hand and kicked his legs in excitement.

Lior's island drew closer. Sorrow rose in Seren, remembering the mighty creature whose influence brought her to Avaris. Lior made it possible for her son's existence. In her heart, Seren thanked the great white dragon.

The eroded sandstone cliffs along with the giant pillars grew larger with the ship's approach. Most of the passengers stood at the rail near her, gazing at the tiny land mass.

"Seems strange," she murmured, positioning Legion so he rested on her shoulder. She patted him on the back in a gentle rhythm. Coos and tiny happy gurgles came from him every few seconds.

"What?" Leo shifted from one foot to the other.

"Last time I came here, I was scared to death." She smiled, glancing at him. "This time, I'm still scared."

He nodded in understanding. "I suppose I'd be the same way." He stood quiet for several moments. He cleared his throat before he faced her. "You sure you want to go back?"

Surprised at his question, she hesitated. Was this what had bothered her these last few days? She'd wandered the deck both day and night, soaking in every second of her time left on Avaris, wanting to engrave each part of this new world in her heart so she'd never forget. She looked over Leo's shoulder to where Paladin stood at the helm. He, too, stared at the island.

No emotion showed on his features. Ever since they'd departed from Durfalin, he'd kept his own company. She tried to decipher what he thought of her leaving, but he revealed nothing, except polite courtesy. She started to go to him several times during this voyage, but her pride stood in the way. He hadn't helped either, avoiding her by attending to one task or another. Besides, if he wanted her to stay, he would ask.

She mentally groaned. Yeah right, after all the times she went on and on about going home to Earth. He'd never come to her. He believed she desired to leave Avaris above anything. And he was right.

She frowned. Wasn't he?

"Of course it is. That's all I've thought of since I came here." Her smile faltered. "This place isn't for me. I'd never completely fit in. You even told me how hard it was for you."

"But in the end, I did. You could too."

Unable to argue with his logic, she stayed quiet. The ship flew alongside the island. The dragons waited. She counted six, the golden one absent. She glanced at Ren. He stood with his feet braced apart, one hand holding his staff. He stared at the empty pedestal where the great beast should have sat.

Disappointment flashed across his face. She wanted to step to him and reassure him, but it'd do no good. He didn't believe the dragon existed. Nothing she said would change his opinion. He had to see it with his own eyes.

Just on the other side of the wizard, Paladin oversaw the placing of the off ramp. Wood thumped against the stone. Seren jumped at the sound. A few more minutes and she'd return home. Moments from now, she'd never see him again. Her chest tightened. Her eyes burned but she fought to keep the surge of overpowering emotions inside. *I have to stay strong.*

One sailor loped across the ramp. He tied the end off with a length of rope around natural protruding rocks. When he finished, Seren's gaze flew to Paladin. He gripped the railing with one hand, the knuckles white. His chest expanded and he released his hold to turn to her. Their glances met and locked. Her breath froze in her chest. Hope sparked within her. If only he'd ask her to stay. She was more accustomed to this world. If only…

He inclined his head and held a hand out. The moment fled in the salty sea breeze. Instead of going to him, she went straight to the ramp. Swallowing the sorrow growing in her heart, she hurried across the wood planks to the solid ground on the other side. Her resolve weakened once she stepped on the island. She looked over her shoulder. He followed, his jaw clenched, the muscle ticking with each step he took.

For the best. Her grandmother loved to say those words whenever something failed to happen. Well, in this case the old lady was right. This was for the best. Paladin had been reinstated as king. The dragons had accepted the role humans played on Avaris, and Arcane, the mystic dragon had been all but destroyed. Now she was leaving. All for the best.

She waited for him to pass her and take the lead. He walked toward one of the caves, going to the center where Lior's cave was situated. Ren came behind them, Leo after him.

The small party worked their way through the narrow tunnel until they came to a ledge across from the huge slab in the middle of the island. A wide gap with the sea below separated them from it. Ren stepped to the edge. He mumbled a spell. Glittering blue light formed a bridge spanning the distance. Without hesitating, Paladin moved onto it, motioning for her to follow.

Why didn't he hold her? She needed his arms around her. She yearned for just one more kiss, a touch, anything to prove he still cared for her.

She moved onto the lighted bridge. After she reached the slab, she brushed by him. The slight contact with his body weakened her knees. All her concentration centered on staying on her feet and not collapsing from the stress. Legion cooed. She sniffed back the rising tears. Wrong thing to do. She drew in a deep breath of sandalwood, his scent. It would haunt her for life.

From the dark inner sanction of Lior's cave, a smoothcheeked young man emerged. His entire body shook, the trembling carried through to his white robes. By his looks, he appeared no more than fifteen. She glanced over at Paladin. His face softened, and he smiled at the boy, extending a hand to him.

"Sachel, it is good to see you."

The boy nodded in response, gripping Paladin's hand. He sneaked a quick look at her. She smiled, hoping to put him at ease.

Paladin motioned at her. "Seren, this is Sachel, my uncle's youngest son. He has trained under Bask's hand since he was a small child."

Heart softening for the boy, she nodded and said. "Glad to meet you."

"My lady." He bowed low before her. "I hope my service here will be a blessing to you."

Oh, yes, she liked him. Polite, courteous, nothing at all like Bask. Still, a twinge of grief went through her over the loss of the great wizard.

Looking from her to Paladin, Sachel almost stuttered with his next question. "Shall we begin?"

Unable to resist, she stared at Paladin. He swallowed and inclined his head. He showed no signs of asking her to stay with him.

"Very well. Step to the edge, and I will inform Melina the conjunction between the great dragons may begin." The boy turned. He leapt into the air, glistening white wings appeared on his back, unfurling and carrying him to the new clan leader.

So, this was it. In the next few minutes, she'd be home in New Orleans. After a while, this world would be like a dream with some good and bad parts. Her throat tightened. She blinked to fight the rise of tears. Damn it, her nose burned. She clenched her teeth, determined not to let Paladin see her cry.

After a brief conversation between the young wizard and the mighty clan leaders, Sachel descended to the slab. He stood separate from the rest of them with his staff held before him. The dragons leapt away from their pedestals, soaring in a circle the same way as when they'd purified her blood.

So long ago with a flood of events between.

The dragons came to a stop, facing Sachel, with the black beast on bottom and each of the others halting above the one in front until, Melina hovered at the top. Stacked in a multicolored tower, they released their fiery breath at the dragon stone tip in Sachel's staff.

A light beam reflected from the stone, coming to rest in the center of the slab. Brilliant white light lengthened and widened across the area. In the center, a door appeared.

Heart racing, excited over seeing Earth again, Seren took a step to the door.

Two more steps and Legion cooed. She glanced at him.

His gaze, so clear and innocent, held hers. "It's okay. We'll be home soon."

She walked the remaining distance without stopping. Reaching the door, she hesitated. The golden knob sparkled in the gleaming light.

All she needed to do was grasp and turn it. Simple movements, but she froze. Memories assailed her with images from her past.

Her wedding and Mandy's birth. Wonderful thoughts ending in tragedy. First with her daughter's death followed by divorce. With no immediate family, she and Legion would be alone. They'd manage. She had the confidence to realize this. But would it be enough?

What if someone noticed Legion's powers? What would happen to him—to her?

In the middle of these tormenting thoughts, more images came to mind of her time on Avaris. The picnic in the beautiful meadow, dancing aboard the airship, meeting so many new people, and seeing the unique places on this planet. New friends, most were closer to her than even her distant blood relatives back home.

Paladin.

How could she leave him? She loved him.

Struggling to catch her breath, she glanced over her shoulder. Her gaze found him. He stood stiff, staring at her.

A single tear slid over the curve of his cheek.

Her heart shattered.

"I can't do it," she whispered.

His stride devoured the distance between them. His arms encircled her, pulling her against him. Holding tight, he murmured against her hair. "You want to return. It's what you've desired."

"No." She buried her face into his shoulder. "Not any longer."

"Then what? Tell me."

She lifted her gaze to meet his. Vision blurry, she sniffed and tried to smile. "For you to love me."

"You have that. Can you doubt it?"

She shook her head. She slipped an arm around his waist. "If I leave, I'll never see you again."

"Probably, but I am willing to let you go if it will bring you happiness. When I first married, I tried to make my wife happy, but she spurned my attempts. With you, though, all I desire is for your peace and joy. Nothing for myself, all for you."

She smiled through her tears. "And that's a good thing for you?"

"Always."

"I guess you'd better tell them I'm not going. Maybe

one day, when Legion is older. When he can control his power. We'll go visit my world so he can see it." She hoped so. Her child was a part of both Avaris and Earth.

"I see no reason why this cannot be." Paladin leaned away and stared into her eyes. "I do love you, Seren."

Those words stopped time for her. They shone from his eyes with pure truth. Her heart caught with the realization he did love her.

He kept an arm around her shoulder and turned to the others waiting on the side of the slab. "Enough, Sachel. The dragons can release the spell. She has decided to remain with us."

Within a second after Paladin made this announcement, the dragons broke free from the tower, spinning off. They circled to land on their pedestals.

Leo moved to meet them, a wide grin stretched across his face. "You won't regret it. I was hoping you'd stay. Even to the point that I almost made a wish."

"Hush," Seren said. "Only one wish per decade and Paladin used it."

She glanced at him. Placing a hand against his neck, she tugged him down to her. "And I'm glad he did." She rose to meet him, sealing her words with a gentle kiss. "Let's go home."

A word about the author...

Born and raised in the South, Judith makes Southwest Louisiana her home. She is a dreamer. Her writing is a doorway to her imagination and she loves to share with the world. Reading--living in other worlds-- has always been a part of her life, and she decided to let others visit the places in her imagination. Her muse set free, she writes mostly paranormal fantasy and futuristic stories, but she also dabbles in contemporary romance fiction. She is a widow, having lost her husband of 43 years last spring. She has three sons, and three very spoiled dachshunds and two cats. When she's not busy writing, she enjoys reading fantasy, romance.